Enter the unique w...
A world of high adven...
and people you will never forget.

TERRY GOODKIND

WARHEART

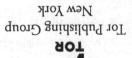

Tor Publishing Group
New York

NOTE: If you purchased this book without a cover, you should be aware that this book is stolen property. It was reported as "unsold and destroyed" to the publisher, and neither the author nor the publisher has received any payment for this "stripped book."

This is a work of fiction. All of the characters, organizations, and events portrayed in this novel are either products of the author's imagination or are used fictitiously.

WARHEART

A Tor Book

Published by Tom Doherty Associates/Tor Publishing Group
120 Broadway
New York, NY 10271

www.tor-forge.com

Tor® is a registered trademark of Macmillan Publishing Group, LLC.

ISBN 978-0-7653-8309-9

Our books may be purchased in bulk for promotional, educational, or business use. Please contact your local bookseller or the Macmillan Corporate and Premium Sales Department at 1-800-221-7945, ext. 5442, or by email at MacmillanSpecialMarkets @macmillan.com.

First Edition: November 2015
First Mass Market Edition: November 2016

Printed in the United States of America

16 15 14 13 12 11 10 9 8 7

This book is dedicated to my readers, who have lived this grand journey with me. Writing Richard and Kahlan's story has been one of the greatest honors and joys of my life, but these stories don't exist in my mind alone. They live because they exist in yours as well. It is your love for this world that has helped breathe life into these characters. Because of your passion, Richard and Kahlan and their world will live on. You now carry this sword, and for that you have my deepest gratitude.

WARHEART

Feeling hot and light-headed, Kahlan stiffened her back as she stood at the head of the funeral pyre, staring down at Richard's body laid out before her. The light mist and fitful drizzle felt cold on her face, like ice against the grief burning inside her. Wet cobblestones glistened in the late-day light. Irregular pools of standing water reflected parts of the citadel rising up beyond and the stone guard tower nearby, with the occasional tears of rain distorting those reflections.

Although the mist and bouts of rain had soaked the neatly stacked wood of the pyre, she knew that it would burn. Thick layers of pitch had been slathered over the lower planks so that once the torches were tossed in, the entire stack would ignite and burn hot, even in the drizzle, and Richard's worldly remains would be consumed in the flames.

Kahlan's hopes and dreams would be consumed in them as well.

Everyone's hopes and dreams would be turned to ashes.

The dozen men ringing the funeral pyre had but to toss their torches into the wood and it would be over.

Everything would be over—for her, and for everyone.

The dozen grim soldiers gripping the torches all stood at attention, but their gazes were on her. None of these men of the First File, the Lord Rahl's personal guard, would be the one to decide to toss his torch and ignite the funeral pyre. It was up to her alone, the Mother Confessor–Richard's wife–to give the order.

The morning was dead silent but for the low hiss of those torches. Their flames spit and popped as they wavered gently in the damp breath of a breeze, as if waiting impatiently for her to give the word so they could be freed to get on with their grisly work.

Beyond the soldiers holding the torches, no one in the gathered crowd made a sound. Most shed tears silently.

Kahlan, standing at Richard's head, stared down at the handsome face of the man she loved. She hated seeing him still in death. She had feared for his life any number of times, but she had never once imagined one day standing over him laid out on a funeral pyre.

They had dressed him in a black shirt and over that a black, open-sided tunic bordered with a gold band decorated with symbols. The wide, multilayered leather belt that cinched the magnificent tunic at his waist bore the same sort of symbols, many in what she now knew to be the language of Creation. At each wrist crossed over his stilled heart he wore wide, leather-padded silver bands engraved with yet more of the ancient symbols. A cape hooked to his broad shoulders, appearing to be nothing so much as spun gold, lay spread under him so that it looked as if he were an offering being presented to the good spirits.

Where had those good spirits been when she needed them most?

Even as she asked the question, though, she knew that the concerns of the world of life were not the concerns of the spirits. The concerns of the living were those of the living alone.

A glimmer of light reflected off the bloodred stone in the center of the ancient amulet Richard wore on a chain around his neck. Intricate lines of silver surrounding the stone represented the dance with death. The amulet had been made by Baraccus, the war wizard at the time Emperor Sulachan had started the great war. The amulet, like the dance with death itself, had meaning to a war wizard. Richard, likely fated to be the last war wizard, was now laid out in the same, traditional outfit of that calling.

The only thing missing was the tooled-leather baldric with the magnificent gold-and-silver-wrought scabbard that held the Sword of Truth. But that weapon was not really a traditional part of a war wizard's outfit. That ancient weapon had now fallen to Kahlan's care.

She remembered the day Zedd had given Richard the sword and named him the Seeker of Truth. She remembered Zedd pledging his life in defense of the Seeker. It was an oath he had kept.

Kahlan remembered falling to her knees in front of Richard that day as well, head bowed, hands held behind her back as she, too, had pledged her life in defense of the Seeker.

A brief smile ghosted across her face when she remembered Richard's astonished expression as he had asked Zedd what a Seeker was.

That was so long ago, and Richard had come to learn and discover so much. He was the first since the ancient weapon's creation to fully comprehend what a Seeker was and the true meaning of the weapon entrusted to him. He was, in fact, the Seeker in every way.

There could never be another.

Kahlan had wielded the weapon in anger enough times to have an understanding of its power, but she was not its master. Richard was the sword's master. He was bonded to the blade.

Nicci, the sorceress who had stopped Richard's heart to end his life so he could go beyond the veil of life and bring Kahlan back from death itself, stood behind her to her left, the cowl of her cloak pulled up over her head to protect her from the drizzle. Even so, droplets of water formed at the sodden tips of her long blond hair. Tears dripped from her jaw. The woman bore the agony of knowing that Richard, a man she loved but could never have, had died by her hand, even if it was by his command.

Three Mord-Sith–Cassia, Laurin, and Vale–stood behind Kahlan to her right. Richard had only just freed them from bondage. Once free, they had chosen to serve and protect him. It had been the first choice they had made of their own free will since they had been girls. They had made the choice out of love and respect for a man they had only just come to know, and who was now gone.

None of the people gathered in the square spoke as they waited for the imminent conflagration that would consume Richard's worldly form. This was the Lord Rahl, the Seeker, and Kahlan's husband. This was her order to give and none wanted to rush that order.

Everyone seemed to be holding their breath in disbelief at the finality of their beloved leader's death.

Because his body had been preserved with occult magic, Richard looked as if he was merely asleep and might at any moment wake and sit up. But even though his body had been preserved as it had been in life, the life was gone from him. This was an empty shell. His spirit was now beyond the veil in the underworld, being dragged down into eternal night by the demons of the dark.

Kahlan allowed herself to fantasize for just a moment that it wasn't so, that he would wake, smile, and say her name.

But it was a fleeting, empty wish that only made her misery all the more cutting.

As she stood, trembling slightly, she watched the mist on Richard's face gather into droplets that from time to time ran across his brow or down his cheek. It almost looked like he, too, was shedding a tear.

Kahlan reached out and ran her fingers lovingly through his wet hair.

How could she say good-bye to him?

How could she give the order to ignite the pyre?

Everyone was waiting.

She knew that dark, worldly forces would be coming to try to steal his body. Sulachan would want it for his own unholy use.

How could she not release the man she loved more than life itself into the flames that would protect him?

The soldiers waited for Kahlan's order, not wanting her to give that order, yet knowing that she must.

She felt panic swelling in her at the thought of being the one to do so, of never being able to forget the moment of giving such a terrible command.

But she knew that it was what Richard would have wanted. He had done the same for Zedd. Richard had told her at the time that he couldn't stand the thought of animals digging up his grandfather's corpse.

Now there were animals in human form loose in the world.

It was up to the living, to those he'd left behind, to those who loved him, to care for his worldly remains. His ancestors, almost every Lord Rahl before Richard, had been entombed in ornate vaults in the lower reaches of the People's Palace, their ancestral home.

But with Emperor Sulachan and his armies of half people and reanimated dead rampaging across the land, Kahlan didn't want there to be any chance for the enemy to capture the palace and exhume Richard's body as a trophy, or worse. Hannis Arc had used Richard's blood to reanimate the corpse of Emperor Sulachan.

Kahlan didn't want to think of what they might do with Richard's body if they could get their hands on it.

Kahlan couldn't allow any chance of that happening to her husband's remains. It was up to her to see to it that nothing remained of him in this world.

There was only one way to make sure she had done the most loving thing she could do, now, and that was to let the flames consume him. She had but to give the word and it would be done.

So then why couldn't she?

Kahlan's mind raced in a thousand different directions, trying to find a way out of doing her duty, trying to think of a reason not to give that order to toss the torches on the pyre.

She could think of none.

In hopeless despair, she went to her knees, pushed the hood of her cloak back, placed her hands on Richard's shoulders, and bowed her head.

"Master Rahl guide us," she whispered as everyone silently watched her give the ancient devotion to the Lord Rahl. "Master Rahl protect us. In your light we thrive. In your mercy we are sheltered. In your wisdom we are humbled. We live only to serve. Our lives are yours."

Her words echoed back to her as she knelt there in the wet square, her trembling hands on Richard's shoulders.

No one joined her in the devotion. They knew that, this time, it was hers alone to give. It was her good-bye.

Tears ran down her cheeks, through the cold specks of mist and dots of rain, to drip off her face. Sucking back a sob before it could escape her restraint, she finally rose to her feet and took on a Confessor's face that revealed nothing of her inner torment.

When Kahlan looked up, she saw through a gap between the soldiers gathered in the square the distant figure of Hunter sitting quietly on his haunches at the edge of the dark woods. Even at that distance, she could see that Hunter's green eyes were fixed on her.

The catlike creature didn't look the least bit bothered by the drizzle. It ran off his thick fur like water off a duck.

Kahlan looked down again at the only man she had ever loved. Still wearing her Confessor face, she cupped a hand to Richard's cold cheek. Even though his flesh was cold, the magic kept it as soft as it had been in life.

In a way, her own face was like his: still, calm, and showing no emotion.

Richard's soul was now on the eternal journey. She had seen it descending into the darkness, weighed down by the demons of the underworld, their wings wrapped tightly around him. At the time she had been dead as well, or at least on the journey into death. The demons of the dark had been dragging her down into eternal night, away from the lines of the Grace, but Richard passed through the veil to the underworld and drew them away. Once he had pulled them away from her, Kahlan's soul, that mysterious element within the Grace, had been able to return to her body in the world of life.

Though a knife had been plunged through Kahlan's heart, Nicci had been able to heal the damage, and Kahlan's soul had returned in time. Returned because Richard had sacrificed his own life to come after her and save her in time.

Kahlan frowned at the thought . . . in time.

There was no such thing as time in the eternity of the underworld. Time only mattered in the world of life.

Was it possible that Richard still carried with him the spark of life, as she had–the balance to the deadly poison that had touched them both? Was it possible that after all this time he still carried that connection to the world of life, even as he journeyed ever farther into the eternal, timeless world of the dead?

How long could that spark, that connection, exist in such a place? Especially if his worldly form was still preserved by occult magic so that it remained as it had been at the moment of his death? The decomposition of his body had been prevented by magic involving the timeless element of the underworld. In that way, it was in a sense still connected to his soul.

Richard had removed the poisonous taint of death from her, drawn away the demons, and used her spark of life to send her along the lines of the Grace back from the underworld to the world of the living. They hadn't used occult magic to preserve her, but they hadn't needed to because she had only just died. It had seemed an eternity in the underworld, but in the world of life it had been only a brief time.

Richard had been dead for a considerable time, but that had meaning only in the world of life. Time had been suspended for his worldly form by elements of the underworld, where his soul had gone, and in the underworld time did not exist as such.

What if there was a way?

Kahlan glanced up at Hunter watching her from the distance.

She had thought that Red, the witch woman, had sent Hunter as a gesture of condolence.

What if Kahlan was wrong, and that had not been the reason Red had sent Hunter?

Somehow, it was all beginning to make a crazy kind of sense. A Richard kind of sense. His ideas often seemed crazy at first, only to turn out to be true. What if what she was thinking was one of those impossible, crazy kinds of ideas that were actually true?

She was Richard's only hope, now. He had no one but her to find a way. No one but her to fight for him.

Kahlan knew that if there really was a chance, any chance at all to bring him back, no matter how crazy it might seem, she was the one who had to find it.

"I have to go," she whispered.

She turned suddenly to Nicci and said aloud, "I have to go."

Nicci, her brow bunched, looked up from her silent weeping. "What? Go where?"

"I have to go see the witch woman."

Nicci's frown deepened at the urgency in Kahlan's voice.

"Why?"

Kahlan looked at Hunter, then looked back and met the sorceress's gaze. "One of love's desperate acts."

K ahlan ran to the closest of the soldiers holding a torch. She put her hands over his big fists
around the torch and pushed him back.

"No. We can't do this. Extinguish the torches." She
looked around at the others, her voice rising. "All of
you! Put them out!"

Everyone looked confused, but the dozen men with
the torches looked more relieved than anything. They
carried the hissing, crackling torches, flames flapping,
back away from the pyre lest they accidentally ignite it,
then doused them in buckets of water. The flames fizzed
and popped and sputtered in protest, but finally went out.

Only then did Kahlan sigh with relief.

Nicci put a hand on Kahlan's shoulder, turning her
back. "What desperate act are you talking about?"

Kahlan ignored the sorceress and pointed in command up at the citadel for all the soldiers watching her
to see.

"Carry Richard back up to the bedroom where he
was. Place him back on the bed. Be careful with him."

Without questioning the strange request, the big men
of the First File all clapped fists to hearts.

Kahlan turned her attention to Commander Fister when he rushed up in front of his men. "Mother Confessor, what–"

"Have the room guarded. No one but the First File goes in, not even staff. Have the citadel guarded until I can get back."

He gave her a nod. "It will be done, Mother Confessor."

"Kahlan, what's going on?" Nicci asked under her breath.

Kahlan glanced off at Hunter, sitting at the edge of the dark wood. She looked off above the trees to the distant mountains that looked like gray phantoms floating in the hazy light. Somewhere back there in those mountains was a pass where the witch woman lived.

"I have to go find Red, the witch woman," Kahlan told her again.

Nicci glanced toward the mountains. "Why would you want to find a witch woman? Why now, of all times?"

Kahlan's gaze met Nicci's blue eyes. "Witch women can see things in the flow of time. They can see events."

"They can certainly make it seem that way at times," Nicci agreed, "but so can a fortune-teller. They will tell you most anything you want to hear for a silver coin. Exactly what you want to hear and make it sound convincing if the coin is gold."

"Witch women don't ask for silver or gold."

Nicci looked sympathetic. "That doesn't mean the things they see really turn out to be true."

"Red told me that I would be murdered."

Nicci paused momentarily at such news. "And did she tell you that Richard would give his life to go to the underworld to come after you?"

"No. That's the point. That's why I have to go see her."

"What do you mean, that's the point?"

"She told me that Richard is the pebble in the pond, and because he acts of free will, the ripples of those things he does touch everything, so it disrupts what she can see." Kahlan gestured toward the puddles. "The same way ripples from the raindrops disturb the reflection."

"Meaning?" Cassia asked, her wet, red leather creaking.

Kahlan looked to the hope in the eyes of the three Mord-Sith. "Meaning, there may be a way for us to bring Richard's soul back to his body in this world."

"Bring him back to life?" Vale asked in a tone of astonished hope.

Kahlan gave her a quick nod. "Yes."

"But you just said that she can't see what Richard will do," Cassia said.

"That's right—that's my point. She can't see what he will do, but she may be able to see what others will do, what others might be able to do, or have the potential to do. Don't you see?" Kahlan turned back to Nicci. "Red told me to kill you."

Nicci's mouth fell open. "What?"

Kahlan grasped Nicci's arm and pulled her a little farther away from the soldiers. The three Mord-Sith followed, forming a shield from the others.

"Red saw that if you weren't stopped, you would kill Richard," Kahlan said in a lower voice. "She didn't know what Richard would do because she can't predict his actions, but she knew what would happen to others and what you would do. She knew that you would kill him.

"She said that the future—all of our lives—depends on Richard. Without him, we were all lost. That includes her. Do you see? She has a vested interest in Richard surviving because she would not want the Keeper of the underworld to be able to get hold of her outside the natural order of the Grace.

"Sulachan and Hannis Arc want to do exactly that. They intend to break the Grace, break the division between the world of the living and the world of the dead. See what I mean? As a witch woman, she would be doomed to an eternity of torture.

"She says that Richard is the only one who can stop them. You probably know better than I do all the prophecy that names Richard, and all the different ways he is named and the way he always seems to be at the center of everything."

Nicci sighed. "Indeed I do."

"So, Red told me that I had to kill you so that you in turn couldn't end Richard's life. She said he must live in order for everyone else to have a chance at life. She told me that I would be murdered before you killed him, so I had to kill you first.

"She was right about it all. But at the time I told her I didn't believe you would kill Richard. She said you would do it because you love him. That was all true. It happened just as she said, but at the time it made no sense.

"She didn't say that you would do it out of an act of love. She only said you would do it because you love him. I thought it meant that she was saying you would somehow do it out of anger or jealousy or something." Kahlan tried to dismiss the accusation with a quick wave of a hand. "You know what I mean."

Nicci's only answer was to let out a deep sigh.

"That part just didn't seem possible to me," Kahlan said. "I couldn't bring myself to believe you would do such a thing to Richard and I told her so. She said that if you lived, you would. In the end I couldn't seriously consider ending your life on her word when it made no sense to me."

Nicci smiled sadly, then. "Thank you for believing in me."

The sorceress looked over at Richard lying atop the funeral pyre. Men were starting to clamber up over the planks and logs to carefully lift him down.

"Maybe you should have taken her advice," Nicci said. "Had you done as she insisted, Richard would be alive right now. I'd rather it be me lying there dead than him."

"Done is done," Kahlan said, waving off the notion. "We can't change what is done, but maybe we can change what will be."

Nicci looked back at her. "What do you mean?"

"Red felt real sorrow for me, true compassion. I know she did." Kahlan gestured off toward Hunter. "Because she did, I thought that Red sent Hunter as a way of offering her condolences."

Nicci was beginning to look more intrigued. "Now you think otherwise? You think she sent him for some other reason?"

"Yes–maybe. The last time she sent Hunter to me, it was so he could lead me safely to her so that she could tell me what she saw in the flow of time. She wanted to protect Richard and she believed that I was the best one to do that. She said that she could not kill you herself because it is not her place to interfere directly. Her place is to see what she can in order to help others do what must be done. She was right about it all, but I didn't believe her and so I didn't follow her instructions."

Kahlan gripped Nicci's arm. "What if that's what she is doing this time as well? What if that's why she sent Hunter? What if she sees something in the flow of time, something we could do to help bring Richard back?"

Nicci's expression was guarded. "Witch women often seem like they are trying to help you, but that isn't necessarily the case. They have their own agenda and they have an unpleasant way of giving you false hope to serve their own ends."

Kahlan knew that Nicci would do anything, take any chance no matter how crazy, if it could save Richard, so she knew that the sorceress was expressing doubt as a way of testing the strength of Kahlan's theory.

"Her agenda this time is for Richard to survive in order to stop Sulachan. There is no bigger threat to her. What if there really is a way?" Kahlan asked. "What if the witch woman sees something, some way to help Richard? While it's true that they misdirect you at times, it's never with lies—there is always a core of truth in what they say. I actually liked her, Nicci. I think she really cares about all of us."

Nicci regarded her with a skeptical expression but didn't say anything.

"Since I didn't do as she told me to do and stop Richard's death by killing you, that changed events, changed the course and flow of events in time. Richard's act of free will changed the future. What if she now sees something new in the flow of time, something that we could do—something that has only now become a possibility because Richard did what he did by coming after me?"

Nicci looked off toward Hunter.

"Let's go," Cassia said, growing impatient with the discussion. "We're wasting time. Let's get to this witch woman and find out."

"She wanted me to come alone the last time," Kahlan told the Mord-Sith.

Cassia drew her hand down the single, wet blond braid lying over the front of her shoulder. "That's nice. This time you're not going alone. We're going with you. If there is a way to bring Lord Rahl back, we're going with you to help make sure you get there to find out how it can be done, and then get back and do it."

Kahlan knew it was pointless arguing with a Mord-Sith who had her mind made up, and besides, maybe the woman had a point. The Dark Lands were a dangerous place.

"I'm going, too," Nicci said with finality.

"No one is arguing," Kahlan said as she gripped the hilt of the sword and started making her way back through the gathered throng of soldiers and a few of the staff from the citadel. Everyone stepped back, making way for her. All eyes were on her and those eyes were filled with hope, even if the people didn't understand why Kahlan herself suddenly seemed to have found some.

"I have to go see Red. Make sure Richard is well protected until we can get back," she called over her shoulder to the commander.

He hurried to catch up with her. "Mother Confessor, we should go with you for protection. Lord Rahl would insist. You need to have some of the First File with you. You've fought with these men. You know their heart and their strength."

"I do, but I want you all to wait here," Kahlan said to the commander. "This is a witch woman. They are private and secretive. She will not be happy and may not help me if I bring an army."

The big officer's knuckles were white as he gripped the hilt of the sword at his hip. "If it's an army, I don't think there is a lot she could have to say about it."

Kahlan cocked her head toward the man. "To get to where she lives, I had to walk over a valley carpeted with human skulls. It was impossible to take a step without putting a foot on one."

That gave the man pause.

"Nicci is protection enough from things magic," Kahlan said before he could take issue with letting her go without him and his men. "Cassia, Laurin, and Vale are protection enough from other dangers."

The three Mord-Sith showed the commander self-satisfied smiles as they passed him on their way to follow after Kahlan.

Kahlan paused momentarily to look back at the concern on Commander Fister's face. She lifted the sword a few inches from its scabbard and let it drop back. "Besides, I have Richard's sword with me and I know how to use it."

Commander Fister let out a deep breath. "We know the truth of that." Behind him a number of his men nodded in agreement.

Nicci leaned over close as Kahlan turned and started out once more. "What if she can't tell us anything?"

"She will. That's why she sent Hunter for me."

Once they were beyond the square, Nicci gently took Kahlan's arm and brought her to a halt. "Look, Kahlan, it's not that I don't want to try, or that I wouldn't do anything, give anything–including my own life–to be able to bring Richard back. I just want you to be realistic and not get yourself carried away with false hope.

"After Richard died and you came back, it was the other way around–I wanted to grasp at any straw and you were the one who was being realistic. You said we had to accept the hard truth and not wish and hope for what was beyond hope. Remember? If it does turn out to be nothing more than a false hope, it will only make it hurt worse."

"It couldn't hurt worse," Kahlan said.

Nicci sighed as she nodded in understanding. Kahlan started across the empty grounds around the citadel, Nicci at her side.

Thinking about Nicci's words, she finally lifted her fist to show Nicci the ring with the Grace on it. "Magda Searus, the first Mother Confessor, and Wizard Merritt, left this ring for Richard. It waited three thousand years for Richard to find it along with their message and with prophecy. This is what they were fighting for, what Richard was fighting for, what we are fighting for."

Nicci nodded. "When Richard laid your dead body on the bed, before I healed you, he took off that ring and put it on your finger."

Kahlan hadn't known that. "This means something, Nicci. Everything that has happened–all the prophecy that has named Richard, all the different peoples who have recognized him by other names and titles, all the things Richard has learned, the things he has done, finding the omen machine, and finding this ring left for him–it all means something. It has to.

"The flow of time that witch women can see into means something. She sees it for a reason. It has meaning.

"All of those things are connected and have a larger meaning. All of it can't simply come to an end. We can't allow it. We have to fight, for if we don't we will surely all die.

"I was blinded to it by grief for a time. But now I see the bigger picture. I can see it the way Richard would want me to see it." She held her fist up again as she walked. "If Richard put this on my finger, it was for a reason.

"Red can tell us something, Nicci. I know she can. I'm not going to let that chance–any chance–pass me by.

"Besides, what do we have to lose? How much worse off could we possibly be than we are now? Are you willing to let the chance pass, no matter how slim?"

"Of course not." Nicci finally showed the faintest of smiles. "If there is a way, you would be the one to find it. Richard loved you enough to go to the underworld to bring you back. We will try anything, do anything, to bring him back."

Kahlan summoned all her courage to show the woman a smile. "The way ahead may be painful, in ways we can't yet imagine."

Nicci's eyes revealed her resolve. "If it has a chance to bring him back, it will be done."

CHAPTER
4

Kahlan, the baldric now resting over her right shoulder and the sword at her left hip, made her way across the grounds of the citadel toward the wall, the sorceress beside her and the three Mord-Sith in tow.

Although common sense told them that there could be no hope of bringing Richard's soul back from the underworld, the three Mord-Sith looked willing to believe it could be done. Kahlan hoped they weren't all investing hope where there was none. But she couldn't live with herself if she didn't turn over every last stone, even if that last stone was a witch woman.

Kahlan knew that people didn't come back from the dead, but she had been witness to times when someone seemed to be lost to death, only to recover. Richard needed more than merely to recover, as if he had suffered a grave wound or fallen through the ice and seemingly drowned, but where did one draw the line–draw the veil across life?

She worried, though, that her whole life had been dedicated to finding truth. Richard was dead, and her fear told her that she had to accept that truth.

Try as she might, she couldn't bring her internal

argument to some kind of resolution. When, exactly, was dead final? When was the veil closed for good?

Who was to say when life really was beyond recovery?

After all, because of the Hedge Maid's taint of poison in them both, she had carried its balance of a spark of life with her into the underworld after she died, and because of that she had returned. Had she not experienced it herself, she might have difficulty believing such a thing was even remotely possible.

So, despite how remote the hope, it worked for her. If it worked for her, maybe since Richard carried that same touch from the occult they could find a way for it to work for Richard. She couldn't imagine how it could be done, especially after all the time that had passed, but that was why they had to go to the witch woman. If there was a chance, she would be the one who could give them a direction or something useful to help them find a way.

Hunter was sitting quietly on a small, dark outcropping of rock, his green eyes tracking her as she passed beneath the arched opening through the modest stone wall. Kahlan checked in both directions to make sure there were no surprises hiding close. They still had to worry about half people showing up.

As Kahlan approached, Hunter began a deep, murmuring purr, as if he was happy to see her again. Kahlan was certainly happy to see him. He gave her a reason to hope, something to latch on to.

The small animal was unlike any other creature she had ever seen. Although he resembled a cat in some ways, she didn't know what he was, except that he was at least two or three times the size of a regular cat, with long whiskers and the same kind of almond-shaped eyes. But his legs were considerably stockier than a typical cat's, and his body broader, more like a badger's. His paws were disproportionately large, showing that he was immature and had yet to grow into them. The short, tan fur of his back was covered in dark spots. The fur became darker down toward his haunches and shoulders. The creature reminded her of nothing so much as a cross between a lynx and something like a wolverine or badger, with the same kind of muscular shoulders but not the long nose or short legs of one of those animals. The head was more like a cougar's or lynx's, but broader and with a heavier brow. His long, pointed ears had tufts of fur at the ends.

When she had first encountered the creature, Kahlan had pulled a thorn from his paw. As a result Hunter had been rather fond of her ever since. He had even slept curled against her that first night. Still, he was the offspring of a creature that Red had assured her was not simply large but quite menacing. Kahlan would not want to have to battle Hunter, much less his mother. But she and Hunter had become friends in a way, and she didn't fear him.

She hoped, though, that like the last time he had really come to lead her to the witch woman.

Kahlan squatted down before the purring creature and looked into his green eyes. She scratched behind an ear and then ran her hand down his fur. Hunter pressed himself against her hand, liking her touch.

"Red sent you to get me, didn't she?"

She didn't know if Hunter could understand her, but he purred louder before looking off toward the dark woods. It seemed to her like he really did know what she was asking.

Kahlan stood, resting the palm of her left hand on the hilt of the sword as she peered off into the forest. It was a long way to the mountain pass where Red lived. Although there was still plenty of light, it was getting late in the day and it would be dark soon. Being out in the wilds of the Dark Lands at night, exposed to whatever dangers it held, was not a pleasant thought.

Letting Richard slip away from them was an even more unpleasant thought.

More important than the approaching night, time may have been meaningless in the underworld, but it was not meaningless in the world of life. With all kinds of dangers closing in on them, she didn't know how much time they might have, but she knew that it couldn't be much. Hannis Arc along with Emperor Sulachan and his legions of half people were rampaging across D'Hara on their way to take the People's Palace. Along the way, they were raising the dead to help them. Every moment counted.

"We don't have any time to waste," Kahlan said, half to herself. "Hunter, can you take us to your mistress? Can you take us to Red?"

As if he understood, Hunter turned and bounded down off the rock and then across a field of tall grasses. He stopped not far away and turned back to wait and make sure she was following him. He had watched over her and kept her safe the last time. Had it not been for Hunter they might not have found their way and survived.

"I guess he knows where he's going," Nicci said.

"He certainly looks like he does," Kahlan said with a sigh as she started out, watching the spot where Hunter disappeared into the shadows among low-hanging pine boughs.

"Travel until it starts to gets dark, then make camp and wait for first light?" Cassia asked.

"No," Kahlan said. "As long as Hunter keeps going, so do we."

The three Mord-Sith nodded. "Sounds good to me," Cassia said.

Overhead, vultures, with their wings spread wide, rode the gentle breezes below the clouds. Some glided lower, riding the air just above the taller trees. Richard had often talked about signs at the beginning of a journey. She didn't like to contemplate the meaning of this one.

Kahlan scanned the deeper shadows in the distance as they started in among the thick stand of pines. Although she didn't see anything threatening, it felt too quiet. Since this was the Dark Lands and the trackless forests held dangers of every sort, she didn't know if it was normal for it to be so quiet.

The danger that worried her the most was the half people. If there were hordes of half people lying in wait back in the woods, Nicci's magic was going to be of little use. The three Mord-Sith could fight, and of course Kahlan had the sword, but the half people usually attacked in vast numbers.

She reconsidered the wisdom of telling the soldiers to remain behind. But even if she had brought all the men, and even as good as the soldiers of the First File were in combat, out in such level ground in the strange woods they wouldn't stand a chance if there were the numbers of half people Emperor Sulachan and Hannis Arc had sent at them in the past. They would be surrounded and smothered under the weight of numbers.

Kahlan knew that if it came, this would not be a battle they could fight and win. They had to depend on the strange, furry creature to keep them out of a major battle and lead them safely through the woods.

Hunter bounded down a narrow trail, pausing and turning back from time to time to wait for them to catch up. He was in his element and seemed unconcerned about any threat lurking in the woods. Kahlan didn't know if that was because he was confident of his ability to protect himself, or his ability to outrun anything that might come after him.

None of the five women fully shared the creature's apparent confidence.

Hunter stayed out in the lead as they followed him along lazy streams and through mazes of small pools of standing water among fallen dead branches and leaf litter. The deep shade of the tightly packed, towering pines left the forest floor along their way open enough to make a crude path of sorts along the brook. In spots where water tumbled and splashed, the spray fed thick carpets of green moss covering the rocks. In some spots, fallen, rotting tree trunks made big steps that they used to climb to higher ground as the foothills began ascending to meet the still-distant mountains.

The ground to either side rose up even higher. In some places stone walls thrust up to hem them in. The woods to both sides were thick with a tangled growth of brush and thorny vines. Hunter instead took a winding course along the streambed. Tight stands of trees and in places steep areas of scree or rock walls forced them to repeatedly cross the stream to avoid an arduous climb. Occasionally they had to slog through wet areas created by natural terraces. At least it was easier than traveling through the snarl of dense brush.

Although not ideal, the ground they followed up through the areas of runoff was at least open enough to make traveling relatively easy. Out in the wilds of the Dark Lands there were rarely any true paths used by people, and even more rarely roads. Since Kahlan had been forced to travel through much more difficult terrain in the past, she appreciated that Hunter was taking them along the easiest route available.

As he crossed the running water, Hunter bounded from rock to rock with the effortless grace of a cat. In a number of places he could have easily loped off through the small openings in the thorny brush, but he instead kept to areas the rest of them could travel. Still, in places it was not so easy for the five women to find good footing on the slippery rocks in order to cross the rushing stream. Sometimes they all held hands to keep their balance in a kind of human necklace across swirling water.

From time to time they heard calls from back in the thick growth to the sides and up ahead in the hills. Some of those raucous calls Kahlan recognized as the cries of ravens. All five women looked off toward other, more unnerving sounds whenever an unseen animal screeched or growled.

Hunter rarely bothered to look, and even then it appeared to be out of curiosity, not fear. He usually sat and licked his fur with his rough tongue as he waited patiently for them to catch up. Kahlan supposed that the forest was his natural habitat and he was at home with all the sounds and calls off in the woods, even if the rest of them were not.

She supposed that the powerful creature could dart through the brush to escape danger if he had to. On the other hand, he himself was a predator, with intimidating claws and teeth and the muscle to back them up. She had never seen him hunt or fight, but she knew by his calm confidence that he had to be a formidable fighter like his mother and quite the fierce protector.

When it became dark enough to make it difficult to see and even more difficult to navigate across the rocky landscape, Nicci used her gift to ignite a small flame, letting it float away from her upturned palm to follow after Hunter. It wasn't overly bright, but lit their way well enough for them to find their footing. Hunter glanced up, watching the floating flame briefly, and then, judging it not to be a danger, continued on his way.

As they climbed higher, the litter of broken rock lower down began to give way to more substantial rocky outcroppings. Sometimes the bulges of rock erupting through the mosses, grasses, and brush looked like they were being held captive in nets of gnarled roots. Hunter would stop from time to time, sitting on his haunches atop a rock or fat root, watching the women struggling to keep up with him. They were all out of breath from the effort of the climb. As soon as they caught up, Hunter would be off again, as if trying to hurry them along and not wanting to waste any time. As winded as they were, none of the five women voiced a complaint or asked to stop for a rest.

The higher the terrain took them, the closer the dark woods grew in to the sides, until they sometimes had to make their way through a near tunnel of vegetation as they followed the tumbling stream ever upward while it poured over rocks and burbled down steep slabs of stone streaked in green and brown slime.

When Hunter was far out ahead of them, visible only in snatches, a man abruptly stumbled out of the trees to their left, jolting them all out of their private thoughts.

He wore tattered pants and no shirt. His bony ribs were covered with a sheen of blood that also soaked his trousers.

He was initially as surprised at seeing them as they were at seeing him stagger out of the trees. Even though he was obviously grievously injured and disoriented, when he saw them his eyes swiftly filled with hate and bloodlust. By his demeanor as well as the strings of bones and teeth holding his tuft of hair upright at the top of his otherwise shaved head, it was obvious that he was a half person.

Without delay, the man lunged toward Kahlan.

Even as the sword was clearing its scabbard, sending the unique ring of steel through the forest, Laurin grabbed the man from behind with a fist around his upright shock of hair. She snatched his head back and in quick, efficient fashion cut his throat deep enough to sever his windpipe.

The man dropped heavily to his knees at Kahlan's feet, her sword hovering over him. He held both hands over the gushing wound at his throat. She was filled with a rush of anger from the ancient weapon. That rage demanded swift violence, but it was obvious that enough violence had already been done and he was no longer a threat. She stepped aside as he toppled forward, his legs across the bank of the stream with the upper half of his body lying in the shallow stream. As the water splashed over the man, air burbled from his lungs through the gaping gash. Blood gushing out ran down the stream in a red fan.

Laurin looked rather sheepish. "Sorry, Mother Confessor. I would have been quicker"–she flicked her Agiel, hanging by a fine gold chain from her right wrist, up into her fist–"but without the bond to Lord Rahl, this doesn't work. So I had to use a knife. It's slower."

"It was fast enough and that's all that really matters," Kahlan said, gripping the sword tightly as she scanned the dark woods, searching for others she expected to descend out of the woods any moment.

"Besides," Kahlan added, her heart racing, "not knowing what his occult powers may have been, a knife is the only thing we know for certain works."

The three Mord-Sith moved to stand with their backs to Kahlan, protectively surrounding her, all with their knives out.

"Do you sense any more?" Kahlan whispered to Nicci.

The sorceress peered around in the shadows. "No. But that doesn't mean they aren't there. I think that sometimes they may be able to use occult powers to shield themselves."

Kahlan knew that the half people usually howled when they came on a running attack through the woods. She didn't hear any cries from off in the darkness.

Hunter returned to sit on a rock not far up above them. He looked down at the man lying half in the stream, and then yawned.

"He doesn't look too concerned," Kahlan said.

"Maybe it was a straggler," Cassia said. "With the barrier down and the half people on the loose now, there are bound to be some wandering through the forests of the Dark Lands."

"That's possible," Kahlan said, "but we're pretty far out in the middle of nowhere. It's also possible that there are a lot more with him."

Cassia signaled silently to the other two and then the three of them swiftly vanished into the darkness to check. Nicci stood on a small rock, slowly turning all the way around as she tried to use her gift to tell if there were more.

In a short time the three Mord-Sith reappeared.

"Nothing," Vale said.

The other two shook their heads to confirm that they didn't see anything either.

When Hunter turned and started off once again, looking unconcerned, Kahlan and Nicci shared a look.

"I think if there were more, he would probably know," Nicci suggested.

"Let's hope you're right," Kahlan said as she started out once more.

But she kept the sword out just in case.

They traveled deep into the night without further incident. It was nerve-racking to continually fear that every sound might mean an imminent attack. Kahlan had drawn her sword half a dozen times, erring on the side of safety. None of them took lightly the possibility of a surprise attack. They were all tense and wary as they followed Hunter onto ever-higher ground.

Hunter almost never made any sound as he walked, and seemed magically able to avoid stepping on anything that would make noise. He moved like a shadow. They tried to be silent as well, but with less success.

After they had put a good deal of distance between themselves and the dead man, they all began to feel more confident that the man had been a loner.

Not all the half people traveled in groups. Some hunted for souls by themselves, feeling they had a better chance to steal a soul if they were alone. Being greedy about getting a soul, they weren't inclined to share, or wait their turn. When they found prey, even if they hunted in large groups, it was every man or woman for themselves.

As skinny as the man had been, he was probably weak from hunger. On top of that, it was night. It was easy enough to fall in the darkness and be seriously injured.

As exhausted as they all were, Kahlan knew that it was a mistake to keep going all night. Every time she thought of stopping, though, she remembered Richard lying in the bedroom back at the citadel. He had no chance if they didn't find a way to help him.

"How much farther is it to the witch woman's lair?" Cassia asked as she stretched to get a foothold high up on a jut of ledge.

Kahlan realized that she wasn't sure. She was having trouble thinking. With the weight of grief, she'd slept only in brief fits the night before they were to have the ceremony at the funeral pyre. It had been a long and sleepless night. With the long trek through the woods on top of that, she was near to dropping from exhaustion.

She tried to think of how much farther it might be. After leaving Red's valley home the last time, Kahlan had been distraught and distracted. Red had told her that she was going to be murdered within days. With the stress and tension of everything that was happening, to say nothing of the poison she and Richard were carrying within them, Kahlan hadn't been paying a great deal of attention to where they were. Her thoughts had been elsewhere. She had simply followed along with Richard and the rest of them, unable to get Red's words out of her mind, her warning that Nicci would kill Richard if Kahlan didn't kill Nicci first.

"I'm not sure, exactly," Kahlan finally admitted. "The pass is in the mountains, so I don't think we are likely to reach her for at least another day, maybe more. Sorry, but I guess I'm too tired to think clearly."

"From what I remember, I think you're right," Nicci said.

"That's a long way," Cassia said as she had to bend down to give Kahlan a hand in climbing up.

"We're going to need to get some sleep, then," Nicci said. "I would not like to be this tired when we finally reach her."

"I think you're right," Kahlan said as she reached the top of the rock.

She took some dried meat when Cassia handed it to her. Once Nicci was up top, she took a piece as well.

"It's easy to make mistakes when you're tired, especially this tired," Kahlan said. "If that man back there hadn't been alone we could have had a time of it. With the half people one mistake would be the last and then we won't ever have the chance to talk to Red."

Nicci seemed to be appraising Kahlan's state of exhaustion. "We also really need to have clear heads when we talk with the witch woman. There is nothing more important than finding out if there is a way to help Richard. We can't afford to make a mistake."

"There is that," Kahlan agreed.

Kahlan tore off a piece of the dried meat with her teeth. It felt good to chew on something. Besides getting no sleep, she hadn't eaten anything for quite a while.

She realized that she was hungry. She supposed this would have to do unless Hunter was true to his name and caught them some rabbit or something. But she hated the thought of taking time for sleep, much less to cook a meal.

She wished that she had thought to bring along more traveling supplies before she'd started out. Time was of the essence and she had been in such a hurry to go after Red to find out what she could do to help Richard that she hadn't even thought to bring supplies. Fortunately, the three Mord-Sith had the presence of mind to snatch up some things as they had hurried to catch up with Kahlan and Nicci.

Nicci was watching her again. "Kahlan, I really think we would be better off in the long run if we stopped and got some sleep."

"But I don't–"

"Your speech is starting to slur," Nicci advised her. "Do you really want that to happen when you talk to Red? I haven't slept much, either, and I know how weak I'm feeling. You have to be worse."

She sighed. She looked around and saw a recessed area in a short rock wall and stopped. "Maybe we should think about getting at least a couple hours of sleep."

"I hate to stop, too." Nicci heaved a sigh of resignation. "But if we don't get at least a little rest it will diminish our chances of making it to Red and finding out if she can give us any answers."

Kahlan knew that talking to witch women was always a draining experience. She would not want to be half asleep and miss something, some vital clue or nuance.

"All right," she finally said. "Let's lie down here and try to get an hour or two of sleep."

Cassia gestured between herself, Laurin, and Vale. "You two sleep. The three of us will share a watch so that we can get a little ourselves."

Kahlan was too tired to argue. When she nodded, the three Mord-Sith quickly cut bundles of small balsam boughs for a sleeping mat. They covered it with armfuls of dried grasses. It wasn't the most ideal way to sleep, but up against the rock it was partially protected and good enough for a short nap.

Cassia climbed up on top of the rock above them to take the first watch. She sat with her arms around her bent knees as she looked out over the woods. The moon behind the clouds lit the expanse of sky just enough to be able to make out the woods. It wasn't enough light to see detail to travel by, but it would be better than nothing for standing watch. On watch, hearing was often more valuable than sight, because at night sound carried a great distance.

From the perch of a nearby rock, Hunter watched them making preparations. He seemed to possess the curiosity of a cat, and watched everything they did to get ready for a brief sleep. His ears swiveled back and forth as they followed everyone's movements. He yawned, looking like he wouldn't mind a nap himself.

Kahlan flopped down on the rough mat beside Nicci once she and the other two Mord-Sith had settled in. Even though it was far from the most comfortable bed she'd ever used, she was so tired that it seemed to be more than comfortable enough.

Nicci let the small, floating flame extinguish, casting them into darkness. Once the flame had sparked out and her eyes adjusted, Kahlan saw that with the moon lighting the clouds she could see more than she would have thought. She was relieved that the Mord-Sith would be able to see as they took turns standing watch.

Kahlan wished she had a blanket to keep warm in the night chill. She didn't want a fire, though. The light would attract the attention of anyone close and the smoke would reveal their presence for a great distance. If they were going to sleep for longer, she would have asked Nicci to use her gift to heat some rocks. But it wasn't that cold and she was already falling into the numbing embrace of sleep.

She lay on her side, curled up to stay as warm as she could while thinking about all the times she had slept in the woods with Richard. She thought about some of the wonderful times she had cuddled up to him.

As she began to cry softly, Hunter crept in close, purring, and curled up against her stomach.

Kahlan laid an appreciative hand over the warm little creature and fell asleep thinking of Richard.

CHAPTER

7

When Kahlan woke and squinted around she was relieved to see that the sky had just begun to lighten with the approaching dawn. She sat up and spotted Vale waking the other two Mord-Sith. Nicci squatted down beside the brook not far away, splashing cold water on her face.

With the faint light of dawn it was already light enough that they would be able to see where they were stepping without the need of Nicci creating a flame to light their way. Kahlan stretched as she yawned. Daylight would enable them to see if they were being attacked. They would be able to see well enough to run, or fight if they had to.

Although she knew that they had to have slept for a couple of hours, it felt like she had been asleep only a few minutes. She needed more, but at least she did feel somewhat better. As she stood she told herself that it would have to do.

"Nice bed you made for us," Kahlan said in a weary voice to the three Mord-Sith. "We better get going."

They returned the smile as Kahlan started out toward where Hunter was sitting up on a rock waiting for them.

Once he saw them all up and moving in a line, he bounded off, expecting them to follow.

Kahlan's back ached from sleeping on the ground, and she felt stiff all over. She put her hand on her middle and smiled when she felt the warmth still there from Hunter sleeping tight against her the whole time.

As the overcast day brightened under an iron-gray sky, they reached the far edge of a ridge, where they had a view out at the trackless forest ahead. It was disheartening to see the vast wilderness spread out below and the enormity of the mountains rising up beyond.

"When we were in the village of those people living by the witch woman, it was in a mountain pass," Nicci said.

Kahlan nodded, feeling discouraged that the mountains were still far off beyond rugged woodlands. "That means we still have a long way to go."

When hopelessness threatened to overwhelm her, she forced it away by keeping herself focused on what she would say to Red once they reached her. They couldn't afford to fail.

Hunter trotted off down the slope, looking back over his shoulder as if to say, "Come on. Let's go."

Without a word, they all moved out to follow. The slope led them down into densely forested lowlands among craggy hills. Though they weren't mountains, it was still difficult traveling.

Despite the difficulty of the terrain, Hunter found them a way through it all so that they were able to make good time until near midmorning, when they came to an impassable ravine that looked to be a long split completely through the rocky forest. It wasn't far to the opposite side, but it was too wide to jump across.

The five of them stared down at the rushing water of the stream at the bottom. Though roots hung down the sides, they were not stout enough for handholds and the

dirt certainly didn't look stable enough to climb down.
Kahlan could see no way for them to make it down the
overhang. Even if they could, the opposite side didn't
look to have a way to climb back up.

Before Kahlan and the rest of them could begin to
look for a better place they might be able to cross, she
saw Hunter on the opposite side of the chasm. She
frowned, wondering how he had gotten across. When
he saw that she had spotted him, he started loping off
to her left, as if he wanted them to go in that direction.

"Let's see where he wants us to go," Kahlan said as
she started following the edge of the drop. "He obviously knows a way across."

In places the edge of the cliffs had given way and taken
trees with it. In another place they were forced to go
through the woods to get around a spot where the tangled and thorny brush among trees growing right up to
the edge was dense and impenetrable. Some of those
trees leaned out over the drop, trying to find a patch
of light for themselves. Vines hung from some of those
trees, but they didn't look strong enough that Kahlan
would trust trying to use them to swing across.

As they came out of the woods Kahlan saw Hunter
sitting on a log of a tree that had fallen over the chasm.
He waited in the middle until he was sure they had spotted him. Once he knew they were watching, he turned
and crossed the rest of the way over to the other side,
clearly letting them know that this was the way they
needed to cross.

Hunter had no difficulty at all crossing the log. Not
only was he smaller and lower, but he had claws if
he needed them. If he did fall, he was quick enough to
be able to catch the log with his claws. He didn't look
like he feared falling, though. He was catlike in that he
seemed to have no fear of heights.

When Kahlan peered over the edge it made her pulse quicken.

"Hunter," she called across the ravine, "we can't walk over the log like you can."

He sat on the other side watching her, as if to ask why not.

Kahlan knew she couldn't do it. She could balance pretty well for a few steps on a log going across a narrow stream if it meant keeping from getting wet, but she couldn't balance for such a distance over a drop that would be fatal. Making it even more difficult, the humidity and frequent drizzle left the log slippery. Just thinking about trying to cross on it made her heart beat even faster.

Kahlan turned to Nicci. "Any ideas? We can't walk across like he did."

"Sure we can," Cassia said.

Without explaining, she straddled the log and started shimmying across, using her hands as well as her legs to hold on. In no time at all she had made it to the other side. She stood up and smiled at them.

"See? Easy."

Vale shook her head as if it was silliness and walked across the log, arms stretched out to the sides, as if she had been doing such things her whole life.

"You don't need to stand up and walk across like her," Cassia called over the chasm. "It's not that hard if you do it like I did."

Kahlan knew they couldn't afford a delay. She got down and straddled the log. The bark was rough. Gummy sap stuck to her hands as she worked her way along the log, trying to look at the two Mord-Sith waiting on the other side, rather than look down.

Cassia was right. In short order Kahlan and then Nicci and Laurin made it across. It turned out to be a lot less trouble than Kahlan had feared when she first saw Hunter trot across.

Once they were all on the other side, they plunged back into the woods, following after Hunter. Before long they came to yet another ridge, but this one overlooked a narrow valley below that seemed softer because it looked mostly to be leafy trees, rather than the spiky shapes of pine and spruce. Hunter quickened his pace as he galloped down the slope, apparently wanting to hurry them along.

Coming down the slope from the ridge and out of the rough rock, they reached an area of smoother ground. It grew thick with grasses dotted with white flowers. As they moved farther into the area, the grass became increasingly shaded by maple, ash, and oak trees. Once he saw they were following, Hunter bounded away. Kahlan frowned as she watched him disappear off into the trees out ahead. It wasn't like him to run off like that and vanish out of sight.

She wondered if he might be checking some danger or investigating a strange smell, like the stench of half people. Whatever it was, Kahlan found it a bit disturbing the way he had so abruptly vanished into the woods. She lifted the sword a few inches, checking that it was clear and its magic ready, then let it slide back down.

Emerging from a crowded area into a more open cathedral of monarch oaks, they all spotted something ahead. It looked like a person in an expanse of gravel beside a shallow stream.

Kahlan saw Hunter sitting on a rocky ledge in the shadows to the right, beside the crystal-clear water moving slowly past.

"I smell meat cooking," Vale said.

Kahlan smelled it, too. She could see the wisps of smoke from the cook fire.

"It's the witch woman," Nicci said in a low voice, her gaze remaining locked on what she was seeing.

"Are you sure?" Kahlan whispered back. "From this distance I can't make out who it is."

"I don't need to see her," Nicci said. "I can sense her power with my gift. It's hard to miss."

"That's disturbing," Cassia muttered. "I hate magic."

Without waiting to discuss a plan, Kahlan started toward the figure in the distance. Her plan was to find out if Red could help them, and if she could, to make sure she did. It was no more complicated than that.

When they got close enough Kahlan could see that there appeared to be something cooking on several spits above a bed of glowing coals. The witch woman stood bent over, tending to the coals with a stout stick.

As they got closer, Kahlan could see that Red was wearing an elegant gray dress that looked completely out of place in the wilds of the Dark Lands. It looked more like something one would wear to a palace ball. It made Kahlan, who was wet and filthy from mud, her hands dotted with spots of sticky sap, feel like a beggar.

The woman's bewitching sky-blue eyes made her tight thatch of ropy red locks, by contrast, look all the more red. The gray dress, by its lack of color, served to make the dazzling color of the witch woman's eyes and hair stand out all the more. Although it would seem to make sense, Kahlan knew that the woman's red hair was not where she had gotten her name.

The witch woman at last looked up with those piercing blue eyes. "Ah, there you are, Mother Confessor. Right on time."

"On time for what?" Kahlan asked suspiciously as she came to a halt not far away.

Red glanced around and spread her arms as if it were obvious. "Why, lunch, of course."

"You were expecting us?" Kahlan asked.

Red frowned. "Yes, of course." She gestured off toward the ledge outcropping where Hunter sat watching. "I sent your little friend to get you."

Kahlan nodded. "I thought that might be the case." She held a hand out to her right. "This is Cassia, Laurin, and Vale." She lifted her other hand out. "This is Nicci."

Red smiled indulgently. "Yes, I know, the sorceress you were supposed to kill."

Kahlan ignored the reprimand. "I hope you don't mind that I brought them with me."

Red shrugged. "No, of course not. I have my own protection. I don't begrudge you yours. In fact, considering the deteriorating state of affairs, I consider it a mark of wisdom."

"That's what I needed to talk to you about . . . the state of affairs and all that is at stake. At stake for all of us."

"Yes, yes, now won't you all pull up a rock, so to speak, and have a seat? Lunch is ready."

Kahlan and Nicci shared a look.

"You made us all lunch?" Kahlan asked.

"Yes," Red said. "I've been expecting the five of you, and I know that you are all hungry. I don't think it's wise to have a serious discussion about the world of the dead on an empty stomach."

Beside the stream, low rocks lay scattered through the area of gravel in more than enough numbers for each of them to have their choice of places to sit close to the fire. Kahlan had more urgent matters on her mind than lunch, but it did smell good and she was starving.

Red used a forked stick to push sizzling meat off the spits onto a flat rock where a pile of already cooked meat was cooling. It appeared by how much there was that she had been cooking all morning. Not only was there a variety of several different things, from what looked like boiled eggs to rabbit to fish, but there looked to be more than they could all eat. There were even some wild plums to the side.

Red gestured as she handed them each a sharpened, forked stick. "Go on, help yourselves. I know that you have been traveling hard and are all in need of a good meal."

Cassia glanced at Kahlan. When Kahlan gave her a slight nod, Cassia and Laurin stabbed pieces of the rabbit meat. Kahlan started out with a couple of eggs. Nicci chose a piece of fish.

"Snake!" Vale said with delight as she found a long

string of meat in the pile. "I haven't had snake since I was young. It was always one of my favorites."

"I know," the witch woman said without looking up from setting aside the cooking rod. "That's why I prepared it."

"Thank you," Vale said as she held up the string of meat between a finger and thumb. She bit off a long chunk from the bottom and chewed with obvious delight. "Delicious," she told Red.

Red smiled.

Gravel crunched under Kahlan's boots as she went to a rock on the opposite side of the bed of hot coals from where Red sat. Red's rock of choice was taller than all the rest, so that once they were seated she looked down on them a little. Kahlan had seen enough queens holding court to get the point. As the Mother Confessor, she ruled over those queens, but at the moment that was about the last thing on her mind. She was content to let Red hold court if that was what pleased her.

Kahlan cracked the shell of an egg and started peeling it off. "What are you doing here, in this place?" She deliberately glanced around. "What brings you here?"

"Why, you do, Mother Confessor."

"There must be more to it," Kahlan said, not buying the simplicity of the answer. "We were on our way to see you at your home. You would have seen me there. Why come here, instead?"

"Well," Red said with a flick of her hand, "I'm afraid that my place is a bit of a mess right now. I don't mind it, but I wouldn't feel right receiving guests there."

Kahlan looked up from under her brow as she popped the shell off the small end of the egg. "What do you mean, it's a mess? It's a mountain pass. How could it be a mess?"

She bit off half the egg and chewed as Red's sky-blue eyes studied her for a moment.

"Do you remember me telling you how I got my name?"

Kahlan swallowed the egg as she peeled the second one. It was a great relief to be eating something warm and fresh.

"Yes, you said it was because there were times when you made that mountain pass run red with blood."

A small smile spread on the woman's lips. "That's right."

"Are you saying that you had some sort of trouble there?" Nicci asked.

The witch woman ignored Nicci and instead glanced at the Mord-Sith in their red leather outfits–outfits designed to obscure the shocking sight of blood. The sight didn't bother Mord-Sith, but it did others. All three were taking bites of meat off their forked sticks, but their gazes stayed on the witch woman. Kahlan could read Mord-Sith well enough to know that they considered the witch woman to be a potential threat. She was used to having Mord-Sith protecting her and Richard. She was glad to have them along. Like most Mord-Sith, these three were as guileless as they were deadly.

Kahlan missed Cara something fierce, but not as fiercely as she missed Richard.

"You see," Red finally went on, looking from the other four back at Kahlan, "the demon–"

"Demon?" Nicci interrupted again. "What demon?"

The witch woman's unsettling gaze glided to Nicci. "The one who belongs in the underworld. The one who came into this world where he does not belong. The one who would unbalance the worlds of life and death."

"You mean Sulachan," Nicci said, not the least bit intimidated by the look the witch woman was giving her.

"Of course."

"So, what were you going to tell us about this demon, Sulachan?" Nicci asked.

"He seeks to bend the forces of the Grace until they break. In his time he–"

"We know," Nicci said as she licked white flakes of fish from a finger. "What does this have to do with your home being a mess?"

Red idly rolled a red lock of hair around a finger as she studied Nicci with a hint of disapproval. "You are a very forward woman, aren't you?"

Nicci shrugged as she stabbed another piece of fish from the pile on the rock. "We didn't come for a social visit," she said as she sat back down. "Every moment counts if we are to send the demon back to the under-world where he belongs. Time is precious–at least it is here in this world. I don't think we have a lot of time to lose."

Red conceded the point with a nod. "Well, from what I saw in the flow of time, he knew that you had escaped those he sent after you. He wanted all the soldiers an-nihilated. He wanted some, like Lord Rahl, the Mother Confessor, and anyone else gifted, captured and brought to him. He had plans for all of you and was furious that you escaped his grasp.

"The demon knew where you were headed, so he sent another force of his half people after you. A large force. He believed that this time they would not fail him."

Kahlan glanced at Nicci out of the corner of her eye. This was news. She had expected that Sulachan might send more half people after them, but didn't know that he had.

"So what happened?" Kahlan asked.

"The route you traveled to get to Saavedra took you through the only mountain pass in that area of the mountains. If the horde of half people wanted to get to you, they had to follow the same route and come through that same pass, my home, first."

Kahlan swallowed some of her egg. Nicci paused eating her fish.

Cassia's eyes widened. "You mean the half people chased you out of your home?"

The witch woman frowned at the Mord-Sith. "I don't get 'chased out' of my home by anyone."

"How close are they?" Nicci asked. "How much time until they reach us?"

Red clasped her fingers together around one knee. "I don't think you understand."

Kahlan did. "You killed them. You slaughtered them all."

Nicci looked up, her gaze moving suspiciously from Kahlan to Red. "Witch women can't personally take direct action to alter events of consequence."

"True." A smile widened on Red's lips. "We don't interfere with events in the flow of time—events of consequence, as you put it. While we see such events and try to use what we see to help those involved, those events must be allowed to run their course.

"For example, I told the Mother Confessor that you would kill Richard, and that she must kill you if she was to prevent that from happening. She chose a different path. As much as I advocated against such a choice, it was her choice to make. I could not kill you myself, I could only let her know what was going to happen if she did not act. The flow of time played out as I feared it would. It played out as I had warned."

Cassia frowned and looked up before taking another bite of rabbit from the forked stick. "If you knew something bad was going to happen, like Lord Rahl dying, and you did not act to prevent it, then the death is your responsibility."

"It might seem that way to someone who does not understand such things, but we can't impose ourselves overtly, directly. That is just the way it is for witch women. While it might seem to others, like you, that such action would be the right thing to do, what others don't see is that our altering events directly endangers the Grace itself."

Cassia clearly wasn't satisfied with the answer. "How does it do that?" she pressed.

"The Grace may seem simple," the witch woman said, "but it is complexity beyond what most people could begin to understand. The demon understands such things. By using forces within the Grace, he seeks to destroy it. For example, he used Richard's lifeblood to breach the veil. Things such as that endanger the stability, the balance, of the Grace and therefore of the world of life.

"It is the same way with a witch woman. It would be difficult to explain the tenets of our existence to one who is not specifically gifted as a witch woman, but take my word for it that restrictions exist for me just as they exist for you."

Cassia looked first to one side and then to her sister Mord-Sith on the other side. "We have no restrictions. Except to follow orders."

"Does your Agiel work?"

"Well, no."

"That's because it needs the bond to the Lord Rahl in order to function. That's a restriction. That's why your Agiel doesn't work. Even if it does, there are restrictions to how it works. For example, you can't use it on a Confessor—unless of course you want to die a horrific death."

Cassia stared down at the meat on her stick without answering.

Red gestured around herself. "My restrictions have to do with the nature of all things, and they exist for sound reasons. One of those restrictions is that we can, if we choose, use what we find of events in the flow of time to help those involved understand the choices they have in the events that are to unfold, but we are not free to directly take part in those events we see. You might say that our place is to be advisors.

"If we directly, personally, take part in that flow, take actions ourselves, then the balance is destroyed because we would be acting on what we see. That is an unbalanced use of power, and all power must be balanced or it can be destructive. We could lose much more than we could ever gain."

"You acted with Emperor Sulachan's forces," Cassia pointed out. "The Mother Confessor said that you killed them."

"That was different. That army of half people took a route that brought them into the sanctuary of my home. That is sacred ground. That changes everything.

"Once they came, they intended to rip my flesh from my bones and devour it, thinking it possessed my soul and they could take it for themselves. They would have killed me to steal something that is not able to be stolen.

"The balance within our nature allows for us to respond to a direct threat to our lives." The witch woman's expression turned icy. "My valley pass ran red with their blood," she said in a chilling, quiet tone. "Their corpses lay in heaps and mounds, food for my worms."

Cassia finally swallowed her bite of rabbit. "Your worms?"

"Don't ask," Kahlan told the Mord-Sith under her breath. "So you killed them all?" she asked Red, wanting to get back to business.

"All but one." Red looked up from the memory. "I'm afraid that it left the pass a bloody mess. Their blood ran in rivers and covers everything. And that is to say nothing of all the viscera and rotting corpses. The stench is quite unpleasant, I can assure you. Hardly the place to receive guests until they are all turned to nothing but bleached bones beneath the grasses. Besides, by coming here I met you somewhat in the middle and that saves you precious time."

Red looked deliberately at Nicci. "You expressed a concern about time. I saw the flow of time, of course, and I knew the urgency of why you would come to me, so I thought to help you by meeting you partway."

"That isn't a violation of directly participating?" Cassia asked.

Red smiled indulgently. "No. That isn't how it works. I came to advise. That is something I am born to do."

"What do you mean you killed all but one?" Kahlan asked. "You said you killed all but one."

"It's rather complex, but basically since I interfered with events directly, even though I had every right to defend myself, I had to leave one of the enemy alive."

Kahlan thought that was rather odd. "Why would you need to leave one of them alive?"

"To balance what happened. Even one is enough to fulfill the need for balance."

Kahlan wasn't satisfied. "How does leaving one alive balance killing a horde of them?"

She gestured among the five women before her. "I had to leave one for you to kill, since you are the ones this horde was after. You are the ones central to events. I had to leave one for you to kill to bring you into direct contact with the event in the flow. That makes you part of it. That is the balance, not the numbers involved."

Red's gaze finally moved deliberately to Nicci. "Speaking of killing, and the events in the flow of time, you realize that the Mother Confessor drastically altered the flow by sparing your life. She made the conscious decision to save your life."

Nicci didn't show any reaction. "It's only fitting."

Red looked genuinely puzzled. "In what way?"

"Her husband saved my soul."

A small smile finally returned to Red's lips. "You may have the chance to return the favor and save his."

That's what we're here about," Kahlan said, eager to get to the heart of the matter. "I was murdered–just as you predicted–but I came back from the world of the dead. We need you to help us do the same for Richard."

Red watched her, but her expression showed nothing. "You failed to do as I told you you must. As a result, Richard Rahl's life was lost, as I told you it would be."

An edge crept into her voice. "He was the only chance we had of stopping Sulachan and preserving the world of life. I told you how to save him, and yet you chose not to heed my warning. Now he is in the grip of the dark ones, being dragged ever downward on a long descent into eternity."

"I know that. We need you to help us get him back. We need you to tell us what we can do."

Red blinked. "You can't do anything. He's dead."

"So was I," Kahlan said. "If I came back, maybe there is a way he can as well."

Red shook her head. "I told you how to save his life. You chose not to take that chance offered in the flow of time. All that can be done now is for us to try to free his soul from the clutches of evil in the underworld so that he might have a chance to stop Sulachan from the other side. That is the only chance I see in the flow of time."

Kahlan did her best to keep her temper under control. "I have fought my entire life for others. I have fought that they might live and so they could live the lives they want to live. Now, I fight for myself, for my own chance to live the life I want to live . . . with Richard."

Red's expression darkened. "I gave you the chance to save him, Mother Confessor. You chose not to take it. You made the choice. Because of that, he is lost to us."

Kahlan's fists tightened. "You are not the only one who has restrictions, who must balance things. I, too, have to live by my own sense of what life means. I can't take an innocent life. I couldn't kill Nicci or I would be violating who I am and what I stand for."

"We are near the tipping point," Nicci said before Kahlan lost control of their purpose. "Once such forces as Sulachan controls are loosed, there will be no one and nothing able to put them back where they belong. Once everything has spun out of control, it is only a matter of time before it is all over. Life–existence–would be extinguished.

"Emperor Sulachan and Hannis Arc arrogantly think they will be able to control the forces of chaos, use them to rule what they will bring about. They are deluded.

"Your abilities are powered by what the Grace represents. Sulachan wants to bend those forces until they break. That threatens the entire world of life–it means your very existence is at stake as well."

"I know what is at stake," Red said in warning. "In this case, acting upon that danger is dangerous in and of itself."

"What do you mean?" Kahlan asked.

The witch woman leaned forward. "You are seeking to meddle in the world of the dead, in the forces of the underworld."

"What is it you think we are here for?" Kahlan growled.

Red blinked. "To help Richard's soul escape the trap he is in and go to the good spirits. If he does that, he has a chance to marshal those forces to cut off Sulachan's power. His power is both Subtractive and occult—both are underworld forces. If Richard can do something about that from the other side, we might be able to stop the darkness that will soon smother the world of life. In that way you will also help the man you love so much to find eternal peace."

"He can work to do that from this side," Kahlan insisted. "We need his soul brought back to the world of life."

Red was momentarily struck speechless with anger. "He's dead!"

"Prophecy says that he is the only one with a chance to stop the grim fate Sulachan and Hannis Arc are trying to bring about."

"Yes, prophecy says he is the one. The flow of time tells me he is the only one with a chance. But from the other side. That is how the flow of time tells me he has a chance to stop Sulachan. With him dead, now, that is the only way."

Kahlan wiped a trembling hand back across her eyes. Before she could say anything, Nicci spoke first.

"Red, I lived at the Palace of the Prophets. I lived there a very long time. While I was there, I studied prophecy, as all the Sisters did. Richard is named in many ways in many of those prophecies. I saw him mentioned throughout thousands of years of writing, although at the time I did not fully comprehend it all or connect it to him.

"Our prelate knew who he was, though, and she protected Richard since before he was born. She knew he was the pebble in the pond, the one who would be born to do what must be done. Many prophecies named him as the only one who would be able to stop one with Emperor Sulachan's power by ending prophecy itself. They don't say how, only that he is the one who can.

"Richard is the only chance we all have. He is the only one with the potential to save the world of life. To save life, he must be here, in the world of life.

"Even the first Confessor, Magda Searus, saw that three thousand years ago and did what she could to help him." Nicci gestured to the ring with the Grace on it that Kahlan was wearing. "The first Confessor sent this ring across time by leaving it for Richard to discover along with the message that he is the one meant to fight for what the symbol on this ring represents, to fight the battle begun by Sulachan in her time. That ring, that duty, has now come full circle, from the first Confessor, to the last, just as Sulachan first threatened the people in the time of Magda Searus, and he has now returned to threaten life in our time.

"The Mother Confessor, the descendant of the very first Confessor, has now come here to you, come with the weight of the responsibility she carries across the ages, to ask you for your help in finding a way to do what must be done.

"If you do not help her, then Richard's soul will be lost for all time. Our only chance will be lost. We all will die. You will die—not only die, but fall into the hands of the Keeper of the underworld.

"To do those things, Richard needs to be here in this world. Every prophecy says as much."

Blood went to Red's face as she leaned toward the sorceress. "Do you now begin to comprehend what I saw in the flow of time? Do you now begin to see why she should have done what I told her to do? Had she done as I told her she must, Richard would be alive."

"No he wouldn't!" Nicci said as she shot to her feet.

"Don't you see? Your view is limited because you can't see what Richard will do. His involvement obscures your view of the flow of time with events involving him. Had the Mother Confessor done as you said, what would actually be the result?"

Red swept an arm out in an angry gesture. "Richard would be alive to do as you say he must to stop Sulachan."

"No, he wouldn't. That's the point. Because you see the flow of time it sometimes blinds you. You can't see Richard's actions because he is a pebble in the pond. You can't see what more there is in that flow."

Red cooled a little and folded her arms. "I'm listening."

Nicci gestured down at Kahlan. "What would have happened had she killed me? She would still have been murdered, just as you saw, right?"

"Well, yes."

"But I would not have been there to heal her damaged body."

"Right," Red said, "so you also would not have been there to end Richard's life. He would be alive."

Nicci was shaking her head emphatically. "No. Only for the moment."

The witch woman frowned down at Kahlan a moment before turning her gaze back up to Nicci. "What are you talking about?"

"Richard would have done it himself. Had I not been there to do it, he would have ended his own life in order to go after Kahlan. When he asked me to stop his heart, he told me that he didn't want to live in a world without her. He said that if I wouldn't do it he would use the sword to do it himself.

"Had I not been there to heal her body right after she was stabbed to death, and then stop Richard's heart, Kahlan would be dead, her body damaged beyond the ability to be a vessel for her spirit, with no hope of being healed, but Richard would have done the same thing. He would still have ended his own life to go to the world of the dead to either try to find a way to bring her back, or to protect her from the dark ones so she could have eternal peace and he could be with her there."

Red paced off a ways, considering. Kahlan couldn't see her face. After a time she turned back.

"Dear spirits," she whispered. "You may be right. He is as headstrong as they come when he has the bit between his teeth.

"With such a free will, and being gifted, it can't be foreseen how the ripples he creates will interact with other people and other events. Doing as I said very well might have resulted in events turning out exactly as you say, with him dead in the end, and the Mother Confessor as well."

"I know they would," Nicci said. "Not because I can see the flow of events in time, but because I know the man's heart. He has often said that he would go to the underworld to get Kahlan. He meant those words. He was dead serious. He would have ended his own life to go after what matters to him more than life itself.

"Had it happened your way, the three of us would all be dead. Instead, with the way it happened, it leaves Kahlan and me still alive. That means we can work to change things. Had it not happened this way, there would be no hope, but now, with us alive and able to work on the problem, there is at least a chance.

"Sulachan and Hannis Arc must be stopped before they can ever bring the insanity of their scheme to pass. You may know about the flow of time, Red, but I know more about prophecy than you will ever know, and I can tell you with absolute certainty, that our only chance–your only chance–is Richard."

"Yes." Red swallowed. "And now he is dead."

CHAPTER 10

Y es, he is dead, but so was I," Kahlan said. "I came back and so must he. There has to be a way. It's the only chance we have."

Red slowly shook her head. "I saw you coming, but because your purpose involves Richard, and I can't see events surrounding him very well, I thought you must be coming to seek my help to get his spirit free of the dark ones who have him. That's what I thought you would want. My intention was to help you free his spirit so he could work to help us from the other side of the veil and then go on to find peace with the good spirits."

"That's not good enough," Kahlan said. "You need to help us bring his spirit back to this world, help us bring him back to life so he can stop Sulachan."

Red looked exasperated. "But it's not like it was with you. You were dead very briefly. He is well beyond that point. Sometimes, if it is done quickly enough a person can be pulled back through the veil. But in this case too much time has passed. Richard is beyond that point."

"You know that I had the Hedge Maid's poisonous touch of death in me," Kahlan said. "That touch was tainted with death and brought to this world. But the balance was that in the world of the dead that touch also carried the spark of life. Like me, Richard had the same taint of death in life. That means that his spirit would still have to carry that spark of life. At least for a time."

Red shook her head without looking up. "As remarkable as it was, I understand how it was possible for such a thing to work for you. The difference is he has been dead too long. Your body was healed and you came back to it almost immediately. His soul may indeed still carry that spark, but the connection between worlds weakens in a very short time as his body breaks down and decomposes. Even with that spark, there is nothing viable for his spirit to return to."

"Yes there is," Kahlan insisted. "You don't know all that happened to change that."

Red frowned as she turned back. "What are you talking about?"

"Abbot Dreier was gifted and he also possessed powerful occult abilities. Those are the same powers that were used to create the half people. I was able to get Dreier to use those abilities to suspend the death process in Richard's body."

"Suspend the death process?" The witch woman looked incredulous. "What are you talking about?"

Kahlan stood. "The half people–like the ones who came into your home–live for an extremely long time because they carry a link to the underworld. Emperor Sulachan was once a powerful wizard. He stripped their souls from them and sent those lost souls to wander between worlds, forever lost. He then linked their soulless bodies to the underworld with the use of occult powers in order to suspend time from touching them in the same way it ordinarily touches anything living.

"Emperor Sulachan planned to transcend death. Since everyone he knew, everyone he ruled, would be long dead by the time he returned, he would not have a nation to command, no army to reestablish his rule. In order to accomplish that he wanted the half people waiting and ready to serve him once his spirit returned to this world."

"That's true . . . ." Red frowned as she recollected. "When they came through the pass where I live, I remember feeling within them that terrible connection to elements of the underworld."

Kahlan stepped closer. "That timeless link keeps them from aging like normal people. It keeps time from working on their living body the way it ordinarily would."

"It was the same with those of us who lived at the Palace of the Prophets," Nicci said as she came to a halt beside Kahlan. "Nathan Rahl lived there for nearly a thousand years. The prelate was nearly as old. I lived there for several lifetimes of those outside the spell of power around the place. The link to the timeless element of the underworld works. I'm living proof of it. So is Nathan Rahl. So are the half people."

"By using his occult powers in the same way," Kahlan explained, "Abbot Dreier was able to link that timeless element of the underworld to Richard's body to keep it the same as it was the moment he died. He isn't living, but time isn't ravaging his body, either, as it ordinarily would. Dreier said Richard will remain in that state for quite a long time. He isn't alive, but his body is not exactly dead, either.

"You might say that his life is suspended."

"I don't know. . . ." Red was still skeptical, but she was frowning in thought.

"I do," Kahlan said. "You have only to touch Richard's flesh as I have done to know it's true. He seems so alive, like he is only asleep, except he takes no breath and his heart is still. Yet he never went stiff the way the dead do in short order, nor did his blood pool on the underside of his body. His tongue isn't swelling the way it does in the dead.

"He remains the same now as he was in life, the same as the moment he died, except that his life force, his soul, his connection to the Grace, is beyond the veil."

Red gave Kahlan a disparaging look. "That's a pretty vital element. It is an essential element."

"I know, but he is preserved for now until we can figure out how to bring his life force, his spirit, back into his body. Until then, his body waits, ready to receive his spirit."

"Do you grasp the full meaning of what the Mother Confessor is saying?" Nicci asked Red. "There is a link from this world–from Richard's body–to the underworld where his spark of life is. The Grace still exists. The lines within the Grace are still intact through the boundary of the veil–at least until Sulachan destroys what the Grace represents.

"Until then, death is here, in this world, while life is there, in that one. It's in balance for the moment."

"But that balance can't last–it won't last," Red told her.

"Of course not," Nicci agreed. "That is why we must act, and act quickly, while we still can."

"If it is actually possible. Understanding such complicated connections and balanced elements is one thing. Altering them is an altogether different matter. Hope will not accomplish such things."

"It's hope based in precedent." Nicci gestured off to the southwest. "Sulachan came back from the world of the dead. His demon spirit did, anyway, but his body had not been preserved the way Richard's is so he can never really join fully with it. His spirit returned to a desiccated corpse."

"That's true," Red whispered as she brooded in thought.

Nicci leaned closer to the woman. "And how did Sulachan accomplish such a thing? How did he bring his spirit back? He used Richard's lifeblood. Prophecy names Richard as the bringer of death. In this case, Sulachan used that to bring him, in death, back to the world of life. Richard's body still contains that blood of the bringer of death."

Red arched an eyebrow at the sorceress and then began to pace, hands clasped behind her back. Gravel crunched under her boots as she slowly walked to the stream and back.

"The pebble in the pond, the bringer of death, the Lord Rahl, Kahlan's husband . . . the one named in prophecy so many times and in so many ways, the one meant to stop Sulachan, must be brought back from the world of the dead," Nicci insisted. "If he is the one prophecy names, then there must be a way, otherwise there would be no purpose to all those thousands of years of prophecy."

"Unless it is all false prophecy," Red muttered. She finally paused in her pacing to stare at Nicci. "But this would explain a lot of things that I've seen in the flow of time that haven't made any sense."

"Then you do know of something," Kahlan said as she moved closer to the witch woman.

"Perhaps I was thinking of it the wrong way," she said under her breath to herself as she went back to pacing.

Kahlan listened to the crunch of gravel for a time before her patience ran out. "What do you mean?"

"I wish I could see him more clearly, see the flow of time around him. That husband of yours has been using and confusing prophecy for thousands of years. He likewise muddies the things I see in the flow of time."

"Well, you must be able to see some of it. You have seen the events around him before. If you see a shadow, you know that something is casting that shadow. What part are you able to see?" Kahlan asked. "Maybe that's a place for us to start."

The witch woman cast a worried look at Kahlan. "I didn't have the pieces I needed to understand."

"Understand what?" Kahlan asked. "Have you thought of a way that you can help us?"

Red drew a long breath. "Maybe. I think I may be beginning to understand what you must do." She walked off toward the stream, staring down into the swirling water for a time. "If I'm right, then you should fear the things I would tell you."

"And what would those things be?" Kahlan asked.

The witch woman finally returned to them and studied both Kahlan and Nicci's faces for a time before answering.

"You must make the dead talk to you."

"And how would we do that?" Kahlan asked without pause, already knowing that she would be willing to do whatever it took to get Richard back.

Red put a hand on her shoulder as she turned her blue eyes away, looking off into things only a witch woman could see.

"I must leave you for a little while," she said in a quiet voice. "Keep the fire going. It will be dark when I return. Eat, rest, and wait until I return."

"Where are you going?" Kahlan called after her.

"I must look into the flow of time to seek the answers you need," the witch woman said as she walked off toward the trees.

Hunter bounded down off his rock and followed her as she disappeared into the shadows.

CHAPTER 11

Kahlan stood in a rush when she saw Red emerge from the stand of oaks. Nicci stood beside her. The Mord-Sith were on watch nearby and started back when they saw the witch woman returning.

"So, what did you mean when you said that we have to make the dead talk to us?" Kahlan asked impatiently. "Did you discover what we need to do?"

Even though it was dark, the low fire gave enough light to reveal the troubled expression on Red's face. She looked drawn and tired. She had been gone the entire afternoon and then for hours after the sun had set. Kahlan had worried that she might never return.

"Not you," the witch woman said to Kahlan as she came to a stop before Nicci. "You."

"Me?" Nicci asked. She quickly recovered from the surprise. "All right, if it will help us get Richard back. What is it I need to do?"

Red slowly paced off partway toward the stream, still deep in thought, as if trying to think of a way to explain it.

"This is not something that can be accomplished easily, if at all," the witch woman said without turning back. "We are seeking to bring a soul back from the world of the dead. In order to do such a thing, we are going to need a great deal of help. It's not something that can be accomplished without the help of others."

"What others?" Nicci asked.

"Dead, others," Red told them, still gazing off into the distance.

Nicci took a deep breath. "I don't understand. How can the dead help us?"

"Do you mean we need the help of the good spirits?" Kahlan guessed.

Red turned back and looked at her for a moment before speaking. "Richard is lost in the world of the dead, the spirit world. In order to help him, before anyone can help him, he first must be found in that eternity of darkness. That's a very specialized task. In order to find him, we first need a spiritist."

"A spiritist?" Nicci asked in a suddenly displeased tone.

"Yes. The flow of time does not ordinarily reveal what is sought, but this time I was able to catch a glimpse of factors surrounding potential events. Sometimes the flow is strong and rich in detail, which tells me that it is fixed and a near certainty. The flow I saw of you ending Richard's life after the Mother Confessor had been murdered was that way. It was obscured where Richard was concerned, but I knew what was going to happen with you two.

"The flow I saw this time was only a slender thread, and I was only able to get a fleeting glimpse of it. That indicates there is only a remote chance that events will take this course. Time moves like a river, taking the easiest course. Ordinarily such slender threads are backwaters in time and are to be ignored, since the chances of them cutting a new path for the river in time are so unlikely. The thread exists only to reveal the richness of possibilities, not the probability.

"It is the allowance made for free choice to balance prophecy.

"For it to come about requires a series of events to come about in precise fashion. To help such a thread to strengthen, Richard must first be found. The only one who can do that is a spiritist."

Kahlan looked back and forth between the two women. "What's a spiritist?"

Nicci glanced over at Kahlan. "A gifted woman who can travel the darkness of the spirit world and seek specific spirits. She is gifted with the talent to find and then talk to spirits."

"You mean she communes with the dead," Kahlan said.

"That's the heart of the matter," Nicci admitted.

Kahlan shrugged. "All right. Where do we find one of these spiritists?"

"I'm afraid you can't," Nicci said. "There are none living anymore."

Kahlan looked back at Red, reflections of the firelight flickering in her knowing eyes. "How can we use a spiritist if they are all dead?"

"I told you. You must talk with the dead."

"You're talking in circles," Kahlan said, her temper heating. "How do we talk to the dead if we need a spiritist to do that, and they are all dead?"

Red tipped her head toward Nicci. "She is the only one who can do such a thing."

Kahlan's gaze went to Nicci. The sorceress was frowning.

"What are you getting at?" Nicci asked. "I'm not a spiritist."

"You were a Sister of the Dark."

Nicci's frown tightened. "So?"

Red admonished her with a look. "What is it Sisters of the Dark deal in? They deal in the world of the dead.

They worked for the forces of the underworld. They sought to bring the Keeper himself into this world."

Nicci backed up a step. "I'm not that person anymore. I'm no longer a Sister of the Dark."

Red flicked a hand in irritation. "All but you are dead. That's because all but you chose to stay to that dark path, and it cost them their lives. You chose otherwise because Richard showed you another path. Now, you must use what you know in order to help find his path back. You still have those same abilities. Doing such things is the use of your abilities for the right reasons."

"What abilities?" Kahlan asked suspiciously.

"A sorceress can't delve into things in the underworld the way a skilled wizard can." Red tipped her head toward Nicci without looking at her. "That is why Nicci, like all Sisters of the Dark, killed a wizard and stole his gift to use in dark devotion to the Keeper. Sisters of the Dark possessing the ability of a wizard can make contact with those in the underworld. Like all such Sisters, the Keeper once visited her in her dreams and granted her access to the darkness."

Red's eyes finally turned to Nicci. "Isn't that right?"

The fire crackled as the two women stared at each other for a long moment.

"What does this have to do with finding a spiritist?" Nicci finally asked in a dangerous tone.

"You wanted to know how to bring Richard back," the witch woman said in a quiet voice that was no less dangerous. "I'm telling you what that thread in the flow of time reveals. I'm not saying it can be done. I'm only telling you that if it is to be done, if Richard is to be found, you must do what only you can do.

"We need the help of the good spirits to rescue him and help put him on the path of the Grace so he may return, but first, before anything else can be done, he must be located in that eternity of darkness. The demons

of the dark have their wings wrapped around his soul,
hiding him." She looked right at Kahlan. "Isn't that
right, Mother Confessor?"

Kahlan swallowed at the memory. "I'm afraid it is."

"If you want to find him to have a chance to bring
him back," Red told Nicci, "then you must first contact
a spiritist in the underworld and seek her help."

Nicci heaved a sigh. "All right. Let's just say for a moment that I can find a way to do such a thing. What is
her name?"

"The one you need is named Naja."

"Naja!" Kahlan said in surprise. "Naja Moon?"

Red nodded.

Kahlan rested her left palm on the hilt of the sword–
Richard's sword. "That's the woman Richard said left
messages in the shielded caves in the village of Stroyza.
That's where he found this ring. Naja knew Magda Searus and the wizard Merritt."

The witch woman nodded. "That is the one I saw in
the flow of time." She let out a deep breath. "The problem is, she was a powerful sorceress. She, in fact, once
helped Emperor Sulachan with his evil schemes, but it
was under threat of death and she eventually escaped.
She came to the New World to help in the fight to defeat
Emperor Sulachan. She understood the things he was
doing, and was a great help to those in the New World."

"So why is that a problem?" Kahlan asked. "Nicci
has to somehow contact Naja Moon, in the underworld,
right? Naja knows how to find Richard?"

"Yes, she could do such a thing," Nicci said in Red's
place. "The problem is, spirits of such power are difficult to find."

"It's worse than that," Red explained. "Sulachan traveled the underworld. Naja had turned against him and
he would have wanted revenge for that betrayal. Men
like Sulachan carry grudges beyond the grave. Naja

would have wished to have eternal peace and would have hidden her spirit."

"I can understand that," Nicci said. "I would not want to be found in the underworld by a wizard of Sulachan's power."

Kahlan wiped a weary hand across her eyes. "Can you find her or not?" she asked Nicci, her impatience lending an edge to her voice.

"Maybe, but only if I had the help of a lesser sorceress, a lesser spiritist," Nicci finally admitted. "One less tangled in Sulachan's affairs and the world of the dead. One who understood how to ride the rim between life and death."

"Isidore," the witch woman said with a nod. "Her name is Isidore. She is the one you want."

Nicci's frown deepened. "You saw that in the flow?"

"She, too, lived in the same time and also knew Magda. She was a talented spiritist. The flow of time tells me that Isidore was once involved in the same struggle and so, with such links, she would be the one who would be able to find Naja in the darkness."

Nicci sighed. "The only problem is I'm not sure I can do such a thing—open myself to the underworld and contact spirits."

Red was watching her. "You mean you are not sure that you want to do such a thing."

Nicci didn't answer.

Kahlan gripped Nicci's arm. "This is for Richard. You told me you would do anything."

Nicci swallowed. "I know. But this is . . ."

"What? This is what? Not something worth doing for Richard? Is that what you're saying? That it isn't something you want to do for him?"

Nicci shook her head. "No—that's not what I'm saying. It's just that . . . you don't know what it means."

Kahlan thought she might know what it meant. It

meant that Nicci had to return to her own inner darkness, to that time when she was a Sister of the Dark, a place from which Richard had brought her back.

"That is only the beginning," the witch woman said in a quiet voice. "Finding the first spiritist to find the second so that they can locate Richard is only the beginning of what must be done. Once he is found, then he will need to be pulled away from the dark ones. Even Naja, though she may be able to find him, does not have the power to do such a thing."

Kahlan's frustration was welling up at the ever-increasing complications. "Then who does?"

Red flicked a hand without answering the question. "First things first. Before we can hope to accomplish the other things that must be done, the one called Isidore must be located, and then she must find Naja so that she can then travel the darkness and find where the demons of the dark are hiding Richard. There is only a slim hope that we can accomplish even that much. It is too soon to worry about what must be done once he is found. I still need to look deeper into the flow of time for answers to such questions."

Kahlan turned to Nicci. "Then let's get started. Let's not waste any more time."

With a hand on her forearm, Red sought to slow Kahlan down. "In order for Nicci to do that, we must first get back to where you are keeping Richard's body."

"You're coming back with us?"

Red's features were tense and solemn. "If we do not succeed in bringing Richard back, there is no hope of stopping Sulachan. If he and Hannis Arc are not stopped we are all going to die.

"If there is a way for me to help with this thread of hope, then I can't let the chance go by without offering what advice I can provide. I may be able to give you an idea of the choices that will have to be made."

Kahlan nodded. "Thank you. Your help would be greatly appreciated."

"You must know one other thing." The witch woman paused and shared a look between Nicci and Kahlan. "If he returns, it will be because someone will forfeit their life for him. Someone will willingly trade their life for his. Someone who loves him."

"I don't like the sound of that," Nicci said under her breath.

Nicci had already shown her apprehension at taking up her dark craft one last time in a desperate attempt to contact spirits in the underworld. Kahlan knew that such an attempt would be profoundly dangerous.

"That isn't fair," Kahlan said in frustration. "We can't selfishly ask someone else to die so that Richard might live."

Red shook her head. "No. Not so that Richard might live, but so that everyone else might live. It is the balance that must be kept, much like the balance of the one man I let live for all the ones I killed. On the surface it may not seem equal, but it served the need for balance.

"The worlds of life and death seek balance. In this case, for all the lives that will be saved, one will be forfeit."

Kahlan desperately wanted Richard back. But she didn't want someone to have to take his place.

"Find a place to get some sleep," Red told them. "We leave for the citadel at first light." She looked over at the Mord-Sith. "No need for you to stand watch. You are all safe here tonight."

Sentries spotted Kahlan and the others moving through the woods and signaled back to the soldiers of the First File closer to the citadel. Hunter melted into the shadows rather than come with them. When the six women made their way through the arched opening in the stone wall, a number of armed men were waiting to meet them.

Torches lit the tense faces of the soldiers. They all looked relieved to have Kahlan safely back under their protection. In the flickering light she could see dark green moss growing in some of the joints between the blocks of stone wet from the steady drizzle. As they made their way into the cobblestone square yet more men rushed up to meet them, their hair slick and stringy in the damp weather.

"Mother Confessor!" Commander Fister called out as he lifted a hand in the air. "Praise be to the good spirits for bringing you safely back to us."

Too tired from the day of traveling through the forests of the Dark Lands to want to have a long conversation, Kahlan merely nodded her greeting.

She knew they had a difficult night ahead of them, and her mind was on the ordeal yet to come.

As distant thunder rumbled through the mountains, the commander fell in beside her. After going a short distance, he glanced back over his shoulder, making sure none of the others could hear him. "Who's the old woman you brought along?"

Kahlan held her hood aside as she glanced back to see where he was looking. Red, like Nicci and the Mord-Sith, also had the hood of her cloak pulled up against the miserable weather. The hood and the darkness concealed her identity. Although the woman hadn't said anything about it, Kahlan knew that witch women were secretive and she suspected that Red didn't want people staring at her.

"It's the witch woman," Kahlan whispered as she leaned toward the man, still holding her hood aside. "My advice is to stay well clear of her."

Commander Fister stole a quick glance back, then straightened, directing his gaze ahead.

"Was there any trouble while we were gone?" Kahlan asked him.

He cleared his throat. "The people down in Saavedra are concerned about what D'Haran troops are doing here. They think we are bringing trouble among them."

"Why would they think that?" Kahlan asked without looking over at the man.

"Well," he said with an unhappy sigh, "I'm afraid that there might be half people about."

Kahlan snatched his sleeve and brought him to a halt. "Half people? How many–"

"I don't think it's a large force," he said to calm her down. "They didn't attack the citadel."

Nicci joined Kahlan at her side. "Where did they attack?"

"In an outlying part of the city. It appears they were scavengers hunting the Dark Lands, not a large force. There have been reports of a couple of attacks, but they weren't organized or coordinated. The latest was an attack at the outskirts of the city last night. When some of our men heard the screams they raced to see what was going on. A couple of half people had attacked an old couple. The men put a swift end to the attack."

"The couple that was attacked?"

Commander Fister shook his head with the sad news. "By the scraggly looks of the two men who stormed into their small home, they were lone hunters."

Kahlan scanned the darkness but saw nothing to indicate trouble. "If it was one of the groups Sulachan and Hannis Arc sent, it wouldn't have been just a couple men."

Nicci nodded her agreement. "Richard said there were different kinds of half people, not only the Shuntuk that Hannis Arc uses as warriors."

"You're right," Kahlan said. "With the wall to the third kingdom breached all of them will be free to come out and hunt for those with souls. An isolated place like Saavedra will be irresistible to their kind."

They needed to do something to stop the madness that had been unleashed on the world. If it wasn't too late, only Richard would be able to do something about it. If they couldn't bring him back, then the fate of the old couple would be the fate of everyone.

"I've posted men throughout the city to make sure nothing sneaks up on us," the commander said. "We've told the people in town about half people hunting the Dark Lands. I thought it best if people knew the truth."

Kahlan nodded. "Of course. Where is Richard's body?"

"In the bedroom, on the top floor, where you told us to put him."

"You haven't let anyone go in there, have you?"

"No, Mother Confessor, no one but me and of course I have men posted in the room. The staff has been restricted from the upper floors. The entire citadel is locked down and under heavy guard."

Kahlan wasn't worried about any of the men of the First File. She had fought with these men. She would put her life, and Richard's, in their care without second thought. But there were other dangers about. She didn't know most of the staff. They had spent their lives as servants to Hannis Arc. Although they seemed to be thankful to be free of his rule, Kahlan didn't know for certain where their loyalties lay.

Samantha, the young sorceress, was also on the loose. She had sworn vengeance against Richard. Her first act of retribution had been to stab Kahlan through the heart. Because Richard's first concern had been Kahlan, it had given Samantha the opportunity to escape. These soldiers, as good as they were, could not stop a sorceress with her abilities.

Men standing to either side opened the big double doors for them to enter the grand greeting hall. The immense room was lit by warm lamplight and a crackling fire in each of the two fireplaces. The mellow light revealed rich, deeply colored carpets and tapestries, tasteful chairs and couches in muted tans, and small, polished mahogany tables near the chairs. The aroma of wood smoke helped cover the musty smell.

Kahlan saw soldiers stationed up on the balcony guarding closed doors and halls. Other soldiers patrolled below in the gallery to the side beyond stone columns. The heavy draperies were drawn against the night. A few women in gray dresses and aprons stood waiting between the sides of the split, grand staircase should they be needed. Everything looked peaceful enough, but there were too many threats closing in on them–to say nothing of Richard's condition–for Kahlan to feel the least bit at ease.

Yet more soldiers stood guard beside the spiraled,

marble newel posts. As Kahlan began to ascend the grand staircase, Nicci leaned closer from behind and whispered, "We need to have the top floor cleared of all the men."

Kahlan frowned back over her shoulder. "The whole floor?"

"Yes."

Kahlan didn't argue or ask for an explanation. "You heard the woman, Commander. Have the men pull back and leave us to care for Richard."

He glanced back at Red coming up the stairs ahead of the three Mord-Sith. When she met his look with her piercing blue eyes, he quickly turned back around, his face having lost a little color.

"Yes, Mother Confessor."

He signaled to one of the men with him. "Run ahead and have all the men clear out of the room and stand guard until we get there. Have the rest of the floor cleared."

The man clapped a fist to his heart in salute and ran up the stairs three at a time.

Commander Fister scratched his head, clearly looking uncomfortable. "What is it you intend to do with Lord Rahl, if I might ask?"

Kahlan considered for a moment. She didn't want to say too much.

"Whatever we can," she said, leaving it at that.

She actually didn't know much more herself. Nicci had brooded the entire way back to the citadel. She hadn't wanted to share anything about what she was going to have to do. None of the rest of them were eager to hear exactly what it was that a Sister of the Dark did in regard to the underworld. Whatever it was, it unnerved Nicci, and Nicci was hardly one to be unnerved. Kahlan had left the sorceress to her own thoughts.

Kahlan paused at the door to the bedroom where Richard lay.

Two First File soldiers stood guard beside the door. Each held a pike upright. It was warm on the upper floor and the massive muscles of their arms glistened with sweat.

"The room is emptied, Mother Confessor," one said.

Kahlan nodded her thanks.

"Is the rest of the floor clear?" Nicci asked.

"It is. We're the last two up here."

"Well, let's go, then," the commander said to him. He turned to Kahlan, trying not to let his gaze wander to the silent witch woman. "We will be downstairs if any of you ladies need anything."

Cassia closed the door once they were inside. The three Mord-Sith quietly took up positions to guard the door, making sure that no one could come in, even though the commander had sworn that no one would disturb them. Mord-Sith rarely took anyone's word for anything.

A stand with a dozen and a half candles as well as a lamp on a table softly lit a large, thick tapestry on one of the walls. The tapestry depicted a dark forest scene. It reminded Kahlan of the Hartland woods where she had first met Richard.

The room had one window that revealed only darkness outside the diamond-shaped pieces of leaded glass. Dark, rust-colored carpet muted the sound of their footsteps.

The canopy bed was covered with dark blue-green fabric embroidered with gold edging. Heavy draping of the same blue-green fabric was gathered with ties around the posts at each corner, making the bed look like a holy shrine.

Now, Richard lay dead on that bed as if he were lying in state. Kahlan supposed that in a way he was.

She stood numb at the foot of the bed staring at Richard lying there still in death. Her heart hammered so hard at seeing him that she swayed on her feet.

Red pushed the hood of her cloak back, letting the ropes of her red hair fall free.

"Do you mind?" she asked in a soft voice as she lifted a hand out toward Richard.

Kahlan shook her head, fearing to test her voice.

Red moved to the side of the bed and put her hand against his face, holding it there for a moment. She didn't say anything. Kahlan suspected that she wanted to feel his flesh as well as use her gift to confirm what Kahlan had told her about how his body was preserved.

Once satisfied, she said nothing as she went to stare out the window into the darkness. Kahlan sat on the side of the bed.

"I'm back," she whispered tearfully to him as she took up one of his big hands in both of hers.

"We're coming for you, Richard. Be strong."

Nicci picked up the corner of the dark, rust-colored carpet and threw it back to reveal a plank floor beneath it.

"Can we help?" Cassia asked.

"Yes." Nicci motioned with an arm. "Pull the carpet back out of the way. I need the floor to be clear."

Cassia and Vale quickly rolled the heavy carpet up against the wall. Beneath was a bare pine wood floor marked with centuries of scratches, scrapes, and dents, its color muted with the patina of age.

Kahlan realized that this floor, this citadel, had been constructed back in the time the great wall had been built to contain the threat from Emperor Sulachan and his third kingdom. The citadel had been made as part of the defensive system to protect the world from the terror beyond.

"Time has been suspended in Richard's body," Red said back over her shoulder to Kahlan, "just as you said."

"So then it will work?" Kahlan asked, hope rising in her voice.

Red shook her head. "I'm only saying that if it wouldn't

have been as you said, then there would have been no chance."

"Which means there is a chance," Kahlan pressed.

Red showed a polite smile. "A chance."

Kahlan wished she knew what the woman saw in the flow of time. On second thought, she realized, maybe she didn't want to know. Sometimes, the future only held pain.

A breathless Laurin rushed back into the room and with her foot pushed the door shut. She handed Nicci a scratched and dented metal bowl when the sorceress stood.

"Metal, like you asked for."

Nodding, Nicci took the bowl and only gave it a cursory look before handing it to Kahlan.

"Three fingers deep should do."

Kahlan blinked. "What?"

"I need some of your blood." She seemed distracted as she pointed to a spot inside the bowl. "This much—up to here."

Kahlan stood holding the bowl, not sure what to do as she watched Nicci carefully pacing off distances across the floor.

Red returned from the window. "I'll help you."

"No!" Nicci said, turning back suddenly. She went to the bedside table and extinguished the lamp. "No one but she must touch it."

Red withdrew her hands and watched Nicci from the corner of her eye for a moment but didn't say anything. Kahlan pulled her knife from the sheath at her belt.

Nicci, checking that the window was closed and latched, turned and saw what Kahlan was about to do. "Wait. There is a prophecy that says 'Sacred is the sword when there is no hope but in the blade.' I think it might have to do with this night."

Kahlan glanced toward Richard and then the sword

standing at the wall, leaning against the head of the bed. She looked back at the sorceress.

"Meaning?"

"Don't use a knife. Use Richard's sword," Nicci said in a quiet voice as she went back to pacing off a distance on the floor.

Something about the words "Richard's sword" gave Kahlan a chill. It was a weapon that had drawn so much blood in the defense of life.

Trying not to think about those connections, Kahlan replaced the knife and drew the sword from its elaborate scabbard, sending the soft, distinctive sound of the singular blade ringing around the stone walls of the room. She sat on the edge of the bed and set the bowl in her lap, trying not to think about how much of her blood Nicci needed, or what the sorceress intended to do with it.

Without giving herself any more time to consider it, she pulled the blade across the inside of her wrist. The blade was so sharp that she hardly felt it at first. As a copious flow of blood began to pump out, the cut began to hurt in earnest. Kahlan bent her wrist back over the bowl, turning her hand up out of the way so that the blood would all run into the metal bowl.

Nicci carefully paced off distances in several directions and placed eight candles on the floor in a large circle. With a quick gesture she used her gift to light the candles, then came over to the bed to check.

"That looks like enough," she said as she peered into the bowl. She placed a hand over the cut. Blood ran out between and over Nicci's fingers. Kahlan felt a hot jolt of magic sear into her arm. "That should close it."

She was right. The wound stopped bleeding immediately, even if it did still throb with a sharp ache.

Nicci picked up the bowl and gestured with it. "I'd like you three to wait outside, please. Guard the door.

Don't let anyone in. Don't open the door, no matter what you hear. Not for anything, understand?"

Cassia frowned. "No matter what we hear? What are we likely to hear?"

"I don't know," Nicci said in a distracted voice as she turned back to the open expanse of floor. "The screams of the dead–that sort of thing. Just don't open the door. I must let the underworld free in here. The room needs to remain sealed lest that darkness get out beyond."

Cassia shared a quick look with the other two. "I think we will be happy to keep it closed."

"What if one of you cries out for help?" Vale asked.

"The only one crying out for help will be you, if you open the door."

"Right, then," Vale said. "The door stays closed."

Once the three Mord-Sith had left and closed the door, and even though Kahlan was in the room with a witch woman and the sorceress, she felt lonely. Both of these women dealt in matters Kahlan could not adequately imagine. Worse, Nicci intended to once more take up her skills as a Sister of the Dark.

Kahlan's gaze wandered to Richard. Knowing that he was dead made her feel more than merely lonely. She felt alone and lost.

When she finally turned back, she saw that Nicci had begun using the bowl of blood to make a large circle. She dipped a hand in the fresh blood and used her dripping fingers to paint on the floor with the blood.

"What are you doing?" Kahlan asked the sorceress.

"Drawing the outer circle of the Grace," she said without looking up, "starting with the boundary to the underworld."

Some of Kahlan's earliest memories as a girl had been watching gifted people draw the Grace. Drawing the Grace was both a deeply reverent act and an invocation of magic. It was central to many things in the lives of the gifted. Although a Grace looked relatively simple, the complexities of it took a lifetime of study if they were to be used properly.

Though it could be drawn in only two dimensions, it was meant to represent all four–the three physical dimensions in space and the fourth dimension of time. Converting those four elements into two dimensions of the Grace through the use of the gift was serious business.

Kahlan had very rarely seen anyone dare to draw a Grace with blood.

Much less her blood.

She knew that drawing a Grace with blood could invoke alchemy of consequence as well as dark forces that ought not be called upon. She supposed that this required nothing less.

The creation of the Grace had to be done in precise fashion, the way Nicci was starting it, with that outer circle representing the beginning of the infinite world of the dead out beyond the circle. Out beyond the circle there is nothing else, there is only forever. This was why the Grace was begun with that circle: out of nothing, where there was nothing, Creation begins.

Nicci dipped her hand in the bowl of blood as she whispered incantations in a strange language Kahlan had never heard before. The sorceress used her crimson hand like a brush, dipping it in the bowl for more blood as necessary, and quickly created a precise square to a mathematical formula in her head, to an orientation only the sorceress understood. The square, its points just touching the inside of the circle, represented the veil between the worlds of life and death. The square was always drawn second so that it would be in place to protect the world of life, once it was laid down, from the power of the underworld.

Nicci again dipped her hand in the blood and painted

with it the smaller circle, representing the beginning of
life, just inside the square so that it touched the sides of
the square in the center of each of its four sides. In this
way, life touched and was bounded by the veil, that also
touched the beginning of the underworld.

With more blood, Nicci drew a precise eight-pointed
star inside the smaller circle. The star represented the
light of Creation. Outward from each point of the star,
the sorceress painted a straight, bloody line, crossing the
inner circle, the square, and the outer circle. The first
four rays she drew bisected the corners of the square,
and then the last four crossed the center of each side of
the square.

Each ray beginning at a point of the star crossed the
inner circle and then the square, finally crossing the
outer circle to end at one of the eight candles. Each
flame, once the bloody line reached it, seethed momentarily with shimmering colors.

Nicci, wearing a glove of blood, looked up in the soft
candlelight. "I need a drop of Richard's blood. Use the
sword. Bring the drop on the blade."

Kahlan found the dark nature of Nicci's voice disturbing. Without pause to consider the instruction, she
went to the bed, sat on the side, and pulled Richard's
hand into her lap. With the point of the sword she
pierced the end of a finger. Working her fingers on his,
she squeezed blood out, letting it collect in a fat crimson
droplet on the end of his finger. Using the blade, she
scooped it up near the point. She could feel the magic
within the sword react with anger to the touch of Richard's blood. Kahlan carefully carried the sword over to
Nicci, being sure not to let the blood she had collected
drip off, or let the sword's anger distract her.

This was the same blood that had been used to bring
Sulachan's spirit back from the world of the dead into
the world of life.

Kahlan held the sword out in both upturned palms, offering it to Nicci. The sorceress shook her head, as if not wanting to touch it.

"The Grace is drawn in your blood. You need to do it. Put the drop in the exact center of the circle.

"Although it can't be seen," Nicci said in a solemn voice, "this circle has a true and absolute center point, which is that point at which we come to be, when we are created, when we acquire a soul. But unlike the outer circle, which represents a beginning without end, this circle is finite. It represents an outer boundary so to speak—death—and a point of beginning."

Kahlan held the point of the sword just above the floor in the center of the circle, letting Richard's blood drip off.

"So, then, you are connecting it all with blood," the witch woman said from the shadows. "You are making the Grace viable."

Nicci nodded. "Life and death are connected in much the same way that Additive and Subtractive Magic depend upon each other to define their nature. Thus, there is, in a very real sense, a connection between everything, even something as elemental as light and dark. Where a shadow is cast across the ground, the shadow is not only connected to what casts it and on what produced it, but it also exists through the presence of the negative shape it creates. Thus, all things, even a seemingly simple shadow, are inextricably linked, locked together, both positive and negative, each depending on the other to exist.

"Just as we need dark to show light, the underworld defines life. Death defines life. The blood gives that representation of life, in the Grace, a reality it would not otherwise have.

"This is all part of what the Grace represents—how the elements are not separate, but interconnected."

"It used to be that wizards traveled between worlds," Red said, transfixed by the bloody Grace.

"Since that time," Nicci said, "they have forgotten how to ride the rim, as it used to be called, between the worlds of life and death."

"Not all of them," Kahlan reminded her, drawing Nicci's gaze. "Richard has done that before. He has gone to the underworld and returned."

Nicci nodded. "Another of the things wizards used to be able to do that Richard somehow managed to accomplish instinctively. Another of the things that mark him as the one."

"Can you travel there?" Kahlan asked, wondering how the sorceress was going to contact the spiritist they needed.

Nicci finally spoke into the silence. "I was a Sister of the Dark. Still, I cannot travel the underworld as Richard or those wizards once did. I can, though, part the veil and look beyond."

Kahlan glanced around the room. "How are you going to see into the spirit world?"

Nicci lifted both arms, gracefully turning her hands over. All the candles in the room except the eight around the Grace extinguished. The room out beyond those eight candles seemed to vanish into nothingness.

"Everything about Richard's life emanating from that point of his blood, touches you," Nicci told Kahlan. "Everything he is touches you. In that way, he exists through you. That is how I will reach into the spirit world–through you."

The sorceress gestured. "Sit in the center, beside that drop of your husband's blood."

Kahlan, tears running down her cheeks, carefully stepped over the bloody lines of the Grace and sat in the center beside Richard's blood.

"To see into the spirit world," Nicci said, "I must be able to look beyond this world to that other realm that exists in the same place all around us, at the same time, in the same place as existence, the negative to the positive, the Subtractive to the Additive.

"In a way, it is the shadow cast by life.

"We are all part of all things. We merely need to look beyond what is around us." She gestured to the candles. "The light of those flames will be our anchor to this world, the world of life, our reminder of what actually exists."

Nicci's words brought back haunting memories for Kahlan of being in that dark place where her soul had been drawn.

Nicci closed her eyes then and began a soft chant in the same strange language she had used before. Kahlan trembled slightly at the enormity of dealing with the world of souls, at her abject misery of having lost her soul mate.

As she was lulled by Nicci's soft, throaty chant, she felt a strange tingling run through her, as if a thousand distant voices were all trying to speak through her. The feeling strengthened or lessened somehow with Nicci's words.

Kahlan waited until Nicci fell silent before speaking. "What is that language you're speaking?"

"It is the opposite of the language of Creation. It is the language of the dead," Nicci said softly without opening her eyes. "It is used by Sisters of the Dark to summon that other world all around us that we never see. The language of the dead contains Subtractive threads that bring about the parting of the veil to the underworld."

In a way, it all made sense. It made Kahlan, sitting in the center of the Grace, feel a part of everything. The problem was going to be finding the one they needed out of all the souls in the darkness beyond the veil, out of all those voices she heard.

"Wait," Kahlan said as she frowned in thought.

Nicci opened her eyes and looked up.

"You said 'Sacred is the sword when there is no hope but in the blade.' I think I know what needs to be done."

She scrambled to her feet and retrieved the amulet from around Richard's neck. In its place, she laid the Sword of Truth down the length of Richard's body. She placed his arms across his chest and then folded his fingers around the wire-wound grip and the word TRUTH woven in gold through the silver wire.

"Let the sword's anger help be your beacon," she whispered to Richard. "Let the righteous rage from the sword help you find your way back to the righteous anger against evil and those who would end life. Let anger be your guide back to the fight for life."

She could feel the magic of the sword's anger heat in response.

When finished, she carefully stepped over the blood and back into the center of the Grace. She held the amulet out by the chain and dropped it into Nicci's hand when she turned up her palm. Kahlan tried not to think about how she had just handed an ancient object of power to a Sister of the Dark.

Nicci placed the chain around her neck and let the ancient amulet, made by Baraccus himself, lie against her chest, against her heart.

"Time to dance with death," she whispered into the darkness.

CHAPTER 14

Hannis Arc, standing in the well-used road, gazed with displeasure at the closed gates in the wall around the small city of Drendon Falls. With the heavy gates closing off the road, the sheer cliffs hard against the back of the city, and the forested mountains all around, the place was well protected from threat of conquest. The falls showering down from the cliffs at the back of the city, fed by mountain springs above, provided ample water flowing through waterways that eventually drained underground, so the people of Drendon Falls felt confident they could close the city gates and be able to endure a long siege.

Hannis Arc had no interest in conducting a siege.

Soldiers of their home guard, most armed with bows or spears, manned the tops of the walls ready to repel any assault. They all watched from a position they considered to be safe, and although obviously tense, didn't look overly concerned. None of them had arrows nocked, or spears at the ready. Hannis Arc knew that Drendon Falls had withstood sieges in the past, and had never been conquered.

Of course, there was not much reason for an enemy to bother with putting a lot of effort into conquering

Drendon Falls. The small city lay on a less important trade route in one of the less populated areas of D'Hara. There were bigger and more important conquests to be made elsewhere. That, in large part, and not the walls, was what had kept the place safe from conquest. It also meant that the defenses had never really been tested in the heat of battle.

For Hannis Arc, it was not a matter of conquest, but a matter of respect. He should not need to conquer people he already considered his subjects. They seemed to be unclear on that point. He intended to make it clear to them.

"You dare to close the gates to the city?" Hannis Arc called up to the man in simple robes standing with both hands resting on the edge of the wall.

"We mean you and your people no ill will," the man called down, "but there have been rumors of terrible atrocities being visited on other places. As the mayor of Drendon Falls I must think first of the safety of the people of my city. We make no judgment against you, sir, and certainly intend no offense, but we must err on the side of safety and keep our gates closed."

Hannis Arc glanced over at Emperor Sulachan, the glow of his spirit twisting the face of his long-dead worldly form into a grim smile.

Hannis Arc looked back up at the mayor on the wall. "I sent people on ahead from other cities with instructions that they speak to you of that very matter–the safety of your people. They were to inform you of your fate should you and the people of your city not bow down and show proper respect."

The man on the wall spread his arms. "We deeply respect all people, and we respect them all equally. We do not want war."

"War!" Hannis Arc exclaimed with a grunt of a laugh. "This is not a war." He looked around, feigning incredulity. "There is no war. The war is long over. This is a matter of rule. It is a matter of allegiance to the D'Haran Empire."

"We are loyal to the D'Haran Empire," the man insisted.

"Well, I am Lord Arc, the ruler of the D'Haran Empire."

The man paused, momentarily unsure what to say. "Lord Rahl is the ruler of the D'Haran Empire."

"Not any longer." Hannis Arc dismissed the distasteful notion of the long line of the House of Rahl with a wave of his hand. "I told you, the war is over."

"We heard of no war for rule," the mayor called down.

"Richard Rahl now resides in the world of the dead," Emperor Sulachan said in a voice that caused the armed men on the wall to take a step back from the edge.

"Dead . . . ?" the mayor asked. "Are you certain?"

"My servants in the underworld have taken his soul and carry it into a forever of darkness."

Hannis Arc checked the silent, eager Shun-tuk nation waiting quietly behind. Only a portion of them were visible among the thick growth of trees. So vast were their numbers that their army extended far back into the forested valley, filling it from the mountains on one side to the mountains on the other.

"Do you really think this place worth the bother?" Sulachan asked in a low, gravelly voice. "Shouldn't we be getting on to the People's Palace? That is the seat of power you seek."

Hannis Arc wasn't worried about the seat of power for the D'Haran Empire going anywhere. "We will be there soon enough."

Sulachan regarded him with a dark look. "We would be best served by securing the omen machine."

Hannis Arc returned a look in kind. "I am the one

who awakened it out of millennia of darkness. I alone awakened it to help me in bringing you back into the world of life. The only man besides me who could use the omen machine is Richard Rahl and he is dead."

Sulachan gazed at him with dead eyes that were alive with the menace of his spirit. "Even so, it would be best–"

"It can't cause us any trouble now that Richard Rahl is dead. I rule the D'Haran Empire, now."

The spirit appraised him for a moment. "You will, but only once you take the seat of power for that empire and secure the omen machine. With the help of my army of half people, of course."

"In good time." Hannis Arc looked off toward the southwest, imagining that he could almost see the vast palace up on the heights of the plateau rising from the Azrith Plain. "Unlike these outposts along the way, the People's Palace is not an easy place to take. You, better than anyone, should realize that. You, better than anyone, understand the importance of instilling terror in an enemy.

"This is all a necessary part of the plan to insure that we will have no opposition in taking the People's Palace. Better to break their spirit before we get there. That will make our reception one of celebration."

The spirit considered briefly before shrugging. "I am in no hurry. I have all of eternity. If that is what you want, so be it."

"What I want is a palace from which I can rule." His temper heating, Hannis Arc leaned toward the spirit king. "I don't want to have to reduce the place to rubble."

The unsettling spirit gaze returned. "As long as the omen machine is secured, that is all that matters."

"Richard Rahl is dead, so for all practical purposes it is secure since there is no one else who could use it. You see to it that the dark ones take him into oblivion and I will see to the omen machine."

"You had better know what you are doing. You have a history of taking chances with that man and letting him slip through your fingers."

Hannis Arc jabbed an angry finger against his own chest. "I'm the one who figured out how to use Richard Rahl and the omen machine–blood and prophecy–to bring you back. I'm not the one who is dealing with him this time. You are the one who is seeing that his fate is sealed.

"Richard Rahl has proven in the past to have many people willing to help him. This time he is in your hands, so to speak. He is in your realm. It is you who needs to worry about seeing to it that he can't interfere."

"He is dead."

"So were you."

Hannis Arc didn't like being lectured to by the man he had rescued from the oblivion of the underworld and brought back to the world of the living. Without Hannis Arc, Emperor Sulachan would forever be banished to the eternity of darkness. The man might have laid out careful plans and taken extraordinary precautions to have everything in place for his return, but without Hannis Arc and his talents, without him going to the trouble of having the symbols he needed tattooed on every patch of flesh as he studied and collected forgotten prophecy, all of those plans would have come to nothing and there would have been no return.

The spirit king glanced to the city wall, his gaze following the men on top.

"I think it unnecessary," he said at last, "but if this is your wish as the new ruler of the D'Haran Empire, then it shall be as you say. My army of Shun-tuk will be only too happy to satisfy your desire to send a clear and terrifying message for those still before us."

"Good." Hannis Arc smiled, happy that the spirit king understood his place. "It is settled, then. We make an example of these people for daring to resist obedience to their ruler. I have, after all, been generous to give a clear offer of peace. It will be useful to let others know what happens to those who do not accept the offer of peaceful obedience. The consequences must be both swift and painful so that others will know that I do not permit disrespect.

"Just be sure to have your people let some of the witnesses escape with word of what happened here. They must race on ahead of us to carry that word to the People's Palace."

At last the emperor smiled. "A small taste, then, of what is to come for this world."

Hannis Arc smiled as he turned to Vika. When he gave her a nod the Mord-Sith stepped forward. Dressed in her red leather, she made quite a contrast to the sea of Shun-tuk behind, half naked, their bodies and faces all smeared with crusty white ash.

"Have them bring the captives forward."

Vika bowed her head. "As you wish, Lord Arc."

She ran back to the Shun-tuk and spoke briefly. Soon the captives were dragged forward out of the trees. They were bound and gagged, their spirits broken. Some seemed almost in a trance from the constant terror. The eyes of others were wide with that terror.

Hannis Arc turned back to the man on the wall. "These are some people from the last city that did not bow down in respect to their Lord Arc."

With that he flung out an arm tattooed completely over with ancient symbols. Some of those symbols lit from within as he invoked his power.

Most of the group of nearly a hundred prisoners were snatched into the air by that power, lifted from their feet and sent flying over the wall screaming the whole way until they crashed down inside.

Some didn't make it over, their bones breaking as they crashed into the stone wall. Those who didn't make it over fell to heaps before the wall, most still alive but in no condition to run. Beyond the wall, those who had come falling from the sky cried out in pain from their injuries.

Hannis Arc turned back to the several dozen remaining prisoners. They were the ones with wide eyes, the ones who would do anything they were told.

Before the man on the wall could ask what he was doing, Emperor Sulachan lifted a hand powered by the bluish glow of his spirit.

The power of that gesture blew the gates apart. Splinters of the beams spiraled through the air. Hot shards of iron from the shattered hinges and straps bounced along the ground. Dust boiled up into the still-falling bits and pieces. Through that cloud people beyond were already running. They had nowhere to run, really. The walls held them prisoner for what was to come.

Sulachan turned to his army of Shun-tuk.

"Feed."

With a howl that vibrated the air, the masses of half people, all desperately hungry for a soul of their own, saw the souls inside and charged for them.

The people inside screamed and shrieked as they ran, trying to find a place to hide. Shun-tuk were skilled at finding hiding souls. Trapped inside the city walls, they were run down by the flood of half-naked Shun-tuk racing in through the gaping hole in the wall. The half people, now in a frenzy to have a soul for themselves, fell on the people of Drendon Falls and started ripping into them with their teeth.

For those who now thought to change allegiance and tried to bow down to Lord Arc, it was too late. They had been given a chance to bow down and they had not taken it. Now, even as they fell to their knees, crying out for mercy, they would serve him in a different manner. They would serve as examples.

Hannis Arc turned to the tattered group of prisoners, both men and women, all filthy with dust and dirt. He gestured with a finger and the rope binding their wrists parted. Their gags fell away.

"Go on to the People's Palace and the places along the way. Tell them what is coming, and that their only hope of salvation is to bow down and swear allegiance to Lord Arc."

The group fell to their knees, wailing with relief. They all crowded in around him, taking his robes in trembling fingers, kissing the cloth, thanking him for his mercy. They all swore undying loyalty to him.

Hannis Arc was gratified to have such a show of respect.

"All right. That's enough. Be on your way."

They all scrambled to their feet and ran to do his bidding.

CHAPTER 15

Uncountable arms reached out of the darkness, clawing the air, trying to catch something, anything. Hands all around tried to touch her, to make contact. Despite how desperately they stretched and raked the air, they could not reach her.

Even with her eyes closed, Nicci could see all the arms and fingers wriggling like a thousand snakes. The hiss of the dead only added to the sense of death closing in around her. Out beyond the walls of arms she could hear the screams of others.

She knew who these souls were. She recognized them. They were the souls of those she had killed.

Nicci lifted a hand before her, pushing back the ones in front, reaching for her, the ones who had deserved to die but in their hatred for life didn't fully realize they were dead. Nicci had no fear of them catching hold of her. These were not demons, and not able to do such things as snatch the living to drag them down.

They were the guilty upon whom she had visited justice.

They could no longer touch her.

Before her, in her mind's eye, she kept the soft light of

Kahlan's spirit safe from those things that wanted to drag her back in among them.

Nicci knew that the dark ones wanted Kahlan back.

Fortunately, Richard had drawn Sulachan's minions to himself, drawing them away from Kahlan's spirit.

Unfortunately, those dark demons wrapped him tightly in their dark wings so that Nicci had no hope of finding him on her own. She had searched beyond the veil before and had found spirits, but she would not be able to find Richard.

Sulachan intended for him never to be found. Though Nicci had considerable power, she was not the match for such evil, especially in his realm.

The task before her seemed impossible. The darkness was thick with souls, like grains of black sand on a beach at midnight, all flowing and shifting constantly as inky waves rolled in and tumbled the sand around. Those souls crowded in from every direction, eddies of them swirling around her and making it impossible to see beyond them. Whenever she parted those in her way, there were only more.

As she approached and they saw her, they twisted and turned, shying away from her. She knew what they were doing. She had seen them before. They recognized that she didn't belong, that she had invaded their peace, that she was a dark force in a world of darkness.

She was out of place, and they were trying to push her back out of eternity to the terror of that momentary spark that was life. They didn't like to be reminded of what they could not have again. They wanted to be left in peace to slowly forget.

In the unfamiliar light of Kahlan's soul, those swirling masses flowed through the darkness like dense schools of fish. Endless masses of dark forms made up of millions of individuals billowed and spiraled in to keep Nicci from that light. They were trying to protect that light from Nicci's darkness.

While she felt like weeping at the beauty of that light, she needed to find her way, and she was being swamped by souls that occupied the darkness. She feared that it was an impossible task to search for a particular grain of sand on that endless, black beach.

Nicci felt gentle hands rest on her shoulders.

It was the witch woman, standing behind her, putting her hands on Nicci's shoulders.

When she did, the nature of the darkness shifted, the souls swirling and whirling in a mad surge as they parted and spiraled back. Nicci smiled inwardly at again seeing the guiding light of Kahlan's soul in the center of that Grace constructed of her blood. From that single drop of Richard's blood in the center, the eternal darkness formed into twisting flows moving gracefully through nothingness.

Nicci realized that the witch woman was using the flow of time to reveal the way through the void. The layers of darkness teeming with spirits folded and turned, rolling over and through itself in undercurrents formed out of nothing, reminding her of strands of smoke curling and billowing through still air. Or blood dripping into still, clear water.

It was as terrifying as it was bewitching and beautiful.

And then, following that flow the witch woman was feeding into her, the light of a soul seemed to appear along those lines out of the black forever. It was a soul Nicci recognized all too well.

It was the soul of the wizard she had killed. It was his power she had taken into her own.

It had been done when she became a Sister of the Dark.

It was something that was beyond forgiving.

The light of the spirit diffused and then consolidated into a glowing form as it confronted her, stopping her progress. She knew that spirits used their light to take a recognizable form.

Nicci didn't know what to do. What could she do? There was no way she could ask forgiveness. She had no right.

The light of the spirit reached out and touched her, then. Touched her soul. In that instant, in that timeless connection, she felt everything he would say to her.

She wept with the beauty of it all. He was at peace. He told her that although she had taken it in the cause of evil, in the end she had done more good with his gift than he ever would have. Although what she had done was an injustice, she had gone on to do the one thing that gave him peace. She had chosen to change, to fight evil, and to make up for all the harm she had done to others.

Nicci did not deserve forgiveness, and he understood that, too. He told her that he could not give her any such forgiveness, that it came from within herself, and that was all that mattered. She saw the beautiful light of his soul, and wept at what she had done to him.

He told her that she carried his gift, now, and he was with her in spirit, helping her new calling, in spirit. Her purpose was his, now. His gift was hers, now.

He ran a glowing, spirit hand down her hair as a father might while smiling down on a beloved daughter. It was a moment of such pure love, such pure acceptance, that it left her shaken and weeping with the beauty of it.

At that, he moved aside, holding out that glowing arm, and welcomed her onward, wishing her well in her mission to fight for the world of life, a cause he said was a noble use of the gift she was born with, and the gift she had taken up.

She felt drained, her emotions exhausted by the confrontation and the agony of sorrow that had only lasted a spark of time, but at the same time, in that eternal world, had lasted forever. She felt as if she knew him better than she ever had, knew herself better than she ever had.

In the distance, Nicci could hear Kahlan asking if she was all right, but she was too far away to answer. The witch woman answered in her place, telling Kahlan that Nicci was moving on to search.

With her mission firmly in mind, Nicci summoned her strength to push on into the darkness, riding the flow that continued to swirl onward through the endless night.

She saw the light of countless souls along the way. All looked the same, like a night sky scattered with a blanket of stars. They all floated at eternal peace in the firmament. She didn't know how she would find one star among the countless numbers scattered ahead forever.

But then one of those glowing stars swept in closer.

"I am Isidore," the spirit said in a voice that was like sunlight. "I felt you calling for me."

Nicci saw the glowing form sweep in with effortless grace, taking a shape that mimicked her once-living form, but made of light. Nicci couldn't get out the rush of everything that suddenly came to mind. There seemed too much to convey.

"I must help Richard," she finally said to the spirit. "I need to find Naja."

"I know," Isidore said. "I am here to guide you."

With that, the spirit form moved off into the flow. Nicci thought that Isidore was just about the most beautiful creature she had ever seen. The spirit glowed with an innocent, childlike kindness. Her smile was a warm summer day.

Together, Isidore leading, Nicci being swept along in her wake, they went into a landscape that was darker

yet, with tunnels of blackness through the inky gloom.
It was a disorienting journey that was up and down all
at the same time, twisting, turning, spiraling their way
through places where it seemed impossible to pass.

In a recess of darkness, a deep cavern of eternity, they
came to another spirit that took on human form. Isidore
gently touched the shoulder of the other.

"This is the one you seek."

Nicci drifted forward. "Naja?"

The spirit regarded Nicci with cool detachment,
rather than Isidore's warmth.

"What is one of your kind doing here? Why have you
come to disturb me?"

"It's not what it seems," Nicci said. "I come in the
guise of a Sister of the Dark because there was no other
way. I had to use what only I know, what only I can do,
to do what must be done."

"And what would that be?"

"What you wanted in life, what you worked for . . .
to stop the emperor, Sulachan."

The shadowy spirit hissed as she backed away at the
name.

"Suuuulachan," Naja said with venom. "His vile
spirit haunts the underworld with an intent darker than
death."

"I know that you tried to stop him when you were
alive. You and Magda Searus and the wizard Merritt."

At speaking their names, their glowing spirits came
into view out of the darkness.

"Why have you come here?" the spirit of Magda
Searus asked. Much like that of Isidore, her spirit was
a wonderful, warm glow that instilled a sense of wonder and peace in Nicci.

Nicci turned and held an arm out. "I come to help
her," she said as she moved aside so they would see the
glow of Kahlan's spirit from where she sat in the center

of the Grace beside that single, luminous drop of Richard's blood.

"The Mother Confessor," Magda whispered with a benevolent reverence that only a good spirit could summon. "You brought her spirit here?"

"Only a bit of the light within her," Nicci said. "She powers the Grace that I used to come to you."

"Why have you come?" Magda asked.

Nicci lifted a hand out toward the loving spirit close at Magda's side. "For the same reason."

"For her love," Merritt said with understanding. "The one in life we knew would come one day."

"That's right," Nicci said. "Sulachan has escaped the underworld and again walks the world of life. Richard Rahl is the one who must stop him. In your time, you all worked to stop the emperor and his forces, and worked to lay out the path for the one who would come after you who can stop the demon."

"That is no longer our world," Naja said, the others nodding their agreement.

"Richard Rahl is not in the other world. He is in this world. He is here."

Distress and anguish haunted their features.

In alarm, Merritt glided closer. "That is not supposed to happen. He is supposed to be the one to stop Sulachan. He needs to be in your world to do that. He can't succeed from here. He can't help that world from here. None of us can."

"I know," Nicci said. "That is why I had to come here, why I had to use the same dark talents I once used for evil, but turned around and now used to fight for the world of life."

The light of the spirit of Naja coalesced into a shape that mimicked the exotic form she'd had had in life, but now in light rather than flesh and blood. She moved closer.

"How did such a thing happen? We all took precautions, we guided prophecy, we left all the help we could. How did he die?"

Nicci looked at the spirits all gazing at her. "I killed him," she said, holding her hand out toward the raven current curling away before her, "just as was foretold in the flow of time."

Merritt glided closer still in a manner that Nicci could only interpret as anger.

Nicci swallowed at the look he gave her. "I had to."

"Why?" he demanded.

Nicci again held her arm out toward the glow of Kahlan's spirit. "For her. She had been murdered. Sulachan's dark minions had her soul and they were taking it into the depths of darkness. Richard asked me to stop his heart so he could go after her, trade places with her, and send her back to the world of life. It mattered to him more than his own life."

The four spirits stared at her with the kind of great sadness that can come only from understanding and empathy.

"I came to find a way to bring his spirit back to his worldly form. The world needs him. His body waits for him in the world of life, touched with a link to this world to keep it ready."

"But if he died," Naja said, "then his spirit is where it belongs."

"Ordinarily, yes. But not in this case. Just as with the Mother Confessor, Richard was touched by a Hedge Maid with a poison containing the call of death. It was killing them. But in this world, the opposite–life–taints him with what does not belong here. Carrying that taint of life, he does not belong here. He belongs in the world of life."

"All men die," Naja said.

"Yes, but it is not his time just as it was not the Mother Confessor's time. It was only by the meddling of Sulachan using and distorting forks of prophecy as well as dark elements. Richard belongs in the world of life for now. He must return to stop Emperor Sulachan and fight for life or the veil will be torn apart and the worlds will implode together."

The world of the dead was silent for a moment. It could have been an eternity.

"We must see if we can help him," Magda finally said in a quiet voice filled with compassion. She lifted out a glowing spirit hand toward the light of Kahlan's spirit. "For her."

"For everyone," Nicci corrected.

The spirit of Naja smiled. "Spoken like a true sorceress."

The spirit of Merritt moved to Naja. "You must help her find him. You know Sulachan's demons better than anyone. You helped him create them. Now you must help stop them."

"Much the same way as I worked for evil once, much as she worked as a Sister of the Dark?" Naja asked in a tone of irony. "You think I still need absolution?"

With a glowing visage of compassion, Magda shook her head. "You came to us to fight the evil of Sulachan," she said. "You know that absolution comes from within. Now she comes to you in much the same way. She understands because she has traveled your path."

Naja nodded. "We both have worked for evil, and we both have struggled to change. We both did change." She turned to Nicci. "What you are doing now is for good. I will help you."

As a spirit arm surrounded Nicci and began to carry her away, Nicci looked back to the smiles of Magda and Merritt, following behind. It was about the most beautiful sight she could imagine. It was love and under-standing, peace and joy, confidence and competence, hope and well wishes.

It reminded her of something. At first she couldn't un-derstand what. And then it came to her. It reminded her of the aura of light she saw in Richard and Kahlan.

"You have a very interesting spirit," Naja said to Nicci as they raced through eternity. "It will serve you well in this place."

Even though the darkness of the underworld was beyond dark, Nicci began to sense that they were moving into places darker yet. Where before she had seen the glow of spirits, she now saw spirits drifting through the darkness and those spirits were sometimes so dark they were difficult to see. Some were darker than the surrounding darkness. It was a disturbing sight.

"This is not going to be easy," Naja said as she pulled Nicci ever downward among the churning, pitch-black clouds of souls billowing up from below.

"What do we need to do?" Nicci asked.

"Hope that we can do the impossible."

"And do you know how to do the impossible?" Nicci pressed.

Naja's spirit didn't answer.

Nicci began to notice that the dark shapes seemed to be shadowing them, keeping pace, gathering as they traveled downward with them.

When Naja noticed Nicci looking at them, she drew Nicci closer. "Evil spirits," she said in a low hiss.

"How do we fight such spirits in their world?" Nicci asked, more to herself than to Naja.

Naja lifted her arms out as she sailed effortlessly through the eternal night, and her whole spirit gradually began to glow brighter. It was a divine sight. In the glow of Naja's spirit, the dark ones retreated back into the darkness.

"You can't fight them," Naja said. "Not these. These want you to fight them. They want you to be filled with loathing. That only feeds their hate. Showing them light gives them the kind of pain only their kind can feel. It's a hatred turned inward and burns their soul."

"I wish I could glow like that," Nicci said, again half to herself.

Naja's spirit beamed with a bright smile. "You do. You just can't see it yet. I can. One day you will, too."

Nicci couldn't say she was looking forward to it. But she did envy the sense of peace all the spirits had shown her. Ever since Richard had come into her life, it seemed all she had done was to fight for peace. Seeing it in these spirits was uplifting, a rewarding glimpse of its true meaning.

"The dark ones that have Richard," Naja warned, "are not like these. They are not simply wicked souls. They are wicked souls that Sulachan has shaped into demons to do his bidding. They are his dark army in this dark place. I helped him in this, so I know what terrible creatures they really are. I know their terrible strength. They are like the wolves of the darkness, with fangs and claws that can catch a spirit and drag it down forever into the darkest depths of the Keeper's realm."

Nicci watched off to the sides, watched the darkness shadowing them as they glided effortlessly ever downward.

"Even if we can find Richard, hidden by the dark ones in eternal darkness, I don't know how we can get him out of the clutches of those demons. I don't have that kind of power."

"Why couldn't Merritt have helped?" Nicci asked. "He was a powerful spirit."

Naja leaned forward, stretching her neck out, sailing faster yet through the void. "He was, and he has that kind of power, but he does not have the necessary links."

"Links?"

"You have to have friends, here," Naja said, cryptically. "Spirits with the power and the proper links."

Nicci wasn't sure exactly what that meant, except that it sounded like it meant they were in trouble.

"But far more problematic," Naja said, "even if we find him and even if we somehow can get him away from the demons, we on this side cannot send souls back to the world of life. We don't have that kind of power. Once your soul is here in death, it cannot return."

Nicci gestured to the light of Kahlan's spirit. "Kahlan's did."

Naja's spirit turned sorrowful. "She had Richard here to help her. He is different. That is what I meant when I said you need friends here with the proper links. He has always been different, and could always do what no other could do. He was able to recognize and use the unique conditions of the situation to help her to return. For him, if we can get him free, it would still take help from the other side."

"But he still has a spark of life in his soul."

"He may still carry the spark of life that would let it blossom again, like the Mother Confessor did, but unlike her, he has no one to help carry him back to the light of the Grace so that he can return. It would take someone on the other side to do that for him now."

Nicci considered for a time as they glided effortlessly through eternity.

"The witch woman said that someone would have to give up their life for him to live again." Nicci stared off into the darkness. "I'll do it. I will give up my life so that he may live. He has to live. The world needs him. Only he can defeat Sulachan and Hannis Arc. I will do it. I will stay here and die in his place."

Naja regarded Nicci with a sorrowful look. "It may be necessary. But I don't know if even that would be sufficient."

Nicci felt fear and trepidation at the thought of dying, of giving up the only life she would ever be blessed with, but at the same time it no longer felt quite so terrifying as it once did, nor as vital that Richard return. In the past when she had traveled the underworld as a Sister of the Dark, it had been on behalf of the Keeper for the darkest of dark matters. Much as Naja had been doing the bidding of Sulachan, she had been doing the bidding of the Sisters of the Dark on behalf of the Keeper of the underworld. The world of the dead had been a place festering with evil that filled her with panic and dread, even as she worked toward its victory over life.

It no longer felt that way to her. Despite her fear, it felt rather . . . peaceful. She could sense areas of cruel desolation, but they were somewhere off in the darkness and she was not in those places. They couldn't touch her—at least not while she was being guided and protected by Naja.

Traveling this time with a good spirit was a journey of wonder. She longed for such a sense of peace and contentment.

Sensing something, she looked behind and saw specks of light that seemed to be following.

"Good spirits," Naja explained when she saw where Nicci was looking. "Richard Rahl has made many friends among them. They carry that bond with him for eternity."

"Could they help us, then? You said he needed friends."

Naja was quiet for a time. "No," she finally admitted.

"None among them has the power. They merely hold him in esteem."

Naja's spirit lifted a glowing arm out, pointing. "At last. There. See them?"

"No," Nicci said, shaking her head as she stared as hard as she could, trying to see in the blackness what only the spirit could see. "What is it?"

"Dark ones," Naja said quietly as she leaned closer. "They have him."

Nicci felt a flush of hope. "Richard? It is Richard somewhere in that darkness?"

"It is," the smiling spirit told her as she increased their speed to catch the demons in their swift descent.

"The battle begins," Naja said as she looked over at Nicci. "This is a battle we dare not lose, or we lose it for eternity."

"Dear spirits help us," Nicci whispered as she at last saw dark, winged forms with fangs and claws coming for them.

chapter 17

It was the darkness that hurt. It was not the kind of pain he had felt in life. It was different, and vastly worse. This was pain not merely down to his bones, but down to his soul.

This was the darkness of demons, of the Keeper himself, of being hopelessly lost for eternity.

Richard struggled, as he had for what seemed an eternity, trying to rip away the claws feeling like they were dug into his shoulders and legs, trying to pull off the wings wrapped around him, smothering him. It was a suffocating feeling, but it was a different kind of suffocating than any had been in life.

This was a suffocation in darkness. His soul longed for the light. It was a suffocation of being able to get no light. It was the darkness of doomed souls being forever banished from the light, a soul being condemned to an eternity of abject misery with no appeal, no escape, no way to free himself.

Despite all that, it was worth it. He had saved Kahlan from the same fate, a terrifying journey into forever. He would have done it for her all over again, and then done it again. It was more than worth it. It was worth the price, no matter what that price might be, to have her safe, to have the brightness of her spirit once more in the world of life. The world needed that kind of light to counter the darkness.

It was hard, though, to make sense of any of it. It had been so long since he had been alive. It was an eternity ago. At times, it felt like perhaps this was life–a life of misery, fear, dread, and desolation. That was what life without Kahlan had been like. That was why he had gone after her. Life without her was not worth living.

Something shifted. He paused in his struggle. He felt the claws tear through his shoulder, as if they were being pulled away and the demon was sinking them in deeper to hold on, hooking bones even though there were no bones in this place. He felt the fangs sinking deeper into his middle, even though his middle was only the glow of light. The misery was beyond worldly agony. This was an agony of the spirit.

And then he thought he saw a spot of light in the surrounding blackness. It had been brief, and then it was gone, as if the wings had momentarily lost their grip around him, momentarily parted to let through a sliver of light but then closed in again. Richard took that chance to fight even harder against the darkness suffocating him.

Again, light came in between the dark layers of wings, this time for longer before the wings were able to close over him and lock it away. He struggled and again saw an opening in the darkness, and through that opening a warm glow. He frantically fought toward that light, forcing the powerful wings back, pulling the gap open wider. He dragged the inky wings away from his body, only to have them once more crush in to cocoon him.

But then a blinding flash made the dark ones shriek in rage and pain. Again a blinding flash in the eternal night tore at them. Fangs snapped in the darkness as the demons tried to sink those fangs into him again. Claws snatched for him even as they were being pulled back away.

Yet more flashes came in quick succession. He recognized the flashes–not so much for the way they looked, as the way they felt. They were discharges of magic. It was that magic that Richard recognized.

The dark ones howled with the frightful kind of shriek that could only come from the depths of the underworld. It was a sound that could sear the flesh from the living and break bones. It was the sound of doomed souls realizing their fate.

The flashes came with overwhelming speed, one upon another, hammering the demons. Ropes of light ignited in the darkness. Wings caught in bolts of that luminescence ripped asunder. Screams escaped wide mouths lined with fangs. Gleaming spears of magic lanced through their ulcerous bodies.

A form slipped between him and the dark ones, protecting him, sheltering him.

"I'm sorry, Richard," an intimate voice said. "I'm afraid that you are in the world of the dead, again."

Richard looked over his shoulder at the figure close behind him. Arms draped with glowing white robes opened from their protective embrace. The radiant figure regarded him with a sad smile. He recognized the face.

It was a woman he had once killed.

In the distance beyond her outstretched, protective arms, he saw dark, winged figures with glowing red eyes swoop in closer. The protective arms again circled tighter, shutting him away from the demons.

Behind her, a furious battle raged. Light and darkness intertwined, opposites of power clashing with ferocious violence that was both out of place and at home in this strange place.

"You are safe," the intimate voice assured him.

"Denna?"

She smiled at hearing her name from him, especially from him. It had been so long since he had seen that smile. It had been a long time because Denna had long ago died. He had seen her spirit before. She had helped him before.

Then, beyond the protective embrace of the good spirit, Richard saw another spirit, one he didn't recognize. He also saw a presence with form and yet it was not a spirit. He recognized that form.

"Nicci?"

"I'm here, Richard."

"Is Kahlan all right?"

Nicci shook her head with profound sadness. "No. She mourns for you. Life is as unbearable for her with you gone as it was for you with her gone. You condemned her to live the misery you yourself could not endure without her."

Richard felt such guilt as he had never felt. He hadn't thought of it that way. He had wanted so much for her to live that he had not considered if life would be worth living for her. It wasn't worth living without her, and hers wouldn't be worth living without him.

"Soul mates should not be separated," said a voice Richard recognized.

"Zedd?"

The spirit came closer. Although it did not look like Zedd in exactly the way Richard remembered, it was unmistakable. It was all glowing light, very much like his own glowing soul, and the form of that singular light, like the light of other good spirits, mimicked the vessel it had filled in life. It was the radiant spirit of his grandfather.

Richard's soul was filled with jubilation at seeing Zedd looking glorious.

"Seems you have gotten yourself into some trouble, again, my boy. I came to help."

"I don't understand," Richard said, looking around at spirits he knew and others he didn't recognize.

"The flow of time had need of me here," the old wizard said. "I didn't know it at the time, but there was a purpose in that flow and a purpose in my death. This was the purpose. I had lived my life and done all I could there, and now I needed to be here for you, because life has desperate need of you. I am the only one who could pull those demons off of you."

"What do you mean? Why?"

Zedd's gloriously beautiful spirit smiled. "It takes the gift carried into the underworld, and that gift needs to be connected by blood if it is to be able to help you here."

"To be helped, in a situation such as you find yourself, it takes many friends," the spirit of a woman said. "I am Naja," the spirit said when she realized his confusion.

"Naja. Naja, as in the one who wrote the account on the walls of the caves at Stroyza?"

The spirit smiled. "The same."

"That was an awfully long time ago," Richard said.

The spirit gave him an unreadable look. "Not so long. From here it seems only a moment ago."

"Or an eternity," another spirit said.

Richard didn't recognize her, either, but because she was with Naja, and another spirit was with her, he suspected that he knew who it was.

"Magda Searus?"

The smiling spirit nodded and held out a glowing hand. "And this is Merritt, my soul mate." She lifted her hand back toward the constellation of lights behind. "Baraccus is here with us as well. He was pulled to the amulet he once made. We have all come to do whatever we could to help free you."

Richard saw the spirit of Baraccus, as well as countless others there with him. He saw his friend Warren. He saw Ben, Cara's husband, and legions of soldiers, now good spirits, who had fought with him in the world of life.

"Dark forces have conspired to keep you here," Naja said. "It took many good spirits to fight this battle. Once your grandfather ripped the demons away from you, some of those here were then able to see to it that they sank into the forever of darkness. They cannot return for now."

"But there are other dangers for you, here," Magda said.

"You must return to the world of life," Nicci told him.

"And so must you," Naja's soft voice said, "for the ones who never sleep and walk like men are coming."

Nicci turned in alarm. "What do—"

Naja's glowing finger touched Nicci's forehead.

In an instant Nicci was gone.

"How do I return? Is there a way?" Richard asked as he looked around at all the good spirits. "There are things in the world of life I must do. The lives of a great many people depend on me. I need to get back. I need to help them. I can't let Sulachan have his way with them."

The spirit of Merritt smiled knowingly. "That is the anger of the sword. I recognize it. It is here with you. Even in death, because it is bonded to you, your soul carries the righteous anger of the sword. Only the right person could do such a thing. Only the bringer of death could bring the power of the sword and life itself to the underworld."

"Well, if I'm the one, then I need to get back there. Sulachan and Hannis Arc are going to destroy the world of life."

"Indeed they are," Naja said.

"I can't stop them from here," Richard said, his soul filled with urgency. "I need to get back there."

"The righteous rage of the sword as well as the spark of life you carry still anchor you to the world of life," she said, "but the world of the dead still holds you here. The skrin guard the veil so that none from this world may cross back."

Richard remembered the bone woman telling him about how the skrin, the guardians of the veil, held the dead back in the underworld and kept them from coming through the veil.

"Sulachan crossed back," Richard said.

"With your blood," Naja reminded him.

"Kahlan crossed back."

"With a lot more than merely your blood," Naja said.

"So how do I get back?" Richard asked the constellation of glowing spirits around him. The spirits all stared back but none seemed to want to answer.

When Zedd laid a sympathetic, glowing hand on her shoulder, Naja finally spoke in a somber tone. "You must have a living bridge."

"How do I find this living bridge?"

"You don't," Naja said, "it must find you."

"I don't understand."

Zedd shook his head in great sadness as he drifted closer. "I'm afraid, my boy, that someone would have to give you their life as that bridge. Their soul would have to join us here."

"It's the only way," Naja confirmed.

Denna's glowing arm embraced him protectively. "You need the help of others, Richard. You need the life of another."

"No," Richard said, drifting back, shaking his head. "I can't allow someone to give their life for me. There has to be another way."

"They would not simply be giving up their life for you," Zedd told him in a comforting voice. "They will be giving up their life for everyone, and out of love."

"Until and unless that happens, you have no way back," Naja said. "If it does not happen, you can never return."

"If you can't return," Magda said, "then the fate of your soul mate, the fate of the world, will be in the cruel hands of Emperor Sulachan."

"And I can't help from here?" he asked, anger at his banishment rising in his soul. "There is nothing I can do?"

With great sorrow, Magda shook her head.

Denna's arm embraced him, trying to give him comfort. Richard felt no comfort.

But he did feel rage at Sulachan for bringing this on him and everyone living.

"Good," Merritt whispered. "Let the rage fill you. If you ever get the chance to use it, it will be ready and there with you."

Richard reached for the hilt of his sword, and even though he could almost touch it, it wasn't there. It was on the other side of the veil, in the world of life. Kahlan was there, on the other side of the veil, in the world of life.

So was Sulachan.

CHAPTER 18

Kahlan flinched when Nicci suddenly gasped and opened her eyes. Red flinched as well and jerked her fingers back from where they had been resting on Nicci's shoulders.

The sorceress's face looked gray in the candlelight. Her hands trembled. Her beautiful features reflected the anguish of what she had just experienced. The witch woman, while not as ashen as Nicci, looked gravely troubled.

Kahlan hadn't been able to see what Nicci was seeing beyond the veil, but she felt some of it, even if distantly, and she could read the tension of Nicci's face as tears ran down her cheeks. It was clear that it had been a profoundly difficult journey. What Kahlan most wanted to know, though, was if it had been successful. Nicci gave no clue.

The terrible, inky darkness surrounded them, isolating them inside the circle of light from the candles set out at the points of the Grace. The darkness also shut away the sounds of the world of life around them.

As that darkness gradually began to recede, Kahlan could begin to make out the walls of the room. She saw the window materialize. She could also begin to hear distant sounds.

As the darkness receded, taking the underworld with it, she was finally able to see the bed again. She stood in a rush and carefully stepped over the lines drawn with her blood to get out of the Grace. Once free of it and past the candles, she rushed to the bed and put a knee up beside Richard, leaning over him, looking for a sign, looking for life, expecting–hoping–to see him smile up at her.

His lifeless hands still gripped the sword. He had not drawn a breath. Kahlan had been sure that Nicci would have been able to do something and that now Richard would at last draw a breath. She had hoped against hope that he would somehow return to life, return to her.

She had hoped to see his eyes open to look at her.

Instead, he remained as dead and still as he had been before.

Nothing had changed.

Kahlan laid her fingers tenderly over his big hand. There was no warmth of life in it. His eyes were still closed, closed to the world of life. His soul had not returned from exile to his worldly form.

"Dear spirits," she whispered, "why haven't you sent him back to us?" She felt a tear run down her cheek. "Dear spirits, I need him. We all need him."

She remembered the dark ones enveloping him with clawed arms and black wings. She remembered the terrible sight of him being smothered by those inky demons and taken down into the darkness.

Nicci joined her to stand beside the bed. "Kahlan . . . I'm sorry."

Kahlan wiped a tear from her cheek. "Why didn't it work?"

The witch woman hurried to join Nicci, looking exhausted and confused. "What happened?"

The sorceress shook her head. "It's hard to explain." She glanced back over her shoulder at Red. "With your help at least I was able to find Isidore and Naja. They were able to find Richard."

Kahlan grabbed Nicci's arm. "You found Richard?"

Nicci nodded. "The dark ones had him, just as you said. Zedd and a great many others came to help us. There was a battle among spirits. Zedd helped us free Richard from the dark ones. Because he was there, we won the battle."

"Then why isn't Richard back?" Kahlan asked, trying to control her voice as well as her pounding heart.

She couldn't help thinking of the wood stacked in a funeral pyre down in the citadel square, waiting for Richard if this last hope didn't work. The terror of having to consign him to the flames was returning. She couldn't go on living if that was going to be his fate. She didn't want to live without him.

Nicci's gaze left Kahlan's. "There is more to it. They couldn't send him back. They said–"

When she heard a distant scream, Kahlan turned away from the bed to stare at the closed doors. It was the kind of scream that sent a chill up her spine and made the fine hairs at the back of her neck stand on end.

Red's eyes were closed, as if she was consulting an inner voice. "They come."

Both Kahlan and Nicci turned to the witch woman.

Kahlan frowned. "Who? Who comes?"

"The ones who never sleep. The ones who walk like men," the witch woman said. Her blue eyes opened. "They are close."

Kahlan was about to ask what she was talking about when beyond the door more screams ripped the night. They were a lot closer. She heard heavy thuds and then the sound of furniture breaking.

Nicci grabbed their arms and pulled them both

back toward the Grace just as the doors exploded inward, banging back against the wall and barely hanging by their hinges. A shower of splintered woodwork filled the room.

A roar came from out in the hall and then a man lurched into the room. In the soft candlelight Kahlan could see half a dozen broken spears jutting from the man's chest and back, along with a cluster of knives and several broken sword blades that had completely penetrated his body. There was no blood.

The eyes of the man glowed crimson in the near darkness, as if lit by the fires of the underworld. The torn, withered skin of his face hung down in places. Teeth showed through holes in the dried flesh of his cheeks. His clothes looked like the dirt in which he had long ago been buried. A fine net of tree roots had grown into his clothes, and some of the bigger roots had even grown through his wrist. Maggots wriggled in open wounds of his abdomen. Ribs showed through splits in his rotted shirt.

The gagging stench of death the man brought with him filled the room.

This was probably one of the dead summoned from his grave by Sulachan's minions. Occult powers, rather than life, gave him purpose and strength.

The three women backed away, keeping out of his reach. The dead man, one ankle broken so that his foot lay completely over to one side, staggered forward as he roared at them. His eyes glowed with hatred and fury.

A soldier raced in and with all his strength drove a spear through the dead man. Kahlan heard it splinter bone, but it had no more effect than the other weapons stuck through the man.

Another brawny soldier leaped onto the dead man's back, trying to wrestle him to the ground. The raging corpse seized the soldier by an arm and whipped him around as if he were but a child. A desiccated arm lashed around with impossible speed, ripping open the soldier's chest. An arc of blood splashed across the wall. The soldier dropped in a lifeless heap against the wall. The other soldier ducked back through the door so as to not be caught by the man's arm.

Just as the invader turned back to them, Nicci threw a fist of air at the man. It knocked him back toward the door. He spread his arms, grabbing the wall at the sides to keep from falling through the splintered doorway. From behind, out in the hallway, Laurin rammed her Agiel into the small of his back. Even though her Agiel didn't work, he roared and spun, backhanding her hard enough to send her flying. She hit the wall and slid down into an unconscious heap.

A soldier stabbed his sword through the dead man's chest, but it did no more than the collection of steel already there. Another soldier swung, trying to hack off an arm, but with the dead man's otherworldly strength he effortlessly deflected the strike. The soldiers kept coming but the dead man knocked them back or took them down as fast as they came. The risen dead were not easily stopped by worldly weapons.

Before more of them could join the battle, the soldiers were set upon from behind by howling hordes of half people racing up the hall. The soldiers were forced to turn to meet the new attack.

Kahlan looked across the room to Richard's sword lying along the length of his body. His hands around the hilt were still where she had placed them. That sword could stop these dead men driven by occult magic. She just needed to get to it.

Before she could try to get across the room to grab the sword, the dead man lurched farther into the room, blocking her from getting to Richard. In the gloom, the glowing red eyes looked all the more menacing as they tracked her dodging first left, then right.

Before Kahlan could try to dart around the growling dead man, Nicci pulled her and the witch woman farther back, dragging them both over the lines of the Grace, until the three of them stood in the center beside the drop of Richard's blood. Nicci apparently hoped the Grace would be protection from such otherworldly forces.

They stood close together as the man came to a stop on the other side of the candles. He looked unsure what to do and reluctant to step into the Grace to get at them.

Kahlan wondered how long his reluctance would last. She eyed the sword across the room even though she knew that she had little chance to make it. The dead man would likely snatch her in an instant.

But she also knew that the sword could stop the threat.

Out in the hall a battle raged. Kahlan caught glimpses of half people racing toward the bedroom only to be slaughtered by soldiers of the First File. Other soldiers were dragged down by half people as other men of the First File pulled them off. She saw flashes of the Mord-Sith's red leather as well.

Just as Kahlan was about to again try to make it to the sword, another dead man, this one bigger, stepped through the splintered doorway and into the bedroom. He was more decomposed than the first and smelled even worse. Flaps of dried skin with hair attached hung down over an ear. One arm didn't work right. Even so, he moved well enough. Like the first, his glowing red eyes appraised the room, the bed with Richard on it, and the three women standing in the center of the Grace.

Several soldiers charged in, hacking wildly at the intruders, trying to take them down. It was futile. Their weapons chopped off bits of the dried bodies, but did little to stop the dead men. With a mighty swipe of his one good arm, the dead man knocked down several soldiers.

"We have no power to stop them," Red whispered even as her hands turned, trying to work some kind of witch-woman magic. Whatever it was she was doing, none of it was working.

Nicci again threw fists of air that staggered the first of the dead men back. The second man ducked to the side so that Nicci's next attempt blew out the edge of the doorway, sending chunks of wood flying.

"Are we safe in the Grace?" Kahlan asked.

Almost as if to answer, one of the two dead men charged across the room. He lunged, swinging an arm like a big hook, trying to snag one of the women as they stepped back just in time. He no longer seemed concerned by the lines of the Grace drawn in blood and stepped right into the midst of it.

When he took another step forward, the three of them split up and went in three different directions. Nicci moved around to the side of the man, hammering him with fists of air. It wasn't enough to stop him, but it distracted him, keeping his attention. When she hit him again in quick succession it knocked the man sideways. Because of his broken ankle he stumbled, but caught himself on the windowsill.

As soon as he was at the window, Nicci conjured a ball of wizard's fire between her palms. It lit the room with harsh yellow-orange light as it ignited into being. The sphere of liquid flame tumbled and rolled obediently between her hands, hissing and bubbling with need.

Almost as soon as she had created it, Nicci cast it out. The lethal inferno howled as it raced across the bedroom, lighting everything in blinding yellow-orange light. It hit the man with a thud that Kahlan could feel in her chest.

The liquid flame exploded against the dead man, enveloping him in a sticky, white-hot blaze. The man erupted in flames that rolled up the wall and billowed across the ceiling.

Before it could set the entire room on fire, Nicci threw yet more fists of air, but this time the man, frantically concerned with the impossible effort of putting out the flames, didn't see it coming. The compressed wall of air hit him hard. With a whoosh of swirling flame it knocked the dead man through the window. His burning body tumbled out and fell through the night, lighting the walls of the citadel. Kahlan heard the thud when he hit the ground.

Fire was one of the few ways to stop the walking dead men. As they turned back to the other one, yet another had joined him, so there were again two in the room, stalking the three women.

Kahlan knew that Nicci couldn't do the same thing with the other two unless she also got them near the window. If not done carefully, as she had done with the first man, wizard's fire unleashed inside the room could easily trap them in a burning inferno. It could set the whole place on fire and kill countless soldiers as well.

The sorceress lifted her hands and recalled the power from the wizard's fire she had unleashed. With another gesture she extinguished the burning tapestry before it was too late.

"You were lucky with that other one and knocked him out the window," Kahlan told the sorceress. "Be careful or you will catch the bed on fire. We might be able to run, but Richard can't."

It would be all too easy to accidentally turn the bed into Richard's funeral pyre. It wouldn't take much for it to go up in flames.

Kahlan danced one way and then the other, trying to get past the growling predators. She needed to get to the sword. Either one or the other of the two dead men

matched every move she made, blocking her from getting to the sword. At the same time as they blocked
her, they were advancing, moving the three women back
toward a corner.

Out in the hallways Kahlan could see that a full-
blown battle had erupted.

Half people howled as they attacked, and screamed
as they were cut. Soldiers savagely fought the flood of
half-naked bodies racing up the hallway.

chapter 19

When Kahlan turned toward the bed, trying to dodge one way and then the other around the closest of the two dead men, he stepped to the side each time, matching her moves to block her. Up closer to him the gagging stench of his rotting corpse was overpowering, making it hard to draw a breath. The focus of his glowing red eyes stayed locked on her.

Out of the corner of her eye, Kahlan caught sight of the red leather of a Mord-Sith coming up behind the other man. Mord-Sith were quick, but the woman's Agiel wasn't going to stop this threat. Kahlan hoped that when she found that out she would be quick enough not to be caught and killed like the soldier lying sprawled up against the wall.

The second man, his focus also on Kahlan, swung an arm behind to brush away the Mord-Sith as if she were a petty nuisance. As Kahlan tried but failed to get past the closest man by feigning a move to her right and then her left, she caught a glimpse of the Mord-Sith ducking as the arm of the other man swept by over her head.

When the man missed catching her with his arm, the woman in red stood and rammed what Kahlan thought must have been her Agiel into the dead man's back.

In that instant, the red glow in his eyes extinguished.

He briefly stood as still and stiff as a corpse before toppling forward and crashing to the floor. He was suddenly as dead as he had been before occult magic had pulled him from his grave.

Kahlan saw then that the Mord-Sith wasn't holding an Agiel as she had thought, but instead had used a knife. This, though, was no ordinary knife. She had seen a knife like this before. It was one of the knives created by the half people to stop the living dead. Even though the gloomy light made it hard to see, she knew who had one of those knives.

When the Mord-Sith turned toward the light and looked up, their eyes met. Kahlan saw what she already knew. It was Cara.

Without pause, Cara raced up behind the other roaring dead man menacing Kahlan and rammed that occult weapon into the small of his back. She withdrew the knife and slammed it in two more times in quick succession just for good measure. Kahlan could hear the thuds of Cara's fist hitting his back as the knife in her fist stabbed all the way in.

The red glow in his eyes went dark. His whole body stiffened. As his weight shifted over on the broken ankle, he toppled to his side, his dead weight landing with a heavy thud on the lines of the Grace drawn in blood on the wooden floor.

Kahlan ran to Cara, intending to throw her arms around the woman, but stopped short instead. There was something odd, something in a way distant about her. She looked the same as Kahlan remembered her always looking. She was muscular and tall, endowed with pure, graceful femininity. Her long blond hair was done in the traditional single braid of a Mord-Sith. On the surface she didn't look any different than she had always looked.

But there was something strange and otherworldly about Cara's blue eyes.

She had obviously fought her way into the citadel. She was covered in blood, now, but the red leather hid it well, and besides, being covered in blood was hardly strange for a Mord-Sith. Kahlan could see horrifically wounded bodies out in the hallway lying sprawled atop one another, all bleeding from gaping wounds of one kind or another. Most had been cut down by the soldiers. Some were missing arms, or legs, or even their heads. Some, though, Cara had stopped.

Kahlan saw flashes of steel down the dimly lit hallway as the soldiers still fought half people who raced in to join the frenzy. But there were less of them now than she had seen before.

"Cara," Kahlan said as she stepped closer. "Dear spirits, I've missed you." She couldn't hold back her tears. "You don't know how I've missed you, and all that's happened."

Cara stared back with that strange look in her eyes. "I know."

Kahlan lifted an arm to point, sobs suddenly choking her words. "Cara . . . Richard is dead."

Without looking where Kahlan pointed, Cara only looked into her eyes. "I know."

"I've tried everything . . ."

"I know," Cara said, her voice finally turning to gentle compassion.

"It hurts so much to be without him."

"I know, Mother Confessor. I carry that same pain every moment. It makes life unbearable."

Kahlan nodded. "I miss Ben, too."

Kahlan wanted to hug the woman. She had missed her so. She wanted to tell her the whole story, explain what had happened and what they had done to try to get Richard back. But she could say none of it. Something about the look in Cara's blue eyes made Kahlan keep her distance. It was Cara, and yet it wasn't.

"Cara, are you all right?"

Cara smiled then, like the old Cara that Kahlan knew so well. It was a smile of knowing, of wisdom, of confidence softened with a glimmer of childlike mischief. It was the smile of a woman who had spent her adult life seeing things that no one should ever have to see, and yet still carried a spark of joy for life that had survived in some dark, distant corner of her tortured mind.

It was a smile of compassion and determination laced with madness.

"Yes, Mother Confessor. I am all right, now. Finally, things are about to be right again."

Kahlan ignored the strange feeling and took a step forward to throw her arms around the woman. Cara felt cold as ice. The Mord-Sith reached up with her free hand and half returned the hug, then parted.

"I have to go, now," Cara said in a voice like a mother speaking tenderly to a child.

Kahlan frowned. "Go? Go where? You're home now."

Cara shook her head. "Not yet, but I soon will be."

With icy fingers, she gently touched Kahlan's cheek. She turned then toward the bed for the first time as if she had always known that Richard was there. At the side of the bed, standing over him, she looked back over her shoulder.

"Don't weep for me, Mother Confessor. Know that I love you both, and that I do this by my own choice alone. Know that I will be at peace. This is the way it is meant to be, the way it must be."

Kahlan wanted to ask what she was talking about, but she couldn't seem to find her voice.

Looking down, Cara spread her arms above Richard. It reminded Kahlan of nothing so much as a graceful bird spreading its wings. Or a good spirit.

Kahlan blinked at what she was seeing. The Mord-Sith seemed to have a glow about her, or rather within her. White robes made of light, almost like wings, draped from her arms.

There seemed to be a spirit form made of light in the same place as Cara. Kahlan knew that it was not Cara she was seeing. The features were similar in their graceful femininity, and yet they were different.

Cara bent over and placed her Agiel, hanging from the gold chain, around Richard's neck. She cupped his cheek with a hand for a moment, just looking at him as she and the form made of light smiled lovingly at him.

And then she leaned forward and pressed her mouth to his, as if kissing him, but it was not a kiss.

Nicci stepped up beside Kahlan and whispered, "She is giving him the breath of life."

Kahlan nodded. Richard had told her how a Mord-Sith shared her victim's breath while he was on the cusp of death. It was a sacred thing to a Mord-Sith to share his pain, share his breath of life as he slipped to the brink of death, as if to view with lust the forbidden sight of what lay beyond in the next world. Sharing, when the time came to kill him, his very death by experiencing his final breath of life, and taking it for her own. Kahlan imagined that to some, it was a grotesquely intimate trophy—part of the madness of the Mord-Sith's world and life.

Richard knew because Denna had done that to him when he had been her captive, used the breath of life to keep him alive, keep him on that cusp of death to prolong his agony.

But Kahlan had also seen Cara do that to a woman who had just died. Kahlan had at first thought it was some outrageous ritual of a Mord-Sith, but Cara had told her that she could sometimes give a person back the breath of life.

Cara now breathed that breath into Richard, his chest rising as his lungs filled with the breath she gave him, with her own breath of life.

Cara pulled away a few inches, Richard's chest slowly sinking as she drew another deep breath. Once again she pressed her mouth over Richard's, hand covering his nose, filling his lungs with her deep, life-giving breath.

"What are you talking about?" Red whispered from right behind them.

"She is the living bridge," Nicci said, tears running down her face as well. "She is the one the spirits said he would need in order to return."

Kahlan felt a spike of hope mixed with fear for Cara.

"That is a spirit with her, helping her," Red whispered to them.

Nicci nodded. "It is the spirit of a Mord-Sith I saw protecting him in the underworld."

"Denna," Kahlan whispered, choking on her tears, her chin quivering, hardly able to believe what she was seeing.

What she was seeing was a good spirit joined with Cara in purpose. It was a sight of hope, of love, and at the same time it was horrifying to know what it meant for Cara.

"This is her choice," Nicci said as if reading Kahlan's mind. "She is doing what she must, and doing it of her own free will."

Richard opened his eyes as he gasped in a breath. The world of life seemed to explode into existence.

Out of nothingness, bright light, shapes, and colors began to materialize all around him. At first he sensed only gossamer traces of something more; then tangible matter began to solidify into shape and substance, as if it had always been in the same place at the same time as the void where he seemed to have been for so long. It felt confusing to not have realized what had been there all along.

He began to recognize walls, a ceiling, a floor. There were now limits to the space around him where there had been none. He blinked at candlelight that was too bright, the colors too vivid. The air felt heavy and thick, but he breathed it in greedily, letting it fill his lungs in a heady rush.

With each breath he drew and then let out, he felt himself exhaling an alien void, breaking the connection to that other world. With every breath he let out, that void dissipated, dissolving away as life came back to take its place.

This was where he belonged. He could smell the

nearly infinite variety of the world of life, he could taste it. Some of the smells were sweet perfume he recognized and he relished, while some was a repulsive stench. It all mixed together into the diversity that was the world of life.

The air filling his lungs felt luxurious, intoxicating. He couldn't get enough of it. It was wonderful. It felt as if he had needed to get his breath forever. At last it was coming freely. He could feel his pulse moving through him with every deep breath he drew. Even so, to an extent it was still an unfamiliar effort to breathe.

"Richard!"

Richard smiled, then, at the most beautiful thing he had ever seen in his life. Kahlan was leaning in over him. She was the sweet bouquet he had smelled.

"Are you all right?" she asked, tears running down her cheeks, her voice a mix of panic and expectant joy, as if she was too afraid to believe he was really with her, and afraid he might unexpectedly leave again.

"I was with the dead."

She nodded, half laughing, half crying as tears continued to overflow from her beautiful green eyes.

"I know." She grasped his face in her hands a moment, as if unable to believe it was really him. She looked back then and seized Nicci's hand. She pulled the sorceress forward. "Nicci went to the underworld to find a way to bring you back."

Richard put a hand to his forehead as he saw it all again, but this time in his mind's eye. "The dark ones. I remember them." Gooseflesh tingled down his arms. "They were all around me."

Nicci nodded. "I know. I saw them."

Richard looked up into Kahlan's beautiful eyes, eyes that also revealed the inner beauty of her soul. "Zedd was there, Kahlan. He was somehow meant to be there to help me, to help free me from the grasp of Sulachan's dark ones. He let me know that it was all to a purpose, that his time in this world had come to its end, and he had needed to move on to be where he could help me."

A woman with strange red hair standing behind Nicci was nodding. "It was all part of the flow of time. It was all meant to be." Her gray dress seemed to be moving as if in a light breeze, even though the air in the room was still. "Events happened as they must in order for you to return. You were not yet meant to be finished with this world. Prophecy yet lives."

Though no one said it, he knew that this was a witch woman. "I must end prophecy if we all are to live."

She smiled in a most peculiar manner. "Prophecy helped place events in order so that you might be returned to us. The flow of time revealed that the one closest to you by blood was the one who had to be there to help you, or you would have been lost forever. He was meant to be there, first, waiting for you."

Richard didn't know if that was true or not. As far as he was concerned, prophecy had always been a source of trouble.

Kahlan began gently turning to someone between them, someone else close to him.

Still trying to put all the sights around him into order, Richard realized, then, that the reason he was having some difficulty breathing was because there was something heavy lying over his chest and left arm. He saw blond hair and red leather. Icy realization flashed through him. Even without seeing her, he knew who it was.

He knew the instant he saw her, though, that she was not asleep. In horrified dread, he realized what had just happened. He remembered the warnings that one must die for him to return. He reached up and felt the Agiel now hanging around his neck.

"Cara no," he said under his breath as panicked fear welled up through him. "Don't do this for me. Please don't do this."

Even as he said it, he knew that it was too late. She had already done it. It was already finished and beyond redemption. She had made the sacrifice she had always sworn she would make for him. She had always said it would be her life before his.

Kahlan swallowed as she cupped a tender hand to his face, wiping away a tear with her thumb.

"She's with Ben, now, Richard."

Richard put his arms around Cara, pulling her cold, limp, and lifeless form up to hold her head to his shoulder as he tipped his head against hers and wept with agony for the woman.

"I didn't want this. Dear spirits, I didn't want this. I didn't want anyone to do this for me."

Nicci laid a hand on his arm. "But she did, Richard. She wanted to be the one to be the bridge back, and she wanted to cross over that bridge to be with Ben."

Richard stared up at the sorceress and finally nodded, too choked up to speak. He knew how much she missed Ben. He understood that kind of pain of being left behind. Richard had given up his own life, after all, to go to the underworld to be with Kahlan. Even so, and even though he knew how much she wanted to be the one, Richard didn't want someone else—didn't want Cara—to die so that he could come back.

But he understood it.

He couldn't stand the thought of life without Kahlan, of living in a world empty of her soul. Cara had waited her whole life for love like that, and then she had lost it. Now, she was with him and the other good spirits. Rich-

ard couldn't stand losing her, and yet he understood
why she had done it.

"Make her sacrifice worth it, Richard," Kahlan whispered to him. "Make it mean something."

He nodded as he rolled her to the side and carefully
laid her back. He could see the soft glow of the spirit
that was still within her, a spirit, a sister of the Agiel,
who had come to be with her to help her do what had
to be done, and then to help guide her to that other
world and Ben's waiting spirit.

Richard closed her blue eyes and then kissed her
cheek.

"Thank you, Cara. Please take care of her, Denna."

As if in answer, the glow of the spirit vanished then
back to the world where she belonged, where she, too,
was at peace.

So many good spirits had helped him. He knew that
they rarely did so, but this time it was a spirit from their
world–Sulachan–who was the cause of the trouble. If
the spirit king had his way he would not only destroy the
world of life, he would destroy the peace of that world
as well. This was a struggle for the fate of both worlds.

When Richard sat up and put his hand around the
hilt of the sword, the rage responded instantly with eager intensity. The storm of fury sprang to life, joining
with his own anger at the thought of all that was at risk
because of Sulachan and the man who had helped bring
him back into the world of life, Hannis Arc.

Richard could hear shouts outside in the hall, as well
as the unmistakable sounds of weapons being used in
anger. Men yelled orders. Others cried out with the fury
of their effort. Yet others screamed in pain.

It was a call Richard knew all too well.

Others had given their lives that he might live, that
he might fight for life. They knew that he was the one

born to stop what was happening. They knew that by helping him they were helping in that fight.

His purpose had never felt so clear to him before. Prophecy or not, this was the battle he was born to fight. Emperor Sulachan had started this war three thousand years before, and had come back to the world of life to finish it. Richard had been born to be the one to oppose him.

It no longer mattered that prophecy had seemed to meddle with his life or had tried to preordain what he would do. All that mattered now was that he was the one to see this struggle to the end.

All things had to be in balance. In this conflict, Richard was the balance to Sulachan and his accomplice Hannis Arc. That inexorable pull toward balance in the battle for life didn't say which side would win, only that in the grand struggle they both were drawn in as balance to each other.

Though he was only just back from the world of the dead, and he knew that he had been gone for quite a while, it was beginning to feel like he had been gone for only an instant. It was the timeless element of the underworld, he knew, that made him feel that way. He had been to the underworld several times before and he recognized that sensation of life interrupted.

But now he was back. The battle cries and screams of the injured and dying were a call to the anger within him. These were savages that Emperor Sulachan and Hannis Arc had loosed on the world. So many people Richard knew and cared about had died already. Cara was only the latest warrior to fall. It had to be stopped, and only he had a chance to put an end to it.

He slid off the edge of the bed and stood, feeling the weight of life, feeling the weight of responsibility, feeling life coursing through his veins, feeling the joy and the sorrow and the duty of being alive again.

Life was a gift. He was not going to waste that gift.

Richard lifted the sword, touching it to his forehead as he closed his eyes. In the background he could hear the eager cries of the attacking enemy. They were battle cries his sword was created to meet, cries he was born to counter.

"Blade," he whispered, "be true this day."

chapter 21

The drizzle had started again, making the cool, damp air feel miserable. Tattered-looking, leaden clouds drifted silently by low overhead. None of the gathered soldiers spoke. Most stood with their heads bowed. These men, like all of the First File, had known Cara. She had been Richard and Kahlan's closest protector. Her husband, Ben, had been their general and had been the one who had led these soldiers into the Dark Lands to find Richard and Kahlan and bring them back to the People's Palace. Ben had died while helping them all escape from Hannis Arc's trap in the third kingdom.

The People's Palace was still far off, their mission still unrealized.

Now, Cara's funeral pyre was but a smoldering heap, sending waves of heat and wisps of smoke curling gently up into the dead-still air. The terrible job completed, there was nothing left but ashes and memories.

While Cara was hardly the only one who had died in the struggle against the spirit king and Hannis Arc, or against Emperor Jagang and the Imperial Order before them, she symbolized for those gathered all the kindred spirits they had lost along the way, all those who had paid the ultimate price for what they all believed in. She had been an inspiration as well as a fierce defender.

Richard could never be grateful enough to Cara for all the times she had protected Kahlan when he couldn't be there. Cara, perhaps better than anyone, recognized the importance of a Lord Rahl who not only loved a woman, but loved life. It had been a very long time since that had been true. That was one reason why Cara had fought so fiercely to protect him. She instinctively knew that he, like Kahlan, had come into the world for a purpose. Cara's purpose, taken up of her free will, had been to be part of that cause by protecting him.

Now, Richard felt numb. He could hardly believe that she was gone. Cara had been at his side for so long, fighting for him and with him, that she had come to be a sister to him, an ever-present protector and companion. It hurt all the more knowing that she had given up her life so that he might live.

He felt guilty, felt responsible, for her death.

Richard knew that most of the soldiers were more than a little astonished that he was actually back from the dead, that he was really alive and among them again, but for these men of the First File it was also expected that the Lord Rahl could do the kind of remarkable things that they could not imagine. After all, while they were the steel against steel, he was the magic against magic. That magic was a largely alien mystery to them, but they had many times seen its power.

The soldiers had been stunned when Richard had charged out the broken doorway, once again alive and once again coming to help them fight off the half people that had flooded into the citadel. Though there had been a large horde of the half people invading the place, they hadn't been what Richard had at first expected. They were not Shun-tuk sent by the spirit king and Hannis Arc.

These had been a tribe of half people who had come out to hunt for souls now that the walls closing off the third kingdom had been breached. They were just as intent on devouring the living in the hope of stealing a soul for themselves, but they were not as good at fighting as the emperor's legions of Shun-tuk. Even so, besides invading the citadel, they had also killed a number of people down in the city of Saavedra.

Richard had led the soldiers down into the city to root out the last of them. They weren't hard to find. They didn't run from soldiers. They came out of buildings and alleyways, seeing Richard and the men of the First File as more opportunities to gain a soul for themselves. Instead of getting a soul, they had been cut down with the ruthless efficiency that only the men of the First File and Richard's blade could deliver.

Unlike Cara's farewell, a pit had been dug for the hundreds of dead half people. No one said words over them. No one would miss them. No one would remember them.

As Richard turned to the three Mord-Sith behind him, he reached up and lifted Cara's Agiel off from around his neck.

"I have worn the of Agiel of a number of women who have died for me," he said, trying to keep his voice steady. "I can't bear to wear this one. It will only remind me of all the ways in which I failed her. I would like to pass it on to you, Cassia, in the hope that, instead of pain, some of her strength will pass on to you."

Cassia nodded, fearing to test her voice. Like most Mord-Sith, she didn't know quite how to react to being treated with respect. Once captured as young women and trained as Mord-Sith, they were treated as little more than savage hounds on a chain, beaten to keep them vicious and make sure they followed orders.

Richard placed the chain over Cassia's bowed head,

and then, after rolling the red Agiel in his fingers for a moment, he carefully let it lie against her chest. He reached back and pulled her blond braid out from under the chain so it could rest around her neck, then arranged her braid over the front of her shoulder, admiring Cara's Agiel at the end of the chain.

"Lord Rahl," she finally said when she found her voice and looked up, "I am not the equal of Cara. I am not—"

He put his fingers to her lips, silencing her. "Yes you are, Cassia. You and Laurin and Vale made the same choice as she did to be free. That shows your strength. You are an individual, strong in your own way, with unique talents and abilities. We will be well served if you are simply yourself and don't try to be like someone else."

Cassia nodded, looking a little relieved. "I will carry it with honor. It will give me strength as I remember her strength." She gestured to Laurin and Vale. "The three of us together will be as strong as Cara was."

Richard smiled. "Let's hope you are not three times the trouble."

Her brow twitched with a little frown. "As long as you allow us to protect you as only we can, then we will not be any trouble at all."

Mord-Sith always thought they knew best how to protect the Lord Rahl. Richard shared a knowing glance with Kahlan. She returned a small smile. He was heartened to see her smile.

Cassia flicked her own Agiel, hanging on a fine gold chain from her right wrist, up into her hand. She hesitated for a moment. "But, Lord Rahl, I don't understand. You are back and seem well again, yet our Agiel still do not work. The bond is not there to make them function. We still feel nothing."

At hearing this, Nicci abruptly stepped forward. "What do you mean they don't work?"

Cassia shrugged. "They don't work. We can't feel the bond to the Lord Rahl, so we can't feel any power from our Agiel. It is the same as it was before Lord Rahl died."

Nicci glanced at the other two Mord-Sith. They shook their heads, confirming that they didn't feel the bond, either.

The sorceress turned a suspicious scowl on Richard and without asking placed a hand against his forehead. She jerked her hand back almost as soon as she had touched him.

Looking shaken, Nicci pushed her long blond hair back over her shoulder. "You still have the poison in you from the Hedge Maid's touch." She gestured to Kahlan. "When she came back, it was gone–left in the underworld. You still have it."

It sounded like an accusation. Although he was doing his best to ignore it, Richard could feel the pain of that deadly sickness deep inside. When he had come out of the bedroom to fight the invaders, the rage of the sword had blocked the ache of the poisonous infection. But now that the sword was back in its sheath, he again felt the full weight of the sickness.

"I took that touch of death out of Kahlan when I was there with her in the underworld. I can't explain how I did it. I just did. But I couldn't take it out of myself. I still carry it."

In alarm, Kahlan seized his arm. "You still have that infection in you? You came back to the world of life only to die? Richard, you can't–"

"I came back," Richard said, cutting her off. He had more important things on his mind and didn't want to get into it right then and there. "That's what matters. Even though I carry that same taint of death, I came back so that I can stop Emperor Sulachan and Hannis Arc."

"If you live that long," Nicci said under her breath.

"Richard, you know better than me that if it's not removed, that poison is fatal."

"I do."

"But I don't understand why you couldn't leave it in the world of the dead," Kahlan said, her exasperated expression darkened by fear and dread. "That is the perfect place to leave that vile poison. The world of the dead is the perfect containment field for the touch of death."

"I couldn't do that." He waved away further discussion of the topic. He was already in a bad enough mood over Cara. "Look, I'm back. That's what matters for now. Sulachan is like that poisonous touch of death loose in the world of life. We have to stop everyone from dying, not just me. I came back to do that. That is the priority.

"At least being in the world of the dead for a time caused the sickness to dissipate somewhat. It bought me at least a few more days."

Nicci was beside herself with bottled fury. "A few more days? Are you really sure or are you just saying that?"

"You felt it. For now it isn't as strong as it was before. It's still there, and it will once again advance the same way it did before, but for the moment it's a little better. It will take some time for it to catch back up. That buys me some time."

Not willing to take his word for it, Nicci put her fingers to his temples on either side of his head. He could feel the tingle of her magic probing deep within his skull; then it felt like tiny flickers of lightning dancing down his spine and his arms to his fingertips, stinging as it went down his legs.

She finally pulled her hands away, looking a bit more composed. "He's right. It's not as strong, but it will be within days."

Kahlan glanced impatiently toward the southwest. "We have to get him to the containment field at the People's Palace so you can pull the poison out of him."

Nicci hesitated. "I think the palace may be too far away."

By her answer and by the way the sickness felt, Richard knew that it was too far to make it there in time.

"There are horses here," Kahlan said, not ready to give up so easily.

Richard nodded. "Yes, but Sulachan and Hannis Arc are heading there and they already have a big head start. Even if we race for the palace, getting past those forces won't be easy. Worse, and more likely, if they beat us there then getting through the horde of them surrounding the plateau in order to get into the palace will not be at all easy."

Kahlan folded her arms in frustration as she shook her head. "I don't understand why you couldn't have left the poison there, in the underworld, like you did with me. Why wouldn't it work for you to leave it there?"

"Balance," Red said into the drizzle.

"What?" Kahlan asked, turning to the witch woman.

"Many things had to be in balance for him to return to the world of life. This must have been one of the things that had to be."

Kahlan was clearly not ready to concede this point, either. "Well, I don't see–"

The witch woman suddenly grabbed Richard's arm and pulled urgently. "You need to move."

Richard frowned as she began dragging him away. "Why?"

"That guard tower is going to fall where you are standing."

Richard was at a loss as to why the witch woman so suddenly believed the tower was about to fall, but it was clear that she did. As he allowed her to lead him away he glanced back at the unassuming tower constructed of heavy stone blocks. Constructed back at the same time as the citadel, during the great war, it was as solid as the rock it was made from. It had stood on that spot for thousands of years, watching over the road up from Saavedra below. A couple of other towers on the other side of the citadel watched over the trackless dark forest beyond.

Like so many things in this part of the Dark Lands, it was part of the precautions having to do with the barrier to the third kingdom. This particular guard tower had been invaluable in alerting the men of the First File of the attack by the half people. No doubt that had been a part of its ancient intent. He had trouble imagining why the solidly built tower that had stood for so long would abruptly fall over. But he knew enough about witch women in general to take her seriously.

Richard didn't really know much about this particular witch woman. Kahlan had gone without him to see Red before, so he had met her only after returning from the underworld. She had helped Nicci in that journey into darkness to come and help find a way for him to return.

"Hurry!" Red growled at them, not satisfied at how fast he was moving as she dragged him away. "Move back!"

When he saw that the soldiers were not moving, and looked confused, Richard signaled with his free arm. "Back! Everyone move back!"

Confused men finally scattered at his command.

"What is it?" Kahlan asked as she followed Richard and Red hurrying away from where they had been standing beside the funeral pyre.

Before Red could answer, Richard felt the ground beneath the cobblestones beginning to tremble. The delicate lacework of ash from the funeral pyre collapsed inward, sending sparks and smoke spiraling up into the damp air.

One of the stone blocks at the base of the guard tower suddenly exploded, sending shards of rock and debris out across the square. Pieces of rock tumbled and bounced across the cobblestones, narrowly missing Richard's group as dust boiled up. Richard heard the distinctive sound of granite cracking, and another block at the base of the tower exploded. Fragments of rock whistled past them. A cloud of granite flakes and chunks filled the air, pelting them with small pieces.

"Get out!" Commander Fister yelled up at the two men in the tower. "Hurry! Get out now!"

Richard looked up just in time to see the tower begin to sway as the two men disappeared to race down the interior spiral stairs. With two of the blocks at the base shattered, the tower groaned as its great weight slowly began to keel over.

The two men dashed out of the narrow doorway as fractures crackled up from the corners of the opening. The men raced for their lives across the square.

Another explosion blew apart a third foundation block beside the first two and with a loud grating of rupturing stone the falling tower suddenly gathered speed and came crashing down. With a thunderous roar it toppled across the square right over the top of Cara's funeral pyre. Many of the stone blocks the tower had been constructed from broke apart on impact. Pieces large and small tumbled and rolled away, but most of it disintegrated into a heap of rubble.

It had happened so quickly. One moment it was standing, the next the blocks exploded and the tower lay scattered across the square. Clouds of dust rolled across the ground and up through the damp late-day air.

Had they not moved in time, they would all have been killed. As it was, some of the soldiers had been cut by sharp fragments of flying rock. One man was on his knees, holding his hands over a bloody wound on his head. Had Richard not moved, he would have been directly under the falling tower and now buried under the debris.

When he turned to her, the witch woman was looking into his eyes. "The flow of time."

He knew enough about witch women and the flow of time they dealt in to understand what she meant. It had been a form of prophecy.

"It would be helpful," he said, "if the next time you could look a little farther ahead in that flow."

"It was an eddy that had only just swirled into existence. Events around you tend to be unpredictable and chaotic in that way."

Commander Fister planted his fists on his hips. He looked perplexed as he peered at the rubble. "Lord Rahl, how did you know the tower was going to fall?"

Richard frowned at the question. "Red told me."

The commander cocked his head. "Red?"

"The witch woman," Richard said.

The commander glanced around. "Witch woman? What are you talking about?"

"The woman with the red hair."

The commander's frown drew tighter as he took another look around. "There was a witch woman here yesterday, but I've seen no woman with red hair."

Richard looked for himself. The witch woman was gone. She had been quiet during the ceremony and as they watched the pyre burn. In fact, she hadn't spoken all afternoon until she had told Richard to move because the tower was going to fall on him.

Richard frowned over at Kahlan. "She's gone."

She gave him a look as if to say that she had expected as much. "She told me that witch women have to stay out of events, lest they create havoc in those events. She's leaving what must be done now to us."

"What I want to know is who created that eddy," Nicci said in a way that betrayed her sense of urgency and ignoring the commander's confusion over the unseen witch woman.

Richard was already moving. He knew who had interrupted to create that disturbance in the flow at the last instant. He looked back over his shoulder when he heard boot strikes and saw the whole force of men following.

"Wait here. All of you, wait here."

The soldiers reluctantly slowed to a halt, remaining near the cobblestone square piled with the rubble of the tower. Nicci, Kahlan, and the three Mord-Sith ignored his instructions and followed him without pause. At the moment he needed to catch the person responsible and didn't want to stop to argue with them, but he knew he couldn't let them go all the way.

Rather than go down the road, he instead headed in the other direction, around the citadel. She wouldn't likely be down in the city. She would have come out of the cover of the uninhabited woods.

"Are you thinking what I'm thinking?" Kahlan asked as she walked faster to catch up with his big strides.

Richard nodded. "It has to be her."

"Who?" Cassia asked from behind. "What are you talking about?"

"Samantha," Nicci said.

The Mord-Sith frowned suspiciously. "Samantha. You mean the young sorceress who stabbed the Mother Confessor?"

"That would be the one," Richard said without looking back.

"How could she do such a thing?" Cassia asked.

"It's drizzling and wet," Nicci said to keep the Mord-Sith from distracting Richard as he scanned all the places she could be hiding. "Samantha can use her ability to heat the moisture in solid objects to make it expand and blow them apart–objects like trees and even rock."

"I've never heard of such a thing," Cassia said.

"Your Lord Rahl generously taught her how to do it," Nicci said with obvious displeasure.

"I learned it from you," Richard reminded her.

Nicci's mouth twisted with displeasure but she didn't answer. Richard slowed as he approached the opening in the wall at the edge of the more formal citadel grounds. The gardens were nowhere near as ornate as some of the places Richard had seen, but the maze of hedges, stone walks, and orderly patches of wildflowers were lavish for the small city of Saavedra. Hannis Arc would have had the grounds kept up as a demonstration of his importance, not because he cared about going for a stroll to gaze at wildflowers.

Richard held his arm out as he slowed, stopping all the women. "I want you all to wait here. I mean it. She's dangerous."

"Yes, she is," Nicci said, "and she wants revenge against you."

"And to get that revenge she would love to kill all of you to get back at me, the same way she stabbed Kahlan to hurt me."

Kahlan put an imploring hand on his shoulder. "Richard, she has already done that. She stabbed me. Now she will want to kill you."

"Kahlan is right," Nicci said. "You shouldn't be going out there to face her at all, much less alone. That's what she wants. We can distract her and keep her from–"

"I said stay here." His harsh tone caused them to fall silent.

They knew he was in no mood to argue with them, and they knew, too, that they couldn't afford to waste time and let her get away. Once he was sure they weren't going to argue, he started for the opening in the wall that led to the marshy fields around the citadel grounds that kept the forest back and insured that it would be harder for anyone to sneak up unseen. There was no gate. Hannis Arc was more feared than what was out beyond.

Richard lifted his sword a few inches, checking that it was clear in the scabbard. He let it drop back in place before he moved into the opening, leaning out to check both ways on the far side. Standing under the arch, he gazed out across the field of soggy grasses, looking for anything that didn't belong.

Richard spotted her in the distance among the rushes.

Samantha stood like a statue among grasses taller than her. She was about halfway across the marshland to the dark forest behind her. Richard turned back and held up a hand to Kahlan, Nicci, and the three Mord-Sith, letting them know that he meant for them to stay put and he would brook no argument.

"If she makes it past me," he told Nicci, "you make sure you stop her before she can get to Kahlan again. Understand?"

Nicci stared into his eyes a moment before answering. "I didn't go to the underworld to get you back only to have a girl with a bad temper kill you."

"I asked if you understood."

Nicci pressed her lips tight for a moment. Finally she folded her arms. "I understand."

"Good. Thank you."

"You came back to the world of life to take care of important matters," Kahlan warned him. "Samantha isn't one of them."

"I can't do anything about Sulachan if Samantha kills us all first, now can I?"

Kahlan didn't look at all happy, but she didn't say anything. She knew he was right. The young woman was the one forcing the issue. It wasn't like they had a choice.

When he was confident that they would wait where they were, he started out the opening.

A s he made his way among the thick clumps of grasses and reeds, out across the sodden field toward the young sorceress, Richard reminded himself to keep control of his anger. Samantha had stabbed Kahlan through the heart, and there was nothing else that would ignite his anger the way harming Kahlan would. But he knew that he couldn't focus on that to the exclusion of everything else.

Righteous anger could be a valuable tool, but it needed to be rational anger. Anger against evil. Anger against wrongs. It had to be wielded the same way any weapon was wielded. It needed to be wielded with reasoned wisdom tempered with maturity. It had to be respected for the damage it could do not only to evil, but also to the innocent. He knew that sometimes ability grew faster than the sense to know when not to use it, like a young man who grew muscles before growing wise enough not to be easily provoked into using them.

Although Samantha had been his friend and had helped him a number of times, and had even used her anger to save his life and the lives of a lot of good people, her temper wasn't always governed by reason. It obviously sometimes got the best of her. When it got out of

control in that way, she was capable of anything, capable of hurting anyone, even someone as innocent as
Kahlan.

It was certainly understandable that she would be en-
raged by the sight of Richard killing her mother, but
she didn't know all the facts. She knew him and she
should know that he wouldn't harm someone, especially not her mother, without a very good reason. He
hoped that by coming out and talking to her, he could
convince her to let her better judgment take over.

As he made his way through the tall rushes and
among patches of blue vervain and swamp milkweed,
he could see Samantha up ahead waiting for him. Her
frizzy mass of black hair was stuffed into the hood of
her cloak to protect it from the steady drizzle. Under the
cloak her skinny arms were bare. He thought she had
to be cold standing out in the wet weather. But he knew,
too, that anger could heat a person and make them forget the cold. She stood stone-still, waiting for him, her
dark-eyed glare locked on him as he made his way
among the clumps of the grasses bowed over under the
wet weight of accumulated mist.

The spongy ground was covered with a tangled web
of matted, dead grass. In places it sank down when he
put weight on it, so that clear water rose up over the toes
of his boots. He reminded himself to be careful and not
lose his footing. He wouldn't want to fall and find himself down on the ground with Samantha standing over
him. She had already proven that there were no bounds
on what she could or would do.

"Samantha," he called through the veil of rushes
when he was still a good distance away from her. He
tried to keep a familiar tone she would remember. "I
need to talk to you."

When he stepped out from a screen of grasses, she
spoke in a low voice that was little more than a growl.

"My name is Sammie. You gave me the name Samantha. My mother called me Sammie. The people of Stroyza all called me Sammie. That is my name–Sammie. I don't want a name from you."

"Fine. Sammie, then," he said as he kept weaving his way among the tall thickets of rushes and shorter knots of grasses, steadily making his way closer to her. "We still need to talk."

"There is nothing to talk about. You killed my mother."

"It's not that simple."

"It is that simple. She's dead. You are the one who killed her. I saw you do it."

He thought that there was something odd-looking about the young woman, some kind of shimmering aspect to her, something in her big, dark eyes, but in the dreary light he couldn't tell for sure what it was, or if it was his imagination. He had often seen the aura of power around sorceresses, seen it crackling with menace. He could do that, though, only when his own gift worked. Because he still had the poisonous touch of death in him, his gift didn't work. Still, he was sure that he saw something, even though he couldn't tell what.

He came to a halt when he was close enough to talk to her without having to yell. He didn't want to get any closer if he didn't have to. He knew what a temper she had, and it was true, after all, that he had killed her mother.

"Samantha, you don't understand. You have to listen to me."

"Sammie."

"You drove a knife through Kahlan's heart."

"Because you killed my mother. It was what you deserve. I want you to suffer the same kind of pain I suffer. I want to make you lose everything that matters to you, the same as you did to me."

Richard reminded himself to keep his voice calm, the same as when he had talked to her so often before. He plucked a few yellow buds from a blooming oxeye and rolled them between his finger and thumb as he considered his words.

"Your mother wasn't who you thought she was, Sammie. She wasn't on our side, on the side of the good people of your village of Stroyza, the way we thought she was."

"She was a protector to our people."

"She killed your aunts. She killed Zedd."

Samantha's brow twitched for just a moment before her glare darkened. "You're lying."

"It's the truth." Richard tossed away the oxeye buds and pulled a small black book from his pants pocket. He held it up for her to see. "This was your mother's journey book. Journey books possess ancient magic that allows them to send messages back and forth to each other."

"So?"

"Ludwig Dreier had the twin to your mother's. He probably gave her the one she had on her. She used it to plot with him. She had been working with him for years.

"She knew all about the barrier failing long before she let on. She wasn't really going to warn anyone. She and Dreier were keeping it a secret because they wanted that evil to escape. They wanted to rule over everyone. They wanted power for themselves. They were using the barrier failing as a way to accomplish their ends."

Samantha was shaking her head, objecting to what he was telling her even as he was saying it. "My mother was the sorceress in charge of Stroyza. She didn't even like that much power. She did not want to rule anyone."

"It was an act she put on, the same as Ludwig Dreier hid his own abilities until it was time for him to make his move. It was all part of their plan. No one knew their secret."

"You're making it all up. I know my mother better than you ever could."

Richard held up the journey book again so she could see it. "It's all in here. All of her conversations with Dreier are still in here. These books are twinned. What is written in one shows up in the other. Your mother had this one and Dreier had the other. Her journey book has all of their conversations and scheming going back for several years.

"There were messages from Ludwig Dreier telling Irena the specifics of what he wanted her to do for him, along with promises of rewards for her loyalty and service to him."

"He was using her?"

Richard shook his head. "I'm not going to lie to you, Samantha. She understood exactly what she was doing and she was doing it willingly. He wasn't fooling her into anything. She was a partner in his plot to gain power."

Samantha used a thumb to hook a curly lock of her black hair back off her face. "So you say."

"She says it, in her own words."

When Samantha only glanced at the book he was holding up without saying anything, he went on.

"Ludwig Dreier advised her on how she should react to people, what to say, and how to behave. He told her the things he wanted her to find out for him. She reported those things back to him. She was eager to help him and for their plan to succeed. She let herself be captured by Hannis Arc so that she would be closer to him in order to report on what he was doing to raise the spirit king from the dead. She was keeping him apprised of his progress and what was happening within the third kingdom.

"He told her to be especially careful not to let anyone know of her occult abilities. You didn't even know of the dark talents she possessed, did you? That's because she didn't want you to know.

"She was writing to him the whole time we were traveling here, letting him know our progress. She told Dreier of how she was keeping the act up for our benefit, playing along so that we would think she was one of us.

"Your mother betrayed us, Samantha. She told Dreier that Kahlan and I needed a containment field in order to be healed. She lied to us, Samantha, telling us that there was one here and that she had seen it. You heard her say that. There was no containment field here, so how could she have seen it?

"She used that lie as a way to get us to come here, to the citadel, where Dreier laid a trap to capture us. He told her where he wanted her to say the containment field was located within the citadel, and how to get down there as a way to get us to the dungeons where he could take us by surprise. He laid the trap and she walked us right into it."

"Lies. My mother wouldn't do such a thing."

Richard held up the book again. "It's all in here, Samantha, in her own words, in her own hand. Your mother and Dreier discussed how they couldn't risk any of the gifted in Stroyza learning that the barrier was failing. She wrote to Dreier, telling him that she had killed her sister Martha and Martha's husband when they had gone to see if the reports about Jit were true. She told him that she dumped their bodies in the swamp to make it look like they died on that journey to Jit's lair. Dreier said he would send soldiers to collect her other sister, Millicent, and her husband, Gyles, and take them to the abbey to make sure they couldn't interfere, either. They died there by his hands, but it was by your mother's design.

"Samantha, you have to listen to the truth, even

though the truth is painful. The truth is that your mother told Dreier that your father was starting to ask too many questions. There was no attack by half people. They didn't kill your father and capture her. Your mother is the one who killed your father."

Samantha's hands fisted at her sides. "Lies! All lies!"

"It's the truth. She is the one who killed Zedd. She wrote in this book, 'the old wizard was getting suspicious.' She describes to Dreier how she went about tricking Zedd and then killing him. She called him a troublesome old man. You knew Zedd. You know what a good man he was. She beheaded him for no other reason than that he was good.

"It's all here, Samantha. It's all here in her own words. You can have her journey book and read it for yourself."

Samantha folded her arms. "I told you, my name is Sammie."

"I thought you had outgrown that name when you took on the responsibility of protecting your village and warning people about the barrier failing." He pointed a thumb back over his shoulder. "You helped me rescue all those people back there. You helped me, Samantha. You did the right things, the things the people of Stroyza would have admired. You grew from a girl into a young woman and did the right things. You grew into Samantha.

"This is the moment you must choose. You can either open your eyes to the hard truth, face the facts, or you can remain a child. This is the moment when you must choose to remain Sammie, the child hiding from truth, or to be more, to be Samantha, a brave young woman I admired."

She folded her skinny arms. "I'm Sammie. That is the name my mother gave me. It's what my people called me. Sammie, not Samantha. I don't want the name you want to give me. You have no right to name me."

Richard let out a breath. "Maybe you're right about that much of it. If you won't hear the truth even though it is about your mother–especially if it is about your mother–then maybe you are still a girl, still Sammie, and not really ready to carry the name Samantha like I thought. But you can't hide your eyes from the truth forever."

"I'm not hiding my eyes from the truth. I don't believe anything you say. I don't believe that anything you are telling me really is the truth. I know the truth. The truth is that you're a liar. All those things you're saying about my mother are lies you invented to cover the truth that you murdered her."

"Why would I want to hurt your mother if she was as innocent as you wish to believe? Why would I want to do that? The truth is, I didn't." Richard waggled the journey book again. "It's all in here. You can read it for yourself."

"You expect me to think that proves anything? You got a little book and wrote out those lies yourself. You made it all up to make my mother look bad because she was a nobody from a little village and you think you are so much more important than us because you are the Lord Rahl. You made it up as an excuse for why you murdered her."

Richard nodded. "I killed her. But it was not murder and I don't regret it. I wish it wouldn't have had to be that way, but I don't regret killing her. She was a murderer of innocent people and she deserved to die. She got what she deserved. I won't apologize for doing what was right."

"So you say. You invented a story to make yourself look noble and wrote those things down to try to cover up your own crime of murder. You murdered a good woman and now you smear her memory for your own need to be an important man, a big important ruler over all the people of D'Hara."

"Samantha, we traveled together long enough that you should know me, know my heart. You should know that I wouldn't lie to you. As painful as the truth might be, I would never hide it from you. I'm telling you the truth.

"You need to grow up and accept the truth. You can't live a lie forever. Just because your mother was evil that doesn't mean you are or that you have to uphold a false belief. My father was an evil man. I understand that, I know that I am not him, just as you are not your mother. You stand on your own two feet and make your own way in life. You can still be the woman you thought she was.

"This is a time when you have to live up to your responsibility as a woman and take up the difficult business of using your head to see the truth that's right here before you, even though it may be hard, and even though it may be painful."

Samantha lifted her chin. "I don't believe your invented stories. They aren't the truth."

"The truth is that your mother even talks in here with Dreier about what they should do if you became suspicious."

Her gaze shifted to the book and then back to him. "What lies did you make up about that?"

"None. You can read it for yourself, judge for yourself. Dreier told your mother that she may need to eliminate you like she eliminated the others who became suspicious. Your mother told Dreier that once the rest of us were taken prisoner here at the citadel, he was welcome to take care of you himself in any manner he wished so that you wouldn't become a problem."

Her hands fisted at her sides again. "She wouldn't do that! She loved me!"

Richard leveled a stern look on the young woman. "You were in chains down in that dungeon because she wanted you in chains. How do you think it happened that you were caught with Kahlan, Nicci, and me? Dreier wanted us, and she made sure he had us.

"She was going to let Dreier use his occult abilities to torture you to death the same as he did to so many others who were taken to his abbey and the same as he was going to do to us had we not escaped. He was ruthless and your mother let him have you knowing how brutal he would be in eliminating you. Had we not escaped, you would have been tortured to death along with us because your mother wanted you out of her way. You were an inconvenience to her."

Samantha stood motionless for a moment, only the muscles in her jaws flexing and the tendons in her arms tightening as she fisted her hands even tighter.

Suddenly, she flung her arms out from beneath the cape and toward him. Richard had hoped she would not react in this way, but he had been ready just in case.

He already had his hand on the sword, letting its power seep through him. When he saw her begin to cast magic at him, he drew the sword in a heartbeat. The unique ring of steel filled the murky air and carried out across the grassy marshland.

A bolt of power, crackling and booming like lightning, shot toward him from her outstretched arms. The loud rumble of that lightning shook droplets of water from the grasses all around.

Richard, holding the hilt of the sword in his right hand, gripped the blade near the point with his other hand and held the weapon up like a shield. The thunderous explosion of the lightning bolt smashed into the sword, sending a shower of sparks out to the sides as the flashes curled all around him. The sound of the explosion reverberated across the countryside, echoing back from the forested hills.

When she saw that Richard wasn't harmed, Samantha growled in rage and cast another bolt of power, this one a bluish white color and thicker. It crackled through the air, sending off secondary threads of sizzling power as it came, lighting all the grass and rushes in a harsh glare. Richard bent at the knees, bracing for the impact.

When it hit the sword the force of it knocked him back a step. Upon impact, the flash of glowing power, split by the sword, spread in a shower of sparkling light around both sides of him. The scintillating discharge was so hot it ignited patches of grass and rushes, even though they were wet. Green blades of grass briefly turned an incandescent yellow-orange before crumbling to ash in the heat. An intense inferno whooshed up from those crackling fires, swirling as it rose into the air. The flames died out as the power dissipated.

Samantha slowly lowered her arms, then, staring at something behind him. Richard kept the sword up to shield himself as he looked back over his shoulder at what Samantha was staring at.

It was Kahlan, making her way through the rushes, gracefully pushing them aside with a hand as she approached. She finally came to a halt at Richard's side, her noble demeanor looking every bit the Mother Confessor.

Samantha stopped and stared, her eyes growing wider. She had driven a knife through Kahlan's heart, and certainly didn't expect to see her alive.

"I killed you. I know I did."

"You certainly did," Kahlan said. "Fortunately, Richard kept you from being a murderer. Now, he is trying to keep you from forever losing your way."

Samantha's expression turned icy calm. It was a look Richard knew all too well. The girl was beyond seeing reason.

Her arms came up once more. "Now I'm going to have to kill you again to make him pay, but this time I'm going to make sure he won't be able to bring you back."

Richard stepped in front of Kahlan and held the sword out to deflect a spreading font of blindingly bright orange flame that roared toward them. He and Kahlan both turned their faces away from the dazzling light and intense heat as they crouched behind the protection of the sword.

When they looked back, Samantha was no longer standing there. Richard spotted her just as she disappeared into the shadows back in the woods.

"I have to go after her," he said.

As he took the first step, a hand snatched his sleeve and jerked him back.

"No, you are not going after her," Nicci said through gritted teeth, meaning for him to know that she meant it.

"I have to stop her," he said, pulling his arm from her grip. "She will come back after us."

Nicci gave him an admonishing look. "Richard, have you forgotten that that girl can make all those trees explode? If you go into those woods, she will blow the forest apart, and you with it. We won't be able to find anything left of you to put on a funeral pyre. You would be shredded into nothing."

"You know she's right, Richard," Kahlan said. "Don't do what she just did and avoid the truth because it's ugly. We have to use our heads. We have more important things to worry about. We need to stop Sulachan, not Samantha."

Richard knew that they were both right. He couldn't let himself be distracted by Samantha. He had given her a chance to accept the truth. Those who refused to see the truth were not immune from it.

Richard finally nodded. "I wish I could talk to Red. She saved our lives because she knew what was about to happen with that tower."

Kahlan shook her head. "She's gone."

"Vanished like a ghost," Nicci confirmed.

Richard's expression soured. "Isn't that just like a witch woman."

"She helped you all she could," Kahlan said. "It's not her place to help us any more than she already has."

Richard let out a heavy sigh. "I suppose you're right. Let's go find Mohler, the scribe. We're in the dark about too many things and that leaves us behind events. We need to get ahead of Sulachan and Hannis Arc if we are going to stop them.

"There are prophecies here that Hannis Arc somehow used to bring Sulachan back from the dead. I want to know everything he knew. For the most part we all know what Hannis Arc has done, but key elements of how he did them are missing. If I'm going to stop him, I need to find those key elements."

Kahlan gave him a crooked smile and then put her arm through his as they started back toward the citadel. "That's the Seeker I know so well."

U p on the top floor of the citadel, Mohler, the old scribe, looked back over his shoulder as he lifted the lantern out toward the oak door. With its heavy iron straps it looked like it could be a door to a treasure vault, or a dungeon.

"This is the place, Lord Rahl," Mohler said. "This is–was–Bishop Arc's study. It's the recording room where all the prophecies have always been kept and where he worked most of the time."

Richard wasn't especially happy about getting tangled up in the uncertainties and misdirection of prophecy, but he needed to know what information Hannis Arc had been using as he hatched his plot to bring Emperor Sulachan back from the underworld. It was clear that something he had been using was effective or Sulachan would still be in the world of the dead.

Mohler lifted a finger out from his fist holding the metal ring of the lantern and placed it against the door as he smiled back at Richard, Kahlan, Nicci, and the three Mord-Sith. Richard thought it was more an apologetic smile than one of pleasure.

"Like the scribes before me, I've spent nearly my entire life working in here, devoted to the prophecies kept here, tending the old ones and recording new ones that came in for Bishop Arc."

Richard glanced from the old scribe to the door. "Let's hope there is something in them that will help us stop the man."

The hunched scribe conceded the point with a nod before leaning down even more to pick the proper key from the ring of keys he always had with him. Long wisps of gray hair did little to cover the top of his bald head and the blotches of dark spots scattered across his scalp. Richard lifted the lantern from the man's hand to make it easier for him to select the right key and unlock the door.

Mohler finally stuck the correct key in the lock, and holding the handle, jiggled it in a way the old lock needed to be finessed in order to make the bolt clang back. He pushed the heavy door inward and retrieved his lantern from Richard before leading them into the room. Once inside, cocooned in the lantern light against the darkness, he plucked a long sliver from a small iron cup mounted on the wall near the door and lit it in the flame of his lantern, then let the glass cover back down before rushing around the room using the flaming sliver of fat wood to light candles and lamps along the way. Each flame added its own little bit of light until the room was fully revealed.

There were no windows to allow the night to look in. High beams on the ceiling were all decorated with ornamental carving. The plastered walls had darkened over the ages from the soot of candles and lanterns, leaving them a dark, mottled tan.

Laurin closed the door and then stood before it. The other two Mord-Sith took up posts to either side of the door, guarding it so that no one could disturb them.

Considering the size of the citadel, the recording room was far more expansive than Richard had expected, even though it wasn't nearly as large as many prophecy rooms he had seen before. Since the citadel was primarily a prison to hold those who had been born with occult power leaking out from beyond the barrier until they could be executed, it seemed strange that so much space would be devoted to prophecy.

He supposed that it might not have been intended for such a use when it had been first built, and along the way those who ran the citadel, like many people, became increasingly obsessed with prophecy. Prophecy, too, even false prophecy, gave those controlling it power over people.

Mohler pointed to ledgers lining shelves of tall bookcases to the left side, as if to answer the question in Richard's expression. "I believe that originally, many ages ago, this was the place where information from the condemned was recorded. All those books there hold names and family links. I think that those in charge back then used those ledgers as a way to try to contain the spread of any infection leaking from the third kingdom. But at some point, prophecy became more important to the people who ran this place and the ledgers were forgotten, along with the original purpose of the citadel."

Richard nodded. "I think that the inmates took over the prison, so to speak. Once they were in charge, they came to believe that prophecy was their means of changing their place in the world to one of domination."

"Prophecy certainly was an obsession of Hannis Arc," Mohler confirmed, "and he was obsessed with domination. Especially of the House of Rahl."

"Why would he be so concerned with the House of Rahl?" Kahlan asked.

Mohler turned to look at her. "They murdered his family when he was still a boy."

Richard nodded. "Some of my ancestors murdered a lot of people and made a lot of enemies."

"Well," Nicci said, changing the subject as she looked around, "this is no match for the vaults of prophecy that were once at the Palace of the Prophets."

"Let's hope that what is here at least turns out to be valuable to us," Kahlan said.

Even with all the candles and lanterns Mohler had lit, the recording room was rather dark and gloomy, but more than that, the place was decidedly strange. An odd assortment of various items stood all throughout the expansive room. Glassed display cases held odd collections of smaller objects. Randomly throughout the room were low cabinets, cases, statues, and pedestals grouped in no particular order that Richard could make out, but he did see that everything had been placed in an even grid pattern, so that they almost resembled pieces on a giant game board. Around the edges of the room in several places there were overstuffed chairs, comfortable spots to relax or read.

Richard frowned as he scanned the room, trying to make sense of it, but he decided in the end that maybe it wasn't supposed to make sense. Not everything had to make sense. Sometimes people simply put new things they collected wherever they could find space. Most likely, the items, everything from marble statues to a bronze sundial, were placed in the room as they were collected. Collected, though, by a disorderly mind that would put a sundial in a dark room with no windows, as if hiding it from its purpose. Either that, or Hannis Arc found comfort in chaos.

They walked slowly, silently, past glassed cabinets that held odd collections of items. There were bones from strange creatures Richard didn't recognize, common-looking rocks, small figures made of straw wearing crudely sewn clothes, carvings of people and animals arranged in scenes of country life, and geared mechanical devices the purpose of which Richard couldn't begin to guess.

Although, those geared devices did remind him in a way of Regula, the omen machine. Regula was filled with complex geared workings.

The shelves in the cabinets also held small boxes in a variety of sizes along with round tubes with symbols in the language of Creation carved all over them. Scanning a few of the boxes, Richard mentally translated some of the symbols and saw that each item told a story, not unlike the scenes depicted by some of the little carved figures.

Nicci shook her head as she stared into one of the cases. "I hate to imagine where Hannis Arc would have obtained some of these rare objects."

When she looked at Mohler, he shrugged an apology for not having an answer. "He didn't collect all of them. Some of these things were here since I was young. I know that he did add items from time to time, but others were here before I was born."

There were also a number of preserved animals in different places around the room. Besides more common creatures in common poses such as a deer standing in a display thick with dried grass, a family of beavers posed on a mound of sticks, and raptors, their wings spread as they stood on bare branches, there was also a large bear towering up on its hind legs, jaws spread wide in a silent roar, its claws raised so that it looked perpetually ready to attack.

In various places throughout the room, conforming to the grid pattern, large pedestals stood in random spots within that gridwork, in no apparent order. Each carved wooden or stone pedestal held an enormous open book, each with a heavy leather binding. Some of the books were decorated with gold leaf. Most showed great age and wear, with frayed edges all around their covers. They would have been hard to move because of their sheer size, but because they appeared to be quite fragile they probably had permanent homes on their pedestals rather than on one of the bookshelves against the back wall.

They all lay open to different places in the volumes, places where the latest entries had been made. Some were opened in the middle, others closer to the end. Only a few lay open near the beginning.

Tables near the pedestals holding the books were piled with disorderly stacks of scrolls. Richard unfurled several and it confirmed his speculation that they were prophecies that had come in to the citadel for Mohler to record in the permanent collection of large books. While a few of the prophecies sounded complex, most were simpler than the typical prophecies he had read. The wax seals on many of the scrolls were unbroken, the scrolls waiting their turn to be opened and recorded.

Kahlan had told him the horror of how Ludwig collected prophecy by torturing captives. It was probable that for some of those scrolls, at least, someone had died at Ludwig Dreier's hands. It had to be the ultimate terror to be at the mercy of such a madman.

And yet, strangely, it appeared that Hannis Arc was in no particular hurry to see all the new prophecies lying untouched. Richard was beginning to suspect that something else must have commanded the man's attention, which meant that, for Hannis Arc at least, the prophecies were not the most important thing in the room, and not what occupied most of his time. Something else was. Richard wondered what that something else could be.

Mohler swept a hand of gnarled, arthritic fingers around, indicating the open books. "This has been my life's work, Lord Rahl. These are the books where I recorded prophecy collected from out in the Dark Lands." With a kind of reverent affection, he let the hand settle on one of the open books. "These books are where I would write down all the prophecy brought to the citadel, as scribes before me had done for generations."

"Did all of these prophecies come from Ludwig Dreier?" Richard asked.

"Actually, only a small portion came from Abbot Dreier. He believed that he was the bishop's most important source of prophecy, but actually he wasn't. Most of the scrolls and even ledger books are brought in from various places around the Dark Lands. A number of emissaries from the citadel traveled the towns and more remote areas out among the villages and the cunning folk to collect prophecies from anyone with the talent for such foretelling. Once each foretelling arrived back here, I recorded it in these books."

"You wrote all these books?" Kahlan asked.

"Oh my no," he said with a short chuckle. "I work with these books, record into them, but they predate me by many centuries. They contain the work of a long line of scribes who came before me, going back several thousand years, almost to the time when the citadel was built, I believe. All of it is recorded here. As did those before me, I have worked at this my entire life. Since I was young I have entered new prophecy in these books, most of that time for Bishop Arc."

Knowing what he knew about prophecy, Richard was having a hard time believing that these books of recorded prophecy were the source of Hannis Arc's knowledge and power. Prophecy, especially what he suspected was more folklore than true prophecy, could not provide that level of expertise.

"How do you choose which book to record these

new prophecies in?" Nicci asked the scribe. "Was that also your job, to decide where they belong?"

He looked somewhat puzzled by the question. "They are categorized and then recorded according to their subject. I record them in the proper book for the subject contained in the prophecy."

Richard shared a look with Nicci before he gazed out over the books lying open all over the room. "I was just starting to organize the prophecies at the People's Palace. But it takes a true prophet to read the prophecy first and determine the proper subject."

"Really?" Mohler asked, his eyes brightening. "I had no idea you were interested in such matters. Bishop Arc never cared much about the mundane aspects of my work. He only cared to read the new prophecies once I recorded them. Are there many books of prophecies there, at the People's Palace?"

Richard arched an eyebrow. "The books in this room would not fill one small corner of one of the smaller libraries. There are a great many libraries there. Some of them, by themselves, as large as this citadel."

Mohler's eyes widened. "Really? I would love to see such a sight one day."

"I hope that someday you can," Richard said. He frowned, getting to what he really wanted to know. "Why aren't the prophecies here recorded by chronology, rather than subject? Chronology is ultimately what matters. After all, a prophecy is irrelevant if it's about an event that took place a thousand years ago, or will take place thousands of years from now. You need to know where a prophecy fits in time to know if it is relevant to what is happening today. Prophecy can only be linked, and more importantly put in context, if it can be placed chronologically."

Mohler looked befuddled. "I rarely have any way of determining chronology, Lord Rahl, so I must instead use the subject as the category. That is how it has always been done."

Richard didn't want to tell the man right then and there that his life's work had not only been misguided but was virtually useless. He couldn't let it go entirely, either.

"The subject of the written words is misleading unless you are gifted and can confirm that the subject as written is actually related to the underlying prophecy. Are you gifted?"

Mohler touched a finger to his lower lip. "No, Lord Rahl. But I can read, so I know the subject."

Richard shook his head. "The problem with that is that the words are not really the prophecy."

The old scribe's eyes widened. "They aren't? But how can that be?"

"The meaning of the prophecy is hidden in a layer of magic beneath the words. What most people don't understand is that the words are not actually the prophecy. They are only a trigger for the meaning of the real prophecy. A prophecy, for example, that says it will rain, may actually mean it will rain blood. Or a bounty of good crops. It takes a prophet to be able to see the vision of the real prophecy veiled by the words. The words are what trigger the vision, they don't actually reveal it."

Mohler looked about the room at his life's work, seeming confused and lost, probably for the first time in his career.

"Even using the words," Nicci said, "prophecy often contains references to a number of subjects. How do you determine which subject book to record them in?"

"I had to do the best I could, Mistress. I used my experience and judgment." Mohler pointed. "For example, all the prophecy in that book is about the House of Rahl—a subject of great interest to Hannis Arc." He looked up at Richard. "Do you mean to say that my entire life's work is meaningless? That the categories are meaningless?"

Richard sighed as he looked around at the books lying open on pedestals. "I can't say for sure. All I can tell you is that prophecy says I'm the one who is supposed to end prophecy–whatever that means. So, I guess that ultimately, if I'm successful, none of this will mean anything."

"Isn't that something," Mohler whispered to himself as he stared at all the books as if seeing prophecy for the first time in a new light. "And to think, Bishop Arc spent so much of his life in here."

What bothered Richard most was that if Hannis Arc didn't help in the assignment of prophecy to particular books, that could only mean that the man wasn't as interested in these prophecies as Mohler believed. Something else had been the focus of Hannis Arc's attention and the source of his knowledge.

"The people who used all this didn't really know what they were doing," Nicci said, being more forward about it than Richard. "From what you say," she told Mohler, "the things collected from anyone with the 'talent for foretelling,' means that most of this would be false prophecy."

He looked alarmed. "False prophecy, Mistress?"

Nicci nodded as she looked around at the books. "True prophecy comes from wizards–prophets–not from country folk who imagine they have such talent and dream up prophecy. Those kind usually have a head full of predictions that come from dreams, wishes, fears, or most often their fertile imaginations.

"True prophets are wizards and wizards in this day and age are exceedingly rare. Prophecy among wizards is even more rare. Prophecy is meant to be read by others with the gift at least, and especially by other wizards who were gifted for prophecy. True prophecy is a specialty of wizards, not regular people."

Mohler was frowning with concern. "You mean this in here is . . . not true prophecy?"

Nicci shrugged. "If you make enough predictions, eventually you will get one right, but that is by accident, not design. People focus on the one that turns out correct and from that give credibility to the others they believe have simply not yet come to pass, but forget about the hundreds or even thousands like them that have been forgotten because they have proven to be false.

"This looks to have become an obsession of a few in the beginning who didn't really understand prophecy, and they passed on their beliefs in this kind of 'prophecy' to those who came after them. It's akin to superstition, nothing more.

"At the Palace of the Prophets I worked for a great many years with the prophecy kept down in the vaults. It was prophecy written by wizards who were true prophets. I can tell you from experience that while there might be a few gems here, most of it is just common rocks."

Richard was thinking the same thing. He wondered what Hannis Arc had really been doing in the room. If this prophecy was largely useless for the purpose and of little value, then how did Hannis Arc learn to raise Emperor Sulachan from the dead?

Richard turned to the scribe. "Where did Hannis Arc work most of the time? You said that he spent a great deal of his time working in here. What did he do?"

Mohler shrugged uncomfortably. "I was not privy to exactly what it was he did. He did not discuss such matters with me–I was only his scribe. I do know, though, that he liked to study old documents. At least, that was what I most often saw him doing. I started early in the morning recording prophecy in the books, here, and he usually came in later. He did a lot of his work in here at night after I was gone."

The old man lifted an arm out toward a large desk off to the side of the pedestals that held the books of prophecy. The disorderly desk was piled with everything from decorated bone objects and simple candlesticks to rulers and dividers to papers and stacks of old scrolls. A fat candle in a silver stand rested on top of a stack of worn ledgers. By the way layers of candle wax dribbled down all over one side of the ledgers, their importance appeared to have been nothing more than as a stand to elevate candles.

"Sometimes he would go over to the books and read

prophecy I had recorded. I assumed that he did that when I was gone as well, but I can't actually say for sure. I can't say that I ever saw him paying close attention, though. I think he merely scanned them, looking for anything that might warrant more of his attention later.

"When I was here he occasionally liked to play chess"–the scribe gestured to a small stand with a board set with black and white game pieces–"over there." He turned back. "Mostly, though, he worked there, at his desk."

Standing behind the broad desk, Richard noticed that the closest pedestal, the one not far away on the other side of the desk, was the one holding the book that Mohler said contained prophecies about the House of Rahl. Just beyond that book of prophecy, rising up behind it, Hannis Arc would have had a good view of the stuffed bear standing up on its hind legs to tower over the book. The man probably liked the symbolism. In that light, the placement of objects in the room was beginning to make a little more sense.

Hannis Arc seemed to be a man fixated on symbology.

The books of prophecy around the room were immense, not only physically, but also in that there were collectively thousands upon thousands of pages contained in them. The thought of studying all of those books to try to find out what Hannis Arc had been up to, or to find a hint that might be helpful in stopping him, was daunting. Small numbers of prophecies were difficult enough to consider. The numbers here were overwhelming. But he didn't think that prophecies collected in such a suspect manner were really what had occupied Hannis Arc.

Richard turned his attention back to the desk and unrolled a brittle, ancient-looking scroll lying to the side of the desk. The vellum was stained with what looked to be centuries of dirt and dark, ringed stains from mugs and candles used as weights to hold it open.

Richard was stunned by what he saw written in faded ink.

Nicci did a double take when she saw the look on his face. "What is it? What do you see?"

Richard could only stare at the scroll covered with a complex tapestry of lines connecting constellations of elements that made up the language of Creation. He moved to the side a little as Nicci and Kahlan rushed around the desk to have a look for themselves at what had captured his attention.

"That's the language of Creation used by Regula," Kahlan said. "The omen machine gives prophecies in that language."

Richard nodded as he scanned the symbols, already trying to work out the translations. "It's also the same language used by Naja Moon to leave messages in the caves in Stroyza."

"I wonder if that means they date back to the time of the great war, the time when Naja and Emperor Sulachan were alive," Kahlan said as she leaned in, frowning at the scroll Richard held spread open on the desk. "What does this say?"

Rather than answering her, he straightened and looked over at Mohler. "Are there any more of these scrolls? Ones written in this same language?"

Mohler stretched his neck to glance across the desk and look down at the scroll. He appeared to recognize it.

"Yes, there are some more of them." He pointed. "There is another one of them, there, in that pile. It's that darker one. Bishop Arc called them Cerulean scrolls."

"Cerulean scrolls?" Richard asked. "You're sure?"

"Yes, that's right. He could read them, but I can't. He spent a great deal of his time working with them. Whenever a new one came in he spent all his waking time with it for weeks, but that was a rare event. He was very protective of them.

"Years ago he used to study every detail of the new prophecies that I recorded for him. Although he would still come over from time to time and scan the newest entries I had made, over the years his interest in the books of prophecy dwindled until he became almost entirely focused on the scrolls.

"Sometimes he used those instruments on the Cerulean scrolls, doing some kind of measuring and such. If he worked late into the night and left them out, then in the morning when I came in I would put them away for him, but other than that I never had anything to do with them."

Kahlan looked up from the scroll. "Do you know what 'Cerulean' means?"

Mohler shook his head. "That was what he called them, but he never told me the meaning of the word."

"It's an ancient word," Richard said. "It means 'celestial.'"

Nicci's brow twitched. "Celestial?"

Richard grunted confirmation as he idly pinched his lower lip, deep in thought about the things he had seen in the room where Hannis Arc spent most of his time. The place contained dusty artifacts from ages ago, most appearing to predate Hannis Arc's time. While the place was chiefly dedicated to cataloging and recording prophecy, the man hadn't bothered to open all the newly arrived divinations. Since he apparently didn't read them closely, it would seem that Hannis Arc wasn't all that interested in prophecy. Or possibly he understood that the kind of ungifted prediction that arrived daily at the citadel was not true prophecy and largely useless.

It appeared that the Cerulean scrolls were the center of his focus. Richard wondered if perhaps Hannis Arc was only seeking out prophecy as a pretext to send people in what was really a search for scrolls or books written in the language of Creation. The Dark Lands, after all, seemed to be rich with history from the time of the great war. The caves at Stroyza were covered with information from that time.

"Sometimes," Mohler said, "when I arrived in the morning to record prophecies that had come in overnight, Bishop Arc would still be in here working on a new Cerulean scroll and I would notice, then, that he had acquired more of those strange tattoos. Bishop Arc didn't like me to speak unless spoken to, so I never asked about them. When we played chess I didn't like to look upon those frightening symbols tattooed all over him."

Nicci hooked a long lock of blond hair behind her ear as she leaned over to get a better look at the scroll on the desk. "Was he good at chess?"

Mohler nodded. "Oh yes. He was a master at it."

"So then there are more of these kind of scrolls, with symbols like this one here?" Richard asked as he impatiently waved a finger at the scroll. "These Cerulean scrolls–there are more of them?"

Mohler seemed a little bewildered by Richard's interest in old scrolls. "That's right. Some are written in languages that are slightly different but are similar enough. All of them are kept over there." He gestured to a cabinet against the stone wall. "Let me show you, Lord Rahl."

The man shuffled across the room, weaving his way between a display of a family of stuffed beavers to one side, and a marble statue of a woman in a filmy robe that left nothing to the imagination on his other side.

Richard noticed that from his desk, Hannis Arc would not have been able to see the statue very well, but he would have had a clear view of the scene with the beavers, all busily at work chewing tree trunks and reducing them to sticks and small logs to use in their dam building so they could control the flow of a stream.

When he reached the cabinet, Mohler opened the tall, carved door to reveal a grid of cubbyholes, almost every one of them holding at least one scroll, some stuffed with several. They looked as ancient as the one on the desk. Many had dark, crumbling edges. A quick appraisal suggested that there were probably close to a hundred Cerulean scrolls in the cabinet.

Richard pulled one of them out and carefully unrolled it to have a look. It began with azimuth angles that he didn't recognize. Those celestial observations, he suspected, were meant to show star positions. Richard wasn't entirely sure how, but he suspected that it might be a way of establishing chronology, a key element that prophecy lacked. In that light, the scrolls made prophecy look amateurish and incomplete. It seemed to have been an advanced technique, the mastery of which had been lost over time.

Right at the beginning, after the information about azimuth angles, Richard saw symbols that spoke about prophecy, except that they weren't giving prophecy. Rather, they spoke of prophecy itself, almost as if it were a living thing.

In a strange way, they were revealing prophecy, but only in an oblique manner as they spoke of specific prophecies, using what they said to explain the central subject of the scroll. What, exactly, the subject of the scroll might be, Richard wasn't entirely sure just yet.

Since in the language of Creation each of the symbols formed a complete concept, similar to an entire written sentence, rather than merely a word in a different language, it would take more time to work out the meanings of all the arcane symbols.

Richard rolled the scroll back up and handed it to Nicci. He pulled out another and opened it wide between his outstretched arms. This one, too, was written in symbols, and although the language was very similar it was not exactly the language of Creation. It was substantially the same, but more arcane, more primitive, written in a kind of less-formal slang. Richard felt a chill run through him at the realization that it seemed to be a language that predated the orthodox form of the language of Creation. A quick look was enough to tell him that he should at least be able catch the gist of it, if not translate it in its entirety.

As he scanned the symbols, they, too, appeared to be about prophecy, but in a different way. He frowned as he studied the scroll, trying to figure out what it was saying.

"Look there," Nicci said, leaning in and pointing at a symbol. "Isn't that the symbol for Regula?"

Richard blinked with the realization. "It certainly is."

He rushed to try to read what the scroll was saying about Regula. Right off the top of his head it wasn't making a lot of sense. His sense of alarm was making it difficult to think clearly.

Nicci leaned in, pointing again. "Look at this formula."

Richard puzzled at it. "I don't think I've ever seen it before. Something about death, but I don't know what it means."

"I recognize that particular set of expressions," Nicci said. "They were used by Sisters of the Dark. They have to do with the underworld." She looked up at him out of the corner of her eye. "It's talking about the world of the dead."

"I see it now," Richard said, nodding as he unfurled more of the scroll. "It's speaking of banishment."

"Banishment?" Kahlan asked, peering around the

side of him at the scroll. "Banishment to the world of the dead? You mean like the Temple of the Winds was sent to the underworld?"

Gooseflesh tingled along Richard's arms.

"No. Not to the underworld. This has to do with a banishment from the world of the dead."

"Banishment from the underworld?" Kahlan shook her head. "What could that be about?"

"I don't know," Richard said as he rolled the scroll back up and started pulling others out of the cubbyholes, holding them in the crook of his arm. "Help me take them over to the desk."

"How many do you want?" Nicci asked.

"All of them."

Kahlan looked over at him. "All of them?"

"Yes. Bring them all over to the desk. This is what we came to find. It's not the prophecies that hold what we're looking for, it's these Cerulean scrolls. This is what Hannis Arc used to bring Sulachan back from the dead."

"Are you sure?" Kahlan asked.

Richard waggled one of the scrolls. "Why do you think he has these symbols tattooed all over himself? It has something to do with the scrolls, not prophecy. The scroll has elements and symbols linked to occult magic. It mentioned Regula. It's all tied together with what's in these scrolls.

"I need to know what all of them say. I need to get to work to translate them to find out what Hannis Arc knows and what he is doing."

"Richard," Kahlan said in a confidential tone, "we don't have time for this."

He stopped pulling scrolls out of the cubbyholes to look at her. "What are you talking about?"

"The sickness you carry. We have to get it out of you or you are going to die before you can use any of this to stop Sulachan and Hannis Arc. You need to be cured first."

Richard went back to pulling out scrolls and stuffing them under his other arm. "We can't make it to the People's Palace in time. I told you that before, it's too far. But maybe there is another way. Maybe these will help us to solve that problem in a different way."

As he rushed to pull scrolls out of the cabinet, he saw Kahlan and Nicci share a look. He understood their concern, but he knew he had a limited amount of time before the poison grew strong enough to stop him from thinking clearly. It wouldn't be long after that until it killed him.

He knew, too, that even in the best of circumstances they couldn't make it to the People's Palace in time. Even if they made it there, Sulachan's half people would already have the plateau surrounded, preventing them from being able to get in. They couldn't fight their way through all of Sulachan's forces.

He started back to the desk with his armload of scrolls. The others followed behind, carrying their own armloads of scrolls.

He needed to find out what was going on. He needed to know how Hannis Arc had brought Sulachan back through the veil. Such things weren't supposed to be possible. The dead were supposed to stay dead. He knew that those answers were the key to everything.

For that matter, even though there were some unique circumstances involved, it shouldn't have been possible for Kahlan and him to come back to life. And yet they had. It all made sense, and yet it didn't. Not really. He suspected that those events were related to everything else taking place with Hannis Arc and Emperor Sulachan.

Richard remembered the bone woman, Adie, telling him about the skrin being a force that was a part of the veil between life and death. That force guarded in both directions. The force of the skrin repelled all from the cusp where the world of the living and the world of the dead touched.

The skrin kept the spirits in the underworld from crossing back into the world of life.

So how did Sulachan cross back?

Richard needed to find the answer to that question.

As she came down the hall, walking through patches of early-morning light coming in the windows, Kahlan could see Vale and Laurin, both wearing their red leather, standing at their posts before the door to Hannis Arc's recording room. They would have been there the whole night, making sure that no one could disturb Richard.

Men of the First File stood guard everywhere in the halls of the citadel, always at the ready for any trouble that might arise. On her way back from the kitchen, Commander Fister had asked Kahlan to come get him if she needed anything. She had assured him she would.

Vale reached out as she stepped away from the door, offering to take the tray.

"No, it's all right," Kahlan said. "I have it."

Vale moved back out of the way to let Kahlan through. "Did you get any sleep, Mother Confessor?"

Kahlan nodded. "Yes, thankfully." It had not been enough, but it had been better than nothing. "How about you two?"

Vale gestured to Laurin. "We took turns resting a little now and then."

Kahlan didn't believe that for a moment. The

Mord-Sith would not have left their posts guarding Richard for anything, especially now that there seemed to be a heightened sense of urgency to what he was doing in the recording room. Mord-Sith didn't know much about magic, or about ancient scrolls for that matter, but it was not at all difficult to tell that Richard was stirred up over the discovery.

Kahlan had been up for ages, it seemed. The anguish of returning to the world of life only to learn that Richard had given his life to send her back had been beyond endurance. The realization that Richard was dead had denied her the ability to sleep, except fitfully. After that, the effort of helping Nicci when she went to the underworld to bring him back had been strenuous, on top of having so little sleep.

And then, the euphoria of having Richard return from that dark realm had been muted by Cara giving her life to make it possible.

The wild swing of emotions had been draining. The relief of at last having Richard back was tempered by the fact that the poison of death still infected him, to say nothing of the ordeal of standing all day beside Cara's funeral pyre. Kahlan had been near to dropping from exhaustion. Her lack of sleep had begun to make it nearly impossible for her to think clearly any longer.

When Richard told her to go get some rest, she hadn't had the energy to argue. She wanted him to come with her and get a few hours' sleep, but he said that he had to stay and work on trying to understand what was in the scrolls and what they might have to do with everything that was happening. She'd reminded him that he needed sleep in order to think clearly. Richard had told her that he'd gotten a good long rest while he had been dead. That made her smile.

With Nicci and the three Mord-Sith saying that they would stay and watch over him, Kahlan had given in and made her way back to the bedroom to get some sleep. She'd fallen asleep almost as soon as she hit the bed. It hadn't been as restful as she had expected or hoped, probably because she missed having Richard there beside her. Even as short as it had been, it had at least done her some good.

"It smells delicious," Laurin said of the eggs and bacon Kahlan had on the tray. "Make sure Lord Rahl eats it all. He needs his strength if he is to be the magic against magic."

Kahlan smiled as she nodded. "I asked some of the workers down in the kitchen to bring you up some as well. They should be along shortly. I want you to eat, too. You three need your strength to be able to protect him."

As she opened the door, Laurin promised that they would be sure to eat. Inside the quiet, windowless room, Cassia looked over from her post beside the door. Kahlan saw Nicci curled up in one of the overstuffed chairs, sound asleep, with one arm draped over the side. The scribe, Mohler, had gone off to bed just before Kahlan, and had not yet returned.

"How is everything?" Kahlan asked in a whisper so as not to wake Nicci.

Cassia glanced at Richard briefly before answering. "I can't say for sure, but I don't think things are going well."

Concern tightened Kahlan's brow. "What do you mean?"

Cassia pressed her lips tight as she considered how to explain it. "I don't know. It seems like he is in a really bad mood."

"A bad mood? Why, what happened?"

"Nothing, really. I can't exactly put my finger on anything specific," Cassia said. "I don't know him well enough to know what he is like most of the time, but just from as long as I've been with him, I don't think he is usually this upset. From what I am able to gather, I think he's angry about something he is reading."

"Did he say something?" Kahlan asked the Mord-Sith.

"No, nothing." Cassia drew her hand down the long, single blond braid she had pulled over the front of her shoulder. "But I can see the muscles in his jaw flex from time to time as he grits his teeth. Once I saw his knuckles turn white because he was gripping the hilt of his sword so tightly."

Kahlan didn't at all like the sound of that. "Well, maybe having something to eat will make him feel better."

Cassia nodded. "I hope so. He needs his strength. I can hardly believe that we have him back. I want him to get over his sickness and be well. I want him to be with us forever."

From knowing Cara so well, Kahlan understood what it meant to the Mord-Sith to have a Lord Rahl like Richard come into their lives. Kahlan lifted Cara's Agiel hanging on the chain around Cassia's neck.

"I understand. I am a sister of the Agiel."

Cassia, her eyes widening, tilted her head forward. "You are? Really?"

Kahlan smiled as she nodded. "Sisters of the Agiel know what is best for him. We all have to stick together in order to take care of him."

Cassia flashed a conspiratorial smile. "You have that right."

At the desk, Kahlan set the tray down to the side, out of Richard's way. "The sun is up," she said. "Well, it's actually too cloudy to see it, but it's light out, anyway. I brought you breakfast."

Richard glanced up briefly to give her a perfunctory smile.

"Have some food, Richard. You need to eat."

Without argument he briefly glanced over at the tray and retrieved a piece of bacon. He munched on it as he continued to study the scroll laid out on the desk before him. A candle in a heavy silver base held down one corner, a lantern the other. More scrolls lay in disorderly stacks all over the desk. Beyond the desk, the stuffed bear stood on its hind legs, towering over them, claws raised as it glared in a frozen, menacing roar.

Once he finished the bacon, Richard kept reading. Kahlan handed him another piece. He took it, offering a grunt of thanks, and kept studying the scroll without looking over.

Kahlan leaned a hip against the desk and folded her arms. "So, have you learned anything?"

"Too much," he muttered.

"What does that mean?"

"It means," he said without looking up at her, "that I'm beginning to wish I wouldn't have come back from the world of the dead."

Kahlan took hold of the wooden armrest and pulled his chair around so that he was facing her. She was not going to be ignored. When he started to protest she put a forkful of scrambled eggs in his mouth.

"You need to eat to keep up your strength," she told him. "Fighting off that poison inside you is a constant effort. You need to eat."

He chewed as he watched her eyes. She knew he couldn't argue the point. Without pause, she scooped up more eggs and fed them to him each time he swallowed.

When he had finished eating most of the eggs, she handed him the cup of tea and smiled. "Good?"

He took a swallow, his gray, raptor gaze staying on her the whole time. "Yes, thanks. I didn't realize how hungry I was." He gestured vaguely to the disorderly stack of scrolls. "I've been absorbed in all these."

Now that he had stopped and eaten something, she expected he would be more forthcoming. "So, do you want to tell me about it?"

He finally let out a deep sigh. "I don't know. I guess I feel like the whole world has been turned upside down. It turns out that the things I've learned in recent years and I thought I knew hardly even scratched the surface. They were true, but only in a way, and only as far as they went. It turns out that nothing is like what I thought. I had no idea of what was actually going on beneath the surface—or even how much there was beneath the surface. I feel like I've been kept in the dark."

"Really? Kept in the dark for how long?"

"Remember the day I first met you in the Hartland woods, and I told you that some men were following you?"

"Of course."

"Since then."

Kahlan gave him a smiling admonishment. "Richard, it can't be that bad. Look at all we've overcome already. Besides, just because you're reading something in these scrolls, that doesn't mean it's true. How many times have we thought we understood something because of what we read, only to find out later that it wasn't true?"

"Unfortunately, this has proven to be true."

"How can you be so sure?"

"Emperor Sulachan would not be back in the world of the living right now if it weren't true. You wouldn't be alive if this were not true. I wouldn't be alive. I had no idea of how much more there is to what is going on than I thought."

"What's not like you thought?"

"Everything."

"Everything," Kahlan repeated. "Such as?"

Richard leaned back, letting out a deep sigh as he drummed his fingers on the arm of the chair, apparently considering where to begin.

"Do you know where prophecy comes from?" he began.

Kahlan thought it an odd question. "Real prophecy comes from prophets."

"Dead prophets."

Kahlan tilted her head forward. "What are you talking about?"

"When a prophet—a wizard gifted with prophecy—goes into a trance and prophecy comes to him, that prophecy is coming from dead prophets in the underworld. That is the source of prophecy."

Kahlan gaped at him a moment. "You can't be serious."

Richard looked up from under his brow. "In the language of Creation, the symbol for prophecy can be translated in two different ways. One meaning of the symbol is 'prophecy,' the other translation is 'the voice of the dead.'"

He turned to the desk and swept an arm over a scroll

held open at each side with ledger books. "These scrolls are full of information about the nature of the world of life and the nature of the underworld. I never imagined that this much comprehensive information could be contained in one place. There is more information–important information–in these scrolls than all the libraries at the People's Palace. It's like everything we've ever found before, everything we've ever looked for, everything we've learned, only scratched the surface of what these scrolls contain."

Kahlan didn't like the sound of that. "Such as?"

Richard wearily rubbed the tips of his fingers against his temples. "Everything that has happened ever since I met you–for that matter everything since you and I were born–is in here. These scrolls tie all the loose ends together. They tie everything together."

"Everything?" Kahlan couldn't fathom what he was talking about. "Richard, I'm not following what you're getting at. Everything . . . like what?"

He looked up at the ceiling. "Where do I even begin?"

"Pick a place and start," she said in as calming a voice as she could muster.

His head came down and he fixed her in his gaze. "Everything from the boxes of Orden to Sulachan to Regula to Hannis Arc to me is tied up in all of this. I don't even know where to start or really even how to begin to explain it to you."

Kahlan folded her arms. "Take it one thing at a time, Richard. Start with Regula. What does it say about the omen machine?"

Richard peered up from under his brow. "Regula is part of the power of the underworld. In a way, it's death itself in our world, in our midst, in the world of life."

She held up a hand to stop him. "Back up. It's buried under the People's Palace. Where did it come from?" she asked, trying to be as patient as she could to get him to calm down. "How did it get there?"

Richard tapped the side of his thumb on the desk for a moment. "I'm not exactly sure, yet, of the whole explanation. There are a lot of Cerulean scrolls left to go through."

"I understand, but you said that it was in a way death itself in our midst. You must have a reason for saying that. What does that mean?"

He leaned forward. "Regula–its power, what makes it alive in a sense–was banished to the world of life, banished from the underworld."

Kahlan made a face. "Banished to the world of life? From the underworld? I'm sorry, Richard, but I don't understand."

"Well, remember how the wizards back in the great war banished the Temple of the Winds to the underworld to protect the dangerous magic it contained?"

Kahlan had some pretty unpleasant memories of the Temple of the Winds. "It would be impossible for me to forget that even if I tried."

"Well," Richard said, using his hands as he talked, "part of the bargain–the balance for that–was that the world of life had to take the power of Regula and keep it hidden here."

Kahlan squinted at him. "Wait–what is it? What is Regula? What is the power that was banished here?"

"It's the collective power of prophecy from the underworld. Having it in this world powers prophecy. It enables prophecy to come into this world. It propagates prophecy."

Kahlan pressed her fingers to her forehead, pausing for a moment. She couldn't begin to fathom what he was talking about.

"You're saying that the reason we have prophecy is because Regula is here in this world."

Richard gave her a single, firm nod. "Yes."

Kahlan couldn't believe he was serious. At the same time it was frightening that she could see he was. She flicked a hand toward the scroll.

"Richard, it sounds to me like what it says in those ancient scrolls is just myth–you know, a form of morality tale set down on ancient scrolls. You've heard such fables before from people in the wilds, remember?"

She circled a hand in the air, gesturing toward the sky, weaving the story the way people in the wilds always did. "Stories about how the sun and the moon were once lovers, and they created the grasslands as a secret, sacred place where they could be together. They say that is how the world came to be–it was a place created where the sun and the moon could lie down alone together, away from the stars.

"That's why the people there, like the Mud People, have such reverence for those plains, believing that the grasslands are sacred because they have been kissed by the sun and the moon. Their story about the sun and the moon and the grasslands beneath them is a fable meant to teach innocent children to respect the land. It's a morality tale. They don't believe it literally happened."

Kahlan swept a hand toward the scroll. "That's what this sounds like to me, like a cautionary tale, a fable. A caution to beware of prophecy and not let it rule your life. I bet that's all the scrolls really are, Richard–fables."

He stared at her for a moment. "The scrolls talk about the ancient power of Orden."

"Probably in fable form as well–"

"No, not in fable form, but explicitly," he said, cutting her off. "It explains what happened–what I did. It explains how Orden works, what I was going to do, and why I did it. The power of Orden apparently predates the scrolls, and yet they talk about it, about the events that would surround it into the future, and they talk about me."

Kahlan leaned toward him, her eyes widening. "These ancient scrolls speak of you?"

"Well," he said with an offhanded gesture, "not specifically, but yes. They don't mention me by name, exactly, but they are talking about me. Remember the prophecies that spoke of me as the bringer of death?"

"Of course."

"It's like that. They use names like that for me, names we've seen before like the pebble in the pond, names that can only refer to me. For example they say that the bringer of death will use the power of Orden to initiate a phase change—"

"A what? What's a phase change?"

Richard paused to gather his thoughts. "The power of Orden predates these scrolls, but the people who wrote the scrolls knew a great deal about the subject. Among other tools, they used prophecy, extracted from the underworld, to help them in the understanding of the structure of Orden and all it touches.

"They explain that the power of Orden can bend the nature of existence. Remember the book on Ordenic theory that I found? Remember that it mentioned the power of Orden held in those boxes had the power to distort the nature of existence?"

Kahlan cocked her head. "You mean, the way you bent existence to bring worlds together into the same time and place in order to banish the followers of the beliefs of the Imperial Order to their own world without magic?"

"Yes, exactly." Richard flattened one side of the scroll on the desk and tapped a place on it near the far end. "It calls that event a spectral fold." He looked up at her. "The power of Orden initiates a spectral fold, meaning it distorts the nature of existence. That's how I was able to bring places together in the same place at the same time. It's called a spectral fold."

Kahlan shrugged. "Well, that was a good thing, right? It ended the war."

Richard shook his head. "It bought us time in one phase of events. It ended that war–and that was a good thing, a necessary thing–but in so doing it started a greater war. Through the series of events caused by the initiation of that spectral fold, the great war from back in Magda and Merritt's time was fully reignited. That war was not merely a war between the New World and the Old World, but more importantly a war between the world of life and the world of death.

"Those were the battlefields, those were the factions involved. The war we fought and won was with the remnants of that conflict. We were only fighting at the fringes of the greater war between the worlds of life and death.

"I used the power of Orden to end that particular war with the Imperial Order in that particular manner, but a spectral fold touches all of existence, not only what I did to banish the followers of the Imperial Order. That spectral fold that I initiated may have been absolutely necessary, but it is still in force.

"The Cerulean scrolls call this spectral fold a star shift, because it shifts the nature of everything, the very nature of existence, of the world of existence–which encompasses the whole world of life. I used the power contained in those boxes, releasing it to end the war. In so doing, I initiated a spectral fold, a star shift.

"That was what the creator of the sword knew had to be done, despite the cost. That was why he made the key. They knew it would initiate a star shift, and they knew the cost would be the spectral fold that would bring about the final battle that I would also have to fight. It was, in a way, a prophecy that had been pulled from the underworld in order to create the situation needed to force the event."

"They created a self-fulfilling prophecy?"

"In a way, but only as a tool for the power of Orden so it could do what it was meant to do."

Kahlan felt like her head was spinning. "What else? What else does this power, this star shift, affect?"

"The veil."

Kahlan felt goose bumps raise the hairs on her arms. "The veil."

"Yes. The veil is the power—the force—that keeps the world of life and the world of the dead separate. It's that line in the Grace that separates life and death. Those worlds can't be allowed to mix. The veil prevents that from happening.

"That power is what Adie knew as the skrin. Remember her telling us about the skrin? The power of the skrin is the power contained in the veil that keeps the spirits on that side. It keeps the dead, dead.

"But the spectral fold, initiated through the power of Orden, not only weakened time and space in order to bring the two separate worlds together so I could banish the people of the Imperial Order to that other world, it also weakened the veil as well. In a way, what I did with the separate worlds coming together in time and space, is the same thing that is also happening with the world of life and the world of the dead.

"The only difference is that the veil is a much larger force because it separates existence from nonexistence, so it has taken it longer to begin to show the signs of this weakening. That, and also, since the underworld is involved, that time factor is distorted. Time is meaningless in the underworld.

"That weakening of the veil is what allowed Hannis Arc to bring Emperor Sulachan back from the dead.

That weakening of the veil is also what enables Sulachan to reanimate the dead." Richard tapped a finger
against the scroll. "Hannis Arc learned what the results
of the weakening would be from these scrolls. The cre-
ators of these scrolls learned what would take place
from prophecy, which they extracted from the underworld. In turn, the scrolls predict what Hannis Arc and
Sulachan would do as a result of what I did with the
power of Orden."

Kahlan was having trouble fitting it all together and
even more trouble grasping all the implications. "Dear
spirits" was all she could say.

"Yes, but all things work toward balance, and that is
the important takeaway from what the scrolls are saying. Events can fall off toward one side of that balance
or toward the other because the contrasting sides work
toward balancing each other."

"How?" was all she could ask.

"The balance to the harm that Hannis Arc has the
potential to do is that the weakening of the power of
the veil because of this spectral fold also allowed me to
travel to the underworld in order to send your spirit
back to the world of life. It allowed Nicci to come into
the underworld to get help for me. It allowed Zedd and
all the others already there to help find me and free me
from Sulachan's dark ones. And it allowed me to return
to the world of life.

"It balanced out the things Hannis Arc does because
I am the force meant to balance what he and Sulachan
are doing. The balance to Sulachan coming back to the
world of life is me being able to return as well to be here
to fight him.

"And, in a larger sense, it's all part of a greater balance. There is prophecy in the Cerulean scrolls–"

"Wait–I thought you said that prophecy came from
the world of the dead. How can the scrolls contain

prophecy if they predate Regula and thus prophecy being in this world?"

"Because they draw information directly from the world of the dead as well as the world of life. They are celestial scrolls, so, in a manner of speaking, they draw from the void of the night sky as well as the daytime sky. In other words, they draw from both sides, from all there is on both sides of the veil, from both worlds.

"Just as wizards of old had Additive Magic as well as Subtractive Magic, the gifted back then, the ones who wrote these scrolls, had abilities beyond what you or I can fathom. They had not only regular Additive and Subtractive Magic, but it was combined with the opposite of occult magic. They wielded power in both worlds. They drew from a world where time exists, and from where it doesn't.

"Cerulean, meaning 'celestial,' also refers to the star shift, which is this spectral fold initiated by the use of the power of Orden. I'm the one who initiated its spark."

"You mean it's kind of like starting a campfire to keep you warm and cook your dinner, and that much is good, but then a big gust of wind comes up and blows sparks everywhere and catches the entire forest around you on fire, so what started off good turns into something very bad."

Richard grimaced a little. "That's one way to put it. But in this instance, the entire world is on fire."

Kahlan pressed her hands to the sides of her head. "This is giving me a headache."

Richard grunted a brief chuckle. "You don't know the half of it. I've only scratched the surface. It's a lot more complex than I'm making it sound, and so far I've only given you a few of the meaningful highlights."

Kahlan lowered her hands and stared at him. "You mean to say that there's more?"

"I'm afraid so," Richard said. "And it gets worse."

Y ou see," Richard said, "Hannis Arc knew all this.
He apparently got his hands on some of these
scrolls long ago and read in them about initiating the power of Orden to create this spectral fold.
He collected more of these scrolls over time and has
been using what he was able to learn in them to start
shaping events to his own objectives. He saw from what
he read that this was his opportunity to bring Sulachan
back."

"Hannis Arc is the one who gave Darken Rahl the
last box of Orden," Kahlan said, trying to keep track of
it all in her head. "You mean he did that to help start
this prophecy to unfold? The prophecy he plays a central part in and that he would benefit from?"

"Exactly. He has been moving the pieces around like
pieces on a chessboard in order to bring about the
events the scrolls talk about. It's as if he sees prophecy
of himself doing these things, and then does them to
make the prophecy reality. Mohler said that he was a
master chess player, and from what I've learned about
the game, much of the thinking in the game carries over
to making moves in life.

"He wanted to open this gateway through this spectral

fold, because he needed Sulachan's help to conquer the world of life, so he put the boxes in play by giving the third box of Orden to Darken Rahl. He was making moves that had repercussions later on, all down the line. He knew from the scrolls that giving Darken Rahl the last box he needed to put them in play would trigger the events in prophecy. Unlike us, he knew from the scrolls what the power of Orden really was.

"Hannis Arc was moving a pawn, knowing from prophecy that if the boxes were in play, I would defeat Darken Rahl and therefore go on to become the Lord Rahl leading the D'Haran Empire that would then be drawn into the war against the Imperial Order.

"He knew that I would use the power of Orden to end the war with the Imperial Order, which is a part of the larger great war that Sulachan started so long ago. After all, Sulachan created the dream walkers. Emperor Jagang was a descendant of those dream walkers created by Sulachan so that he would start the war that I would end by using the power of Orden that Hannis Arc would then use, once the star shift weakened the veil, to bring Sulachan back from the dead."

Kahlan pressed her hands to her head. "Dear spirits. And they were using this knowledge of the use of Orden all along?"

Richard nodded. "Hannis Arc had already moved that pawn long ago by giving the box to Darken Rahl to begin the chain of events that would eventually get me to use Orden's power, because he didn't have the key to it, but the scrolls said I would, which would in turn get him what he was ultimately after: to be ruler of the world of life. Which would get Sulachan what he wanted by being able to come back from the world of the dead, which he helped engineer by creating the dream walkers, and so on and so forth."

"But then he was carrying out prophecy that hadn't

happened yet," she protested. "He was creating prophecy, in effect. He was creating a self-fulfilling prophecy."

Richard showed her a smile. "Exactly. You see, prophecy is an underworld power–"

"Wait. How can it be an underworld power? You said that before but I don't think that can be right. Prophecy comes from prophets predicting the future. Hannis Arc saw that prophecy and took the actions he did in order to make sure everything was in place for it to happen as in the prophecy."

"But the prophecy itself came from the underworld in the first place," Richard said. "Prophecy is an artifact of the world of the dead."

Kahlan shook her head. "Prophecy is given by prophets in this world, not the world of the dead."

Richard leaned toward her in a meaningful manner. "So we always thought. And that is the key to it all."

"I don't follow what you mean."

Richard gestured to the scrolls. "Prophecy actually originates in the underworld, from the spirits of the dead, and prophets in the world of life are able to channel those prophecies in this world."

Kahlan took a deep breath to fortify herself against her growing frustration. "I don't understand. How could they originate there, in the world of the dead, from spirits?"

Richard leaned forward again, almost with delight at what he had discovered. "This is where it starts to get complicated."

"Starts? Richard, I don't–"

He held up a hand. "Hear me out, first, and then the bigger picture will all start to make sense."

She pressed her lips tight and remained silent so he could go on. She knew Richard, and she knew he didn't go off on pointless tangents.

"The underworld is eternal, which makes it timeless,"

he began in a calm voice. "We've always understood that much of it. Time has no meaning in an eternal world because there is no beginning and no end of time there, so there is no way to measure a segment of forever. Right?"

Kahlan conceded the point with a nod. "Right."

"One day or a thousand years is the same because with no beginning and no end there are no units of measure for time there—no limits to measure a day, a year, a century."

"So?"

"So, in the underworld, where nothing changes and there is no future as such—because there are no boundaries and no units to measure time—the future is the same as now. There can be no tomorrow, so there can be no future as such.

"The future in the world of the dead takes place in what the scrolls call 'the eternal now.'"

Kahlan scratched an eyebrow. "The eternal now?"

"That's right—the eternal now. In the underworld there is only 'now.'" Richard held up a finger to make a point, reminding Kahlan very much of Zedd when he did so. "Time is a concept that only has relevance in this world, where there are beginnings and ends to things—days, years, lives. In the underworld, a soul never dies. It is eternal.

"The underworld does not have those things needed from which to construct the concept of time. There is no yesterday in the underworld because it's eternally the same there, eternally unvarying, eternally changeless, so there can be no such thing as yesterday. By the same token, there can be no tomorrow. Right? The sun does not rise and set there. It's always the same. There are no 'days' there, nothing to mark time, no end of time. See what I mean? It's all an eternal now.

"Since 'now' in the underworld is an eternity—the

eternal now–there is no future as such there because, in a place with no markers for time, such a thing can't be delineated. This means that what we would think of as happening in the future, here in our world, in the eternity of the underworld actually happens in this homogeneous soup of the eternal now.

"We think of events happening in our future because in our world we have time–a today and a tomorrow–but you can't think of it the same way there."

Kahlan stared off into the memory. "I remember when I was there, in the underworld. I don't recall any sense of how long. I was only there. Always, forever, unchanging."

"Exactly," he said. "In the eternal now of the underworld, those events, which all take place in the eternal now, all happen together and are the purview of a power known as Regula. Regula, you might say, is the sum of everything–everything that can happen, everything that will happen.

"Once the power of Regula was sent to this world, imprisoned in that case buried in the People's Palace, it compressed the future–what we know as prophecy because it hasn't happened yet–into the now, our present, because to Regula there is no future, no past.

"Regula, being an underworld power, can't differentiate between today and tomorrow, or today and a year from today. It only knows everything that will happen, the totality of events, but since it's an underworld power it has no real concept of time, so it doesn't know when those things will happen, or which one of them will happen for that matter, because everything is in a state of constant flux.

"So, to Regula, when it says the ceiling will fall in, that event has already happened. It's not predicting, it's reporting."

Kahlan folded her arms, squinting, trying to reconcile

it in her mind. "That doesn't make any sense. I don't understand."

"Prophecy is a compression of the future into the present. Everything that takes place continually alters the totality of what Regula knows. It contains events without the quality of time. Without time there is no 'future' so it is all happening now.

"That's the specific power that Regula controls: the eternal now."

Kahlan gave him a look from under her brow. "And that is what the scrolls call it? The 'eternal now'?"

"Yes. Here it gets more complex, so you need to let me get through this part and then you'll see how it all fits together."

Kahlan nodded for him to go on, making an earnest effort to listen with an open mind.

"The underworld is timeless, with everything there in the eternal now, right? But here in this world, where there is time, if you reveal the future, then there really is no future as such. You are pulling the future backward to right now. This is an aspect of the underworld, not the world of life. Prophecy compresses what will happen into what we know right now, into the eternal now. But that is an underworld quality and it doesn't belong here."

Richard could apparently see by the look on her face that she was lost, so he came at it a little differently. "In prophecy the future is revealed to us now, right? If we read a prophecy about an event in the future–say a queen having a child–then that future event is pulled backward from its rightful place of where it will happen in the future, back to today. See what I mean? So now, when you read the prophecy, you are reading what will happen, so that future has in a way become real right now. That's why it's called the eternal now.

"Without time in the underworld it's all one long

eternal now. Here, though, it's a perversion of the nature of time in our world. It's a corrupting element. An underworld element. Here, in this world, future events aren't supposed to happen now. That is an underworld contamination leaking into our world.

"That's why I've always instinctively hated prophecy–because prophecy is actually a component of the underworld. Prophecy is an element that in its natural state does not contain an element of time. It belongs in the world of the dead where it came from, where there is no time. It is part of death itself. I've always instinctively recognized prophecy as carrying death within it.

"The reason I instinctively recognized that, is because I'm the one."

Kahlan tilted her head toward him. "The one. You mean, the pebble in the pond?"

"Yes. The balance to prophecy is free will. Now we can understand for the first time exactly why. Acting on free will preempts that eternal now by pulling the future away from the eternal now, pulling timelessness away from it by canceling the prediction with the use of free will–human choice.

"Free choice is the counter to prophecy. It's a living aspect, the balance to the dead aspect of prophecy. Prophecy is an element of the world of the dead, while free will is an element of the world of life.

"The wrinkle in this spectral fold was created by events long ago, but in the underworld those thousands of years are in the eternal now. So, the spectral fold–the star shift–initiated by my igniting the power of Orden does not simply ripple through space with the spectral folds, it ripples through time."

Kahlan gestured to the desk. "But all those things you did to trigger these events were predicted in prophecy and written in these scrolls."

Richard gave her a cunning smile. "Of course they

were. Sulachan sent the prophecy to this world, through prophets in this world, so that they would write it in the scrolls, so that Hannis Arc would read it and initiate it all by putting the boxes of Orden in play. It is all part of Sulachan's grand plan. He began laying the groundwork for it when he was still alive.

"You see, at some point long past, before Sulachan ever came along, the good spirits in the underworld, knowing the danger, wanted to protect the power of Regula from being misused, so they sent the power to this world and hid it for safekeeping—or so they thought.

"But because Regula is part of the eternal now, and exists in that eternal now, there is no accurate way of telling exactly when Regula actually appeared here in this world. What those spirits didn't know when they sent it here was that this power created a breach between worlds, allowing prophecy to cross over through it from that world. Without Regula being there in the underworld to contain it, prophecy continued to leak through the veil along the lines of the Grace."

"So then," she said, "those good spirits didn't actually do the good thing they thought. By sending Regula here they created a terrible problem."

Richard shrugged. "They exist in the eternal now, where all possible futures exist. Perhaps they saw a future gaining strength that was more terrible and more dangerous than we can imagine, so they hid Regula in this world to choke off that terrible future. For all we know, had they not done so, maybe the world of life would have ended thousands and thousands of years ago.

"Anyway, for whatever reasons those good spirits had at the time, Regula was sent here to this world. Because of it being part of the eternal now, it doesn't behave the way we would expect something here to behave so there is no way of knowing precisely when it actually came into being in this world.

"What is known, though, is that sometime later, after it was already rooted here in this world, Sulachan found out about it and he sparked its power, using it to ignite a firestorm of prophecy flooding into this world. All the thousands of books of prophecy written since the great war that we've found in libraries are the flames of that conflagration, a hidden, smoldering part of Sulachan's plan. This is how he brought the House of Rahl and then Hannis Arc into his web to help him in his struggle.

"Wizards came along–prophets–who tapped into this stream of prophecy flowing along the lines of the Grace and, thinking they were doing good, channeled these predictions which unbeknownst to them were flooding through the veil from the underworld. Without knowing it, they were tapping into the eternal now and poisoning our world with underworld power.

"As long as Regula is in this world, as long as it lives, it will continue to poison this world with prophecy."

CHAPTER 30

K ahlan rubbed her arms against the chill of beginning to grasp the enormity of what Richard
had discovered. It was all so overwhelming
that it was making her feel very small and insignificant,
as if she were but a speck of dust in the vast universe.
She supposed that was all she really was.

"I almost hate to say it, Richard, but it's starting to
make sense. It touches on vague doubts I've always
had–things that just never seemed right. For the first
time in my life, all of these doubts and questions are
starting to make sense."

"Good, I'm relieved that you get this much of it because there is more, and understanding this foundation
will help with the rest." Richard took a breath before
going on. "The underworld is not touched by Creation,
so it is not created. Rather, it is chaos in free form. You
might say, since it is death, it is the opposite of Creation.
It is anti-Creation. It is neither good nor bad. It has no
integral nature to define it. It has no inherent order. It is
merely a timeless void that is, in a way, shaped by the
souls that exist there.

"Prophecy, being a power partly involving certain elements of the Grace, is expressed by the souls in the

underworld existing in the eternal now. Touched by the Grace from the moment they came into being, they continue to be connected to it even as they cross over through the veil. That's how the spirits, the souls of the dead, who exist in a world where prophecy is all part of their eternal now, channel it back through prophets in the world of life. It follows those lines of the Grace that cross worlds separated by the veil.

"Some of those souls are good, some evil, some brilliant, some fools–just as they were in life. Our souls, you see, are the sum total of who we are–good, evil, brilliant, or fools. That means prophecy is the product of both brilliant and ignorant souls, good and bad souls, choosing those things in the homogeneous soup of the eternal now which fit their inherent nature. They gravitate toward those outcomes which their soul embraces. It all mixes together into the prophecy that becomes the power of Regula.

"That collective intellect pooled–the web of life and the spirits–creates what the celestial scrolls call the time wave of prophecy. All of the predictions are true, but all can't be."

Kahlan wiped a hand back across her face. "If it can't all be true, then how is it resolved?"

"It isn't. That's the point. In the eternal now of the underworld it doesn't matter–it's all part of the homogeneous soup of the eternal now–but here it all spins out of control and collapses. It's one of the powers that doesn't belong in this world–it's incongruous–but it is leaking through the veil because the veil is weakened by the spectral fold.

"What's called the Twilight Count measures this degradation of the veil."

Kahlan cocked her head. "The Twilight Count? That measures how much the veil is weakening?"

"Yes, that's right. The Twilight Count was begun, like

turning over an hourglass, by the initiation of the star shift of the spectral fold. You could say that the Twilight Count is the sand in that grand celestial hourglass counting down our existence.

"The death of this world through the spectral fold degrading the veil will devour the world of existence and thus our souls. Prophecy is the leper's bell betraying that open gap between the worlds. The very existence of prophecy is a dire warning that the sands of the Twilight Count are running out. Prophecy is contaminating the nature of time in our world, and that contamination is measured by the Twilight Count."

Kahlan blinked in alarm. "How much time do we have?"

"To answer that question we would need some kind of zenith formulas called breach calculations from the star shift."

"You mean to say there was previously one of these star shifts?" she asked. "It's happened before?"

"Apparently. The scrolls are vague about the previous events, but they mention needing, among other things, templates for occulted celestial charts called seventh-level rift formulas if you are to work out these worldly timelines for this star shift. I haven't the faintest idea what any of that means, where to find these things, or how to work them if I did."

Kahlan looked over at the sleeping sorceress draped in the overstuffed chair. "What about Nicci? Would she know, do you think?"

Richard sighed as he shook his head. "She was just as mystified about that part as I was. Except she did say that by the nature of such things she could tell that it would require the use of my gift to work any such calculations. So even if I had the components, I couldn't make them work. But it really doesn't make a lot of difference anymore because we know from everything else, such as Sulachan being back in this world and the barrier to the third kingdom being down, that we are rapidly running out of time. What is happening now is an end phase.

"While it seems that prophecy has been here forever, in the stretch of cosmic existence, prophecy has been coming into this world for only a brief twinkling of time. Now that it has, the timeless nature of the underworld is stealing time away from us. Stealing existence from us. Prophecy is the open link that is draining away our free will, our lives, our existence."

Kahlan snapped her fingers. "That's what it means when it says you can only save us all by ending prophecy."

Richard smiled that she saw it. "Exactly. It really means that I need to end prophecy in this world by closing the bridge between worlds that has been opened up."

"Opened by you."

"Yes," Richard conceded. "When I used the power of Orden, that was the initiating phase of everything that was long ago set into motion when Sulachan sent the prophecy out from the world of the dead. The entire thing is tightly woven together with thousands of different threads." Richard drew a deep breath. "And all of those threads are linked to me."

Kahlan swept some of her hair back off of her face. "So if you end prophecy, you are really sealing the spectral fold and completing the star shift."

He nodded again. "Thus letting life begin a new era. That page needs to be turned—life reset. The open conduit of prophecy must be closed. Only in that way can the star shift be complete. When that happens, life will be reset in a new phase. Life will then be able to go on."

"And without that happening?"

Richard raked his fingers back through his hair. "If I can't end prophecy then the veil will continue to erode

away, which is what Sulachan has been working toward, and everything will be consumed by the chaos of
the underworld. Because he has understood all of this
and has been able to direct so much of it, Sulachan
believes himself to be the master of the underworld, I
guess you could say. He thinks this will unite it all into
one world–life and death existing together–and he will
rule over this new world of souls.

"But what he doesn't understand, or doesn't care
about, is that when the veil finally fails completely and
the worlds come together, everything–even the eternity
of the underworld itself–will end. It will be a form of
death for everything, except the underworld can't die,
as such, since it's already dead. So what happens is that
everything–the world of life and the world of souls–will
simply wink out of existence."

"How can eternity end?" Kahlan asked. "It's eternal."

"Think of it this way: A shadow exists because of
something casting it. If the thing that casts the shadow
ceases to exist, then the shadow ceases to exist."

Richard shook his head. "Only so long as everything
is in balance, as long as life and death–these two opposing forces–are separated by the veil. On its own, without the world of life, the eternity of the world of the
dead is a contradiction–like a shadow with nothing
casting it–and contradictions can't exist.

"In other words, how can something be dead if there
is no such thing as life? The world of the dead is defined
by the world of life, so, once the world of life ends, the
underworld ceases to exist. No world of life, therefore
no world of the dead."

"How can it end," she asked, "if there is no such thing
as the concept of an end in the underworld?"

"It wouldn't exactly end–because, technically, there is
no existence in the underworld to end–it will all simply
cease to exist. It will be as if it never existed, like a

shadow vanishes without an object to cast it. No trace would be left behind. The eternal now will wink out as if nothing ever existed."

He leaned back in his chair, drumming his fingers on the desk. "Unless, of course, I can stop it from happening."

Kahlan nested her hands in her lap, feeling overwhelmed. "You're dying, Richard. You have the poison of death in you. How are you going to do anything to help us if you die?"

Richard considered his answer for a time. When he spoke, he spoke in a quiet, but forceful, tone.

"I'm inextricably woven into the fabric of this, in a number of ways, from using prophecy, to using free will, to using the power of Orden to stop what would have happened had I not. I couldn't not have used the power of Orden.

"Prophecy grows old and corrupt over time, becoming infected with branches that never took place or false prophecy or evil prophecy. Such defective prophecy infects life with that underworld power that is pulling the world of existence apart. Wizards—gifted individuals—have become rare where once they were common. The gift itself is fading away from mankind. Subtractive Magic has virtually vanished from those few who do have the gift. The world has been dying for thousands of years, and we never realized it—or at least never realized why. Prophecy is the talisman that marks everything being taken into oblivion.

"I'm the only one who can stop it. I must stop it."

Kahlan wiped a hand back over her face. She was beginning to see more of the links the more she thought about it, the way everything was inextricably connected, but he still hadn't answered her question of how he would be able to stop any of it if he was dead.

"How are you connected with Sulachan?" she asked.

He looked up from under his raptor brow. "I'm the living bridge that enabled Sulachan to cross over, in much the same way that Cara was the living bridge that allowed me to cross back through the veil. My blood, the blood of the bringer of death, brought the dead man back."

"And Hannis Arc? How is he linked into this?"

"He is basically taking advantage of it all for himself, but in so doing he enables it to happen. For all I know, the end of the Twilight Count may take a lifetime, or ten lifetimes, before it runs out. He wants to rule the world of life in the interim."

"And why would Sulachan help him?"

Richard leveled a look at her. "I'm the living bridge, but Sulachan needed someone on this side to initiate the elements necessary to bring him back. He needed someone on this side of the veil to move the pieces on the chessboard, so to speak. Hannis Arc has the occult powers and the detailed knowledge that were required to accomplish such an extraordinary task."

Kahlan lifted her hands in a gesture of frustration, only to let them drop back to rest on her thighs. "Red told me that Sulachan and Hannis Arc are like two vipers, each with the tail of the other in his mouth. I can see that Hannis Arc needs Sulachan's army of half people to help him take over the D'Haran Empire and rule the world of life, but now that Emperor Sulachan is back in this world, what does he need with Hannis Arc?"

Richard met her gaze. "You know those tattoo symbols all over Hannis Arc?"

"Of course."

He gestured to the scrolls. "Those tattoos are elements of occult magic laid out in these scrolls. They are part of how Hannis Arc was able to pull Sulachan out of the underworld."

"But he's back, now. Why continue to indulge the man?"

Richard smiled. "Those spell-forms tattooed all over the man are the only thing keeping Sulachan in this world. They are his anchor. At the same time, those spells are Hannis Arc's armor, protecting him from being harmed by Sulachan.

"Until he can finish breaking the veil and uniting the world of the dead and the living, he still needs those living spells in order to remain in this world. They secure his spirit here in the world of life and keep the spirit king from being pulled back into the spirit world by the power of the skrin. If Hannis Arc dies, those spells lose their viability.

"My blood brought Sulachan here, but those spells all over Hannis Arc keep him here."

Kahlan blinked in eager astonishment. "So, then, if someone kills Hannis Arc, that would get rid of Sulachan at the same time. Maybe a force of men of the First File?" Kahlan snapped her fingers. "Maybe archers could take him down from up on the plateau when they come to lay siege to the People's Palace."

"Both of them are protected by powerful occult powers." Richard looked away and tapped a thumb against the scroll for a time before answering. "Only a Warheart can stop Sulachan and only a Warheart can kill Hannis Arc."

Kahlan wasn't sure she had heard him right. "A what?"

Richard pulled a scroll out of the pile on the side and unfurled it across the desk. He tapped one of the symbols.

"This symbol, here, means 'Warheart.' It says in this scroll that the only one who can send Sulachan back to the underworld, kill Hannis Arc, and end prophecy to seal the spectral fold to complete the star shift before the Twilight Count trickles down to the end of everything, is the one it calls the Warheart."

Kahlan gave him a look. "Don't tell me, it's someone we know."

Richard nodded. "The bringer of death, the pebble in the pond, and all the other names that have identified me over the ages. A Warheart is an ancient name for a specific kind of war wizard. It's a war wizard who has led a war, who has wielded a sword in righteous anger . . . and a few other requirements."

"Like what?"

"Only a unique war wizard is the true Warheart. That kind of war wizard who has war in their heart must possess the balance to that."

Kahlan frowned. "What is the balance to having war in your heart?"

"The love of one who is virtuous. I am the bringer of death. You are what balances all of those things in me with the meaning of life, with what life is about, with what is worth fighting for, with love for you, and in turn love for life. You are my soul mate. You complete me. You make me whole.

"All of those things make me complete in the fight for life. They made me go to the underworld itself to fight for you.

"And that is the last requirement that names me the Warheart. The scrolls say that only the one who has willingly gone to the world of the dead to take the place of the one he loves is the true Warheart who can end prophecy and close the spectral shift to reset life on its new course, free from the reach of those in the underworld.

"I'm the one with war in my heart—a war wizard—and the only one who can bring death to those two vipers and to prophecy. They fight to rule. In part because of my love for you, I fight instead for what is right and noble about life.

"That's why these Cerulean scrolls name me the War-heart."

The only problem," Richard said into the silence, "is what you mentioned, that I have that poison in me, which means my gift doesn't work, so I don't know how I'm going to be able to do any of those things that need to be done." He lifted a hand and let it fall back to rest on top of an opened scroll. "Without my gift, against these kind of enemies, I don't have the weapons I need."

Kahlan wiped a tear from under her eye as she stood. "You have your mind, Richard. How many times did Zedd tell you that is all you need? Your mind is your weapon. It always has been. It's what has figured all this out."

He smiled a special smile just for her, and that was answer enough. His heart was in the fight. The Warheart was committed to the fight.

"What I remember," he said, "is Zedd telling me that nothing is ever easy."

"Has it ever been?"

"No." He smiled again, this time with a hint of sadness for his grandfather. "I guess not."

Kahlan folded her arms as she paced a short distance and then back. Nicci was still asleep. Having helped

Richard translate the scrolls for most of the night, Kahlan knew that the sorceress would already know most everything Richard had just explained.

Cassia, over by the door, having heard everything Richard had said as well as what he and Nicci had discussed during the night, looked like she was proud to be the Mord-Sith protecting the Warheart. When had Mord-Sith ever had the chance to fight for a Lord Rahl who in turn fought for them? He truly was the magic against magic.

Except that for now his magic was out of his reach.

Kahlan finally slowed to a stop before him. "We have no choice, then. We are going to have to race as swiftly as possible back to the People's Palace. We need to get to the containment field. You can't do any of those important things you've learned about in the scrolls if you're dead. We have to get that poison out of you, first."

Richard raked his fingers back through his thick hair. "I know it sounds like that would be the solution, Kahlan, but it's simply too far. I can feel how the poison is advancing in me, and I know roughly how much time I have, and I know how long it would take to ride to the palace. We wouldn't make it in time—and that's even if we could ride right in without having to first get past Sulachan, Hannis Arc, and all those half people."

Kahlan spread her arms in frustration. "What choice do we have but to try? You won't live long with that poison in you, and if you die then Sulachan wins. We have to try, Richard.

"Maybe the poison won't work as fast as you think. After all, you said that being in the underworld caused it to regress some. Maybe it slowed its advance enough for you to make it to the palace in time.

"Besides, you have to make it. You said yourself that the scrolls say you are the balance, the counter, to what Sulachan and Hannis Arc intend to do."

"They do say that," Richard told her with a sigh as he glanced over at the scroll lying open on the desk, "but they don't say which side will win."

"Well, you can't win if the poison kills you, now can you? That means we have to get there in time," she insisted, "that's all there is to it. Everything depends on it."

As the silence dragged on, Richard rose slowly out of his chair. He wore an expression that Kahlan knew all too well. It was a look that told her that some inner calculation had been running through his head as he tried to fit all the pieces of the puzzle together. The look on his face told her that he might have just found the missing piece.

While it was a look that meant he had thought of something, in the past that something had not always been what she wanted to hear. It was a look that meant some crazy idea had just come to him. It was a look that usually meant trouble and sent them off in a direction she had never expected.

But she also knew that those crazy ideas he came up with often ended up being the solution they needed.

"What?" She took hold of his arms, looking him in the eye. "What are you thinking?"

Rather than look at her, he stared off into the distance, lost in thought and not really hearing her. Kahlan recognized that, too. She knew he was still making mental connections, running through all the possibilities, going down roads and pathways and blind alleys, trying to see where they all led. He was trying to see if there was another way, or if he really had found the right course to guide them.

It was not unlike what she had learned one did when playing chess. You didn't make the move until you had exhausted every possible outcome that you could think of. Of course, sometimes that move still resulted in you losing because you hadn't thought of the one fatal possibility.

"It's too far," he said to himself with an odd frown. He finally looked down at her. "You said it yourself—we have to get there in time. But it's too far to get there in time."

"What of it?"

"Time." He grabbed hold of her arms in the same way she had taken hold of his. "There wouldn't have been enough time for them, either."

"Who?" Kahlan squinted her bewilderment at him. "What are you talking about?"

Richard ignored her as he rushed over to the chair where Nicci was curled up asleep. He shook her foot.

"Wake up. Nicci, wake up."

The sorceress jerked awake. "What is it? What? What's happened?"

"We're leaving."

Nicci wiped her eyes and then looked at Kahlan for an explanation. Kahlan shrugged.

"Cassia," Richard called out.

She leaped forward. "Yes, Lord Rahl?"

"Go find Commander Fister. Tell him that I said we need horses—for us and a dozen of the men. Extra horses we can switch out as well. We will need to leave at once. And tell him I want the guides we used before—the men who grew up in the Dark Lands—to come with us."

Cassia looked confused. "We're leaving? Where are we going?"

"Move!" he yelled at the woman. "There is no time to waste. Do it now. Get going." He called her name when she was almost to the door. She turned back. "And get Mohler," he added. "Tell him that I need him."

Cassia quickly clapped a fist to her heart before turning and racing out the door. The other two Mord-Sith peered around the edge of the doorway, looking back in to try to see what the yelling was all about.

Before they had time to question, Cassia snatched them by their arms and turned them around, telling them to help her find Commander Fister and the guides. All three raced off down the hallway, past bewildered soldiers of the First File.

"Did he tell you about Warheart?" Nicci asked Kahlan as Richard paced off a ways, once again completely absorbed in thought.

"Yes. And the 'highlights' as he put it."

Nicci's blue eyes turned back to Kahlan after watching Richard pace between the desk and the door for a moment. "I know it all sounds far-fetched. I had my doubts about the whole thing at first, but I have to tell you, Kahlan, the more I read, the more I realized he's right—about all of it.

"I've been reading and studying prophecy and prophetic theory for most of my life. I've never looked at any of it in this light before. For that matter, I never even imagined it in this light before. I feel like I'm starting to understand prophecy, really understand it in a fundamental way, for the first time in my life."

"So you're convinced that prophecy really does originate in the underworld?"

Nicci looked over to watch Richard pace for a moment. "Before everything we read during the night, I would never have believed it. It isn't simply reading it, though, but reading it all in context, reading all the explanations of how things are connected going back to the time before the great war that Emperor Sulachan started. Now, I can't believe that I never suspected any of this before. Including the part about me."

Kahlan's brow twitched. "About you?"

The sorceress nodded. "About me taking him to the Old World being part of the prophecy in the scrolls."

"I don't know about that part. He hasn't had the time to tell me everything," Kahlan said.

Nicci held up a finger, asking Kahlan to have patience and wait. "Richard," Nicci called across the room, "what have you thought of? What's going on?"

He hurried over to them. "I'm not completely sure, yet."

"I see," Nicci said. "So we are are going to get on horses and race back to the People's Palace. You're right, that makes the most sense."

It wasn't a question and she obviously knew that wasn't his intent. Nicci obviously knew that Richard had no intention of trying to ride to the palace in time. He was too dead set against it. He had thought of something else but wasn't saying what. Kahlan was a little amazed that Nicci knew exactly how to get his actual intent out of him.

"What is this place for?" he asked Nicci. He held an arm up and gestured around. "This citadel. Why is it here?"

Nicci clasped her hands behind her back, playing along, if reluctantly. "It's a prison outpost. It was meant to hold for execution anyone who had occult powers because that power could only have leaked out of the barrier to the third kingdom. Executing them was the only way to stop the spread of the contamination. If not stopped, it would be the same as the barrier itself failing."

"Right," he said with a nod as he looked back and forth between them. "And what, then, was the purpose of Stroyza?"

Kahlan shrugged, answering this time. "It's a first line of defense, meant to send a warning that the barrier has been breached and the half people and those with occult abilities are escaping. They are meant to watch and when the barrier to the third kingdom failed, they were supposed to go to Aydindril and warn the wizards' council at the Keep."

"There hasn't been a wizards' council at the Keep for ages, but the people of Stroyza didn't know that," he said. "They still think the council rules the New World. So how were they going to get there in time to warn everyone before the half people attack towns and cities, or reached the Keep, first?

"The people on the other side of the barrier were from the Old World. They would have headed for the seat of power, just as Hannis Arc and Emperor Sulachan are doing now. Except back then, that was the Wizard's Keep, not the People's Palace. So, how were the people of Stroyza going to manage to do that–to get to the Keep first, before the hordes of half people?"

"I guess they would have to hurry," Kahlan said, not quite following what he was getting at.

"The people of Stroyza live in a remote area that isn't near roads or even good paths," he said.

Kahlan shrugged. "That's because the people back in the great war put the third kingdom in the most remote area they could find. They wanted it as far away from civilization as possible."

Richard nodded. "That's right. But even so, there are roads closer to the barrier than Stroyza going back in that direction. Even the paths that are near Stroyza go to other places for the purpose of trade and supplies, not toward Aydindril and the Keep. The people of Stroyza live in caves and don't use horses. As Ester told me, Stroyza is their home and they have nowhere else to go, so travel isn't an important part of their lives."

"Maybe they used to travel," Nicci said. "It could be that they forgot to keep horses in the same way they lost so many of the things they were told when Stroyza was founded back in the great war. After all, they don't even know how to read all the messages left for them on the walls of the caves because they lost the ability to read the language of Creation."

"We can use horses," he said, "and we won't be able to get there first."

"That's only because they have a good lead on us," Kahlan said.

"Yes, but even if we caught them, we have to worry about getting past them. They have incredible numbers, many with occult powers. They have a spirit king risen from the dead. They have thousands of half people–tens of thousands. They're spread out across the land. Worse, Sulachan can reanimate as many of the dead as he needs. He's a wizard with great power. He can use occult abilities.

"So how was one lone person from Stroyza supposed to get past all that, keep from being captured, and get to the Keep in enough time for them to mobilize forces to protect people? By the time the people in Stroyza would realize that the barrier was breached, it would be too late to get to the Keep in time to warn them."

Nicci scratched her cheek. "That does seem like a pretty ill-conceived solution to the problem of the barrier."

Richard nodded. "Especially since the people back in the great war–the ones who built that barrier in the first place and put the dangerous half people and occult powers they couldn't destroy behind the wall–knew that it was eventually going to fail. They didn't put Stroyza there in case it failed, they put it there because they knew it was going to fail, and they wanted us to have ample warning to defend ourselves. They didn't take the threat lightly. They wouldn't have let the fate of the world depend on such a tenuous method of warning people."

Kahlan was frowning in thought. "When you put it that way, it doesn't make much sense." She looked up. "So, what are you thinking? You believe they had some other way to warn people?"

"I do."

Before he could say more, Commander Fister rushed in, holding his sword against his hip to keep it from flopping as he ran. He had several men with him. Kahlan recognized the men as the scouts who grew up in the Dark Lands.

CHAPTER 32

L ord Rahl, what is it?" the breathless commander
asked.
"Are the men getting horses together?"

"Of course, Lord Rahl. They are being packed with
supplies, now. Are we to take you and the Mother Confessor back to the palace at long last?"

Richard waved off the question as a dead issue. "No.
We would never make it. Just as the guardian at Stroyza
would never have made it."

The commander frowned as he panted, catching his
breath. He glanced at Kahlan and Nicci before turning a
puzzled look on Richard. "Where are we headed, then?"

"We're going to Stroyza."

Kahlan knew that was where he wanted to go. She
just didn't know why.

"Stroyza! Back across that forsaken, trackless wilderness and over the mountain passes we crossed to get
here?"

"Irena said that there were roads and trails she used
to come here before. I don't know if she really did come
here, but she may have been right about there being
roads." He turned to the three men. "Is that true? Are
there roads and trails we can use to get to Stroyza,

rather than go back across those mountains at Saavedra's back door?"

Without having to think about it, the three nodded.

"There is a pretty good road part of the way," one of
them said, "but partway there it starts heading off in the
wrong direction. From that point, though, we can take
trails used by merchants as trade routes. That will at
least get us close to Stroyza. It's not the easiest of trails,
but far easier on horseback than going back over the
mountains on foot and having to hack our way through
uncharted wilderness."

"All right, then, we need to leave at once."

The commander clapped a fist to his heart. "As you
wish, Lord Rahl. All the men can be ready to go before
you get down to the stables."

Richard looked over at the desk. "No, we're not all
going. I need the men to split up. I only want to take a
detachment of a dozen or so men. More will only slow
us down."

The commander cleared his throat. "I beg to differ,
Lord Rahl. Not one of my men would slow us down.
They would sooner die of exhaustion than slow you
down. Besides, you will need their numbers if we're attacked by any more of the half people."

Richard flashed the man a brief smile. "I understand
your concern." He gestured back at the scrolls. "But
these scrolls are incredibly valuable to me–to all of us.
They have already been in the wrong hands and that
has resulted in all the trouble we now have. We must
keep possession of those scrolls at all cost. They are to
be protected with our lives. Eventually they will have to
be taken back to the People's Palace, where I will need
them. Until then, they must be guarded."

The commander scratched his scalp as he glanced
over at the desk piled high with scrolls. "Do you want
the men to start back with them now?"

Off behind the hulking commander, Kahlan saw the scribe, Mohler, hurrying into the room. He came up behind the soldiers and stopped, waiting to be summoned. Richard urgently motioned him forward.

"Yes, Lord Rahl? What can I do for you?"

"I need you to collect all the Cerulean scrolls, including the ones that have similar symbols on them, and get them all packed up so they are safe to travel."

"They arrived in leather tubes that protected them from the weather," Mohler said. "A number of scrolls will fit in each one. If they are rolled tightly together, it would not take more than maybe ten or twelve of the tubes."

"Are they waterproof?"

Mohler glanced over at the scrolls. "Enough to protect them from rain and such, but not enough if you were to drop them in a river or plunge them under water. They are very ancient, Lord Rahl, very fragile."

"All right," Richard said to the man, "pack them carefully for traveling, then seal the lids with pitch and wax to better protect them. It will also keep them from being opened."

"Then take them back to the palace?" Commander Fister asked.

Richard considered a moment. "Not yet. They would be more vulnerable when traveling. For now they would be better protected here. This place is a fortress, after all. Hannis Arc and Emperor Sulachan have no reason to come back here. For now, I want the bulk of the men to stay here and protect them."

The commander clearly looked reluctant but didn't argue. "As you wish, Lord Rahl."

"And make sure that the men understand that these are incredibly valuable to stopping Sulachan and the half people. These scrolls must never again fall into enemy hands."

The commander clapped a fist to his heart. "I will make sure they understand the importance of their mission."

"Good," Richard said with a nod.

"They will be guarded here, for now, but when would you like them taken to the palace?"

"When I succeed at stopping Sulachan. Then it will be safe to travel with them. If I don't succeed, well, I guess in that case it won't matter much."

Commander Fister didn't understand, but neither did he question. "Lord Rahl, if I may ask, I would like to lead the men who are to go with you. These scrolls may be valuable, but they are not as valuable as you. You and the Mother Confessor are my primary responsibility. I would ask to be at the head of the detachment you take to Stroyza. I would feel a lot better if I was there to help protect you."

"Of course," Richard said. He leaned to the side, looking past the commander to the three Mord-Sith. "I want you three to come with us."

Cassia frowned. "What made you think we would have allowed you to leave us behind?"

CHAPTER 33

Kahlan was glad to be leaving the citadel. It had been a place of sadness and tragedy. Cara had died there, as had a number of others. The fact that Richard was once again back with them in the world of life could not erase the indelible horror of seeing him lying dead, of seeing him on his funeral pyre.

But more than any other, it was the memory of almost giving the order to ignite his funeral pyre that kept creeping back into her mind. She knew that the memory of the order she had come so close to giving would haunt her as long as she lived and be the rich fodder of nightmares.

She mentally shook off the memory. He was alive and that was what mattered. She couldn't dwell on the past or on what might have been. She had to focus on what was and what they needed to do from here on out.

She was also glad to leave the citadel because of the scrolls that Richard had discovered there. She was still disturbed and upset over everything they had revealed. They had contradicted much of what she had learned growing up and been taught by wizards about how magic fit into the world. The scrolls, though, had skewed her understanding of everything to the point that she

felt lost in a world she thought she knew. Her understanding of everything had been turned upside down.

She would like to dismiss the things Richard had told
her, refuse to believe what he had discovered and attri-
bute it to myth or far-fetched theory, but she knew she
couldn't do that. Not only did she trust in what Richard was able to translate and figure out, but Nicci, too,
served to validate everything Richard said. Nicci had a
great deal of trust and faith in Richard, but she cared
enough for him not to allow him to falsely believe something if it wasn't true.

Besides, in a very strange way, Kahlan found the new
knowledge to be comforting. She supposed that was because it all had the ring of truth to it, but as disturbing
as that truth might be, it was also exciting to have discovered a previously unknown mechanism responsible
for so much that everyone simply took for granted. It
was like peeking behind the curtain of Creation.

It was fascinating in the remarkable clarity it brought
to so many things, like prophecy, that she had always
taken at face value without ever questioning. It also
made her feel a little resentful for being duped her whole
life by all the various established authorities who
claimed absolute certainty on such subjects. Richard's
discoveries were like finding the key to so much that
had been proclaimed to be unknowable and beyond the
scope of knowledge of mere mortals.

It was a new world she would have to get used to,
with new rules, and new challenges, but at least she felt
as if the knowledge had given them the tools with which
to fight to set things right. Now they knew what was
really wrong, and that would better help Richard to do
what he needed to do: end prophecy.

The irony of the prophecy that he was the one to end
prophecy wasn't lost on her. In a way, it was poetic justice.

In a very fundamental way, what Richard had learned had already begun to cause prophecy to unravel.

Nicci, as much as she understood the truth contained within the scrolls, had been somewhat shaken by what they had revealed. The sorceress had been a Sister of the Light and had lived most of her life at the Palace of the Prophets, a place devoted to prophecy and teaching the gifted how to use it. But everything Nicci had learned there and thought she knew was built on misunderstanding and deception. When he had been taken there, Richard had peeled back the first layer, shedding new light on prophecy.

Now he had discovered that the entire structure of prophecy had no foundation in reality. The scrolls weren't myth. It was prophecy itself that was really founded in myth.

Of course, Nicci never held any favor with prophecy in the first place, so Kahlan supposed the woman wasn't as disturbed by what they had learned as she might otherwise have been. Nicci had always told them that she had viewed the study of prophecy as an onerous duty, and she had never taken delight in it the way many of the other Sisters had. There were Sisters there who had spent hundreds of years down in the vaults at the Palace of the Prophets, devoted to studying prophecy, delighting in what they believed they were learning, thinking they understood it.

Kahlan wondered what Sister Verna would think of what the scrolls had revealed—if they ever had the chance to see the woman again. There were a number of Sisters besides Verna now living at the Wizard's Keep, in Aydindril. While Kahlan had been somewhat disoriented and confused by learning that many of the things she thought she knew were wrong, she had a suspicion that many of those Sisters would be bewildered and horrified that their whole world, everything they had believed and worked for, was not at all what they had thought. Not even close.

As with all truth, there would be those who refused to believe it and would not even look at the proof.

As they turned down the main street through the city, people in Saavedra stared openly at the dozen big soldiers of the First File riding tall in their saddles along with the three Mord-Sith in red leather, all escorting the Mother Confessor and the Lord Rahl. Kahlan wondered if most of these people even knew who the Lord Rahl was. After all, the only ruler they had known for most of their lives had been Hannis Arc. The Lord Rahl had always been a distant leader in a far-off land.

As they rode through the city, the sound of the horses' hooves on the wet cobblestones echoed back from the warren of narrow streets and tightly packed buildings. Most of those buildings were low and drab, with only the ones on the main street having a second story. The wooden walls Kahlan could see had faded paint, if they had paint, and almost all of the wood was stained with dark, blotchy mold from the constant dampness.

The shops in the lower floors sold basic goods and few luxuries that Kahlan could see. Life in the Dark Lands was about surviving, and few could afford the finer things in life. The entire city was hunched defensively inward, with its back turned to the surrounding Dark Lands and the things living in it. In side streets vendors with small carts of bread, or meats, or general merchandise all watched with somber expressions as the column of horses trotted past. None rushed out to try to hawk their goods to the strangers riding past.

The overcast sky was as dark and threatening as it always seemed to be in the Dark Lands. Kahlan couldn't remember the last time she had seen the sun. The constant gloom was depressing. The accumulating mist soaked the reins and the exposed leather of the saddle.

She shook the hood of her cloak to shed some of the gathered water. At least it was only misting lightly and not raining.

As the rapid clatter of all the hooves echoed through the canyons of tightly packed buildings, Kahlan patted the muscular neck of her bay mare, giving it a bit of reassurance that she would treat it well. Old scars on the horse's rump told Kahlan that previous riders had not been so kind or treated the horse well. They had obviously favored using a whip to make the animal do their bidding. The horse whinnied and tossed its head a little to let her know it had felt the gentle touch.

Richard rode a big black gelding that carried his weight easily. By the way it danced sideways at times when they stopped told her that the horse had some spirit. Richard looked magnificent on the horse. It was good to see him on one again. In the dull light his sword gleamed against his dark outfit. It was good to see him, too, with that glint of purpose in his eyes, even if those gray eyes also carried the shadow of poison.

As they left the city behind, and as happy as she was to be out of the citadel, she was happier still to be out of the depressing city of Saavedra. It felt good to be away from all the eyes on her. She had no way of knowing if any of those people watching would have been loyal to Hannis Arc, or for that matter, to Emperor Sulachan. For all she knew, he could have minions anywhere.

As they left the shelter of the city, though, there were other concerns. There was no telling who might be watching from the leafy shadows of the vast forests carpeting the wilderness. Commander Fister had been more than concerned that they were taking so few men. He wanted more than a dozen total in case they were set upon by half people. Richard told him that their safety depended on speed and escape, not on standing and fighting a battle. To that end, they'd brought a string of extra mounts so they could trade off and give the animals a break.

Cassia had reassured the commander that with three Mord-Sith along, they didn't need more men. His face screwed up with a sour expression, but he didn't say anything. Men of the First File had traditionally been the first line of defense for the Lord Rahl, but then, so had the Mord-Sith.

To Kahlan's knowledge it had never formally been settled among them who took precedence. Mord-Sith didn't think there was any need for formality. They believed that they took precedence and were never shy about making that point.

Richard, along with the commander and other officers of the First File, never contradicted that assertion. Richard didn't see the need. There were always plenty of enemy to go around.

Once they were clear of the city, Richard took the lead and set a pace that would make it difficult for anyone to stop them. The sight of the men with Richard at the lead reminded her of cavalry on the move. Any half people on foot would be at a distinct disadvantage. Still, they had numbers that might even be able to overwhelm a column of horses moving at speed. If any appeared, though, they would move into a gallop. Stepping out in front of a pack of horses in a thundering gallop would be the last mistake they ever made.

Richard pulled his horse to a halt as they reached a place where the road divided. Two of the men who had grown up in the Dark Lands drew their horses alongside him.

"Which way?" Richard asked. "Left or right?"

"The right is the shortest route," one of the men said.

"The left may be a little longer, but it's easier traveling," the other man said.

Richard turned in his saddle to look back at Nicci.
"Do you sense anything ahead on either road?"

Nicci rested her wrists atop one another on the horn
of her saddle as she looked off into the distance down
each road.

"No," she finally said. "I don't sense anyone. But that
doesn't mean anything, really, with them able to mask
their presence with occult powers. If they did that, I
wouldn't be able to sense them."

Richard tapped the side of his thumb on the horn of
his saddle as he gazed down both roads, considering.
Kahlan knew that he was worried about something
other than half people. He was concerned about Samantha trying to catch them out in the open with few men
to protect them. Of course, soldiers would not really be
much of an obstacle to the young sorceress.

Kahlan suspected that the Mord-Sith would not have
any better of a chance to stop her. Mord-Sith had the
ability to capture a person's magic if it was used against
them, but exactly what abilities Samantha had, they
didn't know for sure, so it was hard to tell if a Mord-
Sith's abilities would work the same with Samantha.
About the only thing they did know was that she was
profoundly gifted and inventive in using that gift.

The worst problem for the three Mord-Sith, though,
was that their Agiel didn't work. The Agiel depended
on the bond to the Lord Rahl, so as long as Richard
had that poison in him the Mord-Sith were at a disadvantage. What other limitations that imposed on their
ability to function, Kahlan didn't know.

They were all rightfully concerned about traveling
through dense woodlands, knowing what Samantha
was capable of. Kahlan was glad that the way they were
going, so far at least, was not taking them through any
gorges or along the bases of any cliffs. Samantha had

proven that she could bring a mountain down on their heads if she wanted to.

"Then I'd rather the shortest distance," Richard finally said as he urged his horse onto the road to the right. "We need to make the best time we can."

By the pace Richard was setting, it was clear that they would not have been able to make better time taking the better but longer road. She knew that Richard would make good time no matter how difficult the route. They'd brought relief mounts, so they could change horses in order to maintain a quick pace.

As the day wore on, the road began climbing in a series of switchbacks along the gentle rise of ever-higher slopes. The road was too narrow and rocky to have accommodated a cart, much less wagons. Anyone using the route would have had to use horses or pack mules.

The forest of shimmering leaves smelled of rot. Several times they had to stop so the men could push deadfalls off to the side of the road. The woodland silence was broken each time by the sound of the heavy, wet, rotted trees crashing down the side of the steep bank.

Near dark, they reached a turn in the road that went around a point of the mountain's edge. It afforded them a view off into the distance in nearly every direction except behind. The terrain over their heads was too steep for any attack from above. Anyone who tried to come at them from over the mountain above them would surely fall and plummet to their death. No one could climb up from below, at least not in numbers and not at all quickly enough.

"This gives us a good place we can watch from," Richard said as he stood in his saddle, checking in every direction, gazing down on the expanse of forest spreading out below. "It's getting dark fast. Let's stop here on the road and set up camp for the night." He pointed behind. "There is a lot of grass for the horses growing to the sides, right there."

"You think it best to stop out in the open where half people could spot us?" Cassia asked.

"I'd rather be in a place where we can see them coming from a long way off. They can't get to us going cross-country through the woods, and if they use the road they can only come from ahead or behind. There is no other way to get to us, here. That makes this spot which might seem like it's out in the open actually much easier for us to defend." He gestured to the rock wall at the apex of the curve around the prominence in the side of the mountain. "We can put some tarps there and be protected against the weather if it starts to rain."

"It looks like it will be a damp and miserable night," Commander Fister said. "What about fires to keep warm?"

Richard's mouth twisted. "I'm not liking the idea of starting fires that could be seen or smelled for miles. It wouldn't attract anything good and might tip off anyone searching for us."

"I can use my gift to heat rocks," Nicci offered. "At least they will keep us all warm."

Richard nodded as he swung down out of his saddle. "Post watches in both directions." He held the reins up close to the bit. "No man stands watch alone. Double the men and keep watches short. We have enough men for us all to get some sleep."

"You heard the man," Commander Fister said as he swung down out of his saddle.

Everyone else dismounted and set about the task of stringing up some small tarps to shelter them from the rain and gathering material to keep them up off the wet ground as they slept.

Kahlan smiled to herself. She was finally going to get to cuddle up to Richard for at least a few hours' rest.

As good a rest as she could expect, anyway, with the Twilight Count marking the time until the end of the world while the half people hunted for souls.

Richard circled his big arm around her waist and smiled at her. "What do you say we get something to eat?"

Richard gently drew back on the reins, slowing his horse to a stop. It was an unexpectedly compliant animal that wanted to please and had willingly taken to his directions, but now its nostrils flared as it tossed its head, snorted, and stepped about nervously. The other horses were just as unsettled.

Richard patted the animal's shoulder. "I smell it too," he murmured in a comforting voice. "I don't like it any better than you."

Everyone had come to a halt all around him. The three Mord-Sith had closed in to get as close to him and Kahlan as they could get. Mord-Sith always wanted to be the closest layer of protection. Richard had long ago learned not only that they were capable and worthy of being in such a position, but it was a lot less trouble if he let them protect him in the way they thought best. The soldiers formed an outer ring surrounding the three women in red leather. They wanted to be the first to encounter any attacking enemy and stop them. So, the Mord-Sith and the soldiers of the First File were both content that they had their way.

Before one of the horses could panic and bolt or throw their riders, Richard signaled everyone to dismount.

"What do you think?" Nicci asked as she leaned closer to him after she was down on the ground.

Richard's gaze moved across the shadows back in the woods among the trees and rock outcroppings, checking for any sign of threat.

"Well, there is no mistaking that something is dead up ahead," he finally told her. "The only question is what, or who."

"And who did the killing," the sorceress added.

Richard glanced over at her. "There is that."

Even at the distance they were from whatever it was that was dead, the smell was repulsive. He supposed it could be dead animals, but the hair standing on end at the back of his neck told him otherwise.

Commander Fister held on to the reins to his horse as he stepped closer so he could whisper. "Are we close to the village?"

Richard nodded. He was on familiar ground, now. From the protection of the forested foothills, they all gazed across the open fields toward the cliff face in the distance. The mountain, thick with clinging vegetation, towered over the rough, raw rock face of the cliff.

"I don't hear anything," Richard said in an equally quiet voice as he leaned toward Nicci. "Can you sense anything? You should be able to sense all the people from here, shouldn't you? You should at least to be able to sense the livestock, right?"

Nicci's blue eyes turned from staring into the distance to look up at him. "If there were any people or animals still alive, I would be able to sense it." She gestured to the thick trees towering over them to each side. "I can sense small animals here–some birds, a squirrel just out of sight over there, things like that. There are mice hiding down in holes under the leaf litter where we can't see them." She flicked a finger, gesturing out toward the fields. "There are small living things like that in the fields, but on the other side, toward the village, I don't sense anything."

Richard wasn't at all surprised. That was what his intuition was telling him. Nicci's words were all the confirmation he needed.

He drew his sword.

In the dead silence the ring of steel echoed out across the fields, announcing the arrival of the Sword of Truth in the damp late-day air.

"All right, we're going to have to go have a look. Horses don't like the smell of death. If we take them any closer they may panic and bolt." He gestured with his sword. "Let's picket them back here. Tie the leads so they can get away if they have to."

One of the men stepped in and took the reins from Richard as he peered out across the field, scanning for any movement, any sign of life. One of the other men took Kahlan's horse. Nicci and the three Mord-Sith handed over the reins to their horses when another man came to get them.

The rest of the men drew their weapons.

Kahlan stroked the neck of her bay mare. "Take good care of her," she said with a smile to the soldier. "She has given me an easy ride."

He smiled back with a nod before leading the horse back to a small open area in the woods.

Richard was already in the grip of the anger from the sword. The smell of death only served to make that rage flooding into him from the sword more urgent, joining with his own anger. Together, those twin storms of rage spiraled through him, filling him with fury to prepare him for the fight. With the power of the sword in his hand, there was no mistaking the threat that hung in the air along with the stench of death. The magic of the sword wanted to meet that threat.

Even though he didn't really know how to command

his gift, it was always there, and it always responded to his rage. He was left with a strange emptiness when his gift was out of reach. The sword served to fill that void and more.

With the sword and its power flooding through him, he felt alive with purpose.

He shared a meaningful look with Kahlan, a look they had shared before when facing unknown dangers. He wanted to see her beautiful green eyes one last time before he began the dance with death. She touched his arm in silent answer.

"If you sense anything I need to know about, speak up," he said in a low voice as he leaned toward Nicci before starting down the path between the green fields. She hurried to step in behind him. Kahlan took up a position beside her, both knowing enough to stay out of the way of his sword. Cassia and the other two Mord-Sith followed them. The soldiers guarded the rear, protecting them from anything that might swoop out of the woods.

Richard wasn't sure exactly what Nicci was able to sense with her gift, but he was sure that had his own gift been working he would have been able to see the aura of power crackling around her. Even without being able to see it, it was not at all difficult for him to tell that she was on alert and would respond in a blink with withering force if need be. Kahlan was no less ready for trouble. The three Mord-Sith always expected trouble and were only surprised when there wasn't any.

So far, though, nothing was emerging out beyond the fields—no people, no animals, and no threat.

In the distance, across the slightly rolling ground spread out before them, in the face of the rock wall rising up from the far side of the fields, Richard could make out the dark opening into the cave village of Stroyza. He didn't see anyone standing in that opening.

When he'd left Stroyza the last time he had told the men to post a watch at all times so that no half people or walking dead could sneak up on them again. The people of the village were humble farmers who raised some livestock. They were not warriors. Even so, from up on the face of that sheer cliff, it would have been easy to repel any attackers climbing up the treacherous trail. All it would take was throwing some rocks down at any threat trying to come up to attack the village.

He should have been able to see those lookouts standing watch and also looking out for their livestock below, but he saw no one up in the cavern opening.

On the way toward the cliff, the foot trail passed between large fields, some planted with grain, some with hay, and others with vegetables and fruit trees. Some of those vegetables were mature and ready but remained unpicked. Some were past ripe. Apples, pears, and plums were turning dark, as they were past their prime. More lay rotting on the ground.

Now that they had left the protection of the forest and were out in the open among the fields, Richard felt exposed and vulnerable. The reality was that they would have been nearly as vulnerable back in the woods, but he always felt better when he was in the forests. Even though these woods were different from his Hartland woods, they were still comfortingly familiar. He knew how to live in woods, how to fight among the trees, and how to evade an enemy there.

Bugs flitted and buzzed above the grass, with orange butterflies feeding on small blue wildflowers growing among the grape vines. Swarms of bees fed on both the ripe fruit still on the trees and the rotting fruit on the ground. Other than those bugs, he saw nothing alive and no movement.

In the dead-still air thick with the stench of death, not a leaf, not a branch, not a blade of grass moved. He did hear a low hum, though. He couldn't quite place the vaguely familiar sound.

The last time he had been in Stroyza, there had been animals in the buildings and pens at the foot of the cliff. If they were still there he didn't hear them.

As they made their way past the fields to the split-rail fences, he found out why. Hogs lay dead in their pens. Two milk cows, their legs sticking stiffly out from their bloated bodies, lay in dirty runnels of muddy water. Bloodstained sheep were piled in a tight cluster in the corner of where a fence met a building. Dead chickens lay scattered here and there around the yards. The feathers settled everywhere atop the mud and manure reminded him a little of snow.

"What could have done this?" Kahlan whispered on their way past the dead hogs. She put her hand back over her nose. All the rest of them held up a hand or an arm, trying to block the putrid stench.

The small group made their way through a sprawling boulder field of broken rock that had built up over time as the weather had cleaved rock from the cliff face to accumulate below. In some places they had to walk single-file among the boulders, and in a few spots had to duck in turn under massive slabs of stone that over the millennia had fallen from the face of the mountain to now rest atop the jumble of boulders.

As they came around and through the clutter of boulders, Richard stopped in his tracks when he at last spotted the people of Stroyza. The buzzing noise he had heard had been clouds of flies.

The corpses lay piled in massive heaps atop one another, on top of and down between the rocks at the bottom of the cliff. They all rested wherever they had landed. Arms and legs sprawled at crazy angles. Maggots wriggled in places where flesh had split open.

The all held their noses, wincing, gagging on the

putrefying stench. The air was so thick with the power-ful smell he could taste it.

As he got closer, holding the crook of his arm over his nose and mouth to try to at least partially block the smell, he recognized some of the individuals. He peered out from just over his arm. These were the people who had rescued him and Kahlan. Many of them had pro-tected and helped them. He had fought with these men to stop the animated dead that invaded their cave vil-lage.

He saw Ester, the woman who had helped him and Kahlan when they had first been brought to the village. Now, flies walked across her dead eyes staring up at the sky. Richard waved his sword over her body, chasing the flies away.

"Dear spirits, please protect these dear souls," Kah-lan whispered from right beside him. She put her hand back, pinching her nose and covering her mouth.

Richard signaled with his sword for the men to check around the piles of bodies for any who might be alive. He knew there couldn't be anyone alive, but he had to check. From the way they were piled together and the broken bones stuck out through clothes, it looked to him that these people had all fallen from the cave open-ing high up on the cliff.

Commander Fister shook his head from the far side of the corpses. "Poor souls. All dead. Terrible way to die."

"There are much worse ways," Cassia said. "At least it looks to have been quick for these people. They didn't suffer."

Richard knew she was right, but that didn't make it any easier to see all of these dead people, the entire vil-lage, all lying tangled in death below their village.

He had seen a lot of death, but this was making him feel sick.

"Do you see any wounds from a fight?" Richard asked the commander as the man made his way back around, stepping over the odd legs or arms sticking out from the bottom of the piles.

Commander Fister, looking all business now, shook his head. "It doesn't appear to have been any kind of fight, but it's a little hard to say for sure. If I had to hazard a guess, I'd say they all fell to their death." He scratched the side of his neck. "Strange, though . . ."

"What's strange?" Richard asked.

The commander cocked his head as he looked in at the tangled mass of corpses. "There are some dead cats in among the people."

"Cats?" Nicci asked with a frown.

The commander nodded. "I can see eight or ten, at least."

"There were a lot of cats living up there in the village," Kahlan said. "They must have fallen or jumped along with the people."

Commander Fister was frowning at the dead. "Some of the cats look like their fur has been singed off."

"Probably decomposition," Cassia said. "They've all been here for a while since they all fell from up there."

Nicci looked up at the cave opening high above. "What I would like to know is what would make all these people jump from up there?"

"Good question," Richard said. "Let's go have a look."

Richard led the five women and twelve men to the point where the narrow path started up along the face of the rock wall. Set back behind a tangle of scrubs and small, scraggly maple trees behind the boulders, it would have been easy to miss had he not known where it was. He looked back, taking a count to make sure everyone was with him.

"Lord Rahl," the commander said in a quiet voice, "we don't know what sort of trouble might be up top. Why don't you let me take the men and go up first, ahead of you?"

Richard lifted his sword along with an eyebrow to make his point that there was more safety behind the sword he carried than the soldiers.

Knowing that arguing would be useless, and realizing that Richard was probably right, the commander only sighed. "Would you like me to post any men down here to make sure no one sneaks up behind us?"

"No. I want us to all to stay together." Richard gestured up the cliff with his sword. "I've used the trail before. It would be safer if I go first, then it will be easier for you to follow after seeing the best place to step. If anyone slips and falls, it could take the rest down, so watch where I put my feet and where I use handholds. It's really not a terribly difficult trail as long as you're careful."

After Commander Fister nodded, Richard began the climb upward. Kahlan followed close behind him, then the three Mord-Sith, then Nicci, then the soldiers.

There was no back door, no secondary entrance, no other way up to the cliff village of Stroyza except the path that followed along natural crags and ledges of the rock face. Where there were no natural footholds, the rock had been laboriously chipped away to create them. In places softer rock underfoot had been smoothed by the feet of people, who for thousands of years climbed and descended the cliff wall on a daily basis.

"Be careful," Richard called back over his shoulder to those following behind. "The rock in this section is smooth and the drizzle makes it slippery along here. The people who lived here were familiar with the trail, but we aren't. Pay attention to where you step and use these natural handholds along here, like I'm doing."

In some places, where there were natural lifts of ledge, the path was wide enough to walk comfortably along. Even so, the path was still only wide enough for them to climb in single file. Some places were dangerously narrow and, even without the drizzle, quite treacherous. Fortunately, in those places there were iron bars pinned into the face of the rock so that particularly narrow spots didn't feel so dangerous.

It might have been easier for Richard to climb the trail without having to hold his sword, but he didn't want to put it away. Besides, he felt that he knew the trail well enough by now to manage with his sword out. Most of the men kept their swords out as well, so he kept an eye on them to make sure they were being careful. Some of them were as agile as mountain goats and had no difficulty. The people of Stroyza, using the trail all their lives, had been familiar enough with it to carry supplies up and down without much of a problem.

But the bodies at the bottom only served to bring into stark relief the dangers of the height.

Richard looked back down the face of the cliff from time to time to check on Kahlan and the rest of them. Each time he looked down, he couldn't help noticing the sprawled, tangled remains of the people of Stroyza. He felt profoundly sorry for these simple people living out in the middle of the Dark Lands. They had lived successfully in a dangerous land for generation after generation. He wished he knew who had thrown them off the cliff. . . . Or made them jump.

These were the people who were the sentries meant to be the ones to alert everyone else of the threat from the third kingdom once the barrier was breached. They had never been able to send out that alert. As a result, they had somehow fallen victim to that threat escaping from the north.

He remembered the walking corpses that had attacked not long after Kahlan had been rescued and first taken to Stroyza by the villagers. Had he not been there with his sword, these people might very well have all died at that time. He wondered if more of those walking dead had returned to finish what they had not been able to accomplish the first time. Even if that had been the case, lookouts perched high above should have been able to simply knock any attackers off the wall. It was possible, he supposed, that anything the villagers could have thrown at such beings powered by occult magic might not have been enough.

Other than that possibility, what had happened didn't make sense to him.

When Richard finally made it up to the top and stepped into the naturally formed, broad cavity, he could see that it was dark down all of the cavelike pas-

sageways and tunnels going deeper back into the mountain. Within short order, everyone behind him made it
onto the safe ground of the cavern floor. In the natural
light coming in through the broad cliff opening, the men
rushed to collect torches standing in baskets to the sides
so that they could light their way for a search deeper
into the caves.

After Nicci used her gift to light them, the men held
up the torches, allowing them to peer into dark passageways. Richard led them all a short distance into one
of the broader passageways. There were a number of
rooms built into natural clefts and crags along the way
back into the cavern.

Many more of the rooms and the network of tunnels
had been excavated from the semisoft rock. Lumps of
granite, anywhere from fist-sized to pieces so enormous
that there was no telling how big they might be, were
embedded in the softer rock. Much of the ceiling was
composed of the massive slabs of granite. Those ledges
helped form a strong and stable ceiling. The caves were
excavated from the amalgam of different rock under
that harder stone.

When the cave village had been hollowed out from
the mountain, the tunnels and passageways had to be
dug mostly through the natural veins of softer rock.
Richard remembered how that left a tangled network of
passageways. It was easy to get lost back in those caverns.

The fronts of some of the hollowed-out rooms had
mortared stone walls filling in the gaps. Some openings
had simple wooden doors, while others were covered
with animal skins. The rooms created a community of
small homes.

Richard cupped a hand to the side of his mouth and
yelled into the darkness. "Is anyone here? It's Richard!
I've come back!"

His voice echoed back from the darkness, and when that echo died out, the caves were dead silent. He couldn't say that he was surprised. He thought by the number of bodies at the bottom that it looked like all the people of Stroyza were dead.

Richard turned back to the men and pointed in several places with his sword at the dwellings honeycombed throughout the warren of passages.

"Check in all the rooms. See if anyone is still alive."

Richard suspected, because of the degree of decomposition of the bodies, that whatever or whoever had killed the people of Stroyza, the threat was probably long gone. But he kept his sword out, anyway.

"Do you sense anything alive back there?" Richard quietly asked Nicci as she came up beside him.

She gazed silently down the passageways for a moment. "It's hard to tell. The network of caverns causes reflections that make it difficult to say for sure, but I don't think there is anything down there for me to sense."

Richard took a torch from one of the men, motioning for him to go retrieve another. "Maybe if we go farther in," he told Nicci, "you will be able to tell better."

Nicci went with him to one side, Kahlan staying close on the other side. The three Mord-Sith, each with a torch, stepped out in front to light the way and check for threat. They left the men behind, checking rooms, as Richard and the women moved deeper into the broad cavern. He could see that it would funnel them into a smaller passageway. Intersections branched off to the sides as they cautiously went deeper. The three Mord-Sith momentarily held their torches out toward the branching passageways, checking, but they saw no one.

The soldiers were conducting a more thorough search, taking the time to do a thorough check of each room. The Mord-Sith threw back the hanging over a doorway to their left to take a quick look inside, making sure everything was clear and that there was no threat. Richard saw pillows used as seating in the rooms, but he saw no people.

Behind them a thunderous roar suddenly shook the ground, nearly knocking them from their feet.

A blinding flash of light lit the walls all around.

Richard and the five women with him spun just in time to see the intense flash send an expanding wall of dust and dirt blasting through the cave. The bodies of all the soldiers came apart in midair among the ignition of light before the remains were blown out the cave opening along with bits of rock and rolling dust.

Richard spread his arms as he scooped up the others and slammed them back against the wall out of the way of the blast. Dust and debris thundered past them on its way back into the caves.

None of the men had cried out. They were all dead before they knew what had hit them. What was left of them fell through space to the rocks below to join the rest of the human remains rotting out in the rain.

Richard took quick appraisal of the women with him. They were all panting and wide-eyed from the force of the unexpected explosion but otherwise looked unharmed. With his finger and thumb he pulled what looked like a long bloody splinter of bone from Kahlan's hair and tossed it aside. Seeing that they were all right, he turned, sword in hand, rage thundering through

him, and snatched a quick look back around the curve
in the tunnel, back toward the cave entrance.

He blinked and stuck his head back out for a longer
look at what he had seen, and knew then that he had
been right the first time. Someone small was standing
silhouetted against the light coming in the cavern opening. Richard knew instantly who it was.

Samantha, wearing a dark cloak with the hood containing her mass of dark hair, stepped farther out of an
intersection to the side between Richard and where the
men of the First File had been.

Now, those men were all dead. It had happened in a
blink. The shape of the cavern had directed most of the
force of the blast out the large opening and had taken
the men with it. That had lessened the force of the blast
back in the smaller passageways where Richard and the
others were.

As soon as he spotted Samantha, Richard hooked an
arm around Kahlan's middle and pulled her farther
back in a passageway to the side. At the same time he
used his sword arm to shove back the three Mord-Sith.
Nicci dove in after them just in time as a crackling bolt
of lightning shot past to shatter rock off the wall farther
down the tunnel. Pieces of rock and rubble tumbled and
bounced down the passageway. The floor everywhere
was now littered with debris. Some of it bloody.

Without pause, Nicci immediately returned the attack. A deafening, twisting ignition of both Additive
and Subtractive Magic exploded into being at the ends
of her outstretched hands, arcing its way across the cave
toward Samantha. Richard had seen that kind of fused
power cut through steel.

Rock ripped off the walls where the blinding bolt of
power hit, but to Richard's surprise—and Nicci's—
Samantha merely lifted an arm, casually brushing

aside the deadly lightning as if it were a petty nuisance.

"Samantha!" Richard screamed. "What are you doing!"

"What needs to be done," she said in a strangely calm voice.

"You said you hate me, but you are killing innocent people! You've killed the people you grew up with! You killed the people of your own village!"

Nicci turned and rammed her fist into Richard's chest, driving him back around a curve in a side tunnel just in time as a bolt of crackling lightning from Samantha thundered through the cave, shattering rock and filling the cave with billowing clouds of dust. The intensity of the light was blinding and left an afterglow in his vision that made it hard to see. Some of the others coughed and choked on the dust.

As destructive as it was, he knew she was only toying with him. She wouldn't want him to die that quickly or that easily.

Richard looked back around the corner and saw Samantha walking purposefully toward them. He saw serious scratches on her skinny arms. The scratches looked like they were from cat claws.

It was then, as the light and shadow changed in the way it played across her, that Richard again saw the same faint shape of something in her face that he had seen before when she had attacked him in the field outside the citadel.

As she stepped out of the light and into a deep shadow, even though she was in partial darkness, he saw it more clearly. It was darker than the shadow, darker than black, darker than the blackest night.

Staring in astonishment as she backed through the cave along with the rest of them, Kahlan apparently saw it, too. "What is that? It looks familiar."

When he saw the shape twist and tighten as if an extension of Samantha's dark mood, Richard recognized it then. That same dark shape had once enveloped him, tightened around him. But this time, it had been accepted willingly.

Now he understood the burned cats and the scratches on Samantha's arms. Cats were creatures that could sometimes see spirits in this world.

"It's one of the dark ones," Richard said.

"The dark ones?" Cassia asked, her voice filled with rage and urgency to eliminate the threat. "What are you talking about?"

"From the underworld," Nicci said as she stared at the otherworldly sight. "I recognize it now, too. It's one of the demons that had Richard in the underworld, one of Sulachan's dark ones taking him down into oblivion."

"Then what's it doing here, in this world?" Laurin asked in an equally heated voice.

"The veil is failing," Richard said as he used his free arm to push them back farther while keeping his sword out and an eye toward Samantha. She kept coming, matching their pace, shadowing them. "Sulachan is tearing the veil more all the time. He apparently was able to bring some of his minions through."

"Give yourself over to us," Samantha called out to him, "and we will let the others go."

None of them believed a word of it. Sulachan and the dark ones from the underworld wanted to eliminate Richard because he was the only possible threat to them.

"You give up and give yourself over to us," Richard said.

Samantha answered by abruptly throwing another bolt of otherworldly power, sending it flying back through the cave. It hit the walls, skipping off one side and then the other, sending showers of rock flying as it raced back toward Richard and the others.

This time, there was no cover close enough. Knowing they wouldn't be able to evade it, Richard made a split-second decision and stepped out, holding the sword by the hilt in one hand and the point in the other as a shield. The tumbling fireball split when it hit the sword, sending streamers of lightning and fire crashing into the walls at each side.

Richard's fears were confirmed when he saw that there was not even one soldier behind Samantha. She had killed Commander Fister and the entire detachment of men with them. Richard, Kahlan, Nicci, and the three Mord-Sith were the only ones left.

They had no choice but to withdraw deeper into the caves to try to stay away from the young sorceress.

"Samantha!" Richard yelled out as he backed deeper into the caverns. "You have to stop! Your hatred of me is inviting evil into yourself! Stop! Think about what you're doing!"

Her hands fisted at her sides. "I know exactly what I'm doing!" she screamed. "I'm killing the murderer of my mother!"

"You have to listen to me," Richard called out to her as he took several steps back. "I tried to explain it to you before. You need to stop and talk to me about it. You need to let me tell you what was happening with your mother. Let me help you to reason it out so you can see the truth for yourself. You have to listen to the truth!"

She lowered her head, arms stiff at her sides.

Kahlan grabbed a fistful of Richard's sleeve. "We're in trouble. That's what she did when she blew apart the rock cliffs in the gorge."

"Kahlan's right," Nicci said. "Samantha buried an entire army of the half people when she did that."

"That's why I said we are in trouble," Kahlan said.

Cassia started for the young sorceress, but Richard snatched her arm just in time to yank her back, nearly pulling her off her feet in the process.

"No you don't," he told her in a heated voice. "She will kill you in a heartbeat."

"I can stop her, Lord Rahl. That's what Mord-Sith do. We absorb the magic of anyone who tries to use it against us. We can capture their magic. Let me–"

"No," he said as he moved with them back toward a corner. "My gift doesn't work, so the bond doesn't work, so your Agiel doesn't work, and that means your ability to absorb magic won't work either."

As he looked over his shoulder to make sure they were all moving behind cover, holding a tight grip on the leather at Cassia's shoulder, pulling her with him, Laurin ducked around the other side of him. She darted away before Richard was able to grab her.

The blond Mord-Sith, Agiel in her fist, charged right for Samantha, daring her to try to use magic against her. Richard was able to catch Vale and prevent her from joining Laurin.

Samantha never moved. Her head was bowed, her eyes closed. The shadowy spirit of the demon seemed to writhe with gleeful menace.

Before Richard could do anything to go after Laurin, the air of the cave jolted with a hard impact, as if the entire mountain had been struck with a giant hammer. At the same time, Laurin's form exploded in a shower of black bits, like crystals of a night stone. Her red leather collapsed to the floor, the black crystals that had been Laurin spilling out of the openings at the wrists and ankles. There was nothing left of the Mord-Sith but charred black bits scattered across the floor.

Cassia and Vale both screamed in rage as they charged for Samantha. Richard snatched each one in an arm just in time and yanked them back behind the corner of the intersection.

As he tumbled back with the two Mord-Sith, falling at Nicci and Kahlan's feet, the walls began to shudder as if in a violent earthquake. Thunderous explosions hammered through the cavern, ringing in his ears.

"She's doing it," Nicci said through gritted teeth. "She's bringing the rock down on us."

"We need to get out of here," Kahlan said.

But there really wasn't anywhere to run. All they could do was try to stay out of Samantha's direct line of fire.

To the left, a slab of rock exploded, sending fragments ricocheting and bouncing up and down the passageway as the main section dropped heavily to the floor. One side of another small slab of the granite ceiling let go and fell, coming to rest on the floor while the other half remained lodged up in the softer rock of the ceiling.

Richard pushed the two Mord-Sith back, giving them an unmistakable warning look. Kahlan and Nicci grabbed them and held them back so he could take a quick look around the corner.

When the explosion paused briefly, he was able to peek around the corner to get a good look. He saw Samantha, with that grim black shadow of the demon twisting with rage in the same place as the girl as she marched toward them. Her arms were still stiff, her hands in fists, her head lowered.

When she spotted him she glared with unrestrained rage and hate and kept coming. She was coming for him.

Richard wondered if he could get close enough to her to use the sword. That ruled out using the sword as a shield, first, because it gave her too much time with him in the open. In his mind he planned what he would need to do. He decided that he would race out from cover to draw her attention. She would change the focus of an attack toward him. That shift of her attention would take a fraction of a second, making her redirected attack less accurate. As she rushed to cast out another lightning bolt of power, he could throw himself to the ground, roll under it, and then spring up in front of her. If he could get in that close, he was pretty sure he would be able to take her down with the sword before she could react.

If she didn't miss, though, it would all be over. He would be dead. Sulachan and Hannis Arc would win. Prophecy would live–at least until the world of life died out.

He gripped the sword tighter in both hands and gritted his teeth, readying himself to charge at the young sorceress.

Samantha stopped. She growled in rage, her whole body trembling with fury. When he snuck a quick glance, Richard could see the shape of the demon in the same place as her, in much the way that Sulachan's spirit occupied his desiccated corpse in the same place at the same time.

But Samantha was not an innocent victim who was possessed by an evil spirit. She had invited that hateful spirit into her with her irrational, out-of-control anger and hate. Now they were one in purpose. Now they both were determined to kill.

The dark one was using her, encouraging her, and Samantha was willingly summoning the full power of her unbridled wrath.

As she shook with anger, the rock of the cave trembled in response. He knew what she was doing. He had, after all, taught her to do it.

Richard knew that he had no time to lose. If he was going to stop her, it had to be now, before she brought the rock down on them. He had no hesitation about the need to kill her. If that dance with death had taught him anything, it was that his life and the lives of innocent people couldn't be forfeited for sentiment. A lethal threat had to be recognized for the reality of what it was. Such threats had to be stopped.

Before he could charge out, Richard had to duck when a slab of thicker stone behind them blew apart. Jagged shards of rock whistled through the air, one going over the top of his bowed head, just missing him.

Then another area out in front of him and down a side tunnel exploded apart. All up and down the passageways rock began exploding in a ripping string of thunderous blasts. The cave trembled with the unfathomable force Samantha was focusing into the rock, blowing it apart. The echo of explosions rippled throughout the cave.

Thunderous blasts rang out painfully in the confined space as the explosions of rock came almost one atop another. Richard was pelted with pieces of rock that sailed through the passageway and ricocheted off walls. The whole mountain shook. He had to close his eyes and turn his face away from debris clouds that blew past him. The sound of it was deafening.

And then, out in front of him, where he was just about to charge out at Samantha and tumble under anything she could throw at him, the entire ceiling let out a reverberating, crackling boom as it was abruptly driven downward by a thunderous explosion. The massive section of the mountain above them had suddenly collapsed.

The force of the entire ceiling giving way shook the mountain so violently that Richard, Kahlan, Nicci, Cassia, and Vale were all knocked from their feet. Along with the Mord-Sith, Richard immediately rolled up onto a hand and a knee, with his other foot on the ground, ready to spring into the fight. Kahlan was on her hands and knees, looking dazed. They all turned their faces away from the blast of wind forced out from under the rock as it came crashing down. The blast of the shock wave caught Nicci off-balance and knocked her flat on her back. The two Mord-Sith were also sent tumbling back by the wall of air.

Richard braced for the next blast, looking to the sides to try to find a place for them to run, a shelter where they could get away from the flying rock, but there was no other intersection. There was no immediate route for an escape. Cassia and Vale scrambled to their feet, picking up their torches off the ground as they did so.

The torches hissed and sputtered, but other than that, the debris settled, rocks rolled to a stop, and everything began to go quiet. The rumbling and shaking had stopped. The explosions had stopped. The echoes of it all gradually died out.

Richard wondered what would be coming next, what power Samantha would unleash. He needed to stop her, first.

In the sudden silence he finally peeked around the corner and saw something out ahead of them, beyond the nearly empty red leather Mord-Sith outfit. He took a torch from Vale and cautiously inched out from the protection of the jut of rock where he had been to see if it was what he thought it was.

He stood to his full height when he saw that he had been right. It was Samantha's bloody arm sticking out from beneath a massive section of granite that had collapsed from overhead. It had crushed the young woman.

"Well, isn't that something," Cassia said as she stepped up beside Richard, holding her torch up with one hand as she brushed the dirt off herself with the other.

The wavering light of their torches lit the bloody forearm and fist—the only thing they could see of Samantha. The rest of her was buried under countless tons of stone that had let go and come down atop her.

"She gets so angry, so focused," Kahlan said, "that she forgets about her own safety. When we were in the gorge when the army of half people were chasing us, she was bringing the mountain down atop them and I had to snatch her up and carry her away or it would have come down on top of her, just like this."

Nicci was nodding in agreement. "I saw that immaturity in her. It frightened me from the first. Her ability exceeded her capacity to handle it."

That bloody arm had a ghostly appearance to it, a dark shadow that moved as if it were alive whereas the arm was dead still. As Richard watched, that shadow faded away into nothing. The demon that had been with her, helping her, had melted back beyond the veil. Without a worldly form to possess and hold it in the world of life, it could not keep the skrin from pulling it back into the world of the dead.

For now, some of those forces still held. At least, to a certain extent.

"I can't believe she so willfully killed those men," Kahlan said. "She knew them. She liked them. At least, she did at one time. She had helped them. I can hardly believe she would so easily kill them."

Richard felt a twinge of sadness for the girl whose ability made her so out of place and who had been trying so hard to become a woman. She'd had such potential. He guessed that the potential and talent did her no good in the end when she instead let herself be ruled by hate. In the end, hate destroyed her.

"She killed her entire village as well," Richard said. "The people she had grown up with and had hoped to protect."

Nicci glared at the bloody, splintered arm. "I told you she was dangerous, that her anger was dangerous."

"One of the Wizard's Rules I learned long ago," Richard said. "Passion rules reason. I'm sorry that I didn't see the indications in her sooner. Had I paid more attention to the signs I might have been able to help her to choose positive things rather than the dishonesty of hate. I guess I was blind to it, thinking she just needed to grow up a little."

"A lot," Nicci grumbled. "You couldn't have helped her, Richard. It was what was inside her. It was her inborn nature. None of us could have changed her."

Richard squatted down and touched the red leather that had belonged to Laurin.

"She gave her life trying to protect you, Lord Rahl," Cassia said in comfort. "Any of us would have done the same. She died a noble death."

"As did all those men," he said. "But they are all still dead."

He picked the Agiel out of the black crystallized pieces that were all that was left of Laurin. He stood and showed it to Vale. "Now you must wear the Agiel of a brave Mord-Sith, a sister of the Agiel, as does Cassia, and gain strength from it."

She bowed her head as he placed the chain around her neck. "I'm sorry that those men and Laurin had to die this day."

"Those men of the First File and Laurin died to protect you, Lord Rahl," Cassia said. "That was their chosen calling. They died doing what they wanted most to do. They were all honored by your trust in them. They died heroes in their mission to make sure you and the Mother Confessor were safe, now."

He smiled his thanks for her words.

"We're not exactly, safe, though," Richard said as he looked up at the solid wall of rock. "I'm afraid we're trapped in here."

CHAPTER

38

W hat do you mean we're trapped in here?" Nicci asked with a mix of suspicion and concern. "There were passageways everywhere. There have to be interconnecting tunnels running all through this place. There has to be a way to get around this collapsed section of ceiling."

As his gaze swept over the wall of rock, Richard slowly shook his head. "You're right that the tunnels interconnect. A little farther back we could have gone down some of those side intersections and they would take us a different way around to the opening at the top of the cliff. But not this far back in this particular corridor.

"We're now in a dedicated corridor that runs back deeper into the mountain. This passageway is unlike the rest. It has a primary purpose, so it doesn't have the typical intersecting routes that crisscross in and out of the general network of tunnels. The builders apparently intended to limit access to it.

"It does have side branches with a number of rooms, some of them places where people lived, but those side passageways are all part of this limited-access area, so none of them lead back out. They all dead-end. From

back here the only way back out, back into the general
tunnel complex, is through this collapsed wall of rock."

"Maybe it's not as big a problem as it seems," Cassia
said, trying to sound positive. "Maybe the five of us can
dig our way out. It probably wouldn't be as hard as it
looks."

Richard frowned over at her. "Look at it." He gestured to the wall of rock. "Cassia, it's solid granite. It's
not a pile of rubble that maybe we could dig through.
It's a single, massive block of granite.

"Granite is often layered in thick lifts like this. Some
of those slabs can be dozens of feet thick and they can
run on horizontally for quite some distance. Weather
will create and open up natural breaks, but protected
inside a mountain like this, these lifts are massive. It
must have fractured along a natural horizontal split
higher up in the rock and because of what Samantha
was doing, the unsupported weight all dropped down
into this void."

"Maybe it's not very wide, though," Kahlan offered.
"People cut granite into blocks to use in buildings."

"Sure," Richard said, "but that takes specialized chis-
els and wedges to split the rock. We don't have any of
that."

Kahlan turned hopefully to Nicci. "Maybe you can
use your gift to open up a hole—maybe crack the rock
or something—to get us through to the other side? Move
some of it aside?"

Nicci frowned her incredulity. "There's no way. The
entire face of the mountain was weakened by what
Samantha was doing. Remember what she did in that
mountain gorge? This here all dropped down into the
void of the caverns, like stepping on an anthill. The
whole network of tunnels from this point back is
crushed. It's solid rock from here to what used to be the
mouth of the cavern."

"How far is that?" Vale asked, hopefully.

Richard made a bit of a face at her. "How long were we running to get away from her?"

Vale looked sheepish. "A pretty long way, I guess."

"You guess right. It's hundreds of feet. We might as well be inside the middle of the mountain."

He pointed to the side. "Look at the way the softer stone is pushed out into this void back here. That's a good indication of the massive size and weight of all the granite that came down from above. As extensive as the network of caves may be, to the mountain it's like the anthills Nicci mentioned. From here to the outside there are no longer any caves. They are all crushed. There is nothing to dig through or cut through. The original people who made these caves surely had hundreds of workers and the tools necessary for such an undertaking. We don't."

Kahlan folded her arms. "What are we doing here, Richard?"

Richard looked over at her. "What do you mean?"

"Richard, we're all afraid. We're going to die in here if there isn't another way out. You wanted to come here because you said it was too far to make it back to the People's Palace. There isn't a containment field here where Nicci could extract that poison from you.

"So why are we here? What's really going on?"

Richard pressed his lips together a moment. "Well, I figured you all would think I was crazy, so I wanted to find it first."

Kahlan kept her admonishing gaze fixed on him. "Find what?"

It was clear she expected the truth. It was also clear to him that she deserved it. So did the rest of them.

"A well for the sliph."

The cavern rang with silence for a moment as everyone stared at him.

Kahlan's expression shifted to a frown. "The sliph? You think the sliph has a well here? Why would you think that?"

Richard let out a deep breath as he gestured to the southwest. "Look how far it is back to the People's Palace. It's even farther to the Wizard's Keep in Aydindril." He turned back, sharing a look with both Kahlan and Nicci. "The sorceress in charge here, at Stroyza, was supposed to keep watch and then go to the Keep to warn them that after thousands of years the barrier to the third kingdom had been breached and the greatest threat to mankind that has ever existed was now on the loose. That is Stroyza's purpose, that's why it was built here by the same people who built the barrier, and that's why a gifted person has always lived here."

Puzzled, Kahlan shrugged. "What of it?"

"So you think the builders of the barrier containing that great evil expected this one person to run all the way back to the Keep and warn everyone that the barrier had been breached by that evil? They entrusted the fate of the New World, the fate of life itself, to this one sorceress to run all the way back to the Wizard's Keep?

"The fate of the world depended on her evading half people, staying out of the clutches of a spirit king risen from the dead, his reanimated dead, occult powers, and all the natural threats and difficulties making the journey all the way across the trackless forests of the Dark Lands entailed? She had to make it across wilderness, mountain ranges, and then across more mountains in D'Hara, to finally get to the Wizard's Keep to warn the wizards there? Really? You really believe that people gifted and intelligent enough to build a barrier that stood for three thousand years, build the citadel, and build this place to watch over the barrier would do that—put the fate of the world in the hands of a sorceress from this place successfully making such a long and perilous journey?"

Nicci folded her arms as she glanced over at Kahlan. "I hate to say it, but when he puts it that way it's hard to disagree. The threat was deadly serious and profoundly difficult to handle. If it could have been ended they would have ended it back in the great war rather than lock it away behind the barrier."

"Right," Richard said, "so they wouldn't have depended on one person to travel all that way and put their faith in her making it there safely, much less make it in time for them to do something about the expanding threat.

"She would have faced the same problem we have now: time. She wouldn't be able to make it there in time, and worse, the half people that had escaped would likely already be out ahead of her, so she would not only have to evade being caught and eaten, she would have to find a way to get past them."

Kahlan stared off in thought for a moment before speaking. "A well for the sliph would have given the lookout here a swift and easy way to get back to the Keep. It makes sense."

"It's the only thing that makes sense," Richard said.

Kahlan folded her arms. "So, if there is a well here for the sliph, why didn't we see it when we were here before? Samantha showed you the shielded caves where Naja Moon wrote instructions and where they have the viewing port. So where is this well if there really is one here?"

"I don't know, exactly," Richard admitted. "I never saw it when I was here before. But I saw the shielded areas, so I figure there must be a shielded room with a well for the sliph—like there is at the Keep. All we have to do is find it."

Nicci aimed a thumb back at the granite wall that used to be the ceiling. "What if it's under there?"

"Like I said, this is a dedicated corridor with no other way in. I think that was by design to keep it safe. I think we're in the right passageway."

Kahlan was still staring off in thought. "We could get back to the palace in short order. Nicci could cure you, then. And then you would be able to stop Sulachan and end prophecy."

CHAPTER 39

In the torchlight, Richard lightly touched the Grace carved into the door. Magda Searus had left a ring with the Grace on it in the shielded hallways beyond. The ring was meant to remind him what he was fighting for. He didn't really need the reminder; he was pretty clear on what he was fighting for.

"These are the quarters for the gifted charged with watching over the barrier," he told the others. "Samantha and her mother, Irena, lived here."

"Rather ironic," Kahlan said, "that the gifted here were supposed to be guardians of what the Grace represented, and all the while Irena was working to destroy it."

"And her daughter took up that cause," Nicci said.

"Seems that is often the case with people who rule," Richard said as he pushed open the door, "even those who rule a place as small as this. They work to destroy what it is they are there to protect."

"Not all of them, Lord Rahl. Not you," Cassia said.

He briefly smiled back over his shoulder at her. "Maybe because I never wanted to rule. I just want to live my life in peace."

A few fat candles sitting in puddles of melted wax were burned almost all the way down but still lit. A few others had already used themselves up. A simple but well-made cabinet stood to the side of a low bench. A crumpled blanket had been pushed to the side of a sleeping mat. It looked like Samantha had been living in the room after wiping out the entire village, even the cats. Especially the cats.

Cassia's torch was sputtering and nearing the end of its usefulness, so she took a lantern from a shelf at the side of a dark hallway at the back of the room. She lit the lantern with a splinter lit from the torch before extinguishing it in a wooden bucket of water. The lantern cast its mellow light down the hallway that led them past dark rooms.

Vale thrust her torch ahead of her into each room to check what or who might be inside. "Nothing," she said as she pulled back out of the last one. "They look like extra bedrooms."

Farther down the hallway they passed a recess cut into the wall that Richard remembered. Three plank shelves in the niche held a few simple clay statues. One of the figures was a shepherd standing beside several sheep. Another statue was another shepherd among a small flock, his hand shielding his eyes as he apparently gazed into the distance. It seemed like a typical country theme. Shepherds were supposed to watch over their flock and watch for danger. On the lower shelves were a few books, and some folded linens.

Nicci took a quick look at the books before tossing them back on the shelves. "Nothing that helps us."

After passing several more empty, darkened rooms to the sides and checking that they were clear, they continued deeper yet into the mountain, finally coming to a stop at the face of what Richard knew to be a round stone disc. Carved in the center of the stone blocking the passageway was another grace. It was obvious what concerned the ancient builders of the place.

Richard gestured to the corroded and pitted metal plate set into the wall to the side. "My gift won't work on the shields."

Nicci leaned in and pressed the flat of her hand to the metal plate. At her touch, the stone blocking the doorway shuddered and began to roll to the right, revealing the dark passageway beyond. They all stood in silence, waiting until the heavy stone rolled out of the way to the side.

Nicci stepped through first. "Good, that will be better," she said as she went to a bracket that held a glass sphere.

As the sorceress reached for it, the sphere began to glow. It brightened even more when she lifted it out of the bracket. The sphere sent its distinctive greenish radiance down the long hallway into the distance.

Unlike the rough cave walls of the rest of the village, these walls beyond the shielded stone entrance had been laboriously smoothed and squared with the floor and ceiling. There were no decorations of any kind on the flat walls, other than the very faint natural variations in the creamy consistency of the rock. This was a part of the mountain that was all composed of the softer rock, with none of the granite in it.

Being devoid of so much as a shelf or niche or bench, the hallway had a strangely sterile feel to it. At least back in the previous hallway there had been the niche with shelves holding statues of shepherds and a few books, but beyond the shields there were no such simple amenities. He guessed it seemed logical, because the passage was only a means to get to the areas that mattered.

"Are there any rooms in here?" Nicci asked.

Richard shook his head. "It's just an outer passageway with a shield at the other end. I think it may be designed this way to trap intruders."

Some shields were like that. They allowed people who didn't belong to get in only so far, and then prevented them from getting back out. Such an arrangement discouraged intruders because scouts never returned with reports.

As they went deeper through the dark, dead-silent passage, rather than making sharp turns the corridor curved gently in places, meandering on its way until they reached another of the stone capstones blocking the way forward. As Richard had remembered, there hadn't been a single room in the passageway.

Nicci saw the metal plate for the shield and without delay pressed the flat of her hand to it. As she did so, the light sphere she was holding brightened. Richard suspected that was an indication that the shields sensed that she was not an intruder, but rather someone who was allowed inside.

The second shield stone was much bigger and heavier. The mountain itself rumbled as the enormous round stone disc rolled to the right into a slot cut into the rock. The corridor beyond was wider and its walls were more precisely smoothed and squared, as if to indicate its elevated level of importance. The stone of the walls had also been laboriously polished. Kahlan touched her fingers to the creamy surface, amazed at the work that had been put into smoothing and polishing the walls deep in the mountain.

"Why would they go to this much trouble?" Kahlan asked.

"I think to stress the importance of what was in here," Richard said. "Putting this much care into it showed all the future generations living in the simple caves that it was an important place and they needed to heed their responsibilities."

"Nice theory," Nicci said. "Too bad it didn't work."

Richard conceded the point with a small grunt.

Around a tight curve in the passageway, they began encountering symbols carved into the stone of the walls. Carving the symbols, rather than using paint of some sort, insured that they would endure for many generations.

The carved writing was all done in the symbols of the language of Creation. The farther they went down the passage, not only did the symbols become more numerous until they covered the entire wall to the left from floor to ceiling, but the symbology also became more complex.

"And so are there any rooms in this hall?" Nicci asked.

"No," Richard said. She was clearly making a point that if there was no room with a well for the sliph, then there was no way for them to get out of the tomb of caverns.

Nicci scanned the writing as she trailed farther behind Richard and Kahlan. The two Mord-Sith moved along the opposite side of the hall, gazing silently at the wall of writing. The farther they all went, the brighter the corridor became. Natural light flooded in through a small round hole carved in the wall. The light coming in fell on the opposite wall, lighting the end of the passageway.

"This is it," Richard said, pointing toward the opening. "This is the viewing port they used to watch the barrier."

Kahlan stretched up on her tiptoes to take a quick glance out the port. "Do you think that when Irena saw the barrier failing she told Ludwig Dreier? Maybe he was the one who came up with the scheme for Jit to capture us."

"I suspect that it was actually Hannis Arc's doing," Richard said. "He would have known from the Cerulean scrolls about the barrier failing long before Irena would have seen it. After all, he had long been making preparations for Sulachan's return. I don't see how Jit would have had any knowledge of us, and yet she used a very specific spell to draw both you and me in. Hannis Arc would have had the knowledge to direct her how to do such a thing."

Kahlan sighed as she finally turned away from the port. "I think you're right."

Nicci held the light sphere up to see better as she read some of the writing on the wall. "I agree. Hannis Arc would've had the motive and the means."

Richard nodded. "He has wanted to eliminate the House of Rahl since he was young. He has been plotting it for decades. I suspect he is behind the Hedge Maid being there in the swamp and her using an occult spell to draw us in."

"All the more reason you need to kill him," Nicci said in a distracted voice without looking away from the writing on the wall.

Richard knew she was right about that. The details no longer mattered. It only mattered that if Hannis Arc was not stopped, they were all going to be dead.

"So," Nicci asked as she finally straightened and looked back at Richard. "Where is the well with the sliph so that we can get out of here?"

Richard raked his fingers back through his hair. "I'm afraid that I don't know. We're going to have to find it."

"Find it how?" Nicci asked in a very pointed manner. It reminded him of the time long ago when she had been his teacher, trying to teach him to use his gift.

They all glanced around the hallway. Other than the writing incised into the wall, the place was featureless.

"Lord Rahl, there aren't any other rooms," Cassia said, adding emphasis to Nicci's point without intending it. "There were none on the way in here once we were past the shields."

"Maybe the room with the well is down a different tunnel," Vale offered.

Richard shook his head. "No. Everything that was done here was done carefully, from the viewing port to the smooth walls to the shielding. They wouldn't have put the well in a place that wasn't safeguarded."

Kahlan gestured to the viewing port. "That hole through the side of the mountain isn't very deep, and there is already a hole there, so maybe Nicci could use her gift to break out some of the rock. Then we could get out of the trap of this cave."

"Go stick your head in and have a look," Richard said. "This face of the mountain is a sheer cliff. Even if we could expand the hole, the opening is thousands of feet up the side of a sheer cliff."

"Maybe we could find ropes," Vale offered.

"You looked in all the rooms on the way in here," Richard said. "Did you see any ropes? Thousands of feet of ropes?"

Vale's face showed her discouragement. "I guess not."

"I guess that unless we can fly, that hole won't offer us a way out," Kahlan said, equally discouraged.

"What's more important," Richard said, "is that even if we could get out through that hole and somehow climb down, what good would it do us? We're still too far from the People's Palace to make it in time. With this poison in me I would be dead long before we ever got there."

"You're right," Kahlan said with a sigh. "The only way is the sliph. If there really is a well somewhere in here."

Nicci planted a hand on her hip as she looked around in a thoughtful manner. "When Samantha showed you this place and told you about their mission to warn others of the barrier, she said that her mother had to go to the Keep to warn everyone. She and her husband—on the face of it, anyway–set out on that journey. She always talked of it as a long journey on foot. That's the way it was always presented."

Richard looked up with sudden comprehension. "They thought they had to travel overland to get back there. That means they didn't know about the well with the sliph. They never gave any indication that they had any knowledge of a sliph."

Nicci smiled as she flicked a finger toward the wall. "Because they couldn't read this writing, so they wouldn't have any reason to suspect there was another way other than an overland journey. Over generations, the people here had lost the ability to understand the language of Creation."

Richard tapped a thumb against the hilt of his sword. "If they lost that knowledge, then they likely would have also lost knowledge of the room with the well, especially if it is hidden and shielded."

Kahlan stepped toward them. "Unless the knowledge of such a hidden room was passed down, then they would no more know about it than how to read this writing. They likely lost the link to that room."

Cassia scrunched up her nose. "How could they lose a room?"

Richard ran his hand lightly along the wall with the language of Creation carved into it. "That room would have been important, and also a dangerous way for an invader to come here, so it probably has a secret way in. There would be shields or some means of protecting the well that also kept any enemy from getting into the caves." He looked over at the wall. "It's probably written here, in all these instructions."

"But none of the people here knew about any of this?" Cassia asked.

"No," Richard said. "Over all that time since the great war there were probably missing links in the lineage of the gifted who would have been able to pass on all their knowledge–you know, important gifted people who died unexpectedly before they could teach younger people the language of Creation or other important information, like how they could quickly get a warning to the Keep by using the sliph."

Richard gestured to the wall. "From what I learned when I was first brought here, the gifted people here had only sketchy information about their duty here, and they knew virtually nothing about this writing. That means the instructions were here all along, but useless to them.

"If they couldn't read this writing, they wouldn't know about the secret room."

"You still really think the well is in a secret room?" Kahlan asked.

"Well it certainly isn't in any room we've looked in, and I think we looked in them all. I'm convinced there is a well here. So it has to be hidden, or shielded, or both."

Kahlan sighed as she gazed at all the writing. "I hope you're right, Richard."

He turned to the sorceress. "Nicci, start looking for anything that talks about the Keep, or anything that explains the procedure for when the barrier fails."

"Already looking," she murmured under her breath as she ran her hand along under the writing while she deciphered it in her head.

Richard swept his hand along a section of the wall. "You can disregard this part, here," he told Nicci. "This is Naja Moon's account, and I've already read all of this. There isn't any mention of the well in it."

When he looked back, Nicci was squatted down, leaning in, urgently inspecting a line of symbols. "What? Do you see something?"

Nicci tapped the symbols and looked up at him.

"Maybe. It says here that when the barrier to the third kingdom fails, the people here must protect the flock."

"Well," Richard said, "when you get down to it, that was ultimately their purpose here."

Nicci looked up at him as he came over to where she was reading. "Yes, but look at this symbol, here, at the end of that part. I'm not quite sure what it means."

Richard squatted down beside her to have a look at where she was pointing.

"Do you understand it?" the sorceress asked.

"Odd combination," Richard mumbled to himself as he studied the symbol.

Cassia, Vale, and Kahlan gathered behind him as he translated it to himself.

Richard suddenly stood.

Nicci rose up beside him. "Do you know what it says?"

Richard looked back the way they had come in. "Yes. It says 'Let the shepherd guide you.'"

"Does that mean something significant?" Kahlan asked.

"Yes," Richard said, still staring back up the passageway. "I think I know where the well is."

Everyone followed Richard as he rushed back the way they had come through the dark passageway. Cassia trotted to catch up and stay at his right side, holding the lantern out to light the dark hallway for them once the light from the viewing port had faded into the distance behind them. Kahlan, with Nicci on the other side of her, took long strides to stay close on Richard's left side. The eerie green luminescence from the light sphere played across the smooth walls of the passageway, twisting with every hurried step Nicci took. Vale, still holding a torch, brought up the rear.

Since there was no one else in the caves and it wasn't possible for anyone to get in to surprise them, they hadn't closed the shielded stones. After he went past the second of the huge stone discs, Nicci reached past Kahlan and snatched his shirtsleeve to get his attention.

"Do you really think the room with the sliph's well would be outside the shielded area?"

"Yes," he said without explaining.

"That doesn't seem likely," she insisted.

"It is if that secret room is shielded as well, as I suspect it is."

Satisfied that he must be right, or simply not wanting to argue the point for the moment, she didn't answer.

When they had almost reached the end of the hallway back into the quarters for the gifted of Stroyza, Richard came to a stop in front of the small niche with the three shelves.

He gestured to the two small statues of shepherds with their flocks. "'Let the shepherd guide you,'" he quoted from the writing on the wall.

Without questioning, Nicci reached out and took hold of one of the shepherds. Nothing happened.

"There isn't any metal plate for a shield," she said. "The statue doesn't respond, so that can't be the key to the shield."

"Try the other one," Kahlan suggested.

Nicci reached out and grasped the one shielding his eyes with a hand. They all waited, glancing around for any sign, as she kept hold of the statue. The hallways remained silent. There was no sound of a stone rolling out of the way or anything else to indicate there was a shield there.

Nicci let go of the statue. "Nothing."

Richard couldn't believe it. He had been sure that the shepherds were the answer to the words on the wall, instructing them to let the shepherd guide them. He didn't know what else to do. This had been the answer he had been looking for and now that he found it, it didn't work.

"What do we do now?" Kahlan asked.

Richard could only stare at the two small clay statues. "I'm not sure."

"Are you still sure that there is a sliph in here, somewhere?" Cassia asked.

Richard looked to her blue eyes for a moment and then looked back at the statues. Looking into her eyes, he was struck with the realization of how much they all depended on him, in everything both large and small. She was looking to him to be the magic against magic.

He reached out and gripped one then the other of the statues.

"That's kind of strange. They're attached to the shelf."

"Maybe so they wouldn't accidentally be knocked off and broken," Vale suggested.

Richard ran a thumb along his jaw as he stared at the statues, trying to figure out how the shepherd was supposed to guide them.

He squinted at the statue of the man shielding his eyes. More than one thing about it seemed odd.

"It's sitting at a funny angle on the shelf, don't you think?" he asked, looking at the four faces watching him. "And I don't think that it's attached to the shelf so that it can't be knocked off and broken. After all, how would it get knocked off a shelf set back in a niche like this?"

"What are you getting at?" Kahlan asked.

He looked over his shoulder in the direction the statue was looking with its hand shielding its eyes.

He frowned as he glanced over at Kahlan. "Do you see the direction he is looking?"

"I'm all turned around in here," she admitted. "I'm not sure."

Nicci was staring at the statue. "It's looking to the southwest," she said, half to herself.

Richard nodded. "Toward the Wizard's Keep."

He and Nicci shared a look of understanding.

The other thing he thought odd about the statue was that all the details looked thick. Richard had sculpted statues and he understood the process quite well. It wasn't that these two were poorly made, but rather that the details looked too bulky to his eye.

With everyone dead and the cave collapsed and buried, Richard didn't think that breaking the statue was going to be much of a problem. He pulled his knife from its sheath at his belt. Holding it by the blade, he used the handle like a hammer to whack the statue.

The clay shattered in an unexpected manner and a piece fell off. Where the broken piece had been, Richard saw the gleam of metal under the clay. He struck the statue half a dozen times, breaking the clay away to reveal that there was the same metal statue underneath, only properly detailed. The whole thing had been covered with clay slurry to encase it; that was why it looked too bulky to him.

"Why in the world would they make a statue like that?" Kahlan asked as she frowned up at Richard.

"If I'm right, to hide the sliph."

He used his knife handle to hammer the other sculpture and it, too, shattered to reveal metal under the covering of clay. He reached in and broke off the remaining pieces, exposing the two metal sculptures of shepherds with their flocks.

"My gift doesn't work," he said to Nicci. "You try it."

Nicci reached in and grasped one of the statues. They all glanced around the hallway, expecting something to happen, but the hallway remained silent and still.

He gestured to the other. "Try holding both."

Nicci reached in and wrapped her hand around the other shepherd, so that she was holding one in each hand. They all looked around the silent hallway.

Still, nothing happened.

With a disappointed sigh, she let her hands slip off the little statues. "I can't explain why there is metal under the clay, but it apparently isn't a trigger mechanism for a shield. It must simply be an ancient oddity."

They all stared in frustration at the small statues of shepherds, trying to imagine their purpose. Nothing about what the original builders of the sentinel village of Stroyza did was random or pointless. Everything had been carefully planned not according to what was happening and what they feared, but according to the things they knew of the star shift and the Twilight Count. It all had a purpose.

He was at a loss to understand what that purpose was.

Cassia gestured with her lantern. "Lord Rahl, I don't think you are listening to the real meaning of the writing."

Richard's brow furrowed. "What do you mean?"

"It said 'Let the shepherd guide you.'"

Richard opened his hands in bewilderment. "I know. Nicci tried it. Nothing happened."

Cassia gave him a crafty smile. "She isn't our shepherd. You are our shepherd, Lord Rahl. You are the one who guides us."

"But my gift doesn't work."

She tipped her head at him in a meaningful way. "Maybe it isn't looking for the gift. Maybe it's looking for the shepherd."

Richard stared at her for a moment, and then turned and grabbed both smooth metal statues.

He felt them both warm under his touch. The shelves began to shudder. The stone floor trembled. All the way around the niche, the wall began to crack in straight lines. Bits of stone flaked away from the ever-widening cracks as a section of the wall with the niche broke free and started to move in away from the hallway. The stone cracked and popped until the section of wall with the niche jolted free and swung back into a dark room.

"I don't understand," Richard said. "My gift doesn't work."

Nicci looked over at him. "You read the Cerulean scrolls, Richard. We're dealing with forces here that transcend the gift."

Nicci slipped in first to provide light from the sphere she'd brought with her. Richard followed, ducking under the short opening so he wouldn't hit his head. Kahlan did the same, staying close behind him. When the sorceress stepped into the room, a dozen light spheres in iron brackets around the outside of the circular room all brightened at her presence, illuminating the entire room with the same green luminescence common to light spheres.

There, in the center of the room, capped with a domed ceiling, was a short, circular stone wall. It looked like most of the other wells for the sliph that Richard had seen.

Kahlan slipped a hand around his biceps as she stared at the well in amazement. "You were right, Richard. Dear spirits, you were right."

"It's hard to believe this has been here for thousands of years," Nicci said as she, too, stared at the well. "The way the room was sealed, it's pretty clear that no one has seen this since it was built in the time of the great war."

"Richard was right," Kahlan said. "They lost the link

to the knowledge of the past and none of them even knew it was here, right by the quarters for the gifted."

Kahlan beamed with a bright smile as she gazed up at him. She was relieved that they weren't trapped in the caves after all.

"This will get us to the People's Palace," she said. "As soon as we get there, Nicci will finally be able to get the poisonous touch of death out of you."

Richard only smiled back. For now, he couldn't let her know that he could never allow that to happen.

Cassia bent over the edge, holding the lantern high to have a look down inside. "I've seen this kind of well before, at the People's Palace."

"That's right," Richard said. "We've used that one before."

Nicci leaned over the short wall beside Cassia, holding out the light sphere to see better down inside.

"No sliph," she announced.

Richard knew they wouldn't see the sliph yet. He stepped up beside Nicci. "We'll have to wake her."

"How do we do that?" Vale asked.

"I have to call her," Richard said back over his shoulder. "I've done it before."

"When your gift worked," Kahlan reminded him.

Richard let out a deep sigh. "You're right." He gestured to Nicci. "Put down that sphere so you can help me. Add your gift to what I do and maybe together we can wake her."

Richard leaned over the well and crossed his wrists, placing the ancient symbols on the silver bands he wore over one another, pressing them tightly together. As he had done in the past, he envisioned the sliph coming to him. He had called her from her sleep before and brought her to him, but he didn't know if it was actually his gift that powered that call.

He had traveled in the sliph a number of times before. Sometimes he had been reluctant. This time he was eager. Time was running out and he needed to get to the palace.

Nicci placed her hands over his fists, closing her fingers tightly over his. He could feel the tingling warmth of her magic flowing into the bands at his wrists, heating them with that power. It was a decidedly uncomfortable feeling, but not painful. He knew that sometimes magic, even magic being used for good, felt that way.

Richard closed his eyes. "Come to me," he whispered. "I need you. Come to me."

For the longest time, they stood leaning in over the sliph's well, Richard pressing the wristbands together, Nicci's hands closed over his. When he slitted his eyes to check down into the darkness to see if the sliph was coming yet, he could see that the stones lined the inside of the well to quite a depth, but they gradually faded away into the darkness.

He saw that his silver wristbands, covered in symbols made up of the language of Creation, were glowing with an intense yellowish light. That light at his wrists—whether from Nicci's magic or her magic plus something she was pulling from him, he didn't know—was so intense that he could see the bones of his wrists right through his flesh. He could also see the bones in both his hands and Nicci's. That light lit the inside of the dome above them and shot down into the depths of the well, disappearing into the darkness far below as if headed on a mission to find the sliph.

For the longest time they all stood still, barely breathing, as they focused on their need for the sliph to come to them. For all that time there was only silence from below.

Richard felt the soles of his boots tingling, and then the ground abruptly began to rumble. His heart beat faster as the trembling became stronger. Dust was shaken free from the walls.

As he listened, he could hear a rushing sound deep down in the well. Small pebbles and grit on the ground danced with the vibration. Dust rose from the stone floor.

A column of air, driven up from far below, suddenly blew Richard and Nicci's hair upward as it blasted out of the well. They both quickly pulled back, fearing they might be hit by the sliph as she raced up from below.

Silvery liquid shot up to the top of the rim, threatening to explode out of the confines of the well, but it slopped along the sides of the stone enclosure as it abruptly stopped. The roaring sound stopped. The rumbling stopped. The room fell quiet again.

The liquid in the well drew up in the center, rising in a reflective column that looked like nothing so much as molten silver. The continually undulating surface drew into features as a face formed. The face, like a polished silver statue, had risen nearly to eye level with Richard. It looked around the room briefly but then the gaze finally settled on him.

"You summoned me?" the sliph announced. It didn't exactly sound happy about it. The voice had a strange quality that seemed to echo around the room even though the rest of their voices didn't.

"Yes!" Richard said as he urgently leaned toward the sliph. "We need to travel."

"Very well," the sliph said. "Will you be traveling alone?"

"No." Richard swept an arm around the room. "All of us will be going. All of us need to travel."

The silver face coolly appraised the four women before looking back at Richard. "As you wish. All of you will need to step forward to allow me to see who among you may travel."

Richard thought the sliph was being uncharacteristically reserved and distant. Usually she was as eager to please as she was to travel. In the past the sliph had always been solicitous, bordering on pandering, always wanting to travel with him. Although he was somewhat confused by the chilly reception, he ignored it as he urged the others to step forward.

As they stood close around the well, the sliph extended a silvery arm, brushing it briefly across the foreheads of Cassia, Vale, Nicci, and Kahlan, touching Richard last.

"Not ideal," the sliph announced, "but each of you has enough of what is needed. I can take you all if you insist."

"We're trapped in here," Richard said, his frustration with her strange behavior growing by the moment. His annoyance increasingly crept into his tone. "Anyone left here will die. So, yes, I insist that we all travel."

The sliph assessed him for a moment with her liquid quicksilver gaze before finally answering. "Very well."

Richard lifted his sword a few inches from its scabbard and then let it drop back down. "We have no other way out of here. I need to take my sword with me."

"Your need for that object is not important to me."

He had to put an effort into keeping his temper in check. "I know that in the past traveling with it was lethal. Is there a way for me to bring it this time? That's what I need to know."

The lustrous metallic face studied him a moment before the sliph again reached out to glide a silvery hand along his brow, then moved it down to touch the sword resting in its scabbard.

"This dangerous thing belongs to you," the cool voice said.

"Yes. It's my sword."

"I mean, it is linked to you through magic. It is bonded to you."

"Yes, that's right."

"In addition to that link to this object, you now have death in you. Because of the link to you, it will not harm the others."

"What about me?" Richard asked. "Will it harm me?"

The silver face showed no emotion. "I told you. You have death in you."

It wasn't a question. "Yes. What of it?"

"If you did not have death within you, it would kill them once they entered me. That object would bring death to you as well if you brought it with you, except that you already have death in you. Since you already have death in you, it can't bring death into you."

"Why not?" Nicci asked, clearly not convinced.

The sliph lifted her brow at the sorceress. "Because you can't be killed twice. He is already dead. At least, to a degree and as far as the magic is concerned. He is already crossing the veil, already irretrievably beyond hope of escaping that death taking him, beyond hope of remaining alive. Since death already has him in its grip, it can't take him a second time."

"We don't have death in us," Nicci pressed. "So why wouldn't it kill the rest of us?"

The silver face looked displeased to have to explain it. "The object is designed to kill. It seeks to bring death to the living. He is living, but he has death in him, so as long as he is in me along with you, the magic within the object is locked on him. It has a purpose designed into it. It cannot go outside that purpose. You might say that because of his condition, the object is fixated on him for now, so you are able to slip through without drawing its lethal magic."

"So then I can bring it," Richard said, eager not to have to discuss it. Kahlan was already looking more than a little alarmed and he didn't want to get her any more upset than she already was.

"Yes," the sliph said. "But you must understand that it will increase the death in you."

Kahlan planted her fists on her hips. "What does that mean?"

The reflective gaze turned to her. "It means that it will steal some of the life from him and it will add instead to the power of death within him. It will be doing its job. It will move the placement of the veil within him. It will shift the balance toward death."

Kahlan glared. "You mean it will cut the time he has in the world of life so that he will die sooner."

"Yes. Traveling with that object will draw away some of his life and add power to the force of the other side of the veil, add power to the death he already has in him, but since he is already in the grip of death it cannot kill him."

"By how much time?" Kahlan asked. "How much time will it steal from his life?"

"I am no expert and I can't say for certain. But I am able to tell that it will drain away some of his remaining life force."

Kahlan grabbed his sleeve. "Richard, you can't afford to take that risk. You need to leave the sword here."

He remembered the sliph telling him before that when he put her to sleep she went to be with her spirit. That meant that at least some part of her had been called from the underworld, and that concerned him. The sliph would have direct knowledge of that line between life and death.

He turned to Kahlan. "We don't have a way to get back in here, except through her. I can't come back for it, and I can't leave the sword here."

"Yes you can," she insisted. "Richard, this is about your life."

"No, it's about everyone's life." He leaned toward her

and lowered his voice. "It's the key to something. Something mentioned in the Cerulean scrolls." He cocked his head to the side, expecting her to complete that concept without having to say it aloud.

Recognition suddenly appeared in her eyes. The sword was the key to the power of Orden. The power of Orden had to do with the Twilight Count, prophecy, and everything else that was happening. The key to that kind of power was far too valuable to abandon.

The sliph would know of the line and the balance between worlds. He had no doubt that she was correct about the cost of taking the sword with him.

But it was a cost that really didn't matter.

"All right, then," he said, turning from Kahlan back to the sliph. "Let's get going. We need to hurry." He put a foot up on the wall. "We need to get to the People's Palace."

The silvery face frowned. "Where?"

CHAPTER 42

R ichard paused and looked up. "The People's Palace. In D'Hara. We need to travel to the People's
Palace."

The sliph stared without comprehension. "I don't
know of such a place. I can't travel there."

Richard let his foot slip off the wall and back down
on the floor. "What are you talking about? Of course
you can. I've traveled with you to and from the People's
Palace in the past."

The sliph shook her head. Little silver droplets fell
back into the well to join the rolling quicksilver.

"I have never seen you before," the sliph insisted.
"You have never traveled with me."

Richard stared, trying to figure out why she would
say such a thing. "Of course you have." He swept an
arm out, as if to indicate the places far away they had
gone together. "I've traveled with you a number of
times. You have pleased me."

A frown of displeasure grew on the silver brow. "It is
not my responsibility to please anyone, even you. If you
want to travel, we will travel, but I am not required to
please you as well. Now, do you still wish to travel?"

Richard and Kahlan shared a look. He cleared his throat and started over.

"We need to travel. We have to get out of here. You are our only way out of here. We must all travel. If you are no longer able to take us to the People's Palace–"

"I told you, I have never been to such a place. I cannot take you there."

Richard forced himself to be patient. "All right, then, where are you able to take us?"

The sliph looked at him as if he had lost his mind. "To the place I am supposed to take you."

Richard wiped a hand back across the side of his face as he reminded himself to be patient. He dared not anger her and have her vanish. The sliph, after all, was their only way out of the caves.

"Where are you supposed to take us? Are you able to name the place?"

"Of course," the sliph said with cool detachment as the head drew back a bit. "The Wizard's Keep."

"The Keep," he repeated as he stared at her. "You can go to the Keep. And where else can you travel? What other places?"

The frown on her silver brow returned. "Other places? There are no other places. There is only here and the Keep. Those are the only two places. You summoned me. I am here to take you from here to the Keep."

Before Richard could say anything else, Kahlan put a hand on his arm to get him to be quiet so she could speak.

"Sliph, are you saying that you were created for the sole purpose of traveling from here to the Keep?"

The sliph turned her puzzled look to Kahlan. "Of course. Where else would I go?" The displeased frown grew again. "And why do you call me by that name . . . sliph?"

"You mean that's not your name?" Kahlan asked.

"No. My name is Lucy."

Richard looked at Kahlan out of the corner of his eye. "That explains a lot."

Kahlan leaned closer to Richard and lowered her voice. "We have to get out of here if we hope to get to the palace."

Richard nodded. "If she can get us to the Keep we can take the sliph from there to the palace."

Kahlan's gaze stayed on his. "That will work."

Richard turned back to the well. "Lucy, we would be pleased if you could take us all to the Keep."

She shot him a silver scowl. "I told you, I am not here to please you. If you all wish to travel to the Keep, I can take you there. But that is all I am required to do for you."

Richard glanced one last time at Nicci and Kahlan. He turned his tone more official and less friendly.

"Of course. I understand, Lucy. Now, we need to travel to the Keep on urgent business. We need you to get us all there as swiftly as possible, and then you may return to your soul in the other world."

"I would like very much to again be with my soul." She bowed her silver head in a single nod of agreement. "Climb up and I will take you all to the Keep."

"Thank you," Richard said as he climbed up on the wall. He turned and extended a hand down to Kahlan.

Before he could help the others up onto the wall, a silver arm swept out over the side of the well and pulled them all from their feet. He had time only to gasp a last breath before she plunged them down into the silvery liquid.

The world abruptly went dark and silent.

Breathe, Lucy said to them. Her voice was an urgent, oppressive command in his mind.

Richard remembered too late that he had not in-structed Cassia and Vale on how traveling in the living quicksilver worked. He hoped they would heed the sliph's instruction. If they didn't, they would arrive at the Keep dead.

More concerned with everything that he had to do than the process of traveling in a sliph, and being familiar enough with how it worked, he ignored his trepidation and drew the liquid silver into his lungs.

His grip with his left hand around the hilt of his sword tightened as the sensation of drowning tightened his chest.

Mercifully, the sensation and the associated panic eased.

With a feeling something like falling through space and at the same time floating without moving, the long journey began.

Unlike the way it had always felt in the past, this time it was not at all pleasant. It was a rather rough and painful feeling of being dragged, rather than carried along effortlessly. His whole body felt as if unseen forces were trying to pull it apart. The silver liquid burned in his lungs. He could feel the magic from the sword burning into his soul.

He tried his best to keep his mind on where they were going and what they needed to do, rather than on how unpleasant it was traveling in Lucy.

He needed to bring the sword with him, but he could feel the life leaching out of him by the moment as the poison within grew stronger.

*B*reathe, a stern voice in his head commanded.

He couldn't bring himself to obey. He didn't care to obey.

Greenish light felt like an apparition moving to and fro in his mind's vision. Even though his eyes were closed, the light made his eyes hurt as if someone were gouging their thumbs against his eyeballs. He heard harsh, jarring sounds, but couldn't make them out. He also heard echoing voices, as if they were coming to him through a long tube. He didn't know what those voices were saying.

He didn't care what they were saying. He didn't care if he ever moved again. He didn't care if he ever breathed again.

It seemed like too much of an effort to care about anything.

Breathe, the stern voice in his head commanded again.

Someone hooked their arms under his. More hands grabbed his shirt and others his belt at the small of his back. People yelled and cursed as they struggled with him. Despite how hard he tried, he couldn't understand the words. He stopped trying and instead let himself sink back down into the numb, silvery haze.

The hands all over him tugged harder at his clothes, his arms. They finally hauled him up above the undulating surface. The rolling surface tossed his limp form about, making him feel sick. He began to drift away from the hands.

Again the hands grabbed hold and lifted him as the people pulling him to the edge grunted with the effort. They finally succeeded in flopping him over the top of the wall. His head and arms hung down, the silver liquid running off him.

A hand repeatedly slapped him on the back hard.

"Breathe, Richard! Breathe!"

He recognized that it was Nicci's voice. She sounded desperate. He wasn't exactly sure why.

"Breathe!" That time it was Kahlan. She sounded even more desperate. He could hear panicked tears in her voice.

That sparked something in him. He didn't want Kahlan to feel desperate. He didn't want her to worry for him, to cry for him.

"Breathe!" she called out again through gritted teeth.

Richard did as she said and expelled the silver liquid from his lungs. It ran down the side of the stone wall of the well into a puddle on the floor.

He saw blood in the silvery liquid collecting on the floor. He thought that maybe there was more blood than silver liquid.

With his lungs emptied he felt the urgent need for air. He gasped a breath. It burned. He held his breath, not wanting to take another.

"Breathe, Richard!" Kahlan yelled in his ear. "Breathe!"

He drew another breath for her. It was difficult, it was painful, but he did it. His throat made a hoarse noise as he pulled in another breath. More blood ran in strings into the puddle under him.

He ached all over. His head felt like it was being crushed. He recognized that the sick feeling and the pain were from the poison of death in him. It had grown stronger. He could feel that he was running out of time.

Cassia, Vale, and Nicci gripped his arms and belt to pull him the rest of the way out of the well. He couldn't help. As his legs came over the wall, they laid him on the ground. They were panting with the effort.

Richard lay on the ground for a time, each breath shallow and painful. He coughed up more blood. He could feel it running over the side of his face. He didn't think he could get up.

And then he felt a searing jolt of magic explode in his mind as Nicci pressed her hands to the sides of his head. It sent such a shot of energy through him that it made his eyes open wide. It brought him crashing back to the world of life.

He was suddenly and fully conscious again.

He sat up in a rush, panting, wiping the blood from his chin on his shirtsleeve.

"Where are we? Are we there? Are we in the Keep?"

Nicci and Kahlan shared a look.

"What?" Richard asked, looking from one to the other. "What's wrong?"

"We're not exactly sure," Kahlan said. She aimed a thumb over her shoulder at the silver face leaning over, looking down at him. "She insists this is the Wizard's Keep."

"It is the Keep," the voice from the well said.

Richard worked to catch his breath as he drew his knees up and leaned back against the side of the well. He put his elbows on his knees and held his head for a moment. What Nicci had done made him feel much better, but he still felt far from good.

He squinted in the greenish light, looking around, try-

ing to figure out where they were. It most certainly was
not the place where the sliph's well was. The round
room with a domed ceiling was much the same as the
place they had come from. And like the place they had
left in the caves, with the exception of the round well
made of mortared stones, this place was also entirely
carved from soft rock rather than built of granite blocks.
The difference from the caves back in Stroyza was that
there was a doorway with no door.

Instead, just outside the doorway and dimly lit by the
light from the glass sphere and candle lanterns in the
well room, he saw a hanging cloth almost completely
covering the opening. Oddly enough, the off-white,
silky cloth had symbols painted all over it.

Richard at last stood, getting his balance for a moment, then drew his sword. The distinctive ring of steel
echoed around the room as he checked the weapon. The
sword appeared to have suffered no ill effects from being in the quicksilver liquid. It looked fine. In fact, it
looked more than fine. It had a dark metallic gleam to
it, unlike anything he had ever seen before.

When he looked up, Nicci was watching him. "It has
been touched by the world of the dead."

Richard gave her a crooked smile. "It wears death
well."

Nicci and Kahlan both smiled, even though they
hadn't looked like they expected to.

He looked back over his shoulder at Lucy. "How
long? How long did it take us to get here? How long
have we been traveling?"

The silver face regarded him with a puzzled look.
"How long? As long as from there to here. That is how
long it is."

"No, I mean time. How long has it taken us to get
here from back in the caves? How much time?"

"You were in me," she said as if that should explain it. "It was that long."

Before he could question Lucy in more detail, Nicci touched his arm to stop him. "Her soul is in the world of the dead. She is partly a creature of that world."

"Well I don't—"

"A part of that timeless world," Nicci said, lifting an eyebrow at him to prompt him.

He paused. "Oh. I see what you mean."

"We never traveled this far in the sliph," Kahlan said. "By how hungry I feel, I can tell you that it has to be a number of days."

"I would have to agree," Nicci said. "I wish I could say it was only a few days, but I think it was more. It was a long way from the Dark Lands all the way back to the Keep."

Cassia tugged on some loose red leather at her waist. "Long enough for me to lose some weight."

Richard nodded. "By the looks of your faces, I'd say we've all gone without food for close to a week."

"That's about the way my stomach feels," Vale confirmed. "If there are any rats down here, I'd happily eat one."

Richard looked around at the room he didn't recognize, at the strange cloth hanging just beyond the doorway. "So, where in the Keep are we, exactly? We need to go find the sliph. As long as we're here, we ought to let Verna and Chase know what's going on." He glanced at Vale, showing her a small smile. "And maybe grab a bite to eat."

"Well, that's a good question." Kahlan glanced toward the doorway with the cloth hanging over it. "Lucy says that we're in the Keep, but I don't know where in the Keep. I've never seen this place."

"If this really is the Keep," Nicci said under her breath

so that Lucy wouldn't hear her. "It's possible she doesn't really know what she's talking about. Maybe those who created her also deceived her and as a result she is only repeating what she was told. Maybe she is only telling us that this is the Keep because someone wants us to believe that."

Richard frowned at both of them. "I don't understand. Kahlan, you grew up here. If anyone knows the Keep it would be you. One look out there should tell you whether or not it's the Keep."

"You would think," she said, cryptically in a confidential voice.

Richard stood up straighter, finally feeling steady on his feet. "Let's go have a look, then. It shouldn't take long to find out one way or another."

He took a step away from the well, then stopped and turned back. The silver face was staring at him.

"Thank you, Lucy. Is there anything you were supposed to tell us when you brought us here? Any message?"

"Message? No. I was simply to bring travelers to the Keep. That is my purpose."

He considered all he had learned in the scrolls and how the people in the great war, like Sulachan, had been using that knowledge as well as prophecy in moves that spanned millennia. He had a thought and rephrased the question.

"Did you know who you would be bringing here?"

The silver face twitched in recognition. "Before, when I first came to be as I am now and was given my purpose, I was told that I might bring the shepherd here."

Richard glanced at Kahlan before again addressing the restless, undulating quicksilver face. "The shepherd. Anything else you were told? Anything at all?"

"No, just that."

"All right," Richard said as he straightened the baldric on his shoulder and the sword at his hip. "I'm the shepherd, I guess, so you've completed your task. You may go back into the long sleep. There should be no reason to return from where you brought us, so we will likely never have need of your services again, but if we do, I will call you."

"Are you saying that you are the shepherd?"

Richard nodded. "That's right."

"There is one thing I was supposed to tell the shepherd about this place."

"And what would that be?"

"I was told to tell you that when you enter the place out there beyond my room, you must be careful."

Richard looked toward the doorway and the strange cloth hanging just beyond. "'Be careful out there.'" That sounded like good advice, but it seemed strange that they would have wanted to pass that message on but nothing as to why or what the danger might be. "Anything else? Were you told why we were to be careful?"

"No, that was all. I don't know what it means, but that is what I was to tell you."

Richard took a deep breath as he glanced again to the doorway. "Thank you for your service, Lucy. You may go back to sleep and be with your soul. Rest in peace."

"That would please me."

It would please him as well, but he didn't say so.

With that, the reflective silver face melted back down into the churning silver pool, and then the entire liquid mass began to sink with ever-increasing speed. Richard looked over the side and saw one last reflection and then it was gone. He could see only darkness down in the well.

He turned back to the others. "That was strange."

"Not as strange as what is beyond that doorway," Nicci said.

"Well, there was no other way out of the caves of Stroyza except to come here. It's not like we had any choice."

None of them could argue.

Rather than asking Nicci to explain, Richard started for the doorway to have a look for himself. Nicci brought a light sphere, while the two Mord-Sith had lanterns taken from pegs in the far wall where another half-dozen lanterns still hung, covered in a layer of dust so thick it made them look like they were carved from dirt.

Richard came to a stop when he saw the small symbol in the language of Creation carved into the stone over the doorway.

He turned and looked back at the four women. "That says 'Sanctuary of Souls.'"

"Yes"–Nicci tilted her head toward the hanging–"and it fits with all of this."

The thin, silklike material hung dead still over the outside of the doorway. Nicci held the light sphere closer so he could see all of the symbols in the language of Creation covering the sheer material of the cloth. The symbols appeared backward because they had been painted onto the other side with a brush and ink.

Even with the symbols being backward, he could make out the meaning of a number of the more familiar

symbols. He puzzled at others, though, trying to think
if he had ever seen them before. While he recognized
some of the compositional elements, he couldn't make
sense of what they meant when combined. In the language of Creation, the sub-elements worked together to
construct the primary expression, so the meaning of
those sub-elements was to an extent dependent on how
all the parts of the symbol worked together. While he
thought some of the symbols looked somehow familiar,
he couldn't recall where he had seen them.

"I don't recognize some of these symbols"–he gestured to several of the more complex emblems–"like
this grouping, here."

"You probably wouldn't," the sorceress said. "These
are ward spells."

Richard frowned back at her. "Ward spells? What
are they warding?"

Nicci's blue eyes turned up to look at him. "The
dead."

"How do you know?"

Nicci admonished him with a look. "I was a Sister of
the Dark. These are things I recognize. They are dangerous spells and only used for the most dangerous of
places."

Richard couldn't help thinking about the words
"Sanctuary of Souls" above the door.

"And they are meant to ward the dead?"

"In this case, yes. They are designed to stop the dead
or any minions of the world of the dead. They act something like shields. But shields, like those rolling stones
back in the caves in Stroyza, often have to be constructed. For that reason, shields are often difficult to
create. Because these kinds of wards can even be
painted on a piece of cloth, they are considerably easier to put up."

Richard felt the thin cloth between his fingers and

thumb. "Then why aren't wards like this used more often? Why bother with building shields when you can simply paint a few of the appropriate ward spells?"

Nicci gave him a look as if he had asked a stupid question. "Pretty hard to steal a giant rolling stone. Don't you think that for people without the ability to create them on their own, this kind of ward would be much easier to steal and use for their own purpose?"

"I suppose so," Richard admitted as he studied the flimsy hanging cloth. "So these particular wards are specifically meant to stop spirits?"

"Yes. In this case there is no doubt that they are meant to repel the dead from this doorway. Since they are facing anything coming from out there, they are obviously meant to keep spirits of the dead out of the room with Lucy's well."

"So then there are ghosts beyond this doorway?" Cassia asked.

Nicci drew her lower lip through her teeth as she studied the spell-forms on the cloth. "That would be my guess. I do know that spirits of the dead can't cross such wards. These keep them on the other side. They could serve no other purpose. Such dangerous spell-forms would not be here unless it was absolutely necessary."

"You mean they act something like the skrin," Kahlan asked, "repelling spirits from the veil to keep them from crossing through and keep them in the underworld?"

Nicci smiled. "That's a very good way to put it, Mother Confessor."

Kahlan looked back at the cloth hanging. "It's beginning to make sense why what is out beyond is called the Sanctuary of Souls."

"Yes," Nicci agreed. "In a way, while it keeps them from crossing, it also creates a sanctuary for them where they feel safe. The underworld, with the skrin, is like that, too–it keeps them on that side, but it also creates a sanctuary for spirits where they won't be disturbed."

Richard frowned as he studied the symbols. "I just realized where I've seen some of these symbols before."

"Really?" Nicci asked. "I can't think of anywhere you would have seen such wards before."

He turned away from the doorway to look at the sorceress. "I remember seeing some of these same ward spells on the enormous gates leading out of the third kingdom."

Kahlan rubbed her arms. "That barrier to the third kingdom was put there an awfully long time ago, Richard. It was back in the great war. Are you saying that you think these were put here by the same people who built that barrier, and possibly for the same reason? Do you really think these have been here that long?"

Richard considered his answer a moment. "I don't have a way to know for sure, but that would be my guess. I suspect this has something to do with that war and what the people back then were doing to stop Sulachan. If that's true, then we're the first people to enter the Sanctuary of Souls since back in that time."

"That's an unsettling thought," Nicci said.

Kahlan gave them both an impatient look. "Regardless, what matters now is that we need to get to the sliph–if this really is the Keep. Like it or not, this is the only way out so let's get going."

Despite what Nicci had done for him to give him strength, the dull ache of the poison was wearing on him. He knew Kahlan was right.

Richard pulled the cloth aside just enough to peer out into the hallway. It was dark, lit only by the light from the lanterns and the sphere Nicci had taken from a bracket on the wall. At the farthest reaches of where that light penetrated, he thought he saw movement. He stared, trying to see it again, or see what it was, but nothing moved when he looked where he thought he'd seen the movement. He wondered if it could be his imagination. He wished he could believe it was.

Kahlan clasped his arm, gently pulling him back briefly. "Lucy said that she was supposed to tell you to be careful out there. While it's important to remember that, sometimes it's more dangerous to do nothing. We're running out of time—you're running out of time. We need to get going."

Richard circled his arm around her waist. "Spoken like the Mother Confessor."

Richard pushed the cloth aside, letting more of the light penetrate farther into the darkness. It looked like an empty hallway. He slipped past the cloth and stepped out into the desolate corridor.

The hall appeared to have been carved from the soft stone of the mountain, rather than built up of granite blocks the way he had always seen before down in the foundation area under the Keep. The walls, ceiling, and floor of the hallway had been cut square and flat, rather than simply being hollowed out like most of the passageways in Stroyza. It seemed a lot of trouble to go to for what looked to be a useless, empty hallway that merely led to the room with Lucy's well.

It also made no sense to him why this cold, empty place would be a sanctuary for souls.

The rest of them followed Richard out into the corridor. Nicci let the cloth fall back down across the doorway. Richard checked that everyone was close behind him before starting out. He didn't want to have to go looking for one of them in the pitch-black tunnel. As they moved through it in their confining cocoon of light, the only thing he could see was the pale brown stone of the walls. There was no plaster, no paint, no words carved in the wall, no furnishings, nothing to indicate what the place was for, other than getting to the well room.

He kept thinking about the words "Sanctuary of Souls" over the doorway into the corridor. It made no sense why this place had been built. Souls had the eternity of the underworld. What did they need with some stone tunnels?

Before they had gone far, a doorway appeared to the right. When they reached the opening, Richard let Cassia slip in ahead of him with her lantern. The room was good-sized and square, with the ceiling the same height as the hallway. There were no furnishings or markings of any kind. The walls were flat, without any niches cut into them. It was simply an empty, square room.

"Nothing," Cassia said as she stepped back out.

Just as he started away, he thought he caught sight of movement back in the room. He stopped and stared back through the doorway. It seemed something shadowlike withdrew out of the pale light, shrinking back into the inky darkness inside the room.

"What?" Kahlan asked.

Richard stood frozen as he stared for a moment, and then he drew his sword. The sound of steel rang through the hallway, echoing back from the distance.

"What is it?" Nicci asked.

"There is something or someone in that room."

Cassia slipped past him before he could stop her. She raced back into the room with her lantern, looking for what he might have seen.

She stuck her head back out the doorway. "Nothing, Lord Rahl. There isn't anyone in here. There isn't anywhere someone could possibly hide."

"No one alive," Richard said under his breath as he stared into the empty room.

He saw a shadow of movement behind Cassia. His grip tightened on the sword.

Nicci shoved him.

"We need to get out of here, Richard. You heard Lucy. She said to be careful in here. Standing around waiting for something to happen is not being careful. Looking for trouble is not being careful. Waiting for it to find you is not being careful. The sooner we get out of here and up into the Keep, the better."

"You took the words right out of my mouth," Kahlan said.

"You're both right," he admitted as he started out again, hurrying his pace.

They soon came to an intersection with opposing hallways branching off to the right and left. Cassia held her lantern up, looking down the one to the left while Vale held hers up to peer down the opposite corridor. Both passageways looked identical in width and height to the one they were in.

Vale pointed. "I think I see openings down there."

Before Richard could stop her, she darted down the hallway to investigate. The cocoon of lamplight went with her as she trotted down the hallway, looking as if she were in a glowing bubble floating through the underworld. When she came to a doorway she turned to immediately disappear inside. He could see only the light through the opening moving about as she searched inside.

After a long moment of silence she emerged. "Nothing," she called back, her voice echoing. "It looks just like the other room we saw."

She moved down the hallway and looked in a half dozen of the other openings spaced at irregular intervals. After emerging from each she called back to report that it was empty. She searched all of the rooms in the area before finally returning.

Vale pointed a thumb back over her shoulder. "There are more intersections down there. I saw more dark doorways down other halls. Should I go look in them?"

"We shouldn't waste time looking in all of the rooms and down all the passageways," Nicci said. "There is no telling how many there might be, and the rooms aren't what matters. What really matters is that we get out of here."

"Which way do you think we should go?" Kahlan asked him.

Richard stared off into the darkness. He knew how easy it was to become lost in a place you didn't know, especially a place with no landmarks to enable you to keep track or orient yourself. Wandering aimlessly was dangerous.

"I have no way of knowing for sure. For now, let's keep going straight."

They soon came to another cloth hanging to their left. When Richard pulled it aside he saw yet another pitch-black hallway. He let the cloth drop back so he could look at the symbols. These were facing toward him. Some he recognized as messages of comfort of a sort—he wasn't exactly sure of what they were trying to convey—and other symbols he didn't think he had ever seen before.

He gestured at the symbols before looking over his shoulder at Nicci. "Do you know what these mean? They look like they are meant to be comforting."

"That's right. They are attractant spells."

"Attractant spells?" Kahlan asked. "What are they attracting?"

"Spirits." Nicci flicked a hand back the way they had come. "Some of the spell-forms, like back at the well room, are meant to keep spirits away. These are the opposite. They are meant to attract spirits."

Richard imagined they must be something like fish-ing nets. What he couldn't figure out was why these were placed in the underground rooms to attract spirits, and others meant to keep them out.

As they moved on into the darkness the hallway made an abrupt right turn just before a cloth hanging across their way ahead, but when he pulled it aside there was only a wall. Since the hallway didn't continue on straight, they had to take the turn. They encountered more rooms, the doorways of many covered with the strange hanging cloth. Some were the silky material, while others were heavier material, something like burlap.

The rooms they came across, some with empty openings, were just as bare as all the others they had investigated. In each room Richard had the feeling that there was someone in there, in the darkness, watching him. He kept his sword out. He wasn't sure it would be of any use against spirits, but it made him feel better to have it in his hand than in its scabbard.

Moving through the darkness, they abruptly came upon a heavy burlap cloth blocking the hallway. Going around it he realized that it was only one of four cloths forming a square, several with passages behind them. One hanging covered in symbols had a blank wall behind it rather than a corridor.

They tried to continue on a straight course, but soon that became impossible as they found themselves in a complex network of passageways turning repeatedly and branching in every direction. To the sides, a few of the inky black tunnels didn't have hangings covering their opening, while others did.

The hallway split over and over, with intersections everywhere, many at odd angles, making it a dizzying choice of which route to take. In the darkness inside the mountain there was no way to get his bearings. It was as if the angles and corners were intended to disguise direction. Behind some hangings the corridor simply stopped in a dead end, forcing them to backtrack.

Although some rooms had the cloth curtains over them he didn't see a single door on any of them. Each room was completely barren, without any furniture. None of them looked to have ever been inhabited nor did they seem to have any purpose.

In some places they encountered layers of coarsely woven, raw linen hanging motionless directly across the passageway. It was unnerving to abruptly encounter the walls of cloth with symbols suspended in the darkness, seemingly for no reason. The hangings contributed to the confusion of the place, helping to turn it into an incomprehensible maze.

If the place had a purpose, Richard couldn't figure it out. If there was any order to its layout, he couldn't figure that out, either.

The underground hallways were dead quiet in a way that made them all jumpy. Every echoing crunch of crumbled rock underfoot made heads jerk around, searching the darkness behind them.

When he heard a soft sound from behind, Richard spun around, sword in hand, anger rising. There was no mistaking the fact that they hadn't made the sound.

"What is it?" Kahlan whispered.

"We're being followed."

They all stared back into the darkness.

"Followed by who?" Kahlan asked in a whisper.

"If I had to hazard a guess, I would say we are being followed by spirits."

"Spirits . . ." She stared into the dark, empty hallway behind them. "I don't see anything."

"Nonetheless they're down here," he told her. "I don't know why, but this place is haunted with spirits. Lots of spirits. I can feel them everywhere down here."

Kahlan's grip tightened on his left arm. "You can't know that for sure."

Nicci gestured to one of the cloth panels hanging over a doorway to the side. "All of these symbols are meant for the dead. They have no purpose except for the dead. The place is called the Sanctuary of Souls, so it only seems logical that there would be spirits here."

Cassia's eyes widened. "Are you sure? Why would spirits be here, instead of in the underworld where they belong?"

Nicci glanced at the Mord-Sith but didn't answer.

The place smelled dusty and dry. Richard lifted his nose a little, trying to smell anything that didn't belong.

"Do any of you smell anything?"

"Just dust and stone," Kahlan said.

"What do you think you smell?" Nicci asked.

Richard finally shook his head. "Nothing. That's why I'm a bit puzzled. I was wondering if we could smell a trace of sulfur."

Kahlan glanced around. "You think this place is an opening to the underworld?"

"It's the Sanctuary of Souls," he said. "Souls belong in the underworld, don't they?"

Nicci looked skeptical. "Why would someone build an underground maze open to the underworld? I don't think that explains what this place is doing here. It has some other purpose."

"Like what?" Richard asked her.

Nicci finally shook her head. "I don't know. The underworld is infinite. What would it need with some empty rooms and hallways?" She drew some of her long blond hair back over her shoulder as she looked around. "Whatever the purpose of this place, it's not tied to the underworld. The symbols tell me that much. There is obviously some intent with this place."

Richard wasn't really listening to Nicci as he stared back into the darkness. Something else had his attention.

"Wait here. All of you."

Kahlan snatched his sleeve before he could leave. "Where do you think you're going?"

"I want to go back a ways and have a look at something. I want all of you to wait here."

Vale held out her lantern. "Take this, at least."

Richard turned it down with a hand signal. "I need to go have a look. All of you stay here. I'll only be a few minutes."

As soon as he started back, he could begin to feel them. The farther he went back into the darkness, the more they closed in around him. As he felt the spirits crowding all around, he could begin to hear their whispers. He looked back over his shoulder and saw the four women in the distance, huddled together in the light of the two lanterns and one light sphere. They looked tiny and insignificant.

"Fuer grissa ost drauka."

He turned at the whispered words. As soon as he did, he heard the same thing from another side. And then another. Before long the whispered words *"Fuer grissa ost drauka"* seemed to melt together into a hushed moan from the dead all around him.

"What is it you want?" Richard asked into the darkness.

"Help us," a soft voice in the darkness answered. Another added the same call. Soon more joined in.

He looked all around but couldn't see them, and yet he could. He saw amorphous forms and sorrowful, filmy faces out of the corner of his eye, but when he looked toward them, they weren't there. He realized that there were thousands of them. Maybe tens of thousands. As he saw the forms gathering, he knew there were more than that. The available amount of room had no bearing on their numbers. They didn't need space so much as a place. They spilled out of rooms and hallways to the sides, coming to see the stranger in their midst.

Richard turned and hurried back to the others.

"What is it?" Kahlan asked, seeing the concern on his face.

"We need to get out of here. We need to get out right now."

"I'm all for that," Cassia said.

"Me too," Vale agreed.

"How are we supposed to know the way out?" Kahlan asked.

Richard looked around, trying to decide which way to go. He gestured with his sword down at the floor.

"Look. Those are our footprints." He pointed again with his sword. "See there, out ahead? The dust covering the floor out there is undisturbed. No one has been in these hallways before us for probably thousands of years. But these footprints are ours. We've been in this hallway before."

Kahlan looked up from the dusty footprints. "We're lost and going in circles."

When Richard looked up into the distance, it was then that he saw it, up high on the wall at an intersection with a corridor to the right. There were no footprints in that dust out ahead, so he knew that they hadn't been down in that area yet.

He pointed it out with his sword. "Look there. Up on the wall just before that corridor to the side. See it?"

Carved into the soft stone were four horizontal, uniformly wavy lines stacked atop one another with a heavier upright line at the end.

"What is it?" Vale asked.

"It's the symbol for a shepherd. It's meant for me. They marked the way for us. Look for that symbol at every intersection."

Without delay they all hurried down the passageway with the shepherd symbol above it. As they went down the hallway and at every intersection they all scanned the walls, looking around for the mark of the shepherd. When they didn't see one at an intersection, they kept going in the same direction and ignored the hallways to the sides. They passed a number of rooms, but didn't bother to search them. As they rushed past doorways and the light shined in, Richard could see that the rooms were empty. Except, perhaps, they were not empty of souls.

Cassia pointed up with her hand holding the lantern. "Lord Rahl, look. There is one of the shepherd symbols."

"Good for you," he said as he put a hand to their backs and ushered the others into the side passageway with the symbol, "you're learning the language of Creation."

As they rushed down the passageways the sound of their footsteps echoed back to them from the distance. The whole way Richard could feel eyes on him. They were everywhere. He could hear them whisper *"Fuer grissa ost drauka"* as if telling others who was coming. The joined whispers seemed to fill the hallways as it was spoken thousands of times.

"Do you hear them?" Richard finally asked. "Do any of you hear them?"

Nicci frowned at him. "Hear what?"

"I don't hear anything but our footsteps," Kahlan said.

"That's all I hear," Cassia added.

Richard let out an irritated sigh. He wished he weren't the only one hearing them. It made him feel as if he were crazy.

Kahlan glanced back into the darkness. "What do you hear?"

Richard didn't see any point in alarming them any more than they already were. "I don't know. It kind of sounds like whispering."

"Whispering?" Nicci, too, looked back over her shoulder. "Can you make out what they are saying?"

"I'm not sure," he lied. "Let's just keep moving."

"Maybe it's the echo of our footsteps against the stone," Cassia suggested.

"Maybe." He pointed with the sword. "Look. Up there. Another shepherd symbol. Take that hallway."

They followed the corridor with the symbol and then raced past yet more intersections with hanging cloth covered with symbols meant for the dead, and past empty rooms that were packed with lonely, filmy faces watching him go by.

Richard noticed that some of the symbols painted on the hanging textiles were warnings to stay out. Yet more were the wards he had learned to recognize. Some were welcoming motifs offering peace, while yet others were simple geometric patterns, the purpose of which was a mystery to him.

Another one of the shepherd symbols then led them into a long corridor without any rooms or intersections. They came to a halt at the far end when they reached a cloth hung across the hallway. Long-faded colors had been painted in vertical geometric designs infused with wards.

Looking behind the textile, Richard saw an arched opening. Such an opening was different from anything they had so far encountered. They all followed Richard around the hanging cloth into a passageway that made the little hairs on the back of his neck stiffen.

The long corridor was noticeably different from any that had come before. It was wider than the others, with carefully carved straight walls and a precisely flat ceiling. It was also completely deserted and silent in a way that was oppressive.

They finally reached a dark opening at the end of the corridor. Beyond it they discovered tunnels that were not so carefully carved out of the soft stone. The edges between walls and ceiling were irregularly rounded, rather than squared. It was as if the broad corridor they emerged from had been a special place for the dead, and these new passageways were common areas used by the living. The separation was marked by the tingle of magic that set his fine hairs on end.

For the first time they encountered rooms with heavy wooden doors. Vale grabbed his arm.

"Lord Rahl, look."

Richard was stunned when she held the light into the room and he saw that it was lined with shelves from floor to ceiling. The shelves held hundreds of books. Nicci slipped past the two of them to go have a look for herself. She set her light sphere on a shelf and pulled a few books down, inspecting them briefly before replacing them. The more books she looked at, the more her search quickened. She finally turned back to him.

"These books are all rare and valuable. Some are profoundly dangerous books of magic that would be kept away from public areas."

Richard turned to Kahlan. "Do you recognize this place? Are we in the Keep?"

Kahlan shook her head with a look of disappointment. "I've never seen this place before in my life."

"Let's keep going," he said.

The passageway, so small they had to walk in single

file, was lined with rooms. Some were small and empty, with simple openings roughly hewn out of the rock. Some were more elaborate, with metal doors hung on rollers. Those looked to be workrooms of some sort. There were more libraries and rooms with tables, as if for taking meals. Many of the rooms had workbenches, stools, shelves, and a variety of tools. Other rooms had books left lying open on tables, as if people had once been studying them and for some reason not returned. One of the larger rooms had a crude kind of forge. A block and tackle for lifting heavy objects hung from an overhead beam.

They soon arrived at stairs carved into the stone and had to head upward through the caverns. As soon as they reached the higher level they came across niches carved back into the rock. All of the carved-out spaces held bodies wrapped in shrouds. Like everything else, they were all covered in layer upon layer of dust.

The twisting cavern forced them ever upward in a series of crudely cut stairs into continually higher warrens of the dead.

"Did you know the Keep had catacombs like this?" he asked Kahlan as they passed hundreds of hollowed-out spaces holding countless bodies.

Kahlan looked from side to side in wonder. "No. If this is the Keep, I never knew about this place."

"Catacombs were sometimes abandoned for various reasons," Nicci said. "Some would simply get full and people would move on to a new site."

"But people would still want to visit them," Kahlan said. "They would have wanted to pay their respect to ancestors. I grew up in the Keep. If these catacombs had been accessible I would have known about them."

"Not only that," Richard said as he gestured to a room with workbenches, tools, and yet more books, "but people apparently worked down here. The way tools and books are left around, it looks like the people abandoned the place in a hurry. It seems strange that they would have closed it all off."

"Everything we're seeing is thousands of years old," Nicci said. "Everything down here, including the empty hallways, probably dates back to the time of the great war when Sulachan was still alive. The Wizard's Keep was alive back then. It was a seat of power. The war would have been run from here."

"That's right. The gifted in Stroyza were supposed to come here to warn the wizards' council when the barrier failed. That was because at the time, the Keep was the center of power." With a sudden realization, Richard stopped and looked at Nicci and Kahlan. "Sulachan and his wizards could reanimate the dead."

Kahlan lifted a finger as she caught his meaning. "Sulachan's forces could have attacked the Keep–this center of power–by using the dead."

Richard nodded. "It's starting to make sense that they would have abandoned the catacombs."

What didn't yet make sense to him was why there would be a sanctuary for souls down below the catacombs.

As they worked their way up, level by level, they passed hundreds of niches carved from the soft sandstone. All the holes were filled with bodies placed on crudely carved shelves. Above many of the hollowed-out resting places could still be seen a family name in faded paint, or a name and a title of the deceased. Some openings were embellished around the edges with crudely carved decorations. Because they were all different, he figured that they were probably done by family members. The paint and decoration had deteriorated almost to the point where it was nearly invisible and lost to the ages.

As they reached another level higher up, the niches

had been connected and expanded to create small rooms
for the dead. Those rooms were tightly stacked from the
floors to the ceilings with bones. They had likely been
long-dead people who had been gathered up to make
room for the more recently deceased.

Rooms carved from the stone held massive numbers
of bones. Under layers of dust, each room was filled to
the ceiling with neatly stacked bones, sorted by type.
Several of the chambers held only skulls, all carefully
and respectfully stacked facing out. Richard was astonished to think of the vast numbers of people who must
have lived at the Keep, or worked there. If, indeed, this
place really was in the Keep.

They climbed stairs in tunnels so small and tight
that Richard had to duck and pull his arms in as he ascended. Higher up they came to levels where the resting chambers carved into the tall corridor were half a
dozen high. Some of the uppermost niches had a ladder leaning against them because they were so high up.

Most of the bodies laid to rest in the honeycombs of
cavities were wrapped in shrouds that were so old and
dirty that they looked to have been carved out of the
same tan sandstone as the rooms themselves. Richard
saw a few recesses holding coffins, all of them stone,
most with carved decorations, all of them layered in
dust and, like the shroud-wrapped bodies, almost
completely encased within masses of cobwebs. In fact,
the cobwebs were sometimes so thick that the shroud-
wrapped corpses looked like big cocoons.

The soft yellow lantern light and the greenish glow
from the light sphere Nicci had with her revealed a series of long corridors with niches carved into the stone
on each side. In some it looked as if an entire family
had been stuffed into the small hollow in the rock. To
the sides, yet more dark corridors branched off in every

direction. From what they could see, all of those corridors were lined with recesses holding the dead.

As they ascended long runs of steps carved directly
from the stone itself, they had to be careful because the
steps were uneven. Cassia was ahead of him, with Kahlan right behind, followed by Nicci and then Vale.

The light from Cassia's lantern suddenly revealed an
opening that looked more carefully constructed than
the ones down below. Going through it, they emerged
in a spacious cavern. The chamber had been carved out
of the rock, much like the tunnels and rooms below,
with tool marks and drill holes from the excavation still
in evidence on the rough stone walls.

The difference was that the floor, barely visible under
the thick dust, was tiled with light and dark stone in a
circular pattern. A table sat alone in the center of the
room. When Cassia wiped a hand across it, swiping
away some of the dust, Richard saw that it was veneered
in burl walnut. A simple, empty white vase sat in the
center of the table.

At one time that vase must have held freshly cut
flowers to make the place look less harsh for the people
who came to visit relatives. At one time, it must have
been a reverent room welcoming visitors.

At intervals around the room, there were openings
cut into the stone, each leading off into darkness. None
of the nine cavelike passageways were trimmed or decorated, except for symbols in the language of Creation
carved into the stone above each opening.

It looked like this had been a central hub, where visitors then went down the appropriate passageway to
where their ancestors were entombed.

The passageway they had come out of was the ninth
of nine tunnels. The symbols above it were similar to the
rest, naming each tunnel with an innocuous name such

as River of Eternal Rest, or Garden of Lilies, or Peaceful Fields. The tunnel names were apparently meant to help people find loved ones. The one they had come from was named Hall of Souls. It reminded him of the name Sanctuary of Souls he had seen at the other end, back in the room with the well.

From the room with the nine tunnels, a staircase of marble stairs and polished marble balustrade, under a thick layer of dust, started up what was little more than a crude shaft cut through the rock. The meticulously constructed stairs and balustrades were a stark contrast to the roughly cut walls. The staircase was also wide enough that Richard and Kahlan could at last walk side by side–a luxury after the narrow corridors and tunneling stairs.

Each run of stairs ended at a square landing from which the next flight ascended, going ever upward in an exhausting spiral. There were no rooms, just landings and more stairs to climb. At least they were well made rather than the roughly hewn steps that were difficult to negotiate.

Still, they were all getting exhausted. Their energy was waning and they all needed food.

Panting with the effort of the long climb, they arrived at a landing where the marble handrail ended on each side in an ornately spiraled newel post. Before them stood a wall of stone blocking their way out.

"It looks like a capstone," Richard said. "They must have used this to seal the catacombs off. It would be too big and heavy for even Sulachan's awakened dead to have moved."

"Then how are we supposed to open it?" Vale asked.

"Look!" Cassia shouted as she held her lantern out.

Two small statues sat to the side, back in a niche. They were the exact same little statues of shepherds that had been back in the hallway in the gifted's quarters in

Stroyza. Those statues, untouched since the time of the great barrier, had opened the doorway into the well room.

Cassia leaned in and with a big breath blew the dust off the statues. She waved her hand in front of her face and coughed at the cloud of dust it raised. She made a face as she waved her hand a moment, then leaned, eyes closed, and blew at the statues again.

Under the dust, Richard saw the glint of metal begin to emerge. He leaned in himself and blew at the statues, clearing off the layers of dust. Under the dust, both statues looked to be made of the same dull silver metal as the ones back in Stroyza.

"What are you waiting for?" Kahlan asked as she turned her face away and waved at the cloud of dust. "Do what you did before. Go on and see if it will get us out of here."

Nicci frowned as she leaned toward what Richard believed was the capstone. "Do you hear that?"

"No, what?" Kahlan frowned as she stopped waving her hand and cocked her head. "Wait, I do hear it. It sounds like alarm bells."

Even though he was concerned about the distant sound of alarm bells from beyond the capstone, Richard slid his sword back into its scabbard. He needed to be able to use both hands, like before, if it was going to work. When he held a cool metal statue of the shepherd in each hand, they warmed under his touch. He felt the tingle of magic seeping through his palms, along his arms, and up his spine into the base of his skull. This magic was stronger than it had been in Stroyza.

As he felt the vibration of magic at the base of his skull, the stone before them began to tremble almost as if in sympathy. Small bits of dirt and rock fell from the walls and ceiling as the area around them quaked. Pebbles danced on the floor as dust rose around them.

Richard remembered the way Samantha brought the rock of the cave's ceiling crashing down. He glanced up, worried that the rock overhead might come down on them the same way. Unlike the stone walls farther down in the catacombs, this rock higher up was granite, the same as the ceiling that had fallen in.

The capstone suddenly let out a loud crack as the seal broke all at once. Mortar that had sealed the stone shattered and popped out. Finally, the enormous slab of stone began to pivot back out of the opening, grating against the floor as it moved. As it did so, light flooded in, along with the racket of alarm bells.

Squinting in the sudden brightness of natural light, Richard peered around the stone door and out through the opening, trying to see. Cassia pushed past him and shot out the opening to check for danger. When she didn't call out a warning, Kahlan took Richard's hand and ducked under the short opening along with him.

They found themselves in a sheltered entryway for the catacombs. Fluted limestone columns lined either side of the recessed alcove. The small pillars, not much taller than Richard, were topped with long entablatures that provided support for arches elaborately decorated with complex, carved stone moldings framing tiles laid out in dark, geometric patterns. Benches to each side had been intricately embellished to match the forbidding architectural details of the rest of the entry. After the filth and crudely cut stone they had been around for so long, the magnificent, polished stone seemed to gleam.

Larger-than-life stone figures in grim, distraught poses clearly conveyed a sense of grieving and sorrow for what lay beyond the pitch-black opening at the rear. This was, after all, a threshold to the place of the dead. The brooding figures surrounding the doorway were apparently meant to prepare visitors, letting them know that they would find the catacombs devoid of any joy.

Kahlan rushed past Richard to step out of the hidden alcove, looking all around as she stepped into the light. "Dear spirits, I know this place." She turned back in a rush. "We're in the Keep!"

Richard stepped out of the shadowed entry to the catacombs to stand beside Kahlan, looking up at the vast, narrow chamber rising up like an enormous split inside the mountain the Wizard's Keep had been built

into. Tightly fit, fine-grained granite blocks lined the
soaring walls. The chamber was perhaps half a dozen
stories high, yet hardly any wider than the public corridors up in the Keep proper.

Cassia and Vale stood shielding them from a small
group of people crowding around, staring at them as if
they were seeing some of the corpses from below come
back to life. Covered in dust as they were, they probably looked the part.

"Richard?" a deep voice asked.

Richard squinted into the light shining into his eyes
from the slits at the top of the lofty wall opposite him.

"Chase?"

The big man sheathed his sword and rushed forward
to grasp Richard by his shoulders and give him a shake.
"Richard! Praise be to the good spirits! Where have you
come from?"

A woman in a simple blue dress pushed through the
small crowd of people, including some Sisters he recognized. "Richard! It is you! And Kahlan!" She grinned
with unexpected joy. "And Sister Nicci! You're here as
well!"

Nicci bowed her head, ignoring the slight of the title
she no longer used. "Sister Verna, or should I say Prelate, I must admit I'm very happy to see your beautiful,
smiling face."

Verna laughed as she rushed forward, her wavy
brown hair bouncing, to hug Kahlan as if she were a
long-lost sister.

Chase's daughter, Rachel, leaned out from behind
him. "Richard!" She ran up and threw her arms around
his waist.

She seemed to have nearly grown into a woman since
the last time he had seen her. Her arms and legs were
considerably longer. Her beautiful, blond hair had also
grown and was now almost as long as Nicci's.

Verna separated from Kahlan, holding her at arm's length as if not willing to let her go for fear she wouldn't be real. "How in the world did you all come to be in there?"

As happy as he was to see these people he knew, Richard had bigger problems on his mind. He knew that time was dangerously short, and they were far from finished with their journey. He could feel how much stronger the poison inside him had grown. Death was trying to pull him back to that dark world before he could do anything about it.

"It's a long story," he said, hoping to avoid being drawn into a lengthy explanation.

"A story we really don't have time for, I'm afraid," Kahlan added as she glanced at Richard when she recognized his reserved tone.

Verna peered suspiciously at him for a moment and then stepped close to press her fingers to the sides of his temples. She jerked her hands back as she let out a little cry of dismay, as if the touch had burned her fingers.

"Dear spirits," she whispered, her eyes widening. "You, you–"

"We know," Kahlan said. "Like I mentioned before, it's a long story and as you can tell, Richard is in trouble."

Chase made a face as he hooked his thumb on his belt. "When is Richard not in trouble?"

Nicci's face contorted in agreement. "Isn't that the truth."

Richard waved a hand for patience and turned to two small metal statues of shepherds that he had spotted set back in a recess of the alcove. When he grasped them he immediately felt them grow warm under his touch. As he held the statues, the enormous capstone slowly swung closed. Once it had again sealed the catacombs, the alarm bells throughout the surrounding corridors finally went silent.

Chase scratched his head as he peered about. "Well that would explain the alarms, if not what you were doing in there."

Richard ignored the implied question as he cast a stern look at both Chase and Verna. "Don't let anyone go in there. Don't even let anyone try to get in there."

"How would they get in?" Verna asked. "As far as I knew, that wasn't even a cavern. We always thought it was simply a small place to sit on a bench and have a rest."

"It's a little more than that," he said. "Keep people away from it."

A scowl settled comfortably on her face. "How long has that passageway been sealed off?"

Richard glanced back at the stone briefly. "Since the great war, near to three thousand years ago."

Her scowl hardened. "What's in there?"

"The dead," Nicci told her.

Verna straightened a little.

"And the spirits of the dead, I believe," Richard added.

Verna's jaw dropped. "Then what were all of you doing in there?"

"Traveling," Richard said without explaining.

"Do you have anything to eat?" Cassia asked into the empty silence. "We're all pretty hungry. I couldn't find a rat down there to save my life."

Verna stared for a moment at the impassive Mord-Sith, then half turned, holding out a hand. "Well, yes, of course. We will prepare a meal to celebrate–"

"We don't have time for that sort of thing," Kahlan said. "If we could get a quick bite to eat, maybe something we could take with us, that would be best. We need to get to the sliph."

Richard recognized that she was focused on getting him back to the People's Palace and the containment field so that Nicci could remove the poison of death from him. He had to get to the palace, but for other reasons.

Verna shared a worried look with Chase. "The sliph?" She leaned to the side, peering suspiciously behind Vale. "Is Zedd with you?" She caught the look on Richard's face. "What's wrong?"

"Verna, I don't have the slightest idea where I could even begin to tell you everything that has happened and all that is wrong, but one thing you do need to know is that Zedd . . ."

Her eyes widened. "He's dead?"

Richard pressed his lips tight and nodded.

"And everyone else is going to die if we don't get to the People's Palace," Kahlan interrupted. "Richard will be the first to die, but he will soon be followed by the rest of us. You felt the poison in him. You know how serious it is. For now, you need to trust us. We will have to fill you in later."

"Of course. But I thought you brought peace to the world. The war was ended. What could have happened?" Verna frowned with concern as she looked from Kahlan to Richard. "Can you at least tell me what this is all about? We might know something that would help."

Richard started moving down the enormous, dimly lit chamber. "Do you know who Emperor Sulachan is?"

Verna hurried to keep up with them. She touched her fingertips to her forehead, looking down as she tried to think. "Sulachan, Sulachan." Her scowl returned as her head came up. "If I'm not mistaken, wasn't he the emperor back during the great war? He's been dead for . . . what, nearly three thousand years or so?"

"Richard brought him back to life," Nicci said.

Verna was struck speechless.

"Like I told you," Richard said, "it's a very long story,

and right now there are more important things we need to worry about."

"Like what?" Verna asked, not willing to let it go.

"Well, the important thing you need to know is that I have to stop Sulachan or he is going to destroy the veil and with it the world of life."

Verna huffed in disapproval. "Richard, ever since I first met you, you have somehow been tied up in trouble with the veil. You have also been tangled in prophecy from the very first. Prophecy told us of your birth long before you were even conceived. Because of prophecy Prelate Ann was there when you were first born, helping to protect you. You were a child of prophecy."

"Now I know why," he said without explaining as he marched along at the head of the small crowd of people.

Richard saw Sisters he knew among the small crowd accompanying them, along with a number of people he didn't know. They were probably people from down in the city of Aydindril brought up to the Keep to help with bringing the place back to life. There used to be a lot of people from down in Aydindril working at the Keep.

Richard wasn't keen on the idea of people he didn't know hearing anything about what was going on. They might be trustworthy, but he didn't know them. Even if they were, they could overhear something and start rumors or even a panic down in the city. Verna and Chase had no idea of the trouble they were all in, so they would have no reason to be careful of who was around. For all they knew, the world was at peace.

In the distance yet more people made their way through the room as they went about their errands and work. The enormous room was so long and poorly lit that he couldn't make out the faces of those people at the far end.

Richard cast a sidelong glance at Chase, then deliberately looked at the people following along. Chase got the message.

He turned back to everyone. "Why don't you all let everyone know that there is no problem and then check that all the alarms are reset. Verna and I can see to this."

The Sisters and some of the others offered their services if needed and then started turning off to the corridors to the side. Soon only Verna, Chase, and Rachel remained with them.

"Thanks," Richard said in a quiet voice to his old friend.

He remembered that the long, tall room was a central hub leading to a number of important areas of the lower Keep. Besides providing daylight, the slits along the top of one of the walls helped the chamber serve as a ventilation chimney, drawing air through the lower Keep and providing fresh air. He could see small birds sitting on those high sills. Now the slits were letting a little daylight flood into the chamber along with fresh mountain air.

To the right, stone stairs built against the wall led to a narrow balcony high up on the wall. Widely spaced openings dotted the wall at irregular intervals along the balcony. Some of them had doors, while most were simply open into passageways to different areas and levels of the Keep.

It felt rather disorienting, after the places they had been and especially after being in the Dark Lands for so long, to find himself back in the Keep. It was all a bit bewildering to be so suddenly back in civilization. He had thought that perhaps he would never see it again. The Wizard's Keep reminded him of Zedd, and brought back the pain of missing his grandfather.

He would have liked to allow himself to feel safe and relaxed to finally be back at the Keep, with Kahlan very near to Aydindril and the Confessors' Palace, where she had grown up, but there could be no safety anywhere in the world of life as long as Sulachan was still a fugitive from the world of the dead.

It was additionally frustrating not knowing how many days they had been traveling from Stroyza. Even if he saw the moon he wouldn't know for sure how much time had passed in the journey to the Keep. The Dark Lands were heavily overcast all the time, so he couldn't ever see the moon phase.

So much had happened, to say nothing of having been in the timeless, changeless underworld, that he wasn't sure how much time had passed since Hannis Arc and Sulachan had taken their army of half people through the barrier to the third kingdom and headed to the southwest toward the People's Palace. Richard had simply lost track of the days.

The one thing he knew for sure was that the People's Palace was in great danger. He knew why Hannis Arc wanted to get to the People's Palace–he wanted to rule the D'Haran Empire as Lord Arc. While the plan had been profoundly complex, his goal was actually pretty simple. He wanted to usurp the House of Rahl and rule in its place.

But Sulachan was generously obliging him even though he had larger plans of his own. The men were using one another for their own ends, and each needed the other, but it seemed to Richard that Sulachan was not one to be led so easily, like a bull with a ring through his nose. From what Richard could tell, Sulachan was just as eager as Hannis Arc to capture the People's Palace.

He wondered if it could have something to do with Regula. Regula was an underworld power that was alien to the world of life. It was powering prophecy in the world of life. It was choking off life with prophecy.

In a way, it was like the touch of death Richard had in him. That touch was leaching the life out of him. Regula for millennia had been leaching life out of the world of life.

Regula, in a way, was a bridge through the veil, an open conduit between worlds. Sulachan needed that conduit. More than anything else, that was why he was intent on taking the palace. He was simply using Hannis Arc for his goals, much the same as Hannis Arc was using the spirit king.

Kahlan took the prelate's arm. "Verna, it would be very much appreciated if you could see to it that we were brought something simple to eat. Could you do that? We have two Mord-Sith with us who are about to boil me alive and eat me if we don't feed them."

That made Verna's frown melt a bit. She glanced at the two steely-eyed Mord-Sith watching her as they marched along behind Kahlan. Richard needed to eat something to help keep up his strength, and he knew that Kahlan and Nicci had to be starving. They all needed food.

"Yes, of course." She immediately broke away to rush over to some men loading firewood out of a room not far away.

They straightened beside their carts and nodded at her instructions before hurrying off into one of the corridors to the side.

Chase, taking long strides, stepped up closer beside them. "Richard, what can I do to help? What do you need?"

Richard thought about it a moment.

"I wish I knew."

"Well," the big man asked, "where are you headed?"

"We need to get to the People's Palace in a hurry. The sliph is the fastest way."

"What's the hurry?"

Richard glanced over at his lifelong friend. "In the great war, Emperor Sulachan used occult power–"

"Occult power?" Verna interrupted as she returned to their side, the scowl back in her expression. "What's that? What are you talking about?"

Richard let out a long sigh. The sliph wasn't far, and there would be no time to explain everything that had happened, much less everything that was going to happen and why.

"There is far too much to be able to fill you in about it all right now," he said, "but I do need to fill in a little and give you some information that you need to know. Sulachan uses occult power. Occult power is in many ways like magic yet it's different."

"Different?" she interrupted. "Different how?"

"It's a balance to magic. You might say that occult power is the other side of magic. Think of it as the dark side."

"Subtractive Magic is the dark side of Additive Magic," she insisted.

Richard made a face at how complicated it all was, trying to think of how to explain it.

"There are layers upon layers of balance," Nicci said when she saw that Richard was having difficulty trying to figure out how best to explain it. "Subtractive is the underworld side of magic. Additive the living side. They balance each other. But it is still all magic, all part of the same thing. They work together, much the way our fingers and thumbs work together. You might think of Additive Magic as the thumb, working in conjunction with the fingers, or Subtractive Magic."

"So then what is occult power?" Rachel asked, fascinated by such exotic matters.

"Occult power is like a different phase of magic. Magic and occult power are different things. Each can exert force, much like either hand can do." Nicci locked the fingers of opposite hands together. "Each hand is different, and each is powerful, but both hands together are far more powerful than either alone."

Richard wasn't sure that Verna understood, so he went on with what mattered. "Sulachan was gifted with both areas, as were some of the wizards back in his time. They used both those abilities together–because they are stronger together, like Nicci explained–to create weapons out of people. Using this occult power, Sulachan could do things that were thought impossible."

"Like what?" Chase asked, now fully caught up in the explanation.

"He created the dream walkers, for one thing. Emperor Jagang was a descendant of the dream walkers originally created by Sulachan and his wizards. Sulachan then used his ability to create an army of half people–"

Chase put the back of a hand to Richard's arm. "Half people?"

Richard nodded. "People without souls."

Chase frowned as he scratched his scalp. "Why?"

"Because they live an incredibly long time–in much the same way as the Sisters did at the Palace of the Prophets. He wanted this army waiting here for him when he finally found a way to return from the dead."

Verna frowned. "I don't see how it's possible to take a person's soul from them. The Creator–"

Richard waved a hand, not wanting to get caught up in theological arguments. "That isn't the point. Like we said, it's a really long and complicated story.

"What matters for now, what's important, and what you need to know, is that the half people that were created went crazy without their souls–"

"Well I should think so," Verna huffed.

"–and came to lust for them so intently that they began attacking people, tearing them apart with their teeth and eating them alive, believing they could get a person's soul that way and have it for themselves. They hunt people with souls, intent on stealing those souls for themselves."

"Well that's just crazy," Verna scoffed as she folded her arms.

"Tell that to them as you watch them ripping your flesh from your bones with their teeth and eating it," Kahlan said.

"An account I read from back in that time says that the half people are death itself, with teeth, coming for the living. They are often called the unholy half-dead," Richard added.

That sobered the prelate. "If these unholy half-dead people want so badly to eat us for our souls, why haven't we ever seen them, or even heard of them?"

"Now you're getting to what matters," Richard said. "Back in the great war, Sulachan turned these crazed half people on the New World. The people up here managed to lock them all away behind a barrier in a distant, deserted place in the Dark Lands. That's what ended the war. The people back then couldn't eliminate the problem, because they didn't have the power, but they could at least lock the evil away and end the war for the time being."

"But now that evil has escaped," Chase guessed.

"Yes. They've been banished there all this time, waiting for the chance to escape. That barrier finally failed. Once it did, Sulachan was brought back from the world of the dead and now he and his half people are flooding across the land."

"What's more," Kahlan told them, "he and some in his army of half people who also possess occult powers can reanimate the dead. Those dead also do their bidding and fight for them."

"Are you serious?" Chase asked in a low voice.

Richard gestured back to the alcove. "That's most likely why the people back in that time sealed the catacombs. Sulachan could raise most of those dead, or at least the ones still mostly intact. They probably had to seal the catacombs to protect themselves."

"The reanimated dead are extremely difficult to stop,"

Nicci put in. "You need to be aware that magic is of little use against them."

"Because of the occult powers used to bring them back to life?" Rachel guessed.

Nicci smiled at her quick mind grasping the problem. "That's right."

"Surely a sword would cut them down," Chase said, his voice echoing as they all followed Richard into a passageway made of granite blocks.

"If only it were so," Richard told him. "About the only way to bring them down is with my sword or fire."

Chase gestured with a fist. "But surely enough men could–"

Richard was shaking his head. "Even what you would think would be overwhelming numbers of soldiers of the First File can't stop them. They aren't really alive, so regular weapons can't kill them. They are already dead. It's the occult power driving these corpses that gives them such great strength. I've seen these walking dead with a collection of swords broken off in their chests and it doesn't even slow them down."

Richard cast a meaningful look over at Chase as they turned down a hallway paneled with figured mahogany. "Even the heart hounds were easier to stop."

Chase grunted his discontent.

"Anyway, Sulachan is determined to finish what he started so long ago. The time he spent in the underworld was meaningless to him, except that he used that time to manipulate events and gather underworld minions. He and his army of half people and walking dead are pouring across D'Hara right now on their way to take the People's Palace. That will only be the beginning.

"He has with him a powerful wizard, Hannis Arc, who also possesses occult powers. There is no telling how many people they are killing along the way. I have to get to the palace and stop them before they can take it."

"Oh," Chase said in a sarcastic tone, "well, now I see. That doesn't sound like it should be too awfully difficult."

"There is a lot more to it," Richard told them.

"Like what?" Verna asked.

"It involves the power of Orden." Richard gestured ahead. "The sliph isn't far. We need to be on our way."

Verna spread her arms in frustration. "Even if everything you say is true, how can you hope to stop such powerful men that the wizards back in that time–with all their considerable knowledge and power–weren't able to handle?"

Richard cast her a look and waited until her gaze turned to his. "By ending prophecy."

Verna harrumphed. "Out of the rain and into the lake."

"Ahh," Chase said, "well then, that sounds simple enough. I'm glad then that you have it all under control."

Despite everything, Richard couldn't help smiling. He brought them all to a stop in a circular area where several hallways branched off. One of them, he remembered, would lead through shields and then directly to the tower room.

Richard cleared his throat. "Verna, before we go, I have to give you an important message–from Warren."

Verna's scowl melted. She blinked. "What do you mean . . . from Warren?"

Richard looked down at the floor as he stuffed his hands in his back pockets. "Warren wants you to know that he loves you, and will love you for all eternity, and that he is at peace."

"How would you be able to know such a thing? How could you have such a message from him?" Verna swallowed, her eyes brimming with tears. "Warren is dead."

Richard nodded. "I was dead, too . . ." He flicked a hand uncomfortably. ". . . for a while. That was when I saw him."

Verna's brow bunched together as she tried to comprehend what he was saying. "You were dead? What are you talking about?"

"I had been murdered," Kahlan explained, trying to help him and hurry the explanation along, "and while I was dead–"

"While you were dead!" Verna asked incredulously.

"Yes. I was dead. Nicci healed my body here in this world, then she stopped Richard's heart so that his spirit could cross the veil. He went to the underworld and sent me back to the world of life. We thought we had lost him forever."

Verna, a look of horror on her face, rounded on Nicci. "You stopped Richard's heart? You killed him? For five hundred years before he was born it had been known that he is our only hope, and you stopped his heart? What would possess you to do such a thing?"

Nicci shrugged. "He told me to do it."

Verna blinked. "And so you killed him because he told you to? Knowing that prophecy names him as the pebble in the pond, knowing that he is our only hope?"

Nicci looked uncomfortable. "Well, yes. He wanted to die, and I knew he would do it by his own hand if I didn't help him. So I stopped his heart." Nicci scratched her temple as her gaze fell away under the scrutiny of the woman now looking very much the part of the prelate. "If you would have been there, you would have understood."

Verna faltered, trying unsuccessfully several times to start another question. She finally turned back to Richard.

"How can you be alive, now, if you were dead?"

"Well, death isn't what it used to be." He realized how flippant that sounded, even though he hadn't intended it to be. "That's part of the problem we're working on."

"How could you come back to life?" she pressed. "How is such a thing possible?"

Richard cleared his throat as his gaze descended to the floor. "Cara gave her life as a bridge for me to cross back over and return to my body in the world of life."

"But she has a life now with Ben and–"

"Ben was killed protecting us from the half people."

Verna blinked at the tears brimming again in her eyes. "And when you were dead, you saw Warren?"

Richard nodded, offering her a small smile. "He wanted you to know that he loves you and that he is at peace so you shouldn't worry for his spirit."

Verna looked away as she laid a hand over her heart for a moment. "Dear Creator, I don't understand. I don't understand anything anymore. The world seems to be unraveling."

Richard gently grasped her shoulder. "It is. That's why I need to hurry. I have to stop it from unraveling."

With Kahlan at his side, Richard led Nicci, the two Mord-Sith, Verna, Chase, and Rachel through a wide hallway that would take them to the round tower room. The plastered walls helped brighten the passageway. There were occasional tables holding a small statue or vase placed along the wall. They passed a variety of rooms to the sides, some small libraries or casual reading rooms with comfortable-looking chairs and others that were dark and hid their contents.

Both Cassia and Vale chewed mouthfuls of cold roast venison as they casually glanced around along the way, taking in the sights, slowing a little when their attention was snagged by a tapestry or painting. They never seemed surprised or astounded by anything they saw, including a shallow display case holding strange, frame-like items made out of carved bones that Richard knew to be objects invested with magic. Even though Mord-Sith didn't especially like anything to do with magic, they did like to look at it all. He supposed that having originally come from the People's Palace, where Darken Rahl once ruled, they didn't find the Keep nearly as impressive, but there were many strange and unexpected things about the Keep that they apparently liked looking at. They gazed at the art on their way by and noticed the strangely patterned marble floors they walked across.

Along the short journey they had passed through a number of shields. Chase was apparently used to having someone gifted helping him get through the shields. Richard wasn't, because in the past his gift had enabled him to pass through any of them by himself, even ones requiring Subtractive Magic that few others could pass through. Now, with his gift not working, they had to skirt some of the strongest shields protecting dangerous magic and Nicci had to help him get through the rest.

Kahlan had been able to glide through most of them, as she had been doing since she was little and wandered the halls of the Keep on her own. But this was a place, guarded by powerful shields, that she had never seen when she had been a young Confessor in training. Powerful shields that she couldn't get through had kept her out. Richard knew that it was by design. There were dangerous objects of magic that could hurt the innocent or the unsuspecting, so the shields protected those areas. Nicci had to help her pass through those shields.

"Do you want any more?" Verna asked, holding out a wrapped piece of venison to Richard and Kahlan.

Kahlan put a hand over her stomach. "Thank you, no. I've had plenty."

"So have I," Richard said when Verna offered it to him. He'd eaten enough to keep up his strength, but for a variety of reasons he had no appetite. He supposed the headache didn't help. The poison was growing steadily stronger, but that was only to be expected.

Like Richard and Kahlan, Nicci had also had enough. Also like Richard and Kahlan, she had a lot more important matters on her mind than eating.

Cassia and Vale took the meat when it was offered to them. They seemed to have boundless appetites. Despite whatever concerns might have been on their minds, they seemed to have no trouble eating and worrying all at the same time. It reminded Richard of Zedd.

"Take these, too," Rachel said to the Mord-Sith. "Eat them when you have time."

"What are they?" Cassia asked as she took the small item wrapped in linen from the girl.

"Honey cakes," Rachel said with a proud smile.

As they reached the end of the corridor, Cassia made a delighted groan at the sound of honey cakes.

"I made them fresh this morning. Emma—she likes me to call her Mother—is teaching me how to cook."

"That sounds like a useful skill for a girl," Cassia said as she chewed a mouthful of venison while scanning a room to the side. It was filled with long tables and benches.

Rachel pulled one of the knives from a sheath at her belt and twirled it between her fingers, finally walking it across her knuckles, flipping it and catching it by the point. "Chase teaches me to use weapons."

Cassia's face warmed with a conspiratorial smile. "An even more useful skill. You are a girl after my own heart."

"She knows how to cut it out for you, if you'd like," Chase said with obvious pride.

Cassia held up the last three fingers of the hand holding the venison. "No, I believe you."

The corridor ended at a landing partway up the inside of a round tower room at least a hundred feet across. Even though there were slits open to the outside up near the top, the openings weren't very big, leaving the place rather dark. Rainwater running down the stone walls collected in a pool at the bottom. Stairs wound their way up around the inside of the immense stone tower, and at irregular intervals small landings interrupted the steps for doors at different levels along the way.

They all descended the stairs in single file to reach the iron rail of the walkway around the outer edge at the base of the tower. From the openings high above, the weak shafts of light pierced the darkness, but it wasn't enough to banish the gloom from the lower reaches. In the center, at the bottom of the tower, lay the pool of black water fed over time by the rain leaking in. Rocks broke the surface of the water here and there.

Gripping the railing, Cassia and Vale leaned over to peer down over the edge into the inky waters. The big eye of a salamander resting on one of the rocks swiveled to watch them.

Richard's mind was occupied with wondering why there would be a sanctuary for spirits down below the catacombs. He was particularly struck by the cloth hangings covered with wards.

He pointed across the tower to the hole broken through the stone wall, letting Cassia and Vale know where they were headed. It was the opening into Kolo's room, as Richard had once called it because after the wall had been blown open for the first time since the great war, he had discovered the remains of a wizard who had once stood watch over the sliph in case an enemy were to try to enter the Keep that way. Sometime during that war the man had been sealed in and eventually died at his post. He had left a number of journals that had been helpful to Richard in understanding some of the things that had happened back in Kolo's time.

Unfortunately, the journals had not revealed the true extent of what had been going on. He thought that perhaps Kolo didn't know. It was likely that very few people did.

Cassia and Vale swiveled their heads, inspecting the impressive damage as they walked through the broken and partially melted stone of the opening into the large room. Kolo's chair and small table still sat to the back of the round room. Unlike the room with Lucy's well, this room was nearly sixty feet across, and even though it was much larger, it also was capped with a high, domed ceiling that was nearly as high as the room was wide.

The well itself was nearly thirty feet across–considerably larger than Lucy's. Richard speculated that the sliph had more volume to her, and needed a bigger well, because she traveled to so many more places. Maybe Lucy had been created for a singular purpose, whereas the sliph was at one time in frequent use, taking wizards to a variety of places.

As Richard walked toward the waist-high stone well, he was surprised to see the quicksilver face of the sliph rise above the edge of her surrounding stone wall. The rising liquid bulge formed into glossy metallic features that reflected the lamplight and the room itself in what seemed like a living mirror.

The attractive face was smiling with fluid grace. "Master. It pleases me to see you again." The eerie voice echoed around the room. "Have you come to travel?"

"Yes," Richard said, surprised that she was already there and he didn't have to wake her. "But what are you doing here? Why aren't you asleep with your soul?"

The face distorted with concern. "I was with my soul and at peace, but then you came into the spirit world. I saw you. We all saw you. We all saw the dark ones chasing you. You still had life in you. I could tell that you did not belong there. I was worried for you, so I came here, hoping that you would return to this world and come to me again so that I might help you."

Richard stepped closer. "I'm glad you're here. We do need your help. We need to get to the People's Palace as soon as possible."

"I know the place." A smile widened on her face. "Come, we will travel." She drifted closer to him. Her voice lowered to an intimate murmur. "You will be pleased."

"We came here in Lucy," Kahlan said, her tone not at all intimate. "We traveled in her to get here. Do you know her?"

The silver face turned with a cold look back to Richard. "Why did you not come to me? Did she please you more than I do?"

Richard shook his head, eager to dispel the notion. He needed this strange creature to get them to the palace. The last thing they needed would be for her to vanish down her well.

Richard gently put his fingers on Kahlan's arm, urging her to take a step back. "No, it's not at all like that," he told the sliph. "We were trapped in Stroyza. Do you know the place?"

The sliph frowned as she considered. "Stroyza," she said, carefully pronouncing the name. "No, I have not heard of the Stroyza place. I cannot travel there."

With all the other problems he had to worry about, Richard didn't need to have difficulty with a jealous sliph, so he tried to dismiss the significance of traveling via Lucy. "We were forced to travel in her to get here–get here to you."

The silver frown eased. "You wish to travel with me? Are you sure?"

"Yes, I am. We need to travel to the People's Palace. We need to get there quickly. We had to get out of Stroyza and get back here to you so we could travel with you and be pleased. You see? We had to travel in Lucy in order to get back to you."

She regarded him coolly. "So that I could please you."

"Yes, that's right." He waved an arm, gesturing his displeasure. "It was terrible traveling in Lucy. It did not please me at all, but we had to do it to get here to you."

Out of the corner of his eye, he caught a glimpse of

Kahlan folding her arms in annoyance. He didn't know why she would be getting jealous of the sliph, but he could tell by her green-eyed look that she was.

The reflective silver face began to distort as the smile returned. "You returned because you would rather travel in me?"

He tried to make his voice sound more businesslike. "Yes, exactly. We wanted to come back so we could travel in you."

The smile brightened. "You will be pleased, Master. Come, we will travel."

Richard lifted his sword partway from its scabbard.

"When I traveled in Lucy I brought this with me. She said I could travel in her with it."

The sliph leaned over a little, looking down at the sword he was holding halfway out of the scabbard.

"I told you before, Master. That object is not compatible with life while it is in me. If you take it you all will die."

Richard waved a hand at the notion. "I know, I remember. But things have changed. You remember—you saw me in the world of the dead. Lucy said that because I have death in me, now, I could bring it and it wouldn't harm us."

"This other, this Lucy, she let you take this with you in her?"

"Yes, but she said it was only because I have a sickness in me. She said I'm already dead—you said that you yourself saw me in the world of the dead. She said this couldn't kill me again."

The sliph looked skeptical as she considered for a moment before extending a glossy silver arm. The end of it formed into a hand with graceful fingers. She sensuously cupped the metallic-looking hand to his face the way a woman might caress a lover.

The arm withdrew back into the well as concern settled into her reflective expression.

"Master, you are dying."

Kahlan stepped forward, grasping his arm. "Can you help him in any way? Is there anything you could do, since you are partly in that world of death, to help remove the sickness from him and take it back to the world of the dead with you to where it belongs?"

The sliph turned a sad look toward Kahlan. "No, I am sorry, but I can only travel in this world."

"Can you at least tell from touching him how much time he has?"

"No, I am sorry. I can only tell that death already has him and his life force is leaving him."

"I know that much," Richard said. "So, since in a way I'm already dead the sword can't really kill me, right?"

The sliph considered him for a time before speaking. "This is a bad business, Master. It is as you say—you could bring it, and you would not die because death already has you. The object is linked to you, focused on the death in you, so it would not harm the others as it ordinarily would."

"Good," Richard said, sighing with relief. "Then it would please me to take it with me."

An arm rose from the churning quicksilver pool to hold up a hand forestalling him. "Master, it is not that simple."

"Yes it is. I did it before."

"Perhaps because this other did not care what happened to you." The sliph drifted a little closer. "Did this other not tell you what would happen when you traveled with this object?"

"Well, yes," Richard admitted. "She said it would take some of my remaining life."

"And it did," the sliph confirmed. "It took that which

you have very little to give. The life is draining away
from you as death replaces it. That object is created to
bring death. When you traveled, having that object of
magic with you took much of your remaining life. It took
time from you, giving you over to death much sooner."

Richard waved a hand, wanting to get on with it and
get to the palace. "I know. So I can take it. That would
please me."

"It would not please me to do such a thing with you,"
the sliph said in a scolding tone. "You may have done it
once, but now you do not have much life left to give.
Your life is draining away as it is. Traveling with that
object would drain away even more of what little you
have left. By the time you reach the People's Palace, you
would have almost no life left. Where life had been it
would be replaced with death instead.

"Taking that object would not kill you, but it would
cost most of your remaining time in the world of life."

"That settles it," Kahlan insisted. "You can't take it,
Richard. You have to leave it here."

"We only have to get to the palace," he said.

Kahlan leaned closer. He could see the anger in her
green eyes, a deep anger she rarely directed at him. "And
then you must stop Sulachan. You have to be alive to
do that. How is having only a little time left going to
help us all?"

"Sulachan?" the sliph asked in alarm. "You are fighting Emperor Sulachan?"

"Yes," Richard said. "Do you know him?"

The glossy head floated back to the far side of the
well. "I know him from the time when I was created.
He is evil. He died and travels the world where my soul
rests. He is evil. He belongs to the dead, now. How can
he be here, in this world?"

"I'm afraid that he has crossed back over," Richard
said, not thinking it would be useful to tell her how. "He

is on his way to capture the People's Palace. If he does, he will tear the veil and destroy all of us—both those living and those souls in that world. I have to get to the palace to stop him. I need to send him back to the world of the dead where he belongs."

"Come, we will travel," she said with a sense of urgency as she floated closer. "You will be pleased."

"I need to bring my sword."

"No, you don't need to bring your sword," Kahlan said through gritted teeth. "It will do you no good if you are dead, or if you don't have enough life left in you to fight. We haven't come this far, gone through this much, to have you throw away your life—all of our lives—just to hold on to your sword. You have to leave it here. The sword isn't what's important right now."

"It will be if Sulachan sends the dead against us. The sword can stop them. How am I supposed to fight his army of the dead without my sword?"

Kahlan leaned close, fire in her green eyes. "If you send Sulachan back to the underworld, then there will be no dead to worry about, now will there? We need to get going. You need to take the sword off and leave it here."

"You should listen to her, Master. What the Mother Confessor is telling you is wise advice. She is one who pleases you, too. You should do as she says."

"Thank you," Kahlan told the sliph, but not in the kindest of tones.

Richard drew a deep breath, debating what to do.

"I suppose you're both right."

He reluctantly pulled the baldric off over his head. He set the point of the scabbard on the floor and leaned the hilt of the sword up against the stone wall of the well.

"No one will bother it, Richard," Chase offered. "I will see to it. No one will come in here. You can rest easy, knowing the sword is safe for now."

Rachel offered him a confident smile. "Once you fix everything, you can come back and get it. We'd really like to see you again and spend more time with all of you."

Richard wished he shared her confidence. Even though he didn't, he smiled to her as if he did.

He climbed up on the wall, then wasted no time in helping to pull the four women up with him.

Before he stepped off into the rolling quicksilver, Verna lifted a hand, catching his attention.

"Richard . . . if, if things don't work out, the Grace carries us all into the eternal world of peace. We know you will do your best, but if things don't work out, well, we will all be together again in that world."

Richard slowly shook his head. "No, if things don't work out, we won't."

She touched her fingers to her chin. "What do you mean?"

"Without victory, there is no survival," Richard said. "Of anything."

He looked back over his shoulder. "Sliph, we need to travel. Please take us to the People's Palace."

"Come into me, Master. You will be pleased."

All of them holding hands, he looked to Nicci and Vale on his left, then Kahlan and Cassia on his right. "Like the last time, let your breath go and breathe her in. Try to keep hold of one another so we can stay together."

Both Mord-Sith, even though they looked apprehensive, nodded.

With that, and the urgency of the situation displacing any second thoughts, he stepped off the edge with the rest of them into the silvery pool.

Gliding through the sliph was an otherworldly sensation, unlike anything Richard had ever been able to relate it to. Each time it felt familiar, and yet completely unexpected. There was a sense of still peacefulness, of a velvety eternity around him, combined with a dim awareness of savage speed.

He tightly held Kahlan's hand in his right, Nicci's in his left. He hoped that the two Mord-Sith were holding on to each of them as well.

There was nothing to see, as such. With his eyes closed he saw colors flash by, but when he opened them there was only darkness. When he closed his eyes again, those colors, spinning and swirling as if carried on a fitful wind, filled his mind. The hues and tones spread through empty space like vivid dyes through crystal-clear water.

There was no way to judge time in the sliph, any more than there had been a way to judge the passage of time in the underworld. While in the underworld Richard couldn't tell if he had been dead for mere moments, or a thousand years. It was all the same. In the past, whenever he had asked the sliph how long they had been traveling, she always said that she was long enough, as if that was somehow answer enough.

He used that stretch of time suspended to consider what he needed to do. He analyzed it from every angle. As far as he could tell, the pieces he did have all fit. Try as he might to come up with another way, and as much as he might wish there were one, there wasn't.

He was the bringer of death, and only he could do such a thing. He understood why every different source, from prophecy to the Cerulean scrolls, said as much.

Breathing the quicksilver fluid of the sliph was at once a giddy experience and a terrifying one. It tended to be giddy as long as he didn't think about what he was actually doing. When he thought about how he was breathing in the silvery fluid instead of air, it switched to terrifying.

Light and shadow in blocky shapes suddenly flooded in around him.

Breathe.

It was the sliph telling him to let go of the fluid he was holding in his lungs and to breathe air instead. In the past he had never wanted to let go of the warm, silken, quicksilver sliph and take that first painful breath of cold air, but in this case he had urgent matters that he was focused on and the sensation of the sliph was a distant secondary thought.

He tilted his head back as he popped up above the surface of the rolling silver waters inside the well, and expelled the fluid of the sliph. With forceful, deliberate effort he drew in a deep breath of air. It hurt, as he expected, but that pain was only a distant consideration.

He looked around as he panted, catching his breath, once again getting accustomed to breathing air, and saw that the others were doing the same. He slipped one arm around Kahlan's waist and grabbed the top of the wall with his other hand. When she threw her arms over the top, he helped lift her up and out of the well. Once she was out, a hand reached down and seized his arm.

It was Nathan's.

Another hand took his other arm. It was Rikka's. Through his still-blurred vision he could see that she was wearing her red leather—always a worrisome sign with Mord-Sith. He was relieved to see both Nathan and Rikka. That told him immediately that Hannis Arc and Emperor Sulachan had not yet captured the People's Palace.

Together, the old wizard and the Mord-Sith helped lift him up and over the edge. The sickness inside him was sapping his strength. Besides Kahlan, Nicci and the two Mord-Sith were already out of the well. Nicci held her stomach, bending forward as she panted. Cassia rested with a hand on the stone wall of the well. As she caught her breath, Vale checked her single blond braid, marveling that it was not wet and dripping silver fluid.

Richard turned back to the well. "Thank you, Sliph. For now it would please me if you would stay here in case I need to travel again."

The silver face smiled. "You were pleased, then, Master?"

Richard nodded, still catching his breath. "Yes. Always."

Content with the answer, she said she would remain there. Her face melted back down into the choppy little waves of the quicksilver liquid and the pool gradually stilled until it was a quiet, mirrored surface of silver.

"Why would we need her again?" Kahlan asked, suspiciously.

"Who knows," Richard told her, leaving it at that and hoping she didn't ask anything else.

Fortunately, she instead turned to the prophet. "Nathan, what are you doing down here?"

"I came to greet you, of course," he said, lifting an arm with a grand gesture a king might give an adoring crowd.

Nathan's full head of straight white hair hung to his broad shoulders. His hawklike Rahl glare hooded his penetrating dark azure eyes. He was clean-shaven and ruggedly handsome, despite being nearly a thousand years old after having lived for most of his long life in the spell around the Palace of the Prophets that slowed time. Rather than the traditional robes of a wizard, he was wearing high boots, dark trousers, and a ruffled white shirt under an open dark green vest. He was also wearing a sword sheathed in an elegant scabbard at his hip.

A sword was about the last thing a wizard of Nathan's ability needed, but he liked carrying one anyway. Most of his life he had dressed in the traditional simple robes of a wizard, as was required of him at the Palace of the Prophets. Now free of that place, he liked to dress in his image of an adventurer from many of the books he'd read. Richard had often wondered if because he had never had a normal childhood, Nathan was living it out now that he was free to do so.

Nathan, looking serious, gestured to Richard's hip. "Where is your sword?"

Richard flicked a hand back at the well. "I couldn't bring it through the sliph."

"Ah" was all Nathan said.

The tall, blond Mord-Sith shared a nod with Cassia and Vale before turning her attention back to Richard.

"Lord Rahl, if I may ask, where is Cara? Why isn't she protecting you? She should be with you."

Richard's breath caught at the name. Before he could answer, Cassia lifted Cara's Agiel, worn around her neck, and answered in his place.

"She is, in a way. Cara died as all Mord-Sith want to die—giving her life for Lord Rahl. I carry her Agiel so that she may be with him in spirit, and so that I can always be reminded of her strength."

Richard saw only a slight pause in Rikka's breathing.

"And where have you two been all this time?" she asked, looking between Cassia and Vale. She sounded like a mother unhappy with children who had not shown up for dinner.

Richard spoke up for Cassia and Vale. "They and the others with them were captured and forced to serve the man who is coming here to kill us all. The rest of those women, except Vika, are dead. Some of them died defending us."

The harsh edges of Rikka's expression eased as she looked back at the two Mord-Sith. "Glad to have you both back to help protect Lord Rahl and the Mother Confessor."

Cassia revealed the slightest of smiles. "From my experience, they require a lot of defending. Lord Rahl, especially, wouldn't last long without at least one of us watching over him."

Richard turned his attention back to Nathan. "How did you know we were coming? How is it that you were down here waiting for us?"

Nathan shrugged his broad shoulders as if it should be stone-cold obvious. "I'm a prophet. Prophecy came to me, saying that you would arrive down here, so we've been down here waiting."

Richard didn't like the sound of that. He cocked his head. "A prophecy."

"Yes," Nathan said. "Oddly enough, I have been having a flood of prophecy lately. Prophecy of every sort. It's quite exciting actually. I've been visited by more prophecies in recent weeks than I've had my entire life. It's quite extraordinary, if the truth be told."

"It's trouble," Nicci said, as if reading Richard's thoughts.

"How so?" the prophet asked, not liking being contradicted. "How is knowledge trouble? It simply is what it is."

Nicci waved away the question and asked one of her own instead. "There is an army on its way. Have you seen any sign of it, yet?"

Nathan's demeanor changed. He looked from Nicci to Richard.

"I think you had better come with me. There is something you need to see." Without waiting or explaining, Nathan turned and headed for the door.

Outside the room with the sliph's well, the broad service corridor was filled with men of the First File. They were all heavily armed and looked in a grim mood. Colonel Zimmer, the big D'Haran commander and the highest-ranking man at the palace, rushed forward when he saw everyone emerge from the sliph's room. He scanned all the faces before leaning to the side, checking back in the room to see if anyone else would be coming out.

The colonel tapped a fist to his heart. "Lord Rahl, welcome back to the palace. I can't tell you how relieved I am to see that you and the Mother Confessor are safe. We have all been terribly worried." It was clear by the look on his face that he meant it. The man cleared his throat. "If I might ask, Lord Rahl, why didn't you ride back with General Meiffert and the men who went to see you safely home? We expected to see you safely returned to the palace in their care."

"I told you they would be coming through the sliph." Nathan folded his arms, clearly feeling smug about the accuracy of his prophecy.

Richard was caught off-guard. It seemed like all he ever did was tell people about all those who had died.

"I'm afraid that General Meiffert, Commander Fister, and all the men they brought with them lost their lives fighting to protect us. We would not be alive if not for the sacrifice of all of those brave men."

The colonel's face reflected the shock of the news. "Dear spirits . . . all of them?"

Richard confirmed it with a solemn nod. "There isn't much time and we have urgent problems that need to be addressed. I'm afraid that I am going to have to ask you to step up and take the place of General Meiffert. I am appointing you general of the First File."

General Zimmer clapped a fist to his chest. "I take on the duty, Lord Rahl, but with a heavy heart."

Richard joggled the man's shoulder. "I know. You're the right man for the job, and I know you will make those who came before you proud, those under your care safe, and those under your sword terrified."

"Yes, yes," Nathan said. "Appointment made. I already told the man that he would soon be promoted to general. As I told you, I have been having a number of prophecies of late. Now, we need to go have a look at the trouble we have."

Richard had wondered why the man had shown so little reaction. General Zimmer glanced up at Richard.

"It's true, he did tell me that not long ago. I thought he meant many years from now. I didn't expect it to be so soon."

Nathan waved a hand irritably. "Prophecy does not name the day, I told you that. Prophecy only–"

"You said you needed to show us something," Richard said.

Nathan paused to scrutinize him for a moment. "Yes, this way." He flicked a hand in the direction of the hallway with all the men.

Richard saw that the men at the head of all the soldiers had bows nocked with red-fletched arrows. They wore special black gloves for handling the deadly arrows. He turned to Nicci.

"Do you think those might stop the dead?"

Nicci's blue eyes turned to the nearest man with the red-fletched arrow nocked in his bow. "Possibly."

"If I might ask, Lord Rahl?" the new general said as he scratched the hollow of his cheek. "What do you mean about stopping the dead?"

Richard skipped the explanations and went right to the part that mattered most. "The man who is coming to lay siege to the palace can reanimate the dead. Once brought back in this way, they are incredibly difficult to bring down. Regular weapons don't work because these corpses are driven by magic mixed with occult powers."

Nathan turned and stared off down one of the halls, frowning.

A number of the soldiers shared looks at this news.

"How do we stop them, then?" General Zimmer asked.

"Stabbing them doesn't work, since they are already dead. If forced to fight them, do your best to hack off limbs. Fire stops them, so if you can throw pitch on them and set them ablaze that might work. Nathan and Nicci can lay down wizard's fire, and that certainly works, but the problem is with their numbers. My sword works against them. At least it would if it was with me."

Richard started down the broad hallway but took only a few steps before coming to a halt and turning back. "What is that odd smell? It smells like something is burning."

Nathan cast a brief glance toward a marble stairwell. "Do you know the crypts where the Rahl ancestors are laid to rest?"

Richard nodded. "Yes. Each is in a separate vault, each in their own ornate stone coffin."

"Well, some of the stone down there is melting."

Richard looked up from under his brow. "Melting?"

Nathan pulled on a long strand of gray hair. "Yes, melting."

Richard raked his fingers back through his own hair as he tried to remember something about that happening before, a very long time ago. He finally looked up at the tall prophet.

"Shortly after I had killed Darken Rahl, I remember a man who said he was the master of the crypt staff coming to report the stone walls down in Panis Rahl's crypt melting."

Nathan's bushy brows rose. "Really?"

Richard rubbed his chin as he stared off into the memory. "Yes. Zedd told the man to use white stone to seal it over." Richard snapped his fingers and looked back at Nathan. "Zedd told him it had to be white stone from the quarry of the prophets. Zedd gave the man a pouch with some kind of magic dust and told him to mix it in with the mortar. He said to seal the crypt shut or the whole palace would melt."

"That's the stone that's melting," Nathan confirmed. "That wall of white stone. It's so hot down in that passageway that men can only go in there just long enough to throw a bucket of water at it to try to cool it down, but that's not helping much."

"Is it some kind of magic that's melting it?" Richard asked.

Nathan shrugged. "None I recognize. We have been rather distracted by other matters, so I haven't been able to investigate it." He held his arm out in invitation to continue what they had been going to do.

Richard turned to the men of the First File watching him.

"Could someone get me a sword, please?"

Almost instantly, a dozen of the nearest men pulled off their weapon belts and held out the hilts of their sheathed weapons to Richard.

Richard took a sword from a man who still had a battle-axe hanging on a hook at his hip. Richard thanked the man as he strapped the belt around his waist. He drew the sword and held it up, turning it, taking a quick look at it and checking its weight. It was a blade, and that was what mattered.

Richard slid the sword back into its sheath. "Let's go."

The men moved aside to let him and those with him through. Rikka immediately stepped out in front of him. Absent Cara, she was determined to make certain he was protected. Cassia and Vale fell in behind Kahlan to guard Richard and Kahlan from behind. It had been a long time since the two Mord-Sith had been in the palace—since Darken Rahl had ruled. Although they had, in a way, taken possession of Richard in Cara's place, they seemed willing to let Rikka take charge. How they wordlessly determined such things, Richard didn't know.

The large force of the First File closed in behind them.

Richard had a lot of questions for Nathan, but he was more interested in what the man thought was so urgent that Richard see.

CHAPTER
51

Nathan rammed his shoulder against the heavy oak door. It finally, reluctantly, opened outward on rusty hinges. In the silence, the bottom scraping against the stone floor of the rampart sounded all the louder. As soon as the door opened, wind rushed in, lifting Kahlan's and Nicci's hair from their shoulders. That wind carried an unmistakable stink. The smell was so thick Richard could almost taste it.

Fleecy clouds of bright white with tattered, dark shadowing lay stacked in layers across the sky. At least it wasn't heavily overcast like the Dark Lands. By the direction of the light, Richard judged that it had to be late afternoon.

Nathan grabbed Richard's sleeve. "Easy, Richard. No good can come from letting them see you."

Richard nodded as he carefully moved out onto the east rampart. This particular projection in the wall stuck out almost even with the edge of the immense plateau below them, itself rising up from the Azrith Plain. Calling the place atop the vast plateau a palace was misleading. The palace, with its sprawling footprint, myriad of connected sections, levels, towers, bridges, all with different roofs, multistory segments that rose up in various places, and many open courtyards, was actually a city.

The central stairway rising up deep inside the plateau itself probably held more people than the palace. That central area in the plateau was filled with shops and living quarters for their owners and guests. Many people who came to the palace to trade only frequented the interior shops and rarely made it all the way up to the top.

Archers of the First File crouched in the battlements overlooking the plains far below. They all had arrows nocked and ready. The men kept out of sight from what might be down on the plain, but peeked out from time to time to check.

Richard moved in a crouch as he made his way across the rampart to a wide merlon. He stood up behind it so that he couldn't be seen from below. Kahlan and Nicci, arms protectively around each other's waists as they crouched, hurried out to join him. The Mord-Sith waited back just inside the door, watching them.

Nathan leaned close and spoke in a low voice. "Careful now. You never know who may be looking up here or what they might unleash against you."

Richard nodded and then carefully leaned over to look out the crenellation between the tall, thick merlons to the Azrith Plain below. From that vantage point one could see for a vast distance. The weather was clear enough that he could see all the way to the mountains at the horizon.

He froze at what he saw below.

The plains were covered with half-naked people. It was a gathering of half people, in greater numbers than he had known existed. They stood in dead silence all across the plains, arms hanging at their sides, all watching the palace. It was so quiet that Richard could hear the call of distant ravens hunting the plains.

Most of the half people wore only pants, or remnants of pants. The majority of their heads were shaved, but some had topknots or closely cropped hair and beards. Richard knew from experience that some of them could wield occult powers. Some of them could even raise the dead.

The unwashed horde was the unmistakable stench he had smelled. He had bad memories of those stinking swarms chasing him through the woods. They were relentless, not caring how many casualties they took. None of them cared much about what happened to their fellow half people, or in their lust to steal a soul, even their own safety. Each one of them figured that any others that fell merely meant that they had a better chance to capture a soul for themselves.

While they had a common purpose, when it came down to it, their single-minded purpose was getting a soul for themselves. Driven by that need, the Shun-tuk followed their spirit king and did his bidding. No doubt, Sulachan had promised them all the souls they could capture along the way.

Richard pulled back out of sight, pressing his back to the wall. He snatched another quick look several times, scanning the masses of naked flesh looking for two who would be darker and stand out. He saw neither Sulachan or Hannis Arc.

Kahlan leaned over and peeked out. "Dear spirits," she said as she pulled back, her eyes wide. "I knew they had a lot, but I didn't know they had that many."

Richard turned to sneak another look. He rolled back against the wall. Kahlan put an arm around him, pressing in close.

"You're right," he said. "That's a lot of half people wanting to eat all of us."

"They outnumber everyone in the palace many times over, that's for certain," Nathan said.

Richard gestured to the west. "What about around on the other sides of the palace? Are there any over there on that side?"

Nathan leaned close with a sour expression. He pointed a finger down and then circled it.

"They are all around us. I can't even guess at their numbers. Common sense says that they can't get in here."

"But prophecy says otherwise," Richard guessed.

Nathan admitted it with a grunt.

"How long have they been here?" Richard asked.

"A few days," Nathan told him.

"Don't tell me," Nicci said, "that was about the time the walls down in the crypts started to melt."

Nathan inclined his head toward her. "You even needed to ask?"

Nicci's face contorted with displeasure as she considered what they might do.

"Fortunately," Nathan said, "the great door down below is closed and the bridge is up. There is no way for them to get in here. I have heard people here say that the People's Palace has survived long sieges before and it can survive this one."

"I don't believe that for a moment," Richard said. "Someone who engineered his return from the world of the dead and managed to come through the veil to get into the world of life will certainly be able to find a way to get in here."

"Well I don't know how," Nathan insisted.

"Neither do I, but have no doubt he will. We need to start figuring out how we are going to defend ourselves inside the palace once they get in. If we can halt them at some key choke points, and then use wizard's fire, it might be possible to keep them at bay, and even reduce their numbers."

Nathan took a rather long, worried look out of the

crenellation. "You should know, Richard, that this is the first time they have been quiet. For days they've been down there hooting and hollering, screaming for our blood, taunting us day and night, promising to eat us all. It's strange the way they've gone silent all of a sudden."

"Not strange at all," Richard said. "They went silent because I'm here. They know I'm up here right now."

Nathan looked dubious. "You came through the sliph and you haven't shown yourself. How would they know you're here?"

"Sulachan would know," Richard said.

"How?"

Richard ignored the question as he met the old wizard's gaze. "Do you know anything about the Cerulean scrolls?"

Nathan frowned. "That's an odd question to ask right now."

"Do you?" Richard pressed.

Nathan drew his fingers and thumb down his chin as he stared off in thought. "Well," he finally said, "several hundred years ago there was one at the Palace of the Prophets. None of the Sisters had the slightest idea how to read it. At the time, neither did I."

"Do you know what it was about?"

Nathan squinted one eye as he searched his memory. "Like I said, I couldn't read it, but I remember some of the Sisters, the ones who told me it was a Cerulean scroll, referred to it as the Warheart scroll."

"If they couldn't read it, then how do they know it was called the Warheart scroll?"

Nathan shrugged. "I don't know, Richard. I don't even know where it came from."

Richard let out a sigh. "And I suppose that it disappeared and no one knew what ever happened to it."

"As a matter of fact, I believe it was traded for a number of rare books of prophecy."

If the situation hadn't been so serious, Richard might have laughed out loud. "That figures."

"Why?" Nathan asked.

"I've read the Warheart scroll. I was just wondering if you had seen any others like it, here at the palace."

Nathan leaned in with surprise. "You found it and you read it? What was it about?"

"It was about me," Richard said as he stretched up looking over rooftops. He pointed. "That's the glass roof of the Garden of Life."

Nathan looked back over his shoulder at where Richard had pointed. "Yes, what of it?"

"I need to go there. Right now. I need to go see Regula."

Kahlan came away from the wall, seized his shirt at the shoulder, and pulled him around toward her. "We can go see the omen machine later. Right now we need to get you to the containment field so that Nicci can get that poison out of you."

"Besides," Nicci pointed out, "to understand the omen machine and how it works you would first need to go to the Temple of the Winds to recover the other half of the book, *Regula*–the half that tells how Regula works."

Richard looked back at Nicci. "That book hidden away in the Temple of the Winds is a false lead, much like *The Book of Counted Shadows* was a decoy. It's a fake meant to protect Regula. I don't even need to see it to tell you it's full of misinformation."

"Without seeing it?" Nicci looked incredulous. "How can you possibly say that?"

"Zedd taught me that a lot of powerful magic is protected by such misleading information. Such stories send people off track looking for supposedly authentic information. Even if they do find it, it's actually a fake like *The Book of Counted Shadows,* just meant to mislead people and prevent them from knowing how something really works."

Nathan lifted his arms. "But how can you know that is the case with this book, *Regula?* The half we have reveals that the other half, hidden in the Temple of the Winds, fills in the parts we don't understand. How would you know that it doesn't really reveal how Regula works?"

Richard waited patiently until the old wizard was done. "Because I already know how it works."

Nathan's arms came down. "How could you know such a thing?"

"Because I've read the Warheart scroll."

Nathan stammered, looking like he had so many questions he didn't know where to start.

"We need to go," Richard told everyone before Nathan could put voice to all his questions. "I need to get to the omen machine."

Kahlan snatched his sleeve again. "No you don't, Richard. First we go to the containment field. I can see in your eyes how much worse that poison has gotten, and how sick you are. I remember what it was like and how it grows. The poison is advancing and you can't afford to waste any more time. Against all odds, we've finally made it here. Now that we're here we are going to the containment field and have Nicci heal you before we do anything else. If you're right and Sulachan's forces do get in, we all need you well so that you can fight."

"You're right," Richard said with a sigh. "But Regula is on the way. I just need to stop there first to see that it's safe and nothing has happened to it, and then we will go right to the containment field. All right?"

Kahlan folded her arms as she peered at him from under her brow for a moment. Finally her arms came unfolded and she shook her head as she was overcome with a smile.

"All right, Richard. We'll stop on our way if it will make you happy."

CHAPTER

52

At the bottom of the wedge-shaped, circular stairs, the proximity spheres around the excavated, dead-still room beneath the Garden of Life began to glow. The ancient room made of simple stone blocks had been discovered only when its roof collapsed. It was simple and without any decorations, and they had at first thought it was an abandoned storage room of some kind. There were no doors, and there was no way in except down the narrow shaft of spiral stone stairs.

The first time he had seen the room, it reminded Richard of a crypt of some sort that had been sealed and forgotten. In some ways that was exactly what it was, but it was actually much more than that.

Sitting in the center of the plain room was the imposing, square omen machine. The shielded, heavy metal that housed the power of Regula was decoration enough. Each side of the machine had an emblem in the language of Creation, identifying it, almost as a ward to keep everyone away. Around the edges of the room in neat stacks against the walls were thousands of blank metal strips that when fed through the omen machine allowed it to give prophecy directly.

At one time, the machine must have been used for that purpose. By the supply of blank metal strips, it must have once been in heavy use. Richard wondered how many of the books of prophecy, especially those in the People's Palace, originated with Regula.

Even if books of prophecy were not directly transcribed from the machine, and even if prophecy was not given directly by the machine, Regula was the conduit bringing prophecy into the world of life. Even if it was buried and no longer used to give prophecy directly, it was still in the world of life generating prophecy through the gifted. Even if it had been sent from the underworld to protect it, its presence still constituted a breach between worlds that, much like the poison of death in him, was slowly working toward the extinction of life.

Richard checked the output tray to see if the omen machine had issued any prophecies in his absence. The slot was empty.

Richard leaned over, placing both hands on the cool metal of the machine's flat top. At his touch, the ground shook with a hard thud as the machine came to life.

He now knew that the apparatus itself was not really Regula. Regula was an underworld power and there was no such mechanical mechanism in the world of the dead. The machine itself was something that had been built by ancient wizards called makers.

Makers were gifted with the ability to create things that had never been before. Richard's sword was one such item, an ancillary object, created as a worldly means necessary to interact with the power of Orden. In much the same way, the omen machine was merely a worldly mechanism created by makers to house and protect the actual power of Regula. It was a container, something like the boxes that held the power of Orden, as well as a way for the power of Regula to communicate directly with those in the world of life.

With a dull thud that shook the ground more sharply, light shot up from the center of the machine, like lightning in the near darkness, projecting a symbol in the language of Creation up onto the ceiling. The design, drawn in lines of light, slowly rotated as the gears within turned. It was the same symbol for "Regula" that was etched into the sides of the machine.

Nathan scratched his scalp. "That makes my skin crawl. I've been down here countless times since you've been gone, Richard. The machine never once stirred. Why would it suddenly start up when you touch it? With that poison in you, your magic doesn't even work."

Richard smoothed his hand along the rounded edge, caressing the cool metal, feeling the machine vibrate under his touch as all the gears, levers, and wheels inside went about their work of recording something on a metal strip in the language of Creation.

"Regula is from the underworld," Richard said. "I am *fuer grissa ost drauka*. Death recognizes me."

"Oh great," Nathan muttered. "I didn't know that they had big metal boxes full of gears in the world of the dead."

"They don't," Richard said, ignoring the old wizard's sarcasm. "The machine was built to house the power and give it a way to communicate."

"By who?" Nathan asked.

Richard looked up. "I suspect by the same people who ended up burying it when they didn't like what it had to say."

A metal strip dropped into the output tray. The metal strips were hardly bigger than his finger, and soft enough to bend easily. Richard let it sit there for a moment to cool, in case it was hot. Finally he picked it up gingerly

and tossed it on the top of the machine to continue
cooling, but it had never been hot when it came out of
the machine. He knew what that meant, and wasn't sure
if he was glad about it or not.

He flicked it with a finger, turning it around so he
could read it. Nathan, Nicci, and Kahlan all leaned in
to look at the row of complex symbols burned into the
surface of the metal.

"What does it say?" Kahlan asked.

"It says *'I have been in darkness. I have missed our
talks.'*"

Nathan scowled. "It recognizes you?"

"I told you. I'm *fuer grissa ost drauka*. It's from the
world of the dead. Now I have death in me so I am different than anyone else. I probably seem recognizable to it."

Richard idly rubbed the top of the machine, not quite
knowing what to say. He finally said, "I've learned a lot
about you since I was last here," directing his words to
the machine.

The ground jolted as the machine again started up.
The symbol made of light rotated on the ceiling as the
internal gears went about their task of pulling out a
blank strip to be engraved by the focused beam of light
inside. The metal finally dropped into the tray with a
clink. This one hadn't taken as long, and it, too, came
out cool.

Richard tossed it on top and then leaned in on his elbows as he translated it. He frowned as he read the
message silently to himself.

I know that you are not here for prophecy.

The irony was not lost on him, and in spite of everything, it made him smile. It was almost as if the machine
was being flippant–a fault he had and sometimes
couldn't control.

Regula was right, though. Richard hadn't come for
prophecy. He wanted answers. Without telling them

what it said, he looked up at the people on both sides of him. "I know this sounds a little . . . odd, but I think Regula would respond to my questions better–focus on what I'm asking–if we had some privacy."

Kahlan shot him an irritated look.

"You want us to give you two some time alone?" Nathan asked as he put his fists on his hips.

"It would probably help make it go a lot quicker," Richard said.

Nicci grasped Kahlan by the upper arm and leaned close to whisper. "After reading the scrolls, I think that maybe Richard knows what he is talking about. I think we should do as he asks."

Kahlan relented with a sigh. "All right. But hurry, will you, please? We need to get to the containment field."

Richard showed her a smile with his nod. "Of course."

When they had all gone back through the doorway to the small landing at the bottom of the spiral stairs, he leaned over again and put both hands on the machine. It immediately sprang to life, drawing another metal strip out of the stack of blanks on the other side and pulling it into the internal gearworks.

When it finally dropped into the tray, Richard picked it up by the edges between thumb and first finger, holding it up to read it.

Written in the symbols of the language of Creation, the machine had asked, *Am I going to die?*

The question unexpectedly touched Richard's heart. He had never felt anything for the machine before, but now, after all he had learned and knowing that Regula had been banished from the world of the dead where it belonged, he was seeing it in a different light. It had been sent to the world of life, an alien world, imprisoned in a metal box likely created by makers, and had taken on sentient qualities in order to function in a world where it didn't belong.

Richard smiled a little as he put a hand on the machine. "In this world, everyone must die. None of us has any choice in that. Our choice is how we wish to live."

The machine immediately began rumbling as another metal strip was plucked from the stack of blanks. When it was finished being inscribed in the focused beam of light and dropped in the tray, Richard picked it up and set it on the top of the machine to translate the symbols.

A Wizard's Rule. A very wise one, I believe.

Richard smiled again as he placed his hand on the machine. "Yes, it is."

The machine again started its gears and levers into motion. The stone floor rumbled as the metal strip made its way through the inner workings to have Regula inscribe it and finally dropped into the tray. Richard glanced back over his shoulder at the others. They were huddled close together, speaking in hushed tones to one another, engaged in what looked like a heated discussion. He couldn't make out what they were saying, but they weren't paying attention to him anymore, and that was what mattered.

He picked up the metal strip and was stunned by what he read.

What is it like to be surprised? Not to know what will happen? Not to know all the possibilities?

This was Regula, the underworld power that regulated the eternal now, speaking directly to him about the nature of his world. Regula knew everything that would happen, everything that could happen. Regula was the grand cosmic knot, a jumble of the eternal now consisting of all possibilities.

Or, at least, it knew almost everything. Free will was beyond its scope.

"That," Richard said as he placed his hand back on the cold metallic top of the machine, "is the meaning of that Wizard's Rule. To not know what will happen is to be filled with the possibilities, much the same as you are. For us, it's sometimes hard to choose from those possibilities. Sometimes we must choose things that are hard and even frightening. Sometimes making those choices is the joyous core of what it means to be alive, to be human."

A metal plate immediately started through Regula. When it came out, Richard laid it on top with the others to read it.

The dead talk to me. Even here, I can hear the dead talking. Even if they didn't want to say things when they were alive, they tell me when they are dead.

"That must be . . . difficult."

Another strip was drawn through Regula. Richard saw that it had four symbols inscribed on it. He quickly worked out the translation.

This is a cold world. I used to have constellations of souls all around me, all talking to me. But I was sent away. Here, I have no one. I am alone.

Richard put a hand back on the machine, feeling empathy for it for having been buried and forgotten.

"I understand. I'm so sorry." He said it in a whisper.

Some of the internal gears spun at idle, not producing a metal strip. It gave the machine a quiet humming noise that reminded him of the way a cat might purr.

"Why did they bury you?" he asked when Regula had remained silent, its gears spinning softly, for a time.

He didn't know who had done it, but it was obvious that someone had gone to a great deal of trouble to bury the Regula device and insure that it was not found.

Finally the gears slowly, almost reluctantly, spun up to speed. Levers clacked into the stops, rods rotated, and steel arms turned as the device began using light to inscribe another message on a metal plate.

Richard pulled out the cool metal strip and tossed it on the top, leaning on his forearm as he translated it.

Because I knew too much.

Richard couldn't help but to chuckle. "I guess they didn't know you. You can't help it. You are only behaving according to your nature."

Another metal strip immediately started through and a message burned into it.

You understand. No one before has ever understood. You understand because you are the Warheart.

The last symbol Richard had seen only once before. He had only just learned its meaning from the Cerulean scrolls.

He smiled sadly. "You have just done something against your nature. You have acted of free will and told me something that you did not need to say."

When the answer came through, Richard puzzled over it.

It was not against my nature. It is prophecy, one of them that has been true.

Richard nodded. "I guess that maybe you're right."

Another metal strip ran through and finally dropped out. Richard bent down and picked it up.

Why do I exist?

He sighed. "You are a part of the underworld. You are meant to regulate certain things there–things the dead tell you. You are the keeper of the eternal now."

Immediately another metal strip came through.

That is my purpose in that world. Prophecy says that I was sent here to fulfill my purpose, but not what that purpose is. What is my purpose here, in this world?

Richard stared at the metal box that now somehow seemed alive to him. "You are the keeper of the eternal now. How can you not know your purpose?"

The machine hardly paused before inscribing its answer.

Because you act on free will. You determine my purpose.

It felt like the machine was feeling him out, prodding him to say the right thing.

"I believe you have answered your own question about what is it like not to know what will happen. Not to know all the possibilities. You only have to ask yourself what it is like to be surprised. Maybe you are coming to understand the Wizard's Rule?"

As Regula waited, Richard leaned over and rested both hands on the machine. "My choice is to help you get back to the world where you belong before your presence here destroys the world of life. That will help you be where you belong. Your purpose is to help me."

The machine sat still and quiet, as if considering, or maybe testing his words against some kind of original constraints. The ground suddenly thumped as Regula started up again, snatching a metal strip out of the stack in the bin. Richard peered down through the thick, wavy viewing glass, watching the plate move through the tracks and gears, being pulled along by metal pincers. When Regula was finished inscribing the symbols of the message, it dropped the metal strip into the bin. Richard stared at it for a moment before picking it up and carefully laying it on top of the machine.

He stared at what it said, what it confirmed in his mind.

The lost are among us. You are their only hope. You are the Warheart. Do what you must. Act according to the Wizard's Rule.

He knew exactly what it meant. He remembered Naja Moon's words written on the cave wall in Stroyza.

Before he could say anything, Regula jumped to life again, but this time with an abrupt thud. Four metal plates were pulled into the machine, one right after the other. The machine rumbled as the strips ran their course through the gears and inner workings. This time, though, it sounded somehow different.

When the first dropped into the tray, he saw it steaming. He gingerly tested it with a finger. The metal strip was scalding hot. He knew what that meant.

It said, *My children are coming.*

The second hot metal strip emerged from the machine. He let it cool for a moment before picking it up.

They will devour you all.

The third plate said, *Retribution is finally at hand.*

The last plate plinked down into the tray. Richard plucked the hot strip out of the tray and tossed it on top of Regula.

Here they come.

He knew exactly what was happening. Emperor Sulachan and Hannis Arc had taken control of what the omen machine said. They were using it. They had done it before. When they did, the metal strips always came out hot.

This time they were telling him that the invasion of the palace was about to begin. It was their way to announce their arrival to strike paralyzing fear into their victims.

CHAPTER
53

Richard pressed his hand to the top of the machine in a silent thank-you.

He turned and hurried to the cramped landing for the spiral stairs where the others waited.

Nicci looked up. "So, what was that all about? What did it say?"

"I don't know," Richard said, flicking a hand back toward Regula. "Nothing much, really. Nothing that made any sense. You know the way it likes to talk in riddles. Just more of those same games and nonsense we've gotten from it before."

Nicci made a sound to say that she knew what he was talking about. Nathan looked disappointed.

Richard rubbed the back of his neck. The pain from the poison was making his head hurt so much it was making him sick to his stomach. Kahlan, watching him, could see how he was feeling.

"I knew it was a waste of time. Now can we go to the containment field?" There was no mistaking by her tone that it was not really a question.

He gave in with a weary nod. "Of course. I told you we would go there as soon as I checked the machine. It's fine. I'm done. Let's go."

Kahlan blinked, apparently having expected an argument of some sort. "Well, all right, then. Good."

Richard grabbed Nathan's arm and turned the frowning prophet to get him started up the circular stone stairway. He needed to distract them from the omen machine.

"Are all the defenses in place," Richard asked Nathan, "like I told you we needed in case those unholy half-dead get into the palace?"

Nathan looked back over his shoulder as Richard prodded him upward. "How would they get in? The palace is sealed tight."

"Well, there are catacombs out there on the plains, remember? That's how I got in before. Jagang managed to launch an attack in that same way. Sulachan is one of the dead, after all, so he would likely be aware of such places. And then there are the walls that are melting–"

"You've made your point," Nathan said, holding up a hand. "You go on to the containment field while I check with General Zimmer and make sure that the defenses are in place and ready. If need be, I can always use wizard's fire to hold any invaders back. Happy?"

"Yes, thank you, that would ease my mind if you would coordinate it with him. If those unholy half-dead get in here, we are going to be in a lot of trouble."

"Once I'm done healing you," Nicci said, "I'll go help them. If the enemy breaks in there are plenty of choke points inside where we can keep them contained with the help of fire."

"Good," Richard said with a firm nod, not believing a word of it. There would be no containing such forces, at least not for long.

At the top of the stairs as they went around the empty structural chamber and climbed the ladder up and out of the hole where the floor of the Garden of Life had collapsed, Richard gestured to the prophet. "Nathan, you had better get going while we have the chance. Get General Zimmer and his men in place. The rest of us will head for the containment field."

Back up on the floor of the Garden of Life, surrounded by the heady fragrance of jasmine that grew in great swaths beside the walkway that wandered down toward them in the heart of the room, Richard paused to look across the remaining grass to the altar. There on top of the granite slab where lives were once sacrificed, right where he had left them, sat the three boxes of Orden.

All of their covers were off. Each sinister-looking box was blacker than black. Each looked like a window through the world of life into the underworld itself.

He supposed that in a way that's exactly what they were. The power of Orden could create spectral folds that brought worlds together. Now, the world of the dead was coming together with the world of life.

Richard glanced up at the glass roof over the Garden of Life. The sun had set and the sky was darkening. Richard couldn't yet see the first stars.

"It will be night soon," Nicci said. "Night is the best time to use the containment field, so we will have that on our side to help us."

"We can't get there soon enough to satisfy me." Kahlan gestured around the room. "The Garden of Life is a containment field. Why can't we do it here?"

Nicci shook her head, dissuading them from the notion. "With the breach in the floor down into the substructure and below that into the room with the omen machine, we dare not trust that the containment field would still be intact. We know that the omen machine goes down through the plateau, like a deep taproot. That could drain the power protecting the field right into the ground. We simply can't trust it. The consequences of a field breach would be catastrophic. We

know that the other one, down in that lower library, is
intact. We need to get down there and use that one."

It was a reminder to prompt Richard to stop looking
around the Garden of Life and get moving. Richard
needed to take a last look at it all and get it fixed in his
mind. He had also wanted to make sure that the boxes
of Orden were still where he had left them and that they
hadn't been disturbed. Satisfied, he started up the path
between the small trees.

Outside the great doors carved with a scene of rolling hills and forests and then sheathed in gold, General
Zimmer and a large contingent of the First File waited
to protect him wherever he went in the palace. He was
going to need a way around that, and he hoped Nathan
would provide the excuse.

"General Zimmer," Richard said, lifting a hand to get
the man's attention as he hurried down the hall. "We
need to get down to the containment field in the lower
libraries. Nicci has to heal me there, so we'll be in there
all night. While we're doing that, I want Nathan to take
you and the men and show you where we need defensive positions set up."

The general looked a little confused. "If there is any
breach, we will defend right there, wherever it is."

Richard was shaking his head. "Ordinarily, you
would be right. But this threat is different. It involves
powers we've never had to face before." Richard signaled to the prophet. "Nathan will take you and the men
down and show you the spots where we hope to be able
to contain any intrusion. He will know best where his
magic will work, should it be needed."

The general, more accustomed to acting alone and in
his own way than by elaborate planning, looked back
at Nathan, seeming unsure. Richard gestured again.
"Hurry now. Get going. Once you're done, I'd like you
and the men to stand guard outside the library with the

containment field where we will be. Nathan knows which one it is."

General Zimmer clapped a fist to his heart. "I will see that it is taken care of, Lord Rahl."

With Nathan following closely behind, General Zimmer peeled away as he started down the hall, taking his large contingent of men with him down the nearest staircase. The entire top floor was guarded with a permanent force of the First File who would remain behind to guard the Garden of Life and the boxes of Orden waiting inside.

Richard, with Kahlan at his side, followed Rikka down the grand marble staircases on the other side from the one the general and his men had taken. Nicci, Cassia, and Vale followed him down flights of stairs past landings at several levels. Richard slipped an arm around Kahlan's waist as they descended the marble steps. He needed to feel her warmth, the life in her. He needed to feel the balance to what churned inside him.

At the unexpected embrace, Kahlan looked over at him, not asking anything, not saying anything, simply happy that he had pulled her close to him. She gave him her special smile, the one she gave no one else.

Rikka knew the way to the library with the containment field better than any of them, so when they reached a lower level she led them without hesitation through guarded double doors out of the restricted areas and into the grand halls of the palace. They were immediately greeted by the background murmur of hushed whispers and the scuffing of feet against the ornate stone floors.

Being one of the main public hallways through the palace, it was several stories high. There were people everywhere nervously going about their business, taking care of urgent matters. He could see small groups of people rushing over the bridges that crossed the hallway overhead. Some stopped to look down at the unexpected sight of the Lord Rahl in the palace. It had been quite a while since they had seen him.

Everywhere, people noticed the statuesque blonde with the single braid, dressed in red leather, walking out in front, leading the Lord Rahl and the Mother Confessor through his palace. Richard had forgotten what it was like to have eyes constantly watching them. With that unique skill that beautiful women seemed to possess, Rikka appeared not to notice anyone looking at her, and yet was acutely aware of all the eyes on her.

From a side hall, Nyda arrived to join them. She glanced over to Richard, Kahlan, and those following. She noticed immediately that Rikka marched with purpose, her eyes ahead, and fell in beside her. Rikka and Nyda almost looked as if they could have been sisters. With four Mord-Sith escorting them, surrounding Richard, Kahlan, and Nicci in a wall of red leather, they were drawing even more attention.

Mord-Sith never went anywhere unnoticed. Even if people didn't look directly at them, most people seemed to have a sixth sense that enabled them to know where the Mord-Sith were and casually, without looking at the women in red leather, to move away and give them ample distance.

The People's Palace was so sprawling that it took quite some time to get from one end to the other. Richard was glad when Rikka turned them in to a private corridor and then down service stairs that would cut the distance they needed to travel through the palace.

They finally reached the proper hallway where there were several libraries, most with glassed doors, including the one with the containment field.

"Here we are," Rikka said as she stopped and gestured.

"At last," Kahlan said with obvious relief. "I never thought we would get here."

Just before entering through the double doors with squares of opaque glass, Richard came to a stop. He snapped his fingers.

"I forgot. I have to do something a minute. It will be quick."

Nicci frowned. "What are you talking about?"

Kahlan's frown was more serious. "Richard, you need to get in here right now and let Nicci get that poison out of you."

Richard was nodding reassuringly as she spoke. "I know, I know. This will only take a minute. Wait here. I'll be right back."

"You can do it after–"

"No, I just need to do this first. It will be quick. I'll explain in a couple minutes when I'm back. I will be right back."

Kahlan looked into the dark room and then back to him. "Richard, I don't think–"

"Get the lamps lit and get the place set up," he said, gesturing into the room. "Hurry."

Before Nicci could take his arm, he stepped away and seized Cassia's instead. "I'll take Cassia with me. All right? Will that ease your mind?"

He started moving down the hall, still holding Cassia's arm, ushering her along with him. He waved assurance back at the confused faces of Kahlan and Nicci, and the scowls of the other three Mord-Sith.

Kahlan lifted her hand in confusion. "Richard–"

"Go in and wait for me." He gestured for her to go into the library. "I'll be right back."

As soon as he turned a corner in the hall so that he was out of their sight, he started running.

Cassia ran at his side. "Lord Rahl, what's going on? Where are we going?"

Richard pointedly didn't answer her. He caught the round cap of a newel post in one hand to help swing

himself around as he caught Cassia's arm with his other
hand to pull her along with him and down the stairs.

His mind raced as fast as his feet as he oriented himself in a mental map of the palace, making sure of each
intersection and turn he made so that he wouldn't get
stuck in a dead end with a shield and have to waste time
backtracking. He took several unconventional routes
simply to skirt one place that he knew was shielded, and
a public corridor so that he wouldn't be seen by anyone.

"Lord Rahl, what are we doing? Where are you going?"

Richard slid to a stop as a shield he hadn't realized
would be in that particular hallway lit the air red right
across the hallway. He would have to go back and take
a different route.

"Lord Rahl–"

He turned to face Cassia, still holding her by the arm.
"I'm going someplace dangerous. I have to do something
crazy. I need help. Are you with me? Are you willing to
risk your life helping me?"

Cassia blinked at the question, then lifted Cara's Agiel
from where it hung on the chain at her neck, showing it
to him. "Of course, Lord Rahl. Like Cara, I would lay
down my life for you."

"I'm trying to save all of our lives. I have to do this.
It's the only way–our only chance."

Cassia's face screwed up with a puzzled frown. "Do
what?"

Richard turned her and gave her a shove, starting
her running back up the hall with him. He took the
next intersection, flinging open the door into the Lord
Rahl's private corridor off the service area. There would
be less chance of being spotted in there. He was relieved to see which corridor it was. He remembered the
small painting of a statue on a hillside of wildflowers.

It was a corridor that would take them where they needed to go.

"Stay with me," he said as he hurried down the hallway. "There is no time to lose."

"Lord Rahl, what's wrong?"

"Sulachan and the half people are going to break in soon and start killing people. We have to get back in time to stop them before it's too late and everyone is slaughtered."

"Lord Rahl," she protested as she ran behind him. "What are you going to do? Why couldn't you tell the others? Why would you leave the Mother Confessor without telling her?"

He stopped and turned back a moment, catching his breath.

"That horde of half people spread out across the Azrith Plain are going to get in here at any moment. If I don't do this they will kill everyone in here. The Twilight Count is nearly done. Time is running out. If I don't do this everyone is going to die."

"So why couldn't you tell her that and tell her what you intend to do? And what is it you intend—"

"Even if I succeed in saving the world of life, I will likely die doing it. I couldn't tell her that. If by some chance I live, then I'll have to apologize to her, but I couldn't tell her I'm running off to do something that is likely to get me killed no matter if I succeed or not. This is about everyone, not just the people here."

Cassia smiled a crooked grin. "Lord Rahl, she knows your heart. Whatever it is you have to do, she would understand."

"Not this," he said as he started down the corridor again, heading for the stairs.

At the bottom of the solemn black marble stairs, he raced along the final corridor that would get him to where he needed to go.

"Sliph!" he called out as he ran. "Sliph–I need you!"

He threw open the double doors and stumbled to a stop, Cassia right behind him, both out of breath.

The silver face rising above the silver pool in the well smiled pleasantly. "Master, you wish to travel?"

Richard swallowed, hands on his knees, catching his breath. He straightened.

"Yes, we both need to travel. It's urgent. We need to travel."

"Come," the sliph said, "and we will travel. You will be pleased."

Richard hopped up on the stone wall surrounding her well. "You must not tell anyone where we're going," he said as he helped pull Cassia up beside him. "No matter who asks, you must not let them know where you are taking us."

"Master," the sliph said with a coy smile, "you know I never reveal anything about my clients to anyone."

CHAPTER

54

Kahlan paced down the length of the library, past rows of shelves holding books of prophecy, a thumbnail held tightly between her front teeth as her mind raced. She would look herself, if she knew where to look, but she wouldn't even know where to start. She came to a halt and looked up when General Zimmer rushed into the room.

"Did you find him?"

He shook his head as he caught his breath. "I'm sorry, Mother Confessor, but no. I have men searching everywhere. No one has seen them."

Nicci threw her arms up. "It doesn't make any sense. He's been missing most of the night. He said he was only going to be a few minutes. How could he simply vanish?"

Vale stepped forward hesitantly. "Could, well, could some of those half people have snuck in and snatched them?"

"There would at least have been blood from any such attack," Nicci said in a quiet voice.

When she heard nothing, the sorceress glanced up from under her brow at the general.

The general's face distorted with an uncomfortable

expression. "All I can tell you is that none of the men has spotted so much as a drop of blood."

"Have they spotted anything useful?"

"It's an awfully big place, Mother Confessor," the big D'Haran said, clearly uneasy that he had no good news. "There are a thousand places to look."

Kahlan went back to pacing. "He said he was only going to be gone a few minutes. I felt like something wasn't right. I had a feeling. I should have trusted that feeling and not have let him go." She gestured with a hand, angry at herself, blaming herself. "It's just that he rushed off so fast."

Kahlan pressed her lips tight for a moment. "He needs to be healed. He doesn't have much time left before that poison kills him."

She was on the verge of panic, remembering what it was like seeing him when he was dead. Her whole world had ended. Now, he was near death again from that taint of death within him. Nicci could have removed it. But now he was gone.

Nicci, leaning against a heavy table, watched Kahlan pace. "This is making me start to wonder why he wanted to stop to check on Regula."

"What do you mean?" Kahlan asked without looking over.

"Richard is so honest that I never suspected he might be lying."

Kahlan paused in her pacing and looked up. "You think he was lying?"

"At least not telling us the whole truth." Nicci's arms came unfolded as she stood up away from the table. "Do you think he had to stop there to check on the machine, talk to Regula alone, and it didn't tell him anything he could understand? Since when has Richard been so easily stymied? Kahlan, that's not just a mysterious omen machine. That's Regula, the controller of the eternal now. It's an underworld force that has been brought to life in this world, banished here because it's so dangerous. Spirits sent it here to hide it from Sulachan in the underworld, but Sulachan found it, here, in this world. Richard knows all that."

Kahlan rubbed her arms against the chill of her fears. "What do you think it told him?"

Nicci let her arms flop down against her sides. "Who knows. Regula knows everything that could happen, everything that will happen." She looked up with a sudden thought. "We could go ask Regula what it told him."

Kahlan shook her head. "I don't know how. It only seems to talk to Richard. Besides, Richard wouldn't want to know prophecy from the machine. Wasn't that the point made in the scrolls–that he is the counter to prophecy through free will? He wouldn't ask what was going to happen. For Richard, action is better than reaction. He would act."

"Then that brings us right back to not knowing where he is." Nicci went to one of the long mahogany tables and rested the fingertips of one hand on the polished top as she stared off in thought.

"Did he give any indication–anything at all–that might suggest where he was going?" General Zimmer asked. "Some kind of hint? It might not have seemed important at the time, but maybe he said something to indicate where he was going."

Kahlan looked up at the big D'Haran general. She remembered him so well from when they were fighting in the war. In the mornings, when Captain Zimmer returned from a night of hunting with his men, he would bring Kahlan a string of ears from the enemy they had killed that night.

"Hunt him, Captain," she said, deliberately reminding him of those special missions he was so good at.

He smiled at the memory and caught her meaning. "The men will keep looking. Don't you worry–if he is in the palace, we will find him."

Kahlan nodded as the man left to continue the search. Kahlan looked up suddenly and turned to Nicci.

"If he is in the palace."

"What?"

"If they can't find him, maybe it's because he isn't here in the palace."

Vale frowned at the notion. "Mother Confessor, the entire palace is surrounded by half people. He couldn't take three steps out of here without them seeing him and jumping all over him. There's no way he could leave the palace."

Kahlan stood stiffly, considering it. "Of course there is."

Nicci folded her arms as she stepped closer. "You think he may have gone somewhere in the sliph?"

"It's the only thing that makes sense."

"Then let's go ask her," Nicci said.

"Rikka, Nyda, take us on the shortest route to the room where the sliph's well is located."

Clapping fists to their hearts, they turned and started away, eager to find their Lord Rahl, happy that they now had a real clue as to what happened to Richard and Cassia.

"We're lucky the sliph's well room is in this section of the palace," Rikka said.

"It could take hours to get there if it were at some distant part of the palace," Nyda agreed. "We're not far away from there."

"That's how he vanished so fast," Kahlan said as she followed the two Mord-Sith, angry at herself for not re-alizing it sooner. "That's why no one has seen him, I know it."

"Where would he have gone?" Nicci asked. "And

why? It doesn't make any sense. All of our problems are here. Sulachan, Hannis Arc, and the entire Shun-tuk nation are right outside, surrounding the palace. That's what Richard needed to deal with. There is nowhere for him to go that would get him any help."

Kahlan couldn't argue with that logic, so she didn't.

It had to be that Richard had already left the palace in the sliph. The more Kahlan thought about it, the more it explained how he had vanished so fast and so completely. She was sure of it, but only the sliph could confirm it. Her thoughts raced as she tried to figure out why he would have left.

"He wouldn't abandon us here," Vale said. "Lord Rahl would die before he would abandon us."

"That's what I'm afraid of," Kahlan said under her breath.

The Mord-Sith led them through the private passageways, keeping them away from the crowded public halls that might have slowed them down. With the palace under siege, people were frightened and could become a problem, so it was better to stay out of the public areas if possible.

Everywhere they went, soldiers of the First File, all with weapons to hand, were searching, going into every room off every passageway. When she looked into libraries along the way, Kahlan saw soldiers searching between the rows of shelves, looking for the missing Lord Rahl. Kahlan knew now that they would not find him.

When they reached it, she saw that the door to the sliph's room was ajar. Kahlan pushed it back, letting it swing in. A lamp hanging from a bracket on the wall was lit.

With Nicci beside her and the three Mord-Sith behind her, Kahlan stepped into the room. The sliph, apparently hearing them coming, rose up in a lump from the well. The mound of liquid silver formed into a smiling face.

"You wish to travel?"

"Maybe," Kahlan said.

The reflective gaze turned to Rikka and Nyda. "I know that you two can't travel. You don't have the required properties."

Kahlan glanced over at Nicci. "That's why he took Cassia. He knows she has what is needed to travel."

"But why?" Nicci whispered back.

Kahlan stepped closer to the sliph. "We need to know where your master went."

The sliph smiled politely. "I am sorry, but I do not discuss my clients with anyone."

"I'm his wife," Kahlan said.

The sliph only stared back.

"This is a matter of life and death. Richard–your master–has a sickness and he needs to be cured."

"I told you all before that he has death in him."

"That's right, and it is getting stronger all the time. If we don't take him to where we can get that poison out of him, he is going to die. You don't want that to happen, do you? You don't want your master to die?"

The silver smile faded a little. "I am sorry, but I cannot help you."

"He told you not to tell us, didn't he?" Kahlan asked.

"Do you wish to travel?" the sliph asked in a more formal tone.

Kahlan stepped up and rested her hands on the edge of the well. "Yes, I do wish to travel. Take me to the place you took Richard and Cassia earlier tonight."

"You must name a place if you wish to travel."

Kahlan stared at the silver face that from only inches away revealed her own face in the distorted reflection.

"The place where you took Richard."

The smile widened on the silver face. "Call on me

anytime if you decide you would like to travel. Please know your destination when you come back."

With that, the silver face that was the sliph melted back down into the quicksilver pool.

Kahlan and Nicci shared a look.

"I guess now we know that Richard took the sliph out of the palace."

"It would seem so," Nicci agreed. "But why?"

A hard thud jolted the room. Everyone looked up as dust fell from the plastered ceiling.

"That sounded like wizard's fire," Nicci said.

"Let's go."

Kahlan raced for the door. Everyone followed on her heels. Once they were out in the hallway, Rikka and Nyda closed in to protect Kahlan and Nicci from the front, while Vale protected them from behind. They took several intersections in the plastered halls, and then service stairwells that headed back up into the palace.

As they cleared the top step up into a broad hallway, half people leaped at them from behind the wall to the left. One of them took Nyda from her feet, rolling with her across the floor.

Another, mouth opened wide, sprang at Kahlan.

Before he even got close, a sword swept around and took off the head of the half-naked half person. It was General Zimmer who had acted just in time to protect her. The head bounced heavily on the floor, leaving a trail of blood as it rolled away. Another soldier stabbed the man grappling with Nyda.

Soldiers raced down the stairs and quickly cut down the dozen or so half people in the hallway.

"Sorry, Mother Confessor." General Zimmer wiped blood off his forehead with the back of his wrist. "I tried to stop them before they got that close, but there were a lot of them."

Nyda pushed the dead half person off her and sprang up, furious that she had been blindsided.

"What's going on?" Kahlan asked.

General Zimmer pointed with his sword. "They created a breach of some sort down in the area of the crypts, down where the walls were melting. I wasn't there at the time so I didn't see it. The men said they were trying to keep the enemy from getting out of the area where we have them contained.

"Apparently more of them managed to get in somewhere else and come up behind my men. It was a bloody battle, but they managed to fall back to a secondary defensive zone. Nathan was using wizard's fire to help keep them from breaking through and flooding into the palace."

"Show me the way," Nicci said. "I need to go help him."

Richard! What are you doing here?" Chase asked.
The big man rubbed sleep from his eyes with one hand and used his other for leverage against his knee as he stood. He had apparently been sleeping while sitting against the wall just outside the tower room.

Richard slipped the baldric of his sword over his head and strapped the belt around his waist as he headed for the stairs to the hallway he needed on the next level.

"I'm in a hurry, Chase."

Chase arranged the knives along his belt, then straightened the sword at his hip before checking that the sword strapped over the back of his shoulder was secure.

Chase followed quickly after them. "Well, all right, but where are you in a hurry to?"

"I need to get back to that place we came out of, back to the catacombs."

Chase caught his sleeve, stopping him, and with his other hand pointed down a side hall. "Then this way is quicker."

Richard nodded. "Lead the way." He looked over at Cassia as they hurried down the starkly plain stone corridor. "Are you all right?"

Cassia tugged down the sleeves of her red leather outfit at the wrists. "I'm fine. I'm just not sure I'm getting any more comfortable traveling in that liquid silver."

"What's this about?" Chase asked. "What's going on?"

"Long story."

Chase frowned over as he pointed Richard down a stairwell. "You seem to be full of a lot of long stories. Is there a short version?" Chase snatched Richard's shirt. "Nope. That way shields a library with books of magic. You need to take this intersection to the right, then take the stairs down a level, then the hall, then back up to get around it."

Richard nodded. "The short version is that Emperor Sulachan and Hannis Arc have an entire nation of those half people surrounding the People's Palace. They are soon going to get in, if they haven't already."

"So then what are you doing here?"

"I came to get something I left behind."

"You mean your sword? So you can fight?"

"Yes, that too."

"What did you leave behind in the catacombs?"

"You wouldn't believe me if I told you."

Chase pointed. "That one. Take that hall. The big chamber is just beyond. So try me. What wouldn't I believe?"

Just as he had said, they soon found themselves in the massive room with the entrance to the catacombs. Torches in brackets down each side lit the area well enough. Richard headed for the entrance to the lower world.

"If you want, you can come with us and see for yourself."

"Good. You might need my sword, too."

"Your sword won't be of any help where we're going."

Cassia glanced over at Chase with a long-suffering look. "Don't feel bad. He hasn't told me, either. He said it isn't good to know how you might die."

"Ah," the big man said. "At least he has a good reason."

"I haven't told either of you because in the first place I wouldn't know how, and in the second place I'm not even sure I can do this."

The slits at the top of the chamber revealed that it was night. How deep in the night Richard wasn't sure, but since Chase had been asleep, it seemed pretty clear that it was the heart of darkness.

Richard spotted the alcove set back in shadows and headed for it. Without delay he pressed his palms to the metal statues, closing his fingers around the shepherds. He felt them warm as before, and as before the stone groaned as it began to swing open.

"Get some torches," Richard said.

Chase grabbed one for himself and handed Cassia a lantern. He gave Richard a torch.

Richard started in. "There are lots of steps. It goes down really deep into the mountain. The first flights are constructed, but you need to be careful once we get lower because they are carved from the rock and they aren't even."

"What's the rush?"

Richard turned and looked at Chase. "A lot of people back at the palace are going to be slaughtered by half people before I can get back. It could even be that everyone there will die. I'm hoping to make it back before that happens. But even if it does, everyone else is going to die after that. I need to try to stop what is going to happen. I think this is the only way. Kahlan's life hangs in the balance. Everyone's life hangs in the balance. I don't know if I will live through what I am going to do, but I have to save everyone I can. That's the rush."

Chase grunted his understanding and followed Richard when he started down, taking two steps at a time, half descending stairs, half falling the entire way. They went past landing after landing, racing down.

The torches suddenly revealed the chamber with the round table and the various tunnel openings. Richard ducked under the opening and went into the ninth one on the right, plunging down the shaft cut through the stone, down rough-cut stairs, the torches flapping in the wind as they raced ever downward.

They began encountering the dead in their carved resting places. Richard paid attention to where he was going, ignoring the hundreds upon hundreds of corpses they hurried past. Chase, though, looked to each side with big eyes. He hadn't known the catacombs were there, beneath the Keep all this time. For that matter, generations had lived at the Keep without ever being aware of what lay below.

The long, winding, descending journey finally brought them to the arched opening into the precisely cut, square, broad passageway.

"This place is making the hairs at the back of my neck stand on end," Chase said.

"Me too," Cassia added.

"I know," Richard said. "Come on. This way."

At the end of the broad corridor, Richard stopped before the cloth hanging at the end. On the other side it was painted with wards to keep spirits from crossing.

"What is this place?" Chase asked, looking around at the carefully carved straight walls and precisely cut, flat ceiling, and especially the strange piece of cloth hanging across their way ahead.

Richard turned back to Chase. "It's called the Sanctuary of Souls."

"You mean . . . there are spirits, ghosts, down here?"

"Yes." Richard gestured to the cloth. "There are these

things, these cloth panels, hanging all throughout the
maze. Some, like this one, have ancient wards painted
on them. Those wards are powerful spell-forms that
keep the spirits from crossing. It keeps them on the
other side. Yet other cloth panels have spell-forms meant
to draw the spirits to this place."

"Draw them here?" Cassia asked. "Why?"

"Back in the caves in Stroyza, Naja left a message
about what happened back in the great war."

"Who is Naja?" Chase asked.

Richard waved away the question. "A sorceress who
lived back in the great war. Not important right now.
But the message she left for us is. You see, the half people
don't have souls. Naja says that when the emperor and
his makers created the half people, those spirits, once
pulled from the victim, were not allowed to go to the
spirit world. That was how Sulachan created the half
people. If their souls went to the underworld, then their
bodies here would die. Instead, their souls were ripped
from them, but not allowed to cross over into the underworld."

Cassia ran her hand down Cara's Agiel. "What happened to them, then?"

"Naja said that those souls are unable to go through
the veil into the underworld, so those lost spirits drift
back in this direction and end up haunting this plane of
existence, not knowing where to go. Some of them have
come to me before, seeking my help, but I didn't understand at the time."

Cassia pointed. "So you think some of them might be
in there?"

"This is the Sanctuary of Souls. Look at all the trouble the people back in Naja's time obviously went to in
order to create this place. I think that some of the spell-
forms draw those spirits here, making it safe for them. I
think this maze is a place they can haunt, a place where

they can gather and feel safe. A temporary home, of sorts. Once drawn in, the wards keep them from coming out here."

"Why?" Chase asked.

"Naja says that not all of them who drift back into the world of life are friendly."

The big man frowned. "Why not?"

"They'd probably be pretty angry about what was done to them, don't you suppose? Ripped from their body and not allowed to cross over to a place of eternal peace. Forced to wander between worlds, always torn from the Grace, kept out of reach."

Chase reached back and scratched his neck. "It's making my skin crawl just thinking about it."

"Lord Rahl, that still doesn't answer what we're doing here."

Richard gave Cassia a long look. "I am the bringer of death. I've been in the world of the dead. I've been dead. The dead recognize me as one of them."

"Well . . ." she drawled, "all right, but I don't see—"

Richard yanked down the cloth and handed it to her. "I need you to carry this. Fold the symbols inward. Come on."

As they hurried into the warren of passageways, Richard kept track of the shepherd symbols up on the walls so that he wouldn't get lost in the maze. Along the way, he pulled down cloth hangings and draped them over Cassia's outstretched arm.

As they went farther into the maze of tunnels, he could sense the presence of the spirits gathering around him in great numbers. He could hear their whispered pleas.

When they reached a larger, central hallway, he motioned to Chase and Cassia. "Go back there, to the end, and wait."

With the shadowy forms passing through the torchlight, they didn't need to be told twice.

Richard stood at the far end of the hallway, looking down the length of it back toward Chase and Cassia. As he watched, he saw sparkles, like dust caught in sunlight, begin to gather in what looked like rippling sheets. As more and more of them came together, creating swirling shapes that formed and moved together the way great flocks of birds did, he could sense the thousands of spirits present, come to someone they recognized as one of their own, but different.

As they gathered, their great numbers created sheets of light, like the northern lights Richard had often seen in the night sky. It was a beautiful sight, an underground show of the northern lights, except these lights were made from the specks of souls, all gathering together, all moving with the same purpose, the same longing, the same need.

Richard drew his sword.

The sound rang through the halls. It sounded pure, almost divine.

In the torchlight he could see that the blade still had the dark metallic gleam to it, taken on from having touched the world of the dead. It looked more sinister than it had ever looked, and rightly so. It now was cloaked in death.

He could feel the power of its magic flooding through him, lifting his own soul with the calling of the storm, touching the death he carried within him.

Richard held the sword out in both hands, then, pointed back up the hallway.

"Come home with me," Richard whispered out to the constellation of souls twisting together before him in great sheets of sparkling light, looking like they were moving on an otherworldly wind.

As he held the sword out, the sheets of light began twisting, turning, spiraling in on the sword. The dark, gleaming blade seemed to absorb fold after fold of those sheets of glimmering souls, until at last they had all gone as dark as the blade.

Richard slid the sword back in its scabbard.

"Let's go."

"Where?" Cassia asked.

"Back to the sliph."

Chase led the way as they raced back through the halls, then the catacombs with the countless niches filled with the dead, their souls safely in the world of the dead, up flights of stairs, and then up long runs of steps tunneling ever upward. It seemed like they ran for half the night. Richard felt like he lost parts of that run in a dim haze.

The sickness was overwhelming him. It sapped his strength as they ran up flight after flight of steps. It threatened to take his legs from under him. It threatened to take consciousness from him.

When he thought he could go on no longer, he thought of Kahlan and everyone else back at the palace, and what they faced. Hannis Arc and Sulachan were determined to take the palace. They would unleash the unholy half-dead on the living. When they did, everyone there would be slaughtered. But that would be only the beginning of the dying. It would be the beginning of the end for the world of life.

With that terrible thought uppermost in his mind, he ignored his pain and kept running.

When they reached the top, Richard closed the cap-stone to the catacombs and then dropped onto the bench, panting, trying to gather his strength, finding it hard even to breathe.

"Cassia," he said without looking up.

She put a worried hand on his shoulder. "Yes, Lord Rahl?"

"This is why I brought you. You have to help me make it back. You have to be my strength."

Without delay, she put an arm around him and helped lift him to his feet. Chase draped one of Richard's arms over his shoulders to hold him up.

"I can help you, Richard. At least until we get back to the sliph. I can't travel, but I can get you there. I wish I could travel so I could help you, but I can't."

"I know," Richard said as they made their way through the immense chamber. "Cassia will help me from there."

Richard tried to let Chase take as much of his weight as possible, let his big friend carry the load. Richard's head hung as he gave himself the chance to gather his strength and recover somewhat while Chase helped him. Much of the journey through the Keep to the tower room was a blur. Richard faded out of consciousness for a time, allowing himself to turn the task over to Chase.

By the time they made it down into the round tower, and then the room with the well, Richard had recovered enough to stand on his own.

The sliph was waiting. "You wish to travel, Master? I waited, as you asked. We can travel right away."

Richard nodded as he climbed up onto the wall, starting to feel better. "Yes, we need to travel. We must hurry."

Cassia reached up so he could help pull her up onto the wall.

"Master, you cannot take that object of magic. I told you before, you must not take it."

Richard hoisted Cassia up as he addressed the sliph.

"The last time, you told me that because I have death in me, it wouldn't kill me to travel with it. You said it would drain some of my life force, letting the sickness of death grow stronger. You didn't say I couldn't take it."

The silver face took on a look of concern. "That is true, but you have little life left to give over this time while traveling."

"Do I have enough to make it back alive?"

A reluctant silver hand extended up out of the pool to caress his face and test that inner poison.

"You have enough life left to make it back to the palace, but you will be nearly dead. Death will have grown strong in you. You will have hardly any time before you die."

"Perfect. Let's go." He slipped an arm around Cassia's waist. "Ready? We need to get back. I'm going to need you to help me once we get there."

"Of course, Lord Rahl."

Richard reached out and brushed a tear from her cheek. "Don't cry for me while I'm still alive. Wait until I'm dead, will you, please?"

That made her laugh just a little.

"Chase, thank you."

Chase nodded as Richard, with his arm around Cassia's waist, stepped off the wall into the quicksilver waters of the sliph and inhaled her into his lungs.

*B*reathe.
 Richard expelled the silver fluid and gasped a breath of cold air. It stung deep down inside like a thousand needles. With a great effort, he threw his arms over the stone wall of the well. He hung on to the edge, resting, trying to recover. He ached everywhere.

He knew that the sliph had been right. What he had done had drained away much of his remaining life force. Death was spreading through him, rotting him from inside.

Cassia was already out. She grunted with the effort of helping to pull his dead weight up and over the wall. Richard helped as much as he could. Once out, he collapsed to the floor, panting, recovering his strength, hoping he still had enough to stand. Cassia sat beside him on the floor, panting, recovering her own breath and strength. After a few moments, he was finally able to stand.

"Do you wish me to wait for you, Master?"

Richard looked back at the sliph. "Until this is over, one way or another, I would appreciate it. I may need to at least get Kahlan out of the palace."

He didn't know what good that would really do. It

wasn't only the palace that was in danger. It was the entire world of life. There was nowhere to run, nowhere to hide. Hannis Arc and Emperor Sulachan would see to that.

Once up on wobbly legs, Richard put his hand over the hilt of his sword, making sure that it was still there with him.

"We need to get to the Garden of Life."

"I'll help you, Lord Rahl. Let's go."

Richard shook his head. "I'm all right for the moment. I can walk."

He wasn't, of course, but he thought he had enough strength for a little while longer. It would be considerably faster if he could make it on his own two feet.

As soon as they went out into the hallway, Richard knew that something was wrong. For one thing, the hallway was empty. For another, he smelled smoke.

"Check all the halls before we go down any of them to make sure they're clear," he told Cassia. "We don't want to have to worry about being chased."

Together they moved quickly but quietly through the deserted service halls. At each intersection, Cassia peeked around to check that it was clear. When they reached a set of double doors with a simple geometric design carved into them, Cassia put an ear to the door, listening.

She straightened in a rush. "I hear screaming."

Richard gritted his teeth. "That's what I was afraid of." He pointed to a plastered hallway that led away from the public area. "That way, there. Let's go."

They continued working their way up back servants' stairs and seldom-used corridors, in places backtracking because they heard the sounds of battle. Richard ached to join that battle and drive the enemy back, but he knew that this time, that was not the way, and that this time, while he still had a breath of life in him, he had a more important job to do.

It took a lot longer than he thought it would to find a way to make it up to the Garden of Life. When he finally reached the top of the stairs to the passageway that encircled the outside of the garden, the guards were shocked to see him.

Richard grabbed the nearest man. "What's going on? Give me a report."

Other soldiers rushed in, gathering around.

"General Zimmer told us to guard the Garden of Life at all costs, to the last man if need be. So far the enemy hasn't made it up this far. We think they got in through the catacombs under the plains outside the plateau. I've heard talk of them getting in through the crypts down in the lower levels, melting their way right through solid stone.

"Since they breached the perimeter, they have been flooding in the ways I mentioned, and we've heard through a couple of other spots. At least I think so. The reports we get are confused and sketchy. We've been told that the enemy has those dead with them, the ones you told us about. Nathan and Nicci have been doing their best to help us try to hold them off."

"How long?" Richard asked. "How long have they been in the palace?"

"Since you disappeared, Lord Rahl."

"And how long has that been?"

The soldier pinched the bridge of his nose as he tried to think. Richard saw that, like those of the rest of the men, his eyes were bloodshot and red.

"I can't recall for sure, Lord Rahl. We've been fighting nonstop, day and night. A lot of people have been killed. We push them back, they break through a different way, then we get them contained again. We've had to fight our way in a number of times to rescue trapped men, or trapped people. It's been so long since we've had any sleep, I honestly can't think straight."

"Several days, then?" Richard asked.

"Oh at least. It's been days since we've been trying to hold them back out of certain areas of the palace, trying to control where they are."

"Have Sulachan or Hannis Arc been seen?"

The man nodded. "Oh yes. We've caught sight of them a few times. They seem to be in no hurry. It's like a show for them."

Richard looked around at all the men gathered around him. "I'm going to need all of you to clear out of here. Very soon it's not going to be safe up here. I need you to get all of our people away from the Garden of Life. Understand?"

"Yes, Lord Rahl. How far away?"

Richard shook his head as he sighed. "I'm not sure. Just get everyone back as far away as possible. Also, we need to clear everyone out of the main hallways of the palace."

"The main halls? You mean the major routes, the halls that are stories high?"

"Yes. We need to clear out of those areas and let the enemy have them. Do it immediately. There's no time to waste."

The man clapped a fist to his heart. "Right away, Lord Rahl."

"I need you to get a message to General Zimmer. When the time is right, I want him to stop holding back the horde of half people. When the time comes, get out of their way, defend yourselves, wall yourselves in rooms and defensive positions, whatever you need to do to try to stay safe, but stop holding them out of the palace. Let them flood through the major public corridors through the palace.

"They're going to get in anyway. When the time comes, stop fighting a losing battle and wasting lives. Let them have the main halls, do you hear me?"

The man looked confused. "When the time is right? How are we to know the time is right?"

Richard wiped a hand back across his face. "I can't say for sure, but you will know."

The man clapped his fist to his heart. Richard could tell that the man didn't understand, but there was no way for Richard to be any more clear. He didn't even know if he would still be alive when that time came. He could feel what little life he had left slipping away.

"Do you know where the Mother Confessor is?"

The soldier nodded. "They have a heavily defended section of the palace that has limited access and they set it up as a safe zone, of sorts. Not that any place is really safe. But for now the men are able to hold the enemy off from that area."

"I need you to get a message to her from me."

"Yes, Lord Rahl?"

"Tell her I love her."

The man nodded his solemn oath. "It will be done."

Richard pulled the Grace ring off his finger and put it in the man's palm. He closed the soldier's fingers around it.

"Tell her this is the reason."

"The reason, Lord Rahl?"

Richard nodded. "She will understand."

"I will personally see to it, Lord Rahl."

"By the way, do you know if it is day or night?"

The soldier pointed with a thumb back toward the Garden of Life. "I was just in there to check the place. It's the middle of the night."

Richard nodded. "Thanks. Now, I need all of you to clear out of here. Get everyone away from the Garden of Life. Sulachan and Hannis Arc will come to claim it at any moment. There is nothing up here to defend that is worth your lives."

Richard watched for a moment as the soldiers raced away. He turned back to Cassia.

"You're also going to need to get as far away from here as you can, but first I need you to help me."

CHAPTER 57

In the light of a few fat candles, Richard leaned against the omen machine. He could hardly stand, but he knew that he had to. At least for a little longer. It would be over soon and then, one way or another, he would not have to stand.

Regula was silent. The machine knew that now was not the time for prophecy.

Now was the time when free will would hold sway.

As he waited in the silence, in the dark hole where so very long ago Regula, a power that belonged in the world of the dead, had been buried, Richard thought instead about Kahlan. He made a conscious decision to use his time, if this was to be his last night of life, to think about what had been the best part of his life: Kahlan. He missed her so much it hurt almost as much as the poison of death gripping him.

He pushed his awareness of the pain of the poison away and instead did his best to picture in his mind the first time he had looked into Kahlan's green eyes that day in the Hartland woods and the instant connection he had felt.

That seemed like a lifetime ago.

He had known the moment he saw her that his life

would never be the same again. Thinking back on that first moment when he had looked into the eyes of his soul mate, it made him smile with the sheer vastness of it. She had been more than he could have ever dreamt his life would be.

She had been seeking help to find the wizard who could name the Seeker so that he could find the last box of Orden. Now, all three of those boxes sat on the cold metal top of Regula not far from his right elbow. The power of Orden and the power of Regula, together, in the world of life. Regula had been sent to the world of life for protection, to keep it away from Sulachan, and now here it was in the very heart of danger.

Richard put it from his mind. If these were to be his last moments of life, he wanted them to be worthwhile. He wanted every possible second of them to be spent in happy memories of Kahlan. He didn't want his last moments to be filled with bitterness and regrets. He wanted his last thoughts to be of love, not hate.

He smiled as he thought about some of the funny faces she sometimes made at him, the way she sometimes teased him, the way she always made him live up to the best he could be. He thought about the way she believed in him when no one else did. He thought about the way he could be weak with her, and she would give him her strength.

He thought about all that he wanted to do for her, to be for her. The way he felt when he kissed her, when he made love to her.

Many people lived their entire lives together without being together, without actually sharing their lives the way he and Kahlan had. He smiled in the dark as he thought about it.

It was while immersed in those thoughts that he heard a sound from above. Instantly, he switched to listening in the silence until he heard steady, measured footsteps.

The ladder creaked when weight was put to it. It could only be Sulachan. Sulachan would recognize the death Richard carried. He would be focused on it the way a mountain lion would be focused on a fawn. The time had come for the spirit king to collect what he claimed as his.

Sulachan would be coming for Richard, there was no doubt of that.

Richard waited in silence for the inevitable.

He saw the shadow flow down and over the stone wedges of the circular stairs as the spirit king descended into Regula's room. He would at last have what he wanted—Richard and Regula.

When he reached the small alcove at the bottom, Sulachan stopped, smiling with menace, as he looked in at Richard trapped in the small room with no other way out. In the semidarkness, the spirit was a glowing, bluish, otherworldly shell over the desiccated corpse that was the long-dead emperor. Having returned from the world of the dead, the spirit, brought back to life by the blood of *fuer grissa ost drauka,* seemed to be content with the form it had taken. Life really was precious, even for a dead emperor.

The glowing eyes were focused intently on Richard. "How thoughtful of you to be here, waiting for me, rather than me having to chase you down and pull you out of some dark little hidey-hole."

"I'm not the kind to run," Richard said.

"That is why I knew you would be here," the spirit king said. "I've known about you for a very long time, Warheart."

"What is it you want with me?"

The emperor stepped out of the alcove and into the room toward Richard. "Why, to kill you, of course, so that there will no longer be any chance of you interfering as only you could. You see, unlike my friend"—he gestured back up the stairwell–"Hannis Arc, I don't make the grave mistake of underestimating you. He plots revenge for years. He seeks to make you suffer. I simply eliminate threats."

"So you, a man who has returned from the dead, are worried about me?"

Sulachan smiled as he glared with hatred. "You are a man who has also returned from the dead, are you not?"

"Well," Richard said with a shrug, "it was not nearly the magnitude of the accomplishment you managed."

"You think not? My dark ones were there, waiting for you. They had you. And yet you escaped their talons and managed to get back to the world of life." The emperor waved a bony finger. "No, I do not underestimate you, Richard Rahl. Hannis Arc hates you, but I have great respect for you, much the way one respects a poisonous snake. Oh, sorry, I didn't mean to remind you of the poison that is eating away at you and has almost sucked all the remaining juices of life from you."

"If you know the poison is going to take me soon, then why bother with me? Seems like a lot of unnecessary effort."

The sinister smile returned. "Because, like I said, I don't underestimate you. You are dangerous, and the time has come to put you down so the Twilight Count can finish and everything that has been set into motion can finally reach its inevitable conclusion. I have worked far too long to leave anything to chance by letting you live a single extra moment. I don't need you to witness the fruition of my plans, as Hannis Arc would want. I simply need to eliminate you."

As Sulachan made his way toward Regula, Richard casually moved away, staying out of his reach. On his way by the candles, he pulled off a small blob of soft, warm candle wax, playing with it in his fingers as he kept an eye on the spirit king.

As Sulachan went to the omen machine, Richard casually circled around toward the opening at the alcove to the stairwell.

"Thinking of running away after all?" Sulachan asked, his back to Richard as he gazed at the boxes of Orden.

Richard reached up and gave a tug on the small string dangling down. As he pulled it taut, untying the knot, the cloth with the wards on it was released, unfurling to drop down and cover the doorway.

"No, I'm not going anywhere," Richard said. "And neither are you."

Intrigued by Richard's casual tone of voice, Sulachan turned with a frown. But when he saw the cloth behind Richard, his expression turned from startled to venomous.

"What do you think you are doing?"

As he played with the soft wax between his finger and thumb, rolling it back and forth, Richard used the same hand to gesture at the cloth panel. "I'm sure you recognize the wards. Wards left by those people you were trying to defeat so long ago. Wards specifically created to keep spirits from crossing."

Sulachan swept an arm out, at the same time letting out a chuckle. "Why would I need to worry about such things?"

As Sulachan circled around to the cloth panel, Richard did the dance with him, circling around with him, matching him step for step, keeping his distance, as he moved back around to the omen machine.

Sulachan, glaring at the wards, at first moved toward the cloth hanging like a bull charging a flag, lifting a hand out as if he intended to swipe the cloth aside or rip it down, but as his hand reached out it paused before he could touch the cloth. He snatched back the hand and instead backed up a step.

He spun around to Richard. "You may be smart and you may be dangerous, but this time, you have done something useless." He lashed a hand out toward the cloth. "I am confused as to why you would bother with such trivialities as this." He straightened, gathering his composure. "But it doesn't matter because I am here to end it."

"Me too. You see, the wards on that cloth are meant to make sure you can't leave. I want to make sure that you don't run." Richard showed the emperor an insincere smile. "I wouldn't want to have to chase you down and pull you out of some dark little hidey-hole."

Sulachan glared but made no argument that he could leave if he wanted to. They both knew that he couldn't, at least, not as long as that cloth with the ancient wards barred the door.

Richard turned and laid his hands on Regula. Out of the corner of his eye he saw Emperor Sulachan lift his own hands to conjure his occult powers.

"Time to go home," Richard said with a smile to Regula.

At that he stuffed the plugs of soft wax into his ears, jammed them both in hard with his thumbs, then swiftly pulled the baldric of his sword off over his head and laid the sword, still in its gleaming scabbard engraved with ancient symbols keyed to the power, across the top of the three black-as-death boxes of Orden.

Sulachan's occult power was making the room shudder. Dust came down in little streams from the ceiling. Richard felt that power clawing at him, trying to pull him apart.

Before it was too late, Richard drew a deep breath as he tilted his head back.

His turn.

With all his might, all his strength, Richard let out a powerful scream, releasing the call of death from deep down inside. With the mighty force of his gift lurking below the poison he had layered over the top of it all the way down in the core of his being, he pushed that poisonous call of death out with all his might.

In his own head, because of the wax plugs, he heard only dead silence. But he knew that the scream of death was filling the room. He unleashed the fury of his gift, along with the anger of the sword, from deep in the core of his being, at last giving it the liberty it needed to drive the call of death upward and out.

Sulachan pressed the palms of his hands against his ears.

Arms stiff, Richard fisted his hands as he screamed. Darkness began swirling around the room, picking up dirt and dust with it. Everything shook. The floor shuddered. The neatly stacked metal strips against the walls toppled, spilling the strips out across the floor. As the speed of the spinning darkness increased, it began lifting up metal strips, sucking them into the vortex.

The omen machine itself began to shudder.

The three boxes of Orden atop the omen machine and beneath his sword slammed together into one and exploded with sudden, blinding light erupting from the pit of darkness that was the world of the dead within Regula. The light shot upward, blowing the ceiling open, carrying blocks of stone up and outward. The light from Orden, freed from the Regula room, exploded up through the Garden of Life, shattering the glass roof high overhead as it blasted upward into the night sky toward the stars. Glass and debris were thrown clear of the blast of light as night was turned to day.

In the rotating maelstrom of darkness swirling around the jet of blinding light from Orden, Regula began breaking apart under the power of the forces that had been unleashed. Metal plates ripped off and swirled around in the spinning storm as if they were bits of paper and debris snatched up in a gale. As Richard continued to scream with all his might, letting death escape from *fuer grissa ost drauka,* the machine was torn apart and drawn upward into the spiraling storm of light. The pieces disintegrated into dust as they were drawn upward in the blinding conflagration.

In Richard's head, as he used all his strength to power the scream, it was all totally silent.

Across the room, Sulachan frantically tried to conjure power to save himself, but as soon as he took his hands off his ears to try to direct his occult powers, the call of death instantly ripped into him. The glow of his spirit crackled and flashed in bright colors for an instant before going as dark as a night stone. At the same time his worldly body imploded inward and then came apart in tattered bits that themselves came apart, crumbling to dust as it was all sucked into the whorl of blinding light at the center of the swirling darkness of the void between worlds.

When at last Richard had let his gift expel every last bit of the poison of death from inside him, and it had been sucked up into the light and carried away, Richard could finally stop screaming.

He collapsed to his knees, getting his breath, hardly believing that he had actually done it. As he recovered, he pulled the wax plugs from his ears. They had protected him from hearing death's call while he expelled it.

For the first time in ages, he no longer felt the weight of the poison inside him. He was finally free of it.

He looked over at the collapsed hole where Regula had been. There was nothing left of it. Not so much as a scrap of metal remained. Everything that had been a part of it, all the gears, shafts, levers, and all the bits that made it work, were gone. It was as if it had never been there. Everything that had housed the power and given it the ability to communicate was no more.

Regula had gone home, and it had taken prophecy with it. He felt a twinge of happiness for Regula, going home to where it belonged among the expanse of souls spread out like a field of stars on the darkest night. It would be where it could no longer harm the world of life, or even influence it.

Richard had done it. He had ended prophecy.

The boxes of Orden, too, were gone, finally completing their cycle begun so long ago when the Sword of Truth had been forged as the key to using the power.

With Regula gone from the world of life, with prophecy ended, with the cycle of Orden finally ended, the spectral fold was closed. The breach between worlds was at last sealed.

Richard saw his sword on the ground beside him, the scabbard gleaming as brightly as ever. He put the baldric back over his head as he came to his feet, feeling strong again. He brushed himself off and tested his arms for residual pain from the poison, but there was no pain. He felt normal again. He could also again feel that inner sense of his gift. He had missed it.

The long ordeal with the poison from the Hedge Maid was finally ended.

Prophecy was ended.

But when he heard the distant howls, he remembered that his work was far from done.

He had to do something to stop what was happening if he could. He raced up the circular staircase to the level above the room where Regula had been banished for so long, but that level had been blown apart. He had to make his way carefully around the edge to get over to the side of the room with the short flight of stairs to the landing where the ladder should have been. He cast about and found the ladder under rubble and managed to pull it out. A few rungs were broken, but it was still usable. He stood it on the landing and leaned it up against floor of the Garden of Life.

Richard scrambled up and once on top quickly surveyed the destruction. Giant blocks of stone had been upended; dirt and rubble lay everywhere. The glass roof had an enormous hole blasted through the structure.

Richard started running up the path toward the double doors to get out to where the howls and screams were coming from.

As he raced up the path between the trees, a Mord-Sith in red leather stepped out from the side, blocking his way. Richard skidded to a halt. It was Vika, the Mord-Sith he had encountered once before when he had been a captive of Hannis Arc.

Vika's steely blue eyes seemed to be examining his soul for every nuance of strength, weakness, and character—an idiosyncratic, piercing scrutiny unique to Mord-Sith.

Richard stared at her, trying to decide what to do. There were few people as lethal as a Mord-Sith. Richard knew how easy it was to make a mistake with such women and underestimate what they were capable of. He had learned that lesson the hard way.

He knew that using his sword against her would be a mistake. Using his gift against her would be just as big a mistake. She could capture magic used against her.

"Vika, you remember our talk," he told her in a low, steady voice. "It's your life. Have you thought about what choices you want to make for yourself?"

Behind her, Richard saw movement. From beyond the trees Hannis Arc, every inch of his flesh tattooed with symbols in the language of Creation, made his way down into the Garden of Life.

He was holding Kahlan by her hair, dragging her along behind. He wasn't being gentle about it, either.

Kahlan clawed at his hands, trying to keep from having her hair pulled out as she was dragged along, stumbling, falling, trying to keep up as he twisted her head one way and then the other.

Kahlan's green eyes turned up and she spotted Richard. Those eyes brimmed with tears of pain and fury. He knew without a doubt that if she could have used her power against Hannis Arc, she would already have done so. He also saw that she was wearing the Grace ring Richard had sent with the soldier. Richard hoped that the blood all down the front of her was not that soldier's blood, killed while delivering Richard's message.

Richard started toward her.

Vika strode purposefully out right in front of him and with no warning rammed her Agiel into his gut. The shock of pain doubled him over. He couldn't draw a breath. She held the Agiel in her fist pressed hard into him. The pain became beyond endurance. His vision sparkled with spots of light at the end of a dim tunnel. His ears rang. Every nerve in his body was on fire.

When she pulled her Agiel back, Richard dropped heavily to his knees, unable to do anything but try to gasp a breath. With her boot, Vika shoved him over. Richard collapsed onto his side, tears of pain streaming down his face. He tried to suck in air, but his throat had closed down so tightly that he couldn't draw a good breath.

Vika went to a knee so that she could bend close, put her face close, so that he could see just how angry she was.

"If you know what's good for you," she growled intimately through gritted teeth, "you will stay down. Do–you–understand?"

She slammed her Agiel into his middle again and twisted it just to make her point, her teeth on edge the whole time. "I asked you a question. Do you understand?"

He nodded as best he could, unable to look at her.

Richard felt like his bulging eyes might burst out of his head. He struggled to draw a breath as she rose up and towered over him. All he could see were her boots right in front of him. He held his arms crossed over his middle.

"Leave him alone!" Kahlan screamed.

Hannis Arc twisted his hand, bending her head back, making her cry out in pain. Richard could see how much it was hurting her, but he was in no condition to do anything about it.

Hannis Arc finally tossed Kahlan to the ground, where she tumbled and rolled to a stop not far to the side of Richard.

Hannis Arc, glaring with his red eyes, lifted an arm toward Kahlan, his palm held up. Kahlan put her hands to her throat, gasping in agony at whatever kind of occult power he was using to hurt her. Her face went red, then started going blue.

Richard was beyond fury, but the pain from Vika's Agiel still kept him from being able to use his muscles, much less draw a breath. He couldn't properly focus his vision.

Hannis Arc gestured angrily at Vika for her to get out of his way. She bowed her head and withdrew to stand behind him.

He took several steps closer, glaring down at Richard the way one would inspect an animal in an iron trap. "You think you have won? You think you have spoiled my plans? Quite the contrary. You have unwittingly helped me by eliminating a very, very dangerous associate who had outlived his usefulness. The fool wanted to destroy the world of life. The world of life will find much more favor with me. I only want to rule it.

"Now that you have sent that lunatic spirit back to the world of the dead, the Shun-tuk will soon have subdued the palace, and I will finally–finally–be able to kill the Lord Rahl, and in his own fallen palace, no less."

Hannis Arc took a step forward as he lifted his hands out to Kahlan and Richard, one to each of them.

Vika walked up behind the man, and without a word pressed her Agiel to the base of his skull.

Hannis Arc's arms lifted, shaking and trembling with the agony of what Vika was doing to him. She showed no expression or mercy as she held her Agiel against him. Spittle flew from his mouth as he shook violently.

And then, all the tattoos on him began to smoke. The lines of each tattoo covering his head turned red-hot, like coals in a fire. The flesh bubbled and sizzled, smoke rising from his skin, as the symbols all over him continued to burn down into his flesh. The skin on his cheekbones detached along the lines of one of the symbols and flopped down, exposing burned and bloody bone.

Still, Vika stood emotionless behind him, holding her Agiel to the base of his skull.

As the lines of the tattoos all over his skin burned, the smell of it was gagging. Blood frothed at Hannis Arc's mouth. His eyes bled. Blood ran out of his ears.

The man's legs suddenly twisted unnaturally and he went down in a heap. Smoke rolled up from his burning flesh. There was no need to check that he was dead. The man was dead and his spirit probably already in the underworld, being swarmed by Sulachan's dark demons, taking his soul down into the darkness of eternity.

Vika ran forward and crouched down, helping Richard get back up onto his knees. His hands trembled as he tried to get control of his movements. Before he could even get to his feet, Kahlan flung her arms around his neck, crying with joy to see him alive, holding his head to her. His arms finally able to move as he wanted, he hugged her for what seemed ages, but not long enough.

Finally, as she separated and wiped the tears from her face, Richard stood.

Vika stepped closer to him. "I made my choice, Lord Rahl. I chose you."

"Then why use your Agiel on me?"

"Because I knew that you wouldn't have stood a chance against his occult powers if you tried to fight him like that. I knew he would kill you if I didn't find a way to make sure he was distracted enough so that I could take him out. So I needed to put you down and to have you stay down.

"He never let me come up behind him like that. He knew what a Mord-Sith was capable of. He was a very careful man about potential threats like that."

"So, you used your Agiel on me to throw some raw meat in front of him and distract him."

Looking solemn, she nodded once and kept her head bowed. "Yes, Lord Rahl."

Vika went to her knees before him and held out her Agiel in upturned palms. "We all learn during our training that should we ever use our power on the Lord Rahl like that, it is automatically punishable by death. I chose to do it anyway to save your life and the life of the Mother Confessor. That was my choice, for my life."

She swallowed without looking up at him. "I ask only that you make it quick, so that I do not suffer. I don't wish to suffer. I have suffered enough."

Richard knelt down in front of her. Her head was bowed and she wouldn't look up at him, fearing the worst.

Richard put his hand over both of hers holding out the Agiel, and lowered them. Then, with a finger, he lifted her chin. Looking into her wet blue eyes, he kissed a finger, and then pressed that finger on her forehead.

"That is your punishment."

Vika frowned, tears starting to run down her cheeks. "Lord Rahl, I don't understand. I used my Agiel on you. That is a mandatory death sentence."

"I just did something to you worse than death."

Her brow twitched. "What have you done?"

"If you don't behave, I will tell all the other Mord-Sith that I kissed you. You will never hear the end of it as long as you live."

He showed her a smile, then, a smile that showed her how proud he was of her for making a choice for herself, a choice for life.

Kahlan put an arm around Vika's shoulders and helped her up. "I have to tell you, I'm proud of you too, but you certainly had me fooled there for a while. I thought we were going to die right then and there."

Vika nodded with a genuine smile. "I decided long ago, after Lord Rahl talked to me in the cave prison. I knew, though, that I needed to do more than simply run away. No one runs away from Hannis Arc. He will find you and then take out his revenge for your betrayal. I knew that the only way to save myself, and the only way to save others, would be to kill him. I had to wait for my chance. He was a pig, but I had to wait for the right time. Today was that time."

Kahlan gave the woman's arm a squeeze of empathy. Then she looked back in the direction of the screaming in the distance. "Richard, the half people–"

"I know," he said as he took her hand. "Come on."

CHAPTER 58

W hat are we going to do?" Kahlan asked as she
ran beside him.

Vika raced along close behind.

As they burst through the gold-sheathed double
doors, Richard immediately took the hallway to the left.
It was the shortest route to where he needed to go. After racing down one short flight of stairs, they took a
long corridor lined with white marble. The floor was a
complex wave pattern of a variety of stones, and quite
slippery, so they had to slow a bit.

At the end, Richard burst out of the double doors
onto a balcony above the central hallway. He immediately raced to an arched bridge high over the walkway
below. He skidded to a stop near the center. Since it was
the middle of the night, the skylights were dark. That
meant that the hallway, lit by scores of reflector lamps,
was dimly lit.

Even in the poor light that the reflector lamps provided to the grand hall, he could see that down on the
floor below them it was mass chaos. Half people were
everywhere, outnumbering the people and the soldiers
many times over. There were dead bodies sprawled all
over the place. Almost all of the dead were half people,

but some weren't. Some were people from the palace who had been caught and taken down. Half people crowded around a body, squatting down to feed on it. Blood was splattered and smeared over the marble walls and columns. Richard saw barefoot half people slip and fall on the bloody marble floor.

Richard didn't have time to assess the situation, he simply needed to put a stop to it.

He drew his sword.

The blade came out with the metallic ring that was unique to the Sword of Truth. Richard by now had come to think of that sound as reassuring. It also came out with that same dark metallic gleam from having touched death. With the fighting and panic below, no one noticed the sound or the sight of the sword up on the dark balcony.

Richard pointed the blade out over the edge of the marble balustrade.

"There are your worldly forms," he said. "Go to them. Return to those you were torn from if you can. Some of you will have to go a great distance to find the one to whom you belong. If they are gone from life and you find yourself still caught in this world, then come to me and we will help you cross over to eternal peace."

In the dim light, a curtain of sparkling light peeled off the sword and unfurled out over the hallway, stretching as it went. The curtain of light wavered the way the strange lights in the night sky to the north did. They moved in long, slow, curling, undulating waves. Countless specks of light, each one a soul, together created a display that had some of the people below slowing down. Even some of the half people glanced up.

As the curtains of light drifted out over the hallway, Richard swung the sword. "Go! Find where you belong."

With that, the specks of light scattered. Many others

began to drift downward, like snowflakes in a dead-still air. All the way down the halls, as far as Richard could see, the tiny specks moved out to find the ones to whom they belonged.

"Richard," Kahlan said in wonder, "what in the world is that? What have you done?"

"Remember the Sanctuary of Souls down in the Keep?"

"Yes," she said as she watched the strange sight. "What about it?"

"Well, that place was built back at the time when there were wizards who were makers–like Wizard Merritt."

"Magda's husband?"

"That's right. Sulachan made the half people by pulling out their souls and not letting them go to the underworld in order to keep the bodies alive. I believe that makers back then made that sanctuary for those lost souls. Those people up there at the Keep, even though the half people were sent to kill them, understood the tragic truth and felt empathy for the lost souls who had not chosen that fate, and had themselves meant no harm. So, they made those lost souls a sanctuary."

Kahlan held her hand out toward the hall below with the dots of light drifting down. "But what is this?"

Richard shrugged. "It's the lost souls, the ones that belong to the half people."

Kahlan could barely contain her exasperation. "What are they doing here?"

"I went there and got them and brought them back."

"Richard, are you crazy? You could have–"

"Look," he said with a smile.

Kahlan turned and looked down. Everywhere half people were stopping. They quit running, quit chasing people. The ones near soldiers fell to their knees and raised their arms in surrender. The ones feeding stopped and stepped back, wiping the blood from their mouths in disgust. As the half people quit chasing victims, the screaming died out.

Throughout the halls, all of the half people slowed down and looked around in bewilderment, or amazement, or jubilation. Some started laughing with delight, looking at their own hands as if seeing them for the first time. Soldiers didn't quite know what to make of it, but as long as the half people weren't trying to attack and eat them, they stopped hacking the half-naked people apart.

"Come on," Richard said. "Let's get down there. I'm worried about the others."

The broad stairwell of creamy stone leading down was close, and the descent quick. As they reached the lower halls, soldiers of the First File closed in protectively.

Richard still had his sword out. Along with the sword there was always the anger, but he kept it in check. He held the sword out and shook it to check to see if any more sparkles of souls would come out of it. None did, so he slid it back in its scabbard before he reached for the doors that led out into the hallway. When he opened the doors, they were confronted by the quite strange sight of the masses of half people no longer attacking anyone.

Just outside, Cassia ran over to him. "Lord Rahl! You were right! You did it! Mother Confessor, look!" Cassia pointed out at the half people milling around, blinking, laughing, crying, talking. "That's why he left you and didn't say where he was going. I scolded him for not telling you."

"Yes, she did," Richard confirmed.

Nyda and Rikka escorted Nathan and Nicci across the hall from one of the grand staircases leading up from the lower levels.

"Richard!" Nicci called out. "You're back! We were so worried! If you ever do anything like that again I swear I will have you locked in a dungeon and only let Kahlan visit you once a week."

Nathan peered around. "Richard, would you happen to know what in the world is going on?"

"Yes, what is happening?" Nicci asked. "It's the same down in the lower areas, near the crypts where they were getting in. There's been a battle raging down there for days and then all of a sudden the half people simply stopped fighting. Almost together, almost all at once, they simply stopped."

Cassia casually pointed a thumb back at the strange scene. "Lord Rahl gave them their souls back."

Nicci's jaw fell open. "What?" She pointed in alarm at his hip. "How did you get your sword back? Richard! Don't you dare tell me that you went back to the Keep and you brought the sword back through the sliph!"

"Well, actually–"

"You can't do that! Richard, your life isn't worth the sword." Nicci was beside herself, hardly knowing what to complain about first. "Richard, you were told how it would make the sickness grow, how it would bring you to the cusp of death, how . . . ."

She looked up suspiciously. "Why don't you look sick?"

"Because I'm not. Why, do you want me to be sick?"

Not believing him and ignoring his flippant remark, Nicci pressed her fingers to his temples. She withdrew her hands in astonishment and turned to Nathan. "He's not sick. It's gone. Completely gone." She turned back to Richard. "I could feel your gift. How is that possible?"

Richard took a deep breath. "Do you want me to explain, or would you rather complain?"

Nicci planted her fists on the curve of her hips and gave him a look she had apparently saved from back in the days when she was his teacher, trying to teach him to use his gifted abilities.

Kahlan turned her face away to hide her smile.

"Explain, please," Nicci said with forced patience.

"I figured out that the only way I was ever going to be able to stop Sulachan was to send him back to the world of the dead. The easiest way to do that, since I couldn't hope to overcome his occult abilities, was to use the poison of death I had in me. So, when I was in the underworld, and you and Kahlan brought me back, during that stretch of time in infinity when I had all the time I needed, I decided that rather than leave the sickness of death there in the world of the dead, as I had done with Kahlan, I'd rather have Sulachan in the world of the dead, so I didn't . . . leave it. I kept it."

"You lied to us?" Nicci fumed. "You told us you couldn't leave it there. You lied?"

It was Kahlan's turn to look astonished. "You mean to say that you deliberately kept that poison of death in you? That poison that could easily have killed you? When you know how difficult it would be to remove it in this world?"

Richard shrugged one shoulder. "Sure. It made sense to me."

Nicci looked over at Kahlan. "It made sense to him."

"The problem was, I feared it wasn't strong enough–"

Nicci flicked a hand in the air. "Not strong enough. Of course. Not strong enough."

"–So right when I found out we were going to have to face Sulachan at any moment, I went back to the Keep and retrieved the sword. Traveling in the sliph with the sword drained away most of my life force and made the poison a lot stronger. That was what I needed to kill Sulachan."

Both women stared openly at him.

"Oh yes," he added, "and while I was there I also collected all the souls that have been lost for the last three thousand years or so, and . . ." He held out his hand to where the half people were all cooperating with the soldiers who were collecting them together. He could see half people weeping, apologizing, asking forgiveness.

Nicci started waggling her finger as she shook her head at the same time. "No, no, no. Wait. How did you kill Sulachan with the death that was inside you?"

"I did the same thing the Hedge Maid did. I let it out with a scream."

Nicci was seething to the point of being momentarily speechless. Kahlan was also being overcome with exasperation. She spoke up before Nicci could put words to her discontent.

"But the scream would have killed you, too, Richard. The sound of it is lethal. That is in fact what killed Jit."

"But it didn't kill us."

Kahlan pointed at her ear. "No, because you plugged our ears with wads of cloth. And even though it didn't kill us right away, it wasn't good enough and so it poisoned us."

Richard smiled as he clasped his hands. "Yes, rather poor choice, but all I had available at the time. This time I knew better. I used wax to plug my ears."

Kahlan turned away, shaking her head, muttering about how dangerous and risky that was.

"No, no, no," Nicci said, finally able to frame her objection. "Not so fast. It's not that easy. You can't just scream and have that touch of death come out. It's not that simple."

"Well of course not," Richard said. "That's why I had to use my gift."

Nicci threw up her hand, looking away for a moment.

She turned back, leaning toward him. "Your gift didn't work! The touch of death blocked it from working!"

"Ah, I see why you're getting confused," Richard said, tilting his head back. "That was before."

"Before what?"

"Before I fixed my gift so it would work to do what I needed."

Nathan, Nicci, and Kahlan were all staring openly at him.

Nicci calmed her voice. "Explain, please, Wizard Rahl, how you 'fixed' your gift, and what you did to make it work the way you wanted."

"Well, I used to think it was hard," he said. "But it's not. Not really. Well, in this world, sure, but not there."

"There?" Nathan swished a finger, looking like he was lost.

"In the underworld. You see, when I went there to send Kahlan back to the world of life, I removed that taint of death from her and left it there. In the underworld I had all the time I needed. Once I did it while I was there, I saw how easy it is to do if you are in the underworld. It's kind of like when you're in water. It's easier to lift things in water because they seem to weigh less."

"Your gift?" Nicci prompted, steering him back on subject.

"Well I knew how to take the poison out while there, so I did that, and then I did a similar thing with my gift."

Nathan looked more than a little concerned. "What do you mean? Do you mean to say you removed your gift when you were there?"

Richard scratched his head as he tried to think of how to explain it. "Well, do you know how you can tie your boots without having to think about it, or watch? That's kind of what it's like there, in the underworld.

Certain things just seem easier for me to do there. So, what I did, was to take out the poison, but hold on to it, and then take out all of my gift—"

Nathan was incredulous. "Take out your gift?"

"Well, to an extent. I kind of gathered it up because I wanted to concentrate it in one spot. It's connected to your spirit by all these threadlike structures. . . . Some were broken or attached in the wrong place, so while I was at it I fixed those. . . . Anyway, I took it partially out, gathered it all together, and then placed it in one concentrated place to amplify its power. After that, I put the poison back in right on top of my gift and reconnected the threads of the gift that the poison had broken so that my gift would be able to respond when I called on it and then it could force all the poison out of me in a scream."

Nathan lifted a hand as he half turned away. "Oh, I see. You're right, that was pretty simple."

Richard turned more serious, wanting them to know the important part they didn't know.

"I ended prophecy."

Nathan spun around. "What?"

Nicci held a hand out, touching Nathan's arm to implore him to let her handle it. She knew about the Cerulean scrolls and Nathan didn't.

"Tell us what happened, Richard. Straight answers this time, please. This is nothing to fool around with."

Richard nodded. "You're right. We know from the Cerulean scrolls that Regula is an underworld power. It's not supposed to be here in the world of life any more than Sulachan. I talked to Regula and it understood. It didn't like being here in this world where it doesn't belong. In a way, I guess you could say it was homesick. So, I killed it, which is actually what it wanted because that sent it back to where it belonged.

"I exposed the boxes of Orden, keyed to the sword,

to the call of death, in order to link Orden into both worlds being pulled together in the spectral fold, along with the other elements that were releasing at the same time, in order to allow the power of Orden to complete the spectral fold that had been initiated by me using the sword previously, and by using the other side–death– which had been pulled into this world with Regula.

"You might say I brought both the worlds of life and death together for an instant so they could realign properly. Death took Regula back into the world of the dead, and with it prophecy. Regula, which is the power of prophecy, is now locked in the world of the dead and with it prophecy, which therefore means prophecy died. Prophecy in this world is ended. With the spectral fold complete, and the Twilight Count ended, it can't come back into the world of life any more than the dead can come back to life. At least from here on out. The time when that could happen is over. The phase change is over. Sulachan can't ever come back."

Nicci held her temples between her fingers on one side and thumb on the other. "Thank you, Richard, for not telling Kahlan and me all of this before you left."

Richard made a face. "Really?"

"Yes, because I would have killed you and then Kahlan would be a widow again, and she didn't like it the first time."

Richard saw Kahlan smile.

"Lord Rahl knew that you would be angry with him when we left, but he had it all under control right from the beginning," Cassia said.

"He did, did he?" Kahlan asked.

Cassia nodded earnestly. "He said that he would just ask for forgiveness later."

Nathan laughed out loud. His laughter was infectious and Kahlan couldn't keep herself from laughing with him.

Nicci rolled her eyes. "You did good, Richard. Really. I wish I could have taught you to do half of those things. One day you will have to teach me."

"I promise," Richard said with a smile.

Richard spotted people moving out of the way for someone running. At first it was hard to see because of all the people crowded into the hall, but then his level of concern rose when he caught a flash of red leather.

Soldiers stepped back out of the way for a Mord-Sith running at full speed. She didn't even bother looking at all the soldiers, she simply expected them to get out of her way.

The Mord-Sith raced up and leaped onto Richard, throwing her arms around his neck and her legs around his waist. The impact staggered him back a step.

"Lord Rahl! Lord Rahl!" She squeezed the breath out of him. "I heard you were back in the palace, but I was defending some people and couldn't come until now. I'm so happy to see you. I'm so happy that you and the Mother Confessor are back. I've missed you something fierce."

Richard hugged her and patted her back as he grinned. "I've missed you, too, Berdine."

While her eyes were bright blue, Berdine's wavy hair was brown rather than blond. She was shorter and curvier than most of the other Mord-Sith. She was full of bubbly enthusiasm. Even so, she was no less deadly than any of the other Mord-Sith.

She still had her legs locked around his waist with her ankles hooked together. "Lord Rahl, I've found some books of prophecy that I think you would want to see."

"We're going to have to talk about the books of prophecy."

Berdine flicked her Agiel up into her hand. "It works again. Did you fix it?"

Richard gave her a lopsided smile. "I fixed it."

She patted his chest. "You are a good Lord Rahl."

She turned to Kahlan. "I'm so happy to see you back, Mother Confessor. We've all missed you."

"Nice to see you, too, Berdine." Kahlan gestured at Berdine's legs around Richard. "Leave some for me, will you?"

Berdine giggled and hopped down.

Vika leaned closer. "Lord Rahl, do you allow Mord-Sith to . . . hug you?"

Berdine grinned up at the taller woman. "No, just me. I'm his favorite."

"We don't have favorites," Kahlan said. "We love you all the same."

"I know," Berdine said with a mischievous grin. "He loves us all equally. Except me. He loves me more. Because I'm his favorite."

"You . . . love the Mord-Sith?" Vika asked Richard, looking truly puzzled.

Richard shrugged. "What's not to love?"

He turned when a group of soldiers rushed over to where he and the rest of them were standing. General Zimmer was leading them.

"Lord Rahl, we have a problem."

Richard instantly went on high alert. They were surrounded and outnumbered many times over by half people. He checked that his sword was free in its scabbard.

"What's wrong?"

The general glanced around without looking obvious. "Notice how they are all closing in tighter to you over here?"

"I can't really see much past the closer throngs."

"Well, we've got archers stationed all around you, up high, and they have been watching the way the Shun-tuk are all inching closer to you. They are all saying they want to tell you something. And it's not just inside. They all seem to be able to, I don't know, sense you. It's not just here, either. Men are reporting from all over the palace that they are gathering near this area of the palace on the lower floors. Outside, the multitudes out there have all closed in and are standing there, as if waiting for something."

"Well, what do they want?" Cassia asked defensively.

"They all seem to want to say something to Lord Rahl."

Richard scanned the throng and the area. He pointed off to the left a little.

"There is an old devotion square over there. It's got a short wall around it. I can stand up there so I can see better, and they can see me better. Let's see what they have to say."

The general frowned. "Are you sure? An hour ago they were all trying to eat us. We don't know anything about these people."

"I do," Richard said as he started toward the devotion square. "I know the spirits of these people."

Rikka and Nyda took up a position on the left, with Cassia and Vale on the right. Berdine led the way. Vika guarded their rear so that Nathan, Nicci, General Zimmer, Kahlan, and Richard were pretty securely surrounded by Mord-Sith.

When he reached the old devotion square, Richard stepped up on the short wall around the pool of water. He realized he couldn't see as well as he had hoped, so he climbed up on top of the dark rock in the center. He stood up straight, looking out over the throng, and rested his left hand on the Sword of Truth. Ordinarily there were a lot of people in the palace, but with the Shun-tuk those numbers had swelled considerably.

He noticed Shun-tuk at all the fountains, washing the whitewash and paint that made them look like skulls off their faces.

"I am Richard Rahl," he said out over the masses he saw. They all stared in silence. "I am told you would like to say something to me."

As one the entire mass of people all went down on their knees and bent forward, putting their foreheads to the floor.

And then, in one voice, every person in the vast halls, on every floor, and out on the plains, said,

"Master Rahl guide us."

Richard was stunned at the thousands of voices all speaking as one. The sound was like rolling thunder.

"Master Rahl teach us."

Richard looked to Kahlan. Her eyes brimmed with tears as she looked up at him.

"Master Rahl protect us."

Nicci covered her mouth in awe.

"In your light we thrive."

In unison, the mass of voices all spoke the next lines of the devotion.

"In your mercy we are sheltered."

"In your wisdom we are humbled."

"We live only to serve."

"Our lives are yours."

Richard was too choked up to say anything.

One man rose from the floor. The rest stayed bowed down. He was old and frail, painted with the white-wash, although the skeletal face had been mostly wiped away.

"Lord Rahl," he said in a voice that carried through the entire hall, over the heads of all the people, "you are the first since our souls were torn from us, to help us. Thank you, Lord Rahl, for guiding our spirits back to where they belong, back to us, back to who we are as people."

Richard swallowed. He wiped a tear from his cheek, and could only nod, fearing to test his voice right then.

Richard stood at the massive stone balustrade at the outer edge of the courtyard, staring out at the night. There was no part of the People's Palace that overlooked the courtyard of their bedroom. As high as it was, and the way it projected out over the walls below, it was as if the courtyard were floating above the Azrith Plain. The portion where Richard stood at the railing in the center, between reverse curved railings to each side, was cantilevered even farther out from the palace. With the carefully trimmed juniper trees in large pots along the sides, and the walls of their quarters rising up behind the potted trees, he felt comfortable out in the courtyard.

It had something that was rare and precious: seclusion.

It was the one place they could be alone. Even Berdine never walked in without knocking.

Berdine had been hard at work, culling books of prophecy. Just like the rest of them, she had been astonished to learn that Regula had been entirely responsible for real prophecy being in the world of life. There always had been, and always would be, those who believed they could see into the future. They were either deluded or easily entranced, or thieves looking for a way to pull money from a person's pocket by revealing their own version of the future.

The real books of prophecy, the legitimate ones, the ones that had in reality been a result of Regula, were being burned. There were those who argued that even if untrue, or false prophecy, they were examples of fine craftsmanship and should be preserved. Others wished to hold on to the superstitious notion that perhaps the prophecies were true, and if the books were destroyed, then ill fortune would befall them. A kind of prophecy double bind.

Nathan, though, had spent close to a thousand years with many of those books. He knew most of them. His blood ran with the ink of prophecy. He had been a wizard who had received prophecy. He was a wizard who could have the visions brought on by prophecy. Of course, the prophecy had all been leaked out of the world of the dead.

Richard remembered the countless problems he and Kahlan had had with prophecy. At Cara's wedding to Ben, people who wanted prophecy, as if it were a commodity, a coin of the realm, had started all sorts of trouble. Many people had died.

Still, Richard could understand and sympathize with Nathan's love of those books. He had been locked up in the Palace of the Prophets nearly his entire life, and those books were more than his friends. They were his escape. They took him places beyond the prison walls of the Palace of the Prophets, places he could imagine, or read about, but had little hope of ever seeing.

Richard suspected that was the source of Nathan's love for dressing as an adventurer, a man of the world.

Richard knew, though, that prophecy was an underworld element. It was death itself. It represented the death of free will. It brought about the decay of humanity as people sought prophecy to help them make every decision. All decisions made for them from the world of the dead. Now, they were entering an age of free will.

Still, Richard understood Nathan's sadness at his old friends being burned. So, Richard had told Nathan to pick any library he wanted in the palace, more than one if he wanted, and stock them with whatever books the old prophet wished to preserve.

The rest were going to be burned. Prophecy was ended.

Nathan, of course, was finally getting his chance to be a real adventurer, so books of prophecy very well might end up in his past. There were many places between the People's Palace and the Dark Lands that had been devastated by Emperor Sulachan, Hannis Arc, and the half people rampaging across the lands. Nathan was to be Lord Rahl's official roving ambassador, visiting those places that were hit hard to see what could be done to help them. Many of the Shun-tuk had volunteered to help in that task. Many more had wanted to go back to the only home they had known, in the Dark Lands.

Richard missed Nathan already, and he had only been gone a few weeks.

In a complete surprise to Richard—Kahlan had said she saw it coming from a mile away—Nicci had chosen to travel with Nathan for a time and keep him company, which as far as Richard was concerned meant keep him out of trouble. Richard thought it ironic that the Palace of the Prophets had always sent a Sister with Nathan whenever he had to travel anywhere. With the Sisters, it was always quite clear that they were his minders, and kept the man in an iron collar to control him.

Richard hoped that Nicci could find true happiness in life. He had regretted seeing her leave with Nathan, but he had understood. He missed her as well. She said she didn't know how long she would be gone. It depended on how obnoxious a traveling companion Nathan turned out to be. Richard was actually a little surprised that she wasn't already back. But she would be.

Cassia and Vale were delighted to be back at the People's Palace–under a new Lord Rahl. Cassia liked going on patrols with the men of the First File. The men didn't complain. Vale spent a lot of her time with Berdine. They whispered a lot to each other. Richard pretended not to notice, and they pretended they were fooling him.

Vika was more than pleased to be back. It was a choice she had made for herself. Richard had given her not merely the chance, but the encouragement to make a hard choice for herself.

The result, though, was that she had decided that she was the Mord-Sith who ought to replace Cara as their closest protection.

Richard, of course, had not been consulted in that decision. He had been informed of it.

Truth be told, it suited him just fine.

Vika had never again apologized for using her Agiel on him. He was glad of that, too. It was in the past.

He was also glad that she understood that if she didn't stay in line, he would punish her in the way he promised. So far she had stayed in line. Well, not in line, exactly. Vika actually only considered the line to be a suggestion.

Richard wouldn't have it any other way.

Richard and Kahlan had made a quick trip via the sliph to the Keep. Before she'd left, Nicci had used Subtractive Magic on Vika so that she could travel in the sliph and protect them. At the Keep they had brought everyone up to date on everything that had happened. Much of the news had been a terrible blow to the Sisters. It didn't fit with what they had been taught at the Palace of the Prophets. Verna, to her credit, had been a big help in putting it to the Sisters in ways they could better accept. The biggest issue had been prophecy. Prophecy had been their lives. Richard couldn't make them believe the truth. He hoped that in time they would come to accept it.

Richard had also given Verna a message from Warren. It had meant the world to her. She said that it made her feel like she could move on, really move on, and live her life.

Richard and Kahlan hoped to soon travel back to Aydindril, the Keep, and the Confessors' Palace, then visit Hartland again.

Kahlan glided up beside Richard and slipped a hand over his shoulder. When she pressed up against him he realized she was not wearing much at all.

"Are you coming to bed, soon?"

Richard nodded, then pointed in the direction of the northern sky. "Look there. Look at the northern lights. They're especially bright tonight."

Kahlan watched them for a time. "Do you think they are lost souls? Lost souls gathered together to look for their place?"

Richard smiled. "I think we have all the lost souls found and accounted for. Those who no longer have a place in this world have been returned to the Grace and they've found their place in the next."

"I suppose," she murmured as she looked at the still, cloudless, moonless sky.

Richard glanced back through the open double doors. "The bed does look comfortable."

When he looked into the bedroom, he saw the leather cases for the Cerulean scrolls all lined up in their neat compartments in the cabinet against the wall. One of the scrolls sat on a stand before all the others. It was the Warheart scroll.

The old scribe Mohler had brought them, and at Richard's invitation had decided to live at the People's Palace. Before he'd left on his adventure, Nathan had healed Mohler's gnarled hands and to Mohler's astonishment they were now pain-free.

"Richard, something is wrong."

He turned back. "What is it? What's wrong?"

She pointed up at the sky. "I never really noticed until just now. The stars aren't in the right places."

Richard made a face. "Of course they are."

Kahlan shook her head, looking seriously concerned. "No, I mean it, Richard. They aren't where they belong. The constellations I know aren't there anymore." She put a hand over her heart. He could see that her breathing had increased, and by the vein in the side of her neck, so had her heart rate.

Richard smiled as he reached over and took her hand. He rested his hand holding hers on the balustrade.

"It's all right, Kahlan. They are where they belong."

"No," she insisted, giving him a worried look. "No they aren't. They aren't where they belong."

He tilted his head toward her a little bit. "They are where they belong, now. They aren't the same as before. But this is where they belong, now."

Her brow twitched. "What are you talking about?"

He flicked a finger toward the stars. "The spectral fold has closed. The Twilight Count has ended with the phase change. The star shift is now complete."

Kahlan looked back to the stars and then back to Richard. "You mean the stars will never be the way they were before?"

"That's right. They will never be like they were before. This is the way they will always be from now on. We will have to name new constellations, learn new patterns."

"And they will always be this way now? These positions will stay the same? We can count on these constellations staying put? This is the way our night sky will look from now on?"

"That's right."

She looked out at the night sky that was new to her. "That's actually pretty astounding."

Richard leaned down and kissed her as they embraced. When they finally parted, both their breathing was a little faster.

"So if there has been a star shift, what does that mean for us now? What does it mean for us going into the future? Especially now, without prophecy?"

Richard shrugged. "It means it's the start of a new age."

Kahlan gazed off at the sky. "A star shift, and the start of a new age." She looked up into his eyes. "What sort of age do you think it is going to be?"

Richard showed her a big smile. "With this star shift, everything has changed. This is the beginning of a new, golden age."

She smiled to herself. "I like the sound of that," she whispered.

Kahlan frowned over at him, then, looking skeptical again. "Are you sure that this is the start of a golden age?"

"Positive. I promise you, this is the start of a golden age."

"Wizards always keep their promises."

"Yes they do, and yes that is a promise that the First Wizard, the Warheart, has just given you."